NO NAKED WALLS

THREE STAGES OF MAYHEM

LEE BENSON

For Nicki

Thank you.

Lee Benson

2024.

APS PUBLICATIONS

APS Books,
4 Oakleigh Road,
Stourbridge,
West Midlands,
DY8 2JX

APS Books is a subsidiary of
the APS Publications imprint

www.andrewsparke.com

Cover art by kind permission of Glenn Badham

This book was originally published by APS Publications in three parts 'So You Want To Own An Art Gallery', 'Where's Your Art Gallery Now' and 'Now You're The Artist...Deal With It'.

ISBN 9781789961461

NO NAKED WALLS

PART ONE

SO YOU WANT TO OWN ART GALLERY

PART TWO

WHERE'S YOUR ART GALLERY NOW

PART THREE

NOW YOU'RE THE ARTIST...DEAL WITH IT

PART ONE

SO YOU WANT TO OWN ART GALLERY

WHITE – THE BLANK CANVAS

So, you want to own an art gallery? Are you sure? Let me convince you otherwise. Pour yourself a drink and let's begin.

A few minor details pre-opening, with a week to go.

Where are the electricians? Where is the credit card machine? Where will the computer fit? Why is the desk too low for my long legs?

And by the way, let's ask the obvious...Who do you invite? Especially when you don't know anyone.

Think! What are the main ingredients of a good party?

Wine, red and white, champagne, and I suppose orange juice...there are always a few who don't indulge.

Create a dynamic atmosphere.

Did I mention wine? Then add more wine. Oh yes and rather edible nibbles, or to be posh, canapés, those delicate mouthwatering designs of miniscule food on crackers. Follow that with strawberries smothered in chocolate and balanced on a polished silver tray.

How many times have you been to a so called private view and been offered a glass of wine that would strip the paint off a car, followed by a slightly hard, over-aired, carrot stick from a small cup, usually served by a young assistant in an obligatory black dress with flat mules. And there are people standing there, pretending to look at the art but secretly, or in some cases, deliberately, looking round the room to see if they're being seen to be seen at this private showing. A serious battle of jungle warfare and territorial one-upmanship.

Meanwhile back in the almost happening world of my reality, I have to find suitably gorgeous looking women and dress them to impress. Well not personally dress them, but you...never mind!

Then one needs to have an extra special bouncer, a *meet-and-greeter*, on the door. Let's say a voluptuous wild blonde with high heels, white top

1

hat and tails, long legs that go on forever and a tightly fitted, sparkly but classy, bodice. After all, this is a new venture and one's business just has to be remembered.

Luckily, I know one such woman who fits the bill precisely.

She has that look of *you wish you could afford to bed me, but you can't,* yet her eyes are fiery and dangerous to match a seductive voice. One which when it says *you can't come in - you're not on the list,* will make you melt in disappointment, all with a touch of class.

If I was married, she would be the devil in a white suit, but luckily, I'm not and the temptation to have a frivolous sampling of danger woman is perfectly irresistible. However, there is a very wise saying that, if followed, will lead you on a safe path to success and lack of stress. Never ever poke the payroll.

I can honestly say this statement is true to my personal knowledge. I know a chap who now lives in oblivion, having not heeded that simple rule. Having had a successful gallery, he decided to bed an artist, and that was where his problems began. She became increasingly jealous of any other female artists he might need to meet; stopped him going to visit clients at their homes after hours; wouldn't let him even go out for a drink at lunch time. Engaged in a power struggle which emotionally screwed him up, he aged ten years in a short while and lost the will to continue his business.

Mind you, how many secretaries have married their bosses and become the boss of their relationship, or failing that, taken a large chunk of financial disaster to the next bed?

So that's one thing sorted, a presence and a half on the door. I now have to hire my future staff, utilising Rule 2B; *You, yourself, must always be the least good-looking member of your organization.*

I contact recruitment agencies. It seems a logical place to start. I'm interviewed by what seems an attentive young lady who asks all the right questions. I give her all the right answers and assume all will be well. I ask for tall persons with retail experience, and a good customer manner. I don't require art degrees, let alone art historians.

Eventually I'm presented with three women, all measuring less than five feet tall.

The first we shall call Number 1. She wears six-inch heels, and still manages to barely reach the sixty-inch mark.

I ask a few easy questions. Will she be able to climb a ladder and would she mind opening the front door for me now? I give her the key, and lo and behold, she can't even reach the security lock. Then she admits to being afraid of heights, which renders her not entirely suitable for the job on offer. Mind you, I blame the designers of the building, placing the door locks in such a stupidly high place. However, it is a dire necessity for my staff to be able to open up the joint on a morning.

The one we shall call Number 2 has more makeup than the entire cosmetics floor of a department store. She tells me that she loves art and traveling abroad, freely admits that she's getting divorced and was in a violently abusive relationship. And all I'm asking her is why she wants the job?

Number 3 is a makeup artist who had been living in Spain and been dumped by her chap (the swine). Her girlfriend has put out a contract on his head and she's feeling the pressure of becoming a lesbian again!

Well, excuse my naivety but all I want is a couple of employees to entice and handle the customers (not that way). And if it's not too much to ask, could they be more or less sane?

Feeling exhausted and mentally drained by the experience, I take myself across the road to relax with a well-earned pint of Guinness.

In the pub behind the bar, I find Louisa. Tall, slim, well-dressed and with a lovely smile. She serves me and engages in polite chit-chat. At some point, I ask if she knows anyone who might be looking for a job. She pulls out her order pad and gives me the details of a friend.

Eureka! This seems a more reliable way of getting staff, but first I ring the agency to tell them that none of the applicants are suitable. To my surprise, they berate me for being insufficiently specific in the first place. At what point a height requirement can be deemed an example of inexact criteria, I fail to understand. Although I admit I failed to state that mentally and sexually disturbed short persons shouldn't apply.

Next up my newly acquired Insurance broker shoves his oar in. He knows a well-presented chap who's looking for a job. It seems like he's doing me a big favour. The chap in question is Julian. No obvious evidence of being either a recovering alcoholic or an obsessive personality with four weekly cyclical mood swings. Not at all. His appearance is dapper and he starts out looking a perfect fit for the job.

Meanwhile Belinda, as recommended by Louisa in the pub, also seems perfect.

So, we're ready to take on the world. Well, I say the world, but in a city like ours, anything outside a twenty-mile radius might as well be on another planet.

Somehow by luck and word of mouth, and a few God-awfully early Breakfast Networking meetings, I manage to create a guest list of around eighty useful souls to attend the opening night of my gallery.

The time arrives.

Let's put colour into your life.

It's five minutes to six. Five minutes to the opening. Doors are ready to be unlocked, lights out. Will it work? Will anyone turn up? Will I sell anything?

Three minutes to go and everything and everyone is in place.

One minute to go. Lights on. I look out the window and 'Heavens above!' There's a queue outside. People are actually waiting to be let in. This is scarier than hanging off a cliff by your ankles with the sea crashing over the rocks a hundred feet down below.

The moment arrives. Exactly six o' clock.

The doors are opened and Miss Hat-and-Tails checks the guest list - or makes it up, but she sure looks the part.

Within minutes the place is heaving, the music struggling to rise above the hubbub of conversation. I swear that vast swathes of the audience seem not to have seen each other for years, they have so much to catch up on.

Suited, dinner and casual; evening dresses, plunging necklines, short skirts; fur coats; dirty jeans!!! How did he get in? Somehow, I manage to negotiate my way through the press to the breaker of our unwritten dress code. 'I hope you don't mind' he says with an air of *I can do anything I like*. 'I was walking past and thought I ought to join you.'

I'm just about to escort him out when one of the heaving masses of invitees shakes dirty jeans by the hand and asked him how the filming's

4

going. How should I know he's an actor? A recognised actor, at that. I mean I don't have time to watch television or go to the movies.

There are many emptied bottles within a very short space of time and the trays of food evaporate as soon as they come out. Apparently, the masses are in fact literally starving.

'Ladies and gentlemen' I bellow and wait.

'Welcome to the gallery' I would continue seamlessly but someone pinches my bum, taking me completely by surprise. I turn but can't see who's cheekily nipped my derriere. No option but to keep my sang-froid and focus back on the ever drinking, loudly talking crowd.

The rest of the evening seems to travel at a hundred miles an hour becoming a blur of constant chatter; *Hello, how are you? Who are you? Would you like to purchase this incredible piece of sculpture? Another drink?*

I look down at my watch and it's eleven o' clock. Not one person seems to want to leave. I get on the table to announce 'Sadly this night is at an end but...I do know how to throw a party, don't I?'.

There's a loud cheer.

Mission underway. I own an art gallery. Time will tell if we can make it work.

'Thank you and good night.'

Miss Top-and-Tails slinkily places her arm through mine, reaching up to whisper in my ear, 'What are you doing later?'

CHAMPAGNE IS A COLOUR

The next morning, at the crack of noon, I stroll up to the doors and peer through the glass.

The sight greeting my eyes is total carnage; a wipeout, akin to the aftermath of an all-night rave. There are spilt explosions of wine on the marble floor, plus food, well-trodden-in. It resembles a vaguely abstract installation surrounded by lingering wine bottles with a few drops hiding inside, still in shock methinks.

Good grief. I scan my new establishment. Is this an art gallery or a nightclub? There's even a bright red lacy thong hanging from a spotlight. Admirable, I think. *Someone obviously had more than they bargained for.*

The phone rings rather too loudly. Surprisingly it's still visible on the counter amid the debris. Julian answers it with an air of disbelief. He puts his hand over the earpiece and shouts loudly into the room, so presumably it's for me. 'Someone wants to buy the large landscape on the back wall. She's coming in to see it again in half an hour.'

So, let's get this right; within thirty minutes, three of us will turn this establishment into a place in which nothing at all happened last night. This is going to take a miracle.

Luckily for us art gallery time is rarely a precise science, especially when it comes to taking money. My customer underestimates by over an hour. The place now sparkles and we look like we've won something in hand-to-hand combat. Time to crack open a bottle of champagne. Just as a thank you and sedative.

'Is it going to be like this all the time?' asks Belinda, her hair somewhat disheveled.

'I sincerely hope not,' is all the reassurance I can manage, placing a full glass of fizz in her hand.

At two o clock on the dot, Mrs. C. Topping strolls in carrying half a dozen full, expensive looking, shopping bags. Her credit card has taken a battering already today, obviously. 'I need a drink,' she states.

'Red White or fizz?'

'Oh, how kind. Champagne sounds perfect.'

She drops all her bags in the middle of the gallery and strolls over to the most expensive painting on show.

'I just love it' she exclaims. 'It will go so well in the snug.'

Snug I thought measuring up the six-foot square painting. *Some snug.* Never ever question unless the customer is absolutely, completely and utterly wrong. I smile. 'Would you like it delivered?'

My heart is missing the odd beat. My most expensive painting is about to find a new home. I endeavor to remain calm on the outside.

'Would you mind?' she says, offering me the empty glass. Julian is there like a shot. *What a bar we run.* 'With pleasure'

I say, 'Is there anything else you might like whilst we're coming out to you?'

'Actually' she says, 'It's my husbands' birthday and he loves nudes. *Lucky Mr. Topping.*

'We have a superb couple in the stock room.'

Off goes Julian to retrieve the two paintings. Belinda on the other hand is looking on in dismay; I'm thinking that maybe she's never seen someone spend so much money at once in her life before. I walk over and politely put my hand on her shoulder to grab her attention. 'My dear! Would you mind putting the kettle on. It's in the kitchen.'

She goes off, still in a daze.

Three glasses of champagne later, three paintings are sold. Investment in quality liquid refreshment always pays off.

'Tomorrow would be perfect.' She slurs her words. 'And do you mind taking these few bags as well. I'm off to lunch with the girlies.'

She slips her platinum card out of her wallet and places it in the machine, which whirs briskly. Within seconds, the sum has cleared.

'Thank you, Madam.' I hand her card back to her. 'Call me Tina' she smiles. 'See you at midday.'

Freed of her shopping, Tina wobbles slightly out of the gallery into the retail world of the wealthy.

'Bloody effin hell!' says Julian, losing all his public-school training. 'Did you see the size of the rock on her finger?

GLOWING ORANGE

Open for a week and a great start. Lots of red dots on labels which technically means they're sold.

I'm feeling quite delighted with everyone's efforts, although a touch jaded given that the launch party has lasted three days and is, to a degree, still ongoing after normal closing time.

It's early evening, and I'm attempting to look busy at the computer, catching up on notes and thank-you letters, valuations and the like, when someone walks in through the doors.

I look up to acknowledge a blue hair do with an array of multi-coloured clothing, holding a large, black, art-folder with *Death is Life* emblazoned on the front in dayglow orange.

Saying to her, 'I'll be with you in a minute,' - at a rough guess she's female - I close down the computer, replace my pen and stand up.

To my complete shock, I'm confronted with a naked female, tattooed from head to toe, lying prostate on top of her folder.

'I thought you'd get a better understanding of what I'm about', she says.

Now don't get me wrong, as a member of the male human race, a naked female is very much my kind of woman, to be appreciated and admired.

However, call me old fashioned, but invasive tattoos graffitied over a body of ample proportions doesn't quite do it for me.

I cough and say calmly 'May I request that you get dressed and then you can show me your artwork or leave.'

The artist says nothing and slowly covers herself up, finally shoving her feet into green Doc Martins, with an attitude of protest. 'My theory is to glow from within the painting and I only use glow paints. You must come to my studio, I insist! I want to have sex with you!'

It's at this point that *No* is the only correct answer - on so many levels.

I have to ask, 'Are you taking any medication at the moment?'

She flings her papers all over the gallery floor, 'Why can't people just fuck and have sex and stuff without all the complications. I hate you!'

So now I'm faced with an emotionally frustrated glow in the dark, in the form of a highly explosive female. The rules of engagement have dramatically changed. The solution is simple; I press the new security alarm button.

Within a few moments - that was quick - two of the shopping complex's security guards enter the gallery, with an *Is everything ok you know, eyebrows raised, man and woman in a room alone, know what I mean?* sort of look.

'Thank you, gentlemen, this person would like to be escorted from the premises.'

Well that at least proves the security system works.

RUSSIAN RED

Nudes seem to attract a lot of admirers, both male and female. We're talking paintings here but one of the things that don't usually sell are life drawings. These are a wonderful way of practicing observational techniques, you see - a bit like scales on a piano but no G Minor scale will ever get to be a top ten hit.

There are exceptions though in my gallery.

One day around six in the afternoon, just before we lock up, a tall, dark haired lady walks in with a folder. She walks straight up to me and says in a wonderful *James Bond* Russian spy accent, 'Are you ze owner of zis establishment?'

'I am indeed' I say, intrigued. Who wouldn't be?

'Good! Very good! I want to exhibit my work wiz you.'

There is no hint of doubt in her approach that I will do other than accept her offer. 'I show you my pieces.'

'Usually,' I say, trying to wrest back control of my gallery, 'artists make an appointment.'

'I have not time for zat; you must to show my work.' Her tongue curls around the English language with a seductive tone.

She is in fact right. She places her folder on the clean white floor and produces from it ten superb, powerful, sultry and nude sketches. They have a sort of abstract quality. In my opinion, they're brilliant. Several of them I'd cheerfully buy for my own collection.

'I use my imagination and the model is myself in all zees works'. She takes her long coat off and drapes it over a wooden sculpture. Julian immediately appears to whisk it off the £5000 piece. He hangs it over the back of a chair.

'Where I come from', she says, 'we have close relationship wiz ze owner of gallery. It is ze Russian way.'

I raise an eyebrow 'That is most interesting, but in England, I'm afraid we haven't heard of this practice before.' She looks puzzled as I continue, 'You must have a lot of exhausted gallery owners.'

I try to concentrate on her drawings but she fixes me with a steely-eyed glare. 'We are very specific whom we show our art wiz.'

Whoops, I've been targeted.

The intensity of her gaze doesn't change. I feel like I'm being stripped naked in my own establishment, and then she exclaims, 'Vodka.' Miraculously she pronounces it as we do. None of that *Wodka* rubbish they say in bad films.

Miraculously from out of the folder appears a branded bottle carrying the emblazoned image of a Cossack on the front and not a word of printed English anywhere. 'Zis is how we seal our friendship.'

I decide on the spot that I'm going to make a habit of adopting new traditions.

At 9.30 I lock up and stroll home. Were it not for the images stored in my stockroom, I'd be wondering if any of that really happened. Nastrovia.

PINK AND BROWN

When putting an exhibition together, you need to imagine a blank image jigsaw with many pieces, all wrapped in bubble wrap or sheets or a combination of cardboard, polythene, mother's old blankets etcetera. Anything that can be used to protect artworks - and cause extra wasted time excavating the painting - will be used.

When eventually the work is laid out against the walls, I tend to put one piece in the middle of the gallery and try to create a flowing feel that should sooth and encourage the onlooker and hopefully tempt them into purchasing a new work. One particular exhibition, predominantly figurative, colourful and large, attracts quite a few new customers, I'm pleased to report.

My gallery is littered with semi nudes in forests and gardens or draped over furniture, all very discreet and tasteful, and sometimes with the bold addition of pieces of fruit strategically placed to hide anything that shouldn't be seen.

After three hours, thirty-six paintings are suitably hung, exhibited to their best and well lit; wherever possible, good lighting is mandatory for bringing out the best of a painting; akin to the expensive second coat of nail varnish, it finishes off the look exquisitely.

A smartly dressed businesswoman with an immaculate hairdo and a very expensive scarf strolls in and around the gallery. She wanders in the manner of someone for whom this is more a chore than a delight.

'Welcome to my world' I say. 'May we offer you a glass of something?'

'I don't drink,' the woman retorts.

'Perhaps a cup of tea or coffee instead.'

'Perfect. Earl grey; no milk' She turns away and continues to examine the paintings with an air of supercilious boredom.

'Permit me for saying it, but you look like you've something very specific in mind'

'Pink and brown,' she states. 'My interior designer says only pink and brown will work in the room.'

Staring right ahead of her is a reclining nude, shades of pink, lying on a wooden chez-longue. 'Any particular shade of brown?'

Belinda stalks by me slowly. 'Ice maiden' she mouths in my direction without saying a word and takes herself off to sit behind the desk, looking professionally busy.

'I'd like to see this in the location before I decide.'

'With pleasure ma'am.' It seems appropriate to address her so. The games one plays with clients could be written as a screen play. There are so many possible roles, but what is most important is to indulge the customer who will always like to think they are right. So, I smile, am polite at all times and am happy to guide them gently into thinking they're right to agree with me.

'When would you like to see this painting in situ?'

'I'm busy for three weeks,' she says, checking her Filofax.

'I'm very sorry,' says I, 'but the opening for this artist is tonight and we anticipate a good response. Is there any way you could see if it works any earlier? Like now perhaps?'

She looks me up and down in disbelief. 'Now?' she shouts. 'I need a phone'. Belinda hands her our telephone.

'Sibyl, delay my next appointment till three pm,' and she hands the phone back to Belinda. I suppose that could be taken as a good sign.

'Well,' she says, 'let's go.'

I take the painting off the wall and place it in a protective bag.

'Where to?'

'Follow me.' She pivots and walks straight out of the gallery, expecting me to keep up. In fast pursuit, I cross the courtyard at a rate of knots, trying breathlessly to make small talk.

'I haven't the time or inclination to chat,' she cuts me off.

Silently, we cross two roads, miraculously unscathed despite her indifference to passing traffic, and arrive at one of those new glass and steel buildings. It's a fine example of modern living in the modern city; devoid of any quality of design but terribly functional and with far too many lifts and auto locking fire doors.

She storms through the entrance and the door closes in my face. *Damned magnetic security locks.* 'Excuse me'. I shout after the vanishing woman.

She turns back to open the door for me. 'Come on,' she says, 'I'm very busy.'

We enter a stainless-steel lift with blue mood lighting. She presses the button etched in the aluminum panel. Top floor. Penthouse.

We walk through the front door, and the whole place is dark. She flicks a switch and the silk curtains come to life, opening like a cinema presentation when a wide screen film begins. Everything is in its place. It looks like a show room, as emotionless and sterile as a photo shoot. Not a single grain of dust dares remain in this place

'Where would you like to place the painting?' I ask. I can't see a wall big enough. The room is all glass and curtains.

'In my bedroom,' she says. 'This way.' She marches through another brown door and again presses a button to let in the light. Here the curtains are a soft pink, shot silk. The carpet is a soft pink. The bed is covered in a silk throw, in soft pink with a delicate pink rose embroidered in the centre.

The bed is brown. The identical brown to the shade in the painting. Is this a coincidence? Has the goddess of interior designers looked down on us? It's the perfect tone.

'There is only one place for this painting,' I offer, 'above the bed'. The cupboards are mirrored so it will reflect perfectly.

'Take your shoes off and climb on the bed. I want you to hold it up there.' She points dramatically. A positive instruction.

So, there I am, supporting the painting of the nude, whilst standing on a very deep soft mattress. The pink colour is a perfect match for her soft furnishings. Identical. It's good job there are a pair of cherry red nipples in the picture, otherwise it might vanish into the décor.

To my surprise, the woman, whose name I still don't know, takes her shoes off, and climbs onto the bed. She lies down in the middle and studies the refection in the mirror. I'm more or less straddling her. A balancing act indeed. She raises herself up and leans on one elbow. Then she grabs a book from the bedside table and opens the pages.

'What do you think?' I ask, not daring to move an inch

'It needs a different frame; it has to match the wardrobe.'

'Certainly.' I smile. I bet she wants it back on her wall, reframed, this evening.

I'm about to step off the bed when she says that she wants to hold it against the wall and will I lie down to check it all works.

'Okay.' This is getting a little weird, but the customer is always right.

We swap positions and there I am, lying in my best suit on a strange bed, a fully dressed woman standing over me.

There's always a first time for everything, I think.

RED AND BLACK

I learn very quickly one thing about having a business is that everyone wants your money and every magazine wants you to advertise. So, you're bombarded with ABC best areas, telephone directories, monthlies, quarterlies, rate cards etcetera. At first I'm flattered to think that these people want my gallery in their publication. Ha! Don't think so; take your money and go.

Eventually I snap and when approached by the latest magazines to hit the area, start asking 'How much would you like to pay me to go in it.' That stops most young trainee salesmen and women but one such person, whom we shall call Tracey, won't take no for an answer. She keeps on ringing and leaving messages; speaks to both my team, who fail to fob her off, and despite being told we're not interested, somehow manages to push them into arranging an appointment to see me. I find this out from Belinda passing by for a fleeting moment on her way out of the gallery to an early lunch.

I'm arranging a beautiful glass sculpture on her plinth, enhancing her beauty by moving it an inch to the left, when an unrecognised female voice says, 'Leave it just as it is. I think it's perfect!'

I don't think I've begun hearing voices in my head, so I turn around to meet a tall, sharply dressed lady with an obvious split in her skirt - designed in, not torn, you understand — and as she moves, her knee keeps saying hello to me and to the rest of the world. She's also wearing a slightly over-tight, white blouse with a revealing neckline. Her perfume fills the room, drowning out the wonderful aroma of fresh oil paintings and well-polished surfaces.

'I do love arranging things in my house. I bet I'd be great in a gallery.'

She's already great - greatly trying my patience. I don't tell her that. 'May I help you,' I ask.

'That depends.' She laughs. 'I'm Tracey and you're so difficult to get to see.'

'Well my dear; here I am, in front of you now. So, what can I do for you?'

I'm breaking my own rules here. I've always said, actually preached, never use the word *Can* as in *Can I help you?* It invites answers like *Yes - I want my kitchen decorating and my satin bed sheets need ironing.* Using the word, *MAY*, gives a far more positive platform for ongoing interaction. If you'd like a few more tutorials on my pet hate phrases, stay behind after and we'll sort you out.

'I have the most wonderful offer, which is only applicable today,' she starts. 'Where can we sit down and talk?'

'Well,' I say looking around the gallery; 'any place you like.'

'Somewhere a little more intimate,' she suggests.

Since the gallery doesn't have a bedroom or a lingerie department, wherever could she mean?

Her smile is artificially beautiful. *Let battle commence,* I think.

'What's behind this door?' She strokes the wooden, lacquered surface, caressingly.

'Would you believe a kitchen area?' Mild amusement on my part.

'Let's put the kettle on or...as you're a gallery, how about something stronger?'

'Tea or coffee?' I offer.

'We're not doing too well, are we?' says Tracey.

'It's only a drink,' I say.

'You know what I mean,' she says.

'I know exactly what you mean,' I say with a sigh of relief.

'Oh good,' continues Tracey. 'Where shall we do it?'

'Do it?' I exclaim, raising my vocals two tones. 'The kettle is on, and it won't take too long.'

'I always get my way.' With that, she begins to hoist her skirt, revealing black lace stocking tops, black suspenders and a pair of miniscule, pillar-box red panties.

What's a man to do? Listen friends, I'm not that naïve. However, it's a small kitchen and I say flippantly, 'Have you ever had sex on a ladder?'

That stops her in her tracks. A moment's thought and she says 'Can't say I have.'

My stockroom is adjacent to the kitchen and praying for Julian to understand this is a plea for help, I call out 'Just going to the stockroom; shout if you need me.'

The stockroom is full of shelves stuffed with artworks, along with boxes and rolls of bubble wrap. A ladder stands propped up against the back wall. Tracey climbs onto the first rung, hoisting her skirt again.

'What do you suggest we do next'?

'Are you serious?' I ask.

'What am I going to tell my boss?'

'That sometimes a shag won't get you exactly what he wants you to get. Actually, tell him I want a full page for a tenth of your card rate. That's the deal.'

She pulls down her skirt and straightens her attire.

'Don't you want to have me?' she asks, dejectedly.

'Pretty underwear,' I say. 'However, I shall decline, thank you. '

At that precise moment, the door crashes open and Julian storms through it, raising an eyebrow to convey that two and two make five, spins on his axis, shouts out the word 'Disgusting!' and leaves.

'I think that will be all for today. I'll look forward to hearing from you with a positive outcome.'

The parade back through the gallery is priceless. Belinda's back from lunch; all eyes are on me for sure, but not a word spoken.

Hopefully that'll be the last we hear from Tracey.

CERULEAN BLUE

Dear Sir, I am a sculptor and would like to show you my work. I have enclosed a couple of photos, a bit dog-eared but they show you what I do. Could you come and see me.
Signed *Nick*.

There's a crinkled photograph of a horse's head, obviously carved out of a tree stump with biro scribble across the image; Then there's a female torso, well proportioned, entitled *Emma* and a large felled tree in a field and one word scribbled on the back, *Shark*. I have to say I'm intrigued by its title. As far as one can see, the tree has neither dorsal fin nor tail but I suppose, with the deployment of vast imagination, it could be a shark.

I decide I need a day out. Seeing this sculptor is a good excuse. A hunch says it might even be worthwhile.

I try the mobile number given in the letter. It rings out for ages and then someone answers, shouting 'WHAT!'

'Is that Nick?' I shout back. The background noise reverberating down the line from his end is a tad above dangerous decibel levels.

'NO. It's Pete. Nick is busy. It's his phone though.'

'Tell him I'll come to see him this Wednesday. Midday.'

'Meet in the pub in the village,' comes the reply.

The line goes dead.

Wednesday comes round and I set off on a two-hour jaunt to get there respectably late in accordance with standard pub etiquette.

Blessing the motorway traffic, I actually manage to arrive in the village by one fifteen and it's not difficult to find the pub. There's only the one, a small church, a church hall with a scout's flag flying proudly and a few small cottages littered around as if they've forgotten to build a sensible road. I walk in and the place falls silent.

'You looking for Nick? says the barman in a thick accent.

'I am indeed. Is he around?'

'He be out back - through that door.'

'Thanks.'

In the backyard, sitting on a barrel; well more like slouched and about to fall off a barrel; is a long haired, well-weathered chap of indeterminate years. His lumberjack shirt is covered in wood shavings and dust, while his gigantic black boots should have been thrown away at least five years ago. A t-shirt emblazoned with the words *Revolution my arse* completes his well-selected ensemble.

'About fuckin' time,' Nick says, trying to get off the barrel and falling on to the cobblestones. 'I've been here since eleven.'

'You're pissed,' I merrily observe.

'Not that pissed to know a fuckin' dealer when I see one. You're all the same, you lot, fuckin' suits and leather shoes, all the fuckin' same.' He lunges forward and grabs hold of me; more to steady himself as he carefully dusts himself down and slaps his knees hard with his hand.

'I'm thirsty and I'm hungry.'

Suddenly he pulls himself erect, stares right into my face for longer than could ever be comfortable and politely says, 'That's the intros done with. I hate meeting new people'.

His heel-turn and progress through the back door and into the bar can best be described as deliberately careful. *Surely this is not going to be one of those sorts of days*, I think.

In the bar, the locals are all laughing. 'This one's on me' says the barman. 'You look like you need a snifter.'

Suffice to say that the food is actually rather good; freshly made soup, thick sliced, tasty bread and a cheese-shop quantity of cheese on a plate.

'I want to show you my shark,' Nick says. 'It's not far from here but I better drive.'

I suffer a few moments of dread as to what he might drive and I'm not disappointed. It's an old Land Rover with all its doors missing and an array of ladders, tied down with old ropes, on the roof. Sitting on the driver's seat is a scraggy mutt, while two sleeping cats are moulting nicely on the passenger seat. A massive chainsaw and oil-can more or less fill the rest of the cabin.

'Hop in,' says Nick. No mean feat, for sure.

The vehicle stinks of stale oil, cat wee and old trainers. Thank God for the all-round air conditioning.

The Landy starts straight away and the gears crunch in resentment. There are no safety belts and no sign of anything to really hold onto, apart from one's breath.

We begin to pick up speed, probably because the road becomes a steep hill...downwards.

'Slow down. Please.'

'Can't mate; the brakes are shite.'

This is no time to be an atheist. *Please God let this rust bucket stop.*

Suddenly Nick turns right, into what looks like solid hedge but miraculously is an undefined lane covered in brush and bramble. 'We don't want everyone to know where we're going,' he laughs and the vehicle jumps and bounces and bucks like a manic bronco about to shake off its rider.

At this point the mutt farts and jumps out of the moving car. Next second, the vehicle bounces so hard to the left that I'm thrown out into a ditch full of muddy green, slimy water. The world stops for a few moments. I lie on my back and look up at the sky. It's a perfect summer's day with a clear blue sky; a cerulean blue sky.

'Harrrr!' goes Nick bringing me back to earth. He's also been ejected and is standing watching the Landy's progress. It comes to an abrupt halt, minus a front wheel, which continues bouncing down the field. 'Bollocks,' he adds.

For a moment my thoughts are disorientated and then I think, *what was it the dog knew, us mere mortals didn't?*

'Fuck it,' says Nick. 'It's always coming off.'

I'm soaked. Luckily, I'm unhurt but I'm not sure a dry clean will restore my suit. Bloody stupid idea, wearing smart clothes on an expedition into the country - memo to self.

Nick sets off across the field followed by the two cats. There's something strange about domestic loyalty. Actually, there's a lot stranger about Nick.

We walk for a few hundred yards, and there right in front of my eyes is the exact tree from the photograph, in the flesh, or to be exact, in the wood.

'Is this it? I ask.

'Yessss,' he hisses. 'My shark. It's going to be fucking awesome.'

'It's a bloody felled tree in the middle of a field,' I say.

'Would look amazing in your gallery, don't you think?'

I have an active imagination but seeing the massive log in its raw state takes a lot of creative thinking. 'No,' I state, 'I can't.'

'A couple of grand and it'll look better than the real thing.'

'Are you really expecting me to shell out two grand for a tree?'

'Sharkkkkk' Nick growls. 'It's a fucking shark. It's a statement of pure art.'

He's mad; he's seriously deranged and, I'm beginning to think, possibly dangerous.

'Have you anything else I could see?' I smile hopefully.

'Horses and nudes,' he says. 'Loads of them.' He starts off up the hill with his menagerie following, including the mutt.

'In for a penny,' I say to myself and splodge up the hill, following Nick like a clown in a very particular, not to say peculiar, circus parade. Luckily, we haven't off-roaded far from the village, although on foot it seems more than far enough.

'Here we are. My place,' says Nick, shoving hard at the wooden split barn door. It smashes against the wall and a pot crashes to the ground.

Inside, sitting cross-legged on the floor, holding a baby to her breast is a young woman. She of the inspirational wooden torso.

'You must be Emma,' I say. 'Nick captured you exactly.' It seems like the right compliment to pay.

'Are you any good at changing nappies?' she says. 'He's useless.' She inclines her head in Nick's direction. He doesn't notice. His energies are directed towards rolling up.

It doesn't take long for me to realise that this is no ordinary cigarette. The smell of heavy grass fills the small room. *This is going to be one of these days after all*, I think.

A little toddler stumbles into the room, full of snot and covered in mud. 'Takes after his dad,' Emma says. 'Filthy dirty all the time.'

Despite the grass, I can sense a distinct lack of love and friendship filling the small room, despite the mad sculptor and his young paramour, two kids and three pet animals. Correction, make that three kids - another little girl crawls into the room to join the party.

The hunch which brought me here is taking a spiraling fall in the wrong direction.

One of the cats hisses at the crawling child and Nick throws a folder at it, narrowly missing. It springs open as it hits the floor. What falls out is breathtaking. There are the most superb drawings and sketches of female nudes and lots of horses, beautifully executed.

'Everybody wants to sell these fucking paintings.' Nick sounds upset.

'They're superb.'

'Fuck that,' he says. 'I want to make my fucking shark. My shark!' and then he exits the room, stage right, with all the injured grandeur of a Shakespearean actor

'Well,' says Emma, 'Can you or can't you change nappies?'

This is the last time I'll ever wear a suit to visit an artist again. No matter what.

GREEN...ANY SHADE YOU LIKE

To be a good painter entails mixing your paints so that the palate blends and swirls and every brush stroke has a form wherein the colours hang perfectly.

Never use green straight from the tube. Always mix the blues and the yellows.

'Utter crap and bollocks' said the painter of the hills.

It's true; there are hundreds of tubes and blocks, all of them green. The reality is that you have to understand the rules to be able to break them.

The trouble with owning a gallery is that you don't have time to paint. You're too busy finding artists of quality to sell. Mind you I have a secret weapon. A wonderful lady. She's an artist and sculptor and has *been there* as they say. She's had public commissions, museum exhibitions, and has written several books but now she feels the time is right to excavate her home and studios and put her life in order.

I suppose I should also mention that she chain smokes and has the most sexy, gravelly voice to go with it.

The down side is her attachment to one of those awful, little, attitudinal rats. Yes, a miniature dog that constantly snivels and barks at everything, whether it moves or stays static. She loves it. It's her pet, her beloved companion, and a bloody smelly pain in the whatsits.

'Let's do lunch,' she says on the phone. 'If you're coming out this far, you must eat and we can't stay in - the kitchen ceiling collapsed last week and I'm still waiting for the builders to turn up.'

It seems logical to me.

She adds, 'I know a quaint, old-fashioned tea room where they serve nice food.'

'Lovely. Look forward to meeting you.' And I offer to pick her up.

'Oh no,' she says. 'Dipsy only likes my car. I shall meet you there. It's easy to find.'

She gives me the address and vague navigational instructions. And I duly and vaguely get lost and can't find the place. As the area is one of outstanding natural beauty, there's not a single soul to ask, let alone a sign indicating there might be a café somewhere nearby. I stop the car and get out.

Luckily, I come upon an old chap walking his dog; although I think in truth the dog is dragging the chap along so the man can have some exercise. 'You lost?' he asks. *How do they do that? Power of the bleedin' obvious!*

'I'm looking for the *Teapot and Whistle*.'

'It's not far, but you won't be able to take your car this way. It's over the ridge by that tree. You can just see the smoke.' *Was it burning down then?*

'How do I get there by car?'

'Easier to walk from here,' he says.

Fair enough. I give in, placing urban thinking in the glove box and locking it away.

It seems I have to climb over a small fence with barbed wire and stroll across the field to the next hedge. Which would be easy, except that it suddenly fills up with very woolly sheep. By the mass of wool and dung attached to their lower haunches, I assume they're waiting to be sheared. I slowly set off with about a hundred and fifty eyes staring at me. I've never had such an attentive audience. Then one of the sheep decides to begin moving after me, hastily followed by the rest of the flock.

Miraculously, as I quicken my step, the sheep do the same. I'm being followed by a horde of future jumpers and lamb chops. Now, if this was a playing field, I dare say I might run for it, but it certainly isn't. There are holes and nettles and dung piles everywhere, and something akin to bouncing is more in order, something sheep are better suited to than I am, I discover. Eventually, I win the sheep hurdles by climbing over the next fence. The sheep stop by the barbed wire, looking bemused. *Bastards!*

Well, here it is, the quaint tea shop. In the faded glory of its pre-war splendour, it should be the gathering place for nannies wearing petticoats and frills, pushing the prams of their infant charges. But the building looks like it was last decorated in the 1940s and not a lick of paint seen since. A sign, with faded headings, indicates the service of fresh sandwiches and tea, daily.

There are six old wrought iron tables with matching chairs splattered in a disheveled array in the garden. Most lean over to a precarious degree. It would appear lunch might involve a balancing act.

'Hello, I'm over here.'

I can't see anybody.

'In the corner, Dipsy likes the view.'

I make my way over to the corner of the garden and sure enough, sitting on one of the chairs, is Dipsy next to her owner. A lovely day to be outdoors and such stunning views for a dog to enjoy. I spy landscape, rolling hills and more sheep. The sun plays his part, imparting brightly gilded tones to the green fields.

'Lovely.' I take one of the chairs and try to find a level area to rest it on.

A rather well-preserved lady stumbles out to take our order. 'I recommend the soup; it's fresh; and what sandwiches would you like? We have cheese or fresh crab.'

Sounds dubious to me. The crab would have had to have walked a long way from the sea to be fresh. So, it's two cheese, two soups and a bowl of water for the dog. An easy order to remember, you might think. There's no choice of salad or bread alternatives. Just simple rustic fare.

'I bet they don't get many American tourists here! '

'I'm not fond of them. They're all so loud and brash,' says Sally.

We become embroiled in the politics of art and galleries and how the world doesn't understand. My mission is to agree with everything she says and then worm my way into viewing Sally's art. My timing is obviously off when I raise the matter.

'I'm not interested anymore. It's all stored and I can't be bothered to unpack it.'

I begin to think my quest to find another artist has already ended in forlorn failure but all is not lost. The soup manages to stay in the bowl, mostly, and Sally tells me about two great friends of hers who don't live too far away. She's already prepared a note for me with the relevant information, sliding it carefully over to my side of the table as if playing at secret agents. 'Ring them,' is all she says, lighting yet another cigarette.

The atmosphere changes completely. Sally begins to interview me, asking many way too personal questions with the excitement of a teenager. She even broaches the vexed subject of my sex life, but soon stops when I don't respond. I daren't even begin to think what's going on inside her head. After a while, she smiles and asks, 'Fancy some cake?'

I have to admit she has a certain charm about her.

We finish the afternoon rendezvous. Being a gentleman, I walk her back to her car and close the door on her.

Now the next challenge is how to get back to my vehicle. I stroll back into the café and ask the owner how I can locate my car without having to challenge a field of sheep. Apparently, a quick stroll up the lane, a few turns right and voila. It remains to be seen.

'May I use your landline? My mobile doesn't seem to connect out here.'

'With pleasure,' the headwaiter, cook and cashier answers.

I lift the rather old, sticky telephone, and placing it gingerly to my ear, dial the number.

'Hello! I've been given your name by Sally who said I should contact you. I have a new gallery. May I come and visit? I know it's short notice but I'm in the area.'

There's a moment's pause, followed by 'Okay'.

No more sheep, no more fields and no more hedge-hopping. I manage to find the home of Patricia and Peter with relative ease. It's a magnificent, four-storey Victorian building overlooking the most dramatic landscape. You can see it for miles. They're both artists and have resolved their individual requirements for studio space by each having a separate floor allocated to their work. No need for passport control or intellectual boundaries.

'Cuppa tea ducky? Kettle's just boiled.'

Patricia has stunning, silver-grey hair. Of medium height, she's impish in her movements and has the most piercing of dark eyes. One could say that she probably retains a good figure too, albeit hidden in a black woolen roll neck jumper and loose black trousers. Peter too favours black attire but looks older. His stubble is of at least three days vintage, but his care-worn face is friendly and topped by wildly curly hair.

Their house contains an eclectic array of art, furniture and wall hangings. You could lose yourself for at least a day, wandering around.

'Sally said I should come and meet you.'

'Bet you didn't get anything out of her in the way of art?' Peter smiles. 'We're very fond of her, but that bloody hound goes everywhere with her and it stinks.'

'True enough, but she's a most interesting lady.'

We sit round an old wooden farm table, indulging in fresh scones smothered in homemade jam, washed down with freshly ground coffee. The wonderful truth is I'm rapidly lost in awe of their knowledge and of the amazingly friendly way in which they treat their guests. We talk for hours. It's effortless and losing track of time is de rigueur.

Patricia finally looks up at the large kitchen clock and offers to show me her studio. We trundle up two flights of stairs, passing a great collection of mounted drawings, and enter her sanctuary.

There are more enormous drawings pinned to the walls with tacks. The work is abstract with intent. Lots of notes are pinned up too, and silk and other materials are strewn everywhere. The massive bay window lets in superb daylight over a huge plan chest. I really have seen nothing like her stuff before. It may be challenging, but I fall in love with its drama and colour.

'Do you sell your work?' I ask innocently.

'I tend to exhibit more,' she says. 'I create for myself most of the time. Why? Do you think these would sell?'

'I'd love to try,' I offer.

She opens one of the drawers in the plan chest. It's stuffed with sketches and prints.

'I always make lino-cuts; they're fascinating after all the work I do on the large pieces.'

I find them powerful and tell her so.

'Most of the tapestries are rolled up in the attic. You'll have to come again to see them.'

Then, dismissed, I'm told to look at her husband's work on the next floor.

Peter starts apologetically. 'My wife is the artist. I'm a mere painter,' he says. He looks like a painter. He has paint splashes all over his black cotton tracksuit bottoms. His smock is adorned with the odd splash of paint too, and I can't help noticing a nurse's watch pinned to his chest. 'For telling the time when I get lost,' he laughs.

Peter is at totally the opposite end of the spectrum to his wife. His work is of bold landscapes with bright colours, huge daubs of paint slapped on and over large amounts of canvas. There are a series of six, two-foot canvases hanging next to each other, balanced precariously on nails. 'Work in progress,' he says. 'I love to work in a series.'

This man knows how to paint. 'I have a dealer who looks after me, but I'll let you try a couple in your new gallery.'

Double success.

In the adjacent room everything is so organized; book shelves full of art books, boxes of paints, colour-coded, catalogues, filing folders in alphabetical order, and in the middle of the room a flat, drawing easel bearing a calm watercolour, completely different to the style in the first studio. All I can think is *I so wish I could paint like this*.

We begin to talk watercolours and I say, 'I can't help noticing you use a lot of green.'

'I taught everyone not to use them at University. To mix the colours. But you know what; break the rules. If they're there, use them.'

It seems easy advice he's giving but, believe me, you need to understand how to expertly balance tones to know which rules to break. I suppose after nearly forty years at it, he does know.

This is going to be more than just selling the work. I feel like I've found a mentor. Above all else, he's willing to show me without making me feel like a total prat. It's the most positive and interesting day since leaving school, and that for me was many years ago.

We decide which paintings I can take and load them in my car before he can change his mind. Then returning to Patricia's studio, I collect some of her works on paper, place them carefully in a folder and thence convey them to the car.

I make my farewells and tell them how much I look forward to seeing them in my gallery. I really must thank Sally for the introduction, despite the altercation with the four-legged woolly creatures.

I drive off in the dark with a couple of hours to get home, feeling like a cat that has eaten all the cream and quite possibly the canary too.

REAL BLACK LEATHER

I'm lost in the world of computerised paperwork. It's no mean task for someone who's dyslexic and I hate every minute of it. It's the painful side of owning and running your own business. How anyone gets excited over spreadsheets and yearly accounts fails me. Just as long as I'm making enough money to survive!

The interruption is a large black presence filling the doorway.

'Is it alright if the lady and me have a butchers?'

There stands a giant of a man, easily six feet six or more. He has long black hair and an unruly, overgrown beard. It's almost a cliché to report that he's wearing a leather jacket replete with emblems and studs. Without counting there have to be at least ten rings on his fingers.

Beside him is a tiny, dyed-blonde lass wearing an exceptionally tight t-shirt over a rather amply magnified pair of breasts held up by the grace of God.

'Come on in.' I'm not going to argue with them. Let alone try to stop him.

It's nearly midday.

'Fancy a cup of tea or something stronger?'

'Coffee please. No sugar.' An innocuous request from a man, the sight of whom on a dark night would make you think about crossing to the other side of the road for safety's sake.

His lady giggles and asks for water. It's surreal. A flagon of ale and half a dozen tequila slammers might appear a more appropriate drinks order. Golden rule. Never ever judge a book by its cover.

She stops in front of a nude - a charcoal study. 'My tits are better than hers.'

The giant lightly pats her behind. It too is straining her very tight pair of denims. She continues checking the paintings and stops at a four-grand landscape - one of my classical pieces.

'It'll look lovely in the lounge, Gate. '

He simply produces an American Express Black card.

'Wrap it up please. I'll be back later. Can't take it on me hog.'

I'm astounded and for once keep my mouth firmly shut.

'Thank you.' Regaining my composure, I pull out a signed catalogue of the artist and offer it up as a token of my appreciation.

'See you later.' They leave with her arm up through his.

Let me tell you, sales never happen like that. I only pray a few more do. I might make a living if they did. Maybe I'll have a sign above the door *Bikers welcome*! Especially with Hells Angel art appreciation chapters in mind.

Just before closing, Gate strides back in, unaccompanied this time.

'Good evening. Remember me?'

Let me think. How many money-spending, giant bikers have I served today? Or any day.

'Indeed, I do. I rang the artist and told him the good news. He says he'll write a little piece and drop it in for you to go with the painting. He told me to say the scene is looking out over the Cotswolds.'

'She's from round those parts. '

He places the wrapped painting under his arm and leaves me to it. Not a bad day at all.

About a month later, Gate returns on his own. 'I'm sure you're a master of discretion.'

I smile. 'It's all part of the job.'

'Me ol' lady wants a painting for the home.'

'That's not so difficult. Look around. We do have quite a selection and a stock room out back just in case.'

Gate coughs and leans over me. Leans? He looms.

'That lady was not my Mrs. and you haven't seen me before. Okay?' He stops for a moment's thought. 'She means a lot to me though and I want to treat her to something special too.'

I nod in total approval.

Later that day, Gate and wife come into the gallery and are greeted as new but welcome strangers. Belinda stares at the biker in his full leathers, but totally composed, offers them a selection of drinks. Two white wines are duly served.

'We're looking for something for our lounge.'

Sounds familiar I think.

'Have you something in mind? A particular style or colour.'

'It's got to be big,' says Mrs. Gate.

'Follow me. I think a visit to the stock room is in order.' Gates' wife is almost the spitting image of his lady friend, except perhaps a year or two older.

I believe I should have a little word about my stock room. It's long and full of shelving, hiding just the right paintings for just the right customer. It boasts no windows and has an exquisite oil-paint and varnish smell, entwined with a hint of cardboard.

I pull out three huge canvases, two abstract and a more-or-less contemporary landscape. Gate looks at me in disbelief. I assume buying bikes is a lot easier.

'If you like, I can bring them round to your home and you can test drive them.'

'Brilliant!'

Gate expression clearly says *I'm not sure I want you coming round to my house.*

Back in the main gallery, I let Belinda lead the conversation. 'Did you see anything you like'?

'He's quite cute,' says the wife nodding her head in my direction, 'but he's not big enough for me.'

'There is something about tall men,' agrees Belinda.

'When would you like me to come around?' I say, opening the diary. I'm free Wednesday or Thursday.'

'Why don't you both come around for a bite? Seven pm on Thursday?'

'Perfect.'

Address confirmed and time too.

At no point does Gate ask how much anything costs.

'Will you bring that nude picture over there' Mrs. Gate adds.

'With pleasure and thank you.'

They both leave and I look at Belinda. 'You never can tell a book by its cover.'

'Isn't he fab. I just love his hair.'

Thursday comes and we do both go for a bite and a pleasant surprise.

We arrive close to seven. Always be early, never late.

The house looks quite small on the outside but it's a rabbit warren inside, extending way into what must once have all been back garden. It's immaculately tidy and minimal. Gate has a top of the range, white wooden kitchen with black granite surfaces and a massive American, two-door fridge. Everything is in straight-out-the-showroom condition.

'Have you just moved in?' I ask.

'No. But we've just finished the whole house from top to bottom. Would you like to see around?' We're going to get the full tour.

Gate opens a bottle of champagne and fills four pewter tankards. 'Tastes great out of these and keeps it cold. Cheers! Now come and see my den.'

We exit through French doors, down a cobbled path, to be confronted by a steel padlocked shed. Gate opens up, switches on a light and...

'Wow!'

What we're looking at is a neatly organized room with equipment and tools hanging from the walls. Four huge motorbikes stand there, gleaming and sparkling. Each bike is polished black and dazzling chrome.

'These are my ladies.' Gate can stand without stooping in his shed, despite his height.

I feel like a kid in a sweet shop. I ask if I can sit on the chopper with the extended handle-bars. I'm unsurprised to be declined but can't help a surge of disappointment. 'Just thought you might like to see them' says Gate. He switches off the light and re-secures the building.

Back in the house, Mrs. Gate takes over. 'I want the nude in our bedroom and the picture of the squiggles in the hall. Then I think the colourful one would look great in the lounge behind the couch.' Methinks we've become hanging assistants. She knows exactly what she wants and where to put it. 'That one is going upstairs in the chill-room.' Done and dusted by the sounds of it

Belinda and I hang the paintings except for the nude. The bedroom is off limits apparently. 'I'll hang that one later,' says Gate.

'Are you sure?' asks Belinda. I just know she wants to see the Giants nocturnal domain.

'Let's eat 'says Mrs. Gate. 'I'll show you the bedroom later.' We sit in the lounge and from nowhere she produces platters of cured meats, cheeses and a massive bowl of salad. 'Tuck in.'

'All out of a packet. God bless the supermarket,' says Gate.

At some point in the evening Gate says they'll have all the paintings; he still hasn't raised the issue of prices. 'I'll call in and sort out payment.'

'That's fine,' I say, offering my hand to close the sale. Duly shaken, we bid them goodbye with thanks for their hospitality.

I've been driving for at least five minutes before Belinda says a word. 'I never got to see their bedroom.'

I rest my case.

I suppose you'd like to know how the deal concludes. Normally I never discuss client confidentiality but for you dear readers the total came to a lot. He comes in and pays just as he said he would. The name on the card he uses is Mr.S. Smith.

'Gate?' I ask, raising an obligatory eyebrow.

'It's a long story.'

'Then thank you for your custom.'

'You got to keep the women happy,' he smiles.

Not Belinda though. She still wants to see their bedroom. Maybe she'll get a chance another time.

I must admit, I can't help wondering where all that money comes from, but you know what? Their home looks stunning with their new paintings. Job done. Who are we to question?

ANOTHER SORT OF BLUE

It's raining, or to be more precise, pouring. Rain is bouncing off the pavements and cascading down for a second dousing. I'm on the phone engaged in someone else's malaise because their dog's bitten off the packaging of their wrapped, new painting and eaten part of the frame. Well at least the dog has taste. I'm trying to sound sympathetic and not to laugh.

The front door opens and a drenched assistant, hair completely sodden, pads in, leaving puddles on the floor. An atmosphere enters with her. Even the hinges sigh in momentary sadness.

'Good morning, Belinda,' I say in my usual up-beat manner. 'Looks like the weather's won today. Thanks for making the effort.'

No reply. She crosses the floor and the door to the kitchen closes behind her, rather too loudly for comfort.

Meanwhile back on the phone we're reaching an obvious outcome; the customer will bring the painting in and we'll repair the frame. I suggest not bringing the dog with them.

Wandering off to the back of the gallery, I open the door gently. Sitting on a stool, with water dripping off her nose, is a dejected Belinda, texting on the phone.

'My boyfriend's left me!' she wails.

'I'm sorry to hear that.' In the back of back of my mind I can hear myself acknowledging that this isn't going to be an easy day.

Now I know there are rules and regulations which govern the working environment but I don't think it unreasonable for staff to try and dry themselves off before having their breakdown on the time I pay them for.

'There are some spare clothes in the stock room. Go and change.' There are always emergency situations but a gallery environment can hide quite a few solutions in a well-stocked back room.

Business as usual, starting with putting on some music. The soundtrack to Butch Cassidy and the Sundance kid. Highly appropriate. Raindrops are pouring on my head.

Approximately half an hour later, Belinda wanders in wearing a decorator's overall, the front all poppers and large pockets. She's rolled the legs up and found a spare pair of wedges. Her hair is tied up in a knot and, I have to say, looks stunning. I've never seen overalls look as good on anyone. Mind you, I've never looked at men in decorator outfits that way, ever.

For the moment, she seems to have forgotten about her boyfriend. There is, however, one slight problem. The poppers are quite far apart and every movement, graceful or not, gape to show off her figure, or at least, those parts of her figure not covered by her underwear. Do you remember the statement I made about never poking the payroll? Well, with due respect, Belinda poses a huge challenge to my principles. I begin to think that she's deliberately flaunting herself, an art she performs with absolute precision.

With great mental restraint, I'm just about able to obey the rules and simply enjoy the view. Please forgive me; I'm not a lecherous old man; at least, not yet.

Then without any warning sign, she begins to wail. 'It's not fair. I'm sure he's gay, the bastard. I love him. He's a shit. I don't know why I bother. He won't sleep with me. I hate him; hate him. Aaarrrh!' She turns it into a full-blown wail with arms flying everywhere and falls to the floor. There's total silence.

The door opens to admit a couple of potential customers.

'Can we look around?'

I say, 'Feel free', casually putting my hands under Belinda's armpits and trying to get her off the floor, into a sitting position. She just sighs and sobs. Then she lets me lift her up gently and I half drag, half walk her back into the kitchen.

'Oh God, I've made such a fool of myself,' she says.

'Have a drink' I suggest and leave her to it. I've got sales to make.

'Now then, what might you be looking for?'

TARTAN

Tartan is made up of many colours; rich dark blues, strong reds and hints of yellow, blended in the traditions of tweed and kilt weaving.

The Managing Partner's PA, a lovely lady called Mary, or MPH to her friends, asks me to attend their Burns Night celebration. She's recently purchased a painting from the gallery, and I must admit there's a sort of mutual attraction between us that could be dangerous. But then sometimes you have to experiment.

There's no better time for Scots to wear the full Tartan regalia than Burns Night. It's become the tradition on such occasions to pipe in the haggis and mix wine and whisky. God knows why - it's a lethal combination and causes havoc with the head and the stomach.

Our hosts are one of the top firms of solicitors in the country, with a reputation for ruthlessness, a massive corporate power-base and lots of money to entertain their clients. I suppose it's a nice gesture, even though I'm not Scottish and I certainly can't afford the firm's rates so I'm highly unlikely to commission their services. All right, I'll recommend them to anyone I know who can afford them. One does like to help out wherever possible.

It's quite a large affair - over a hundred and twenty men and a smattering of ladies. Strangely, quite a number of the menfolk are wearing kilts even though few of them sound remotely Hibernian. I go suitably black-tied and no kilt. I do wear trousers though.

On entering the suite, I'm offered a glass of champagne by one of the junior assistants. She's in the obligatory little black dress, and ushers me in. Always a good start.

MPH is wearing a smart long black number which clings in all the right places, fitting her perfectly. In her black patent heels, she's as tall as I am.

I suppose if you like classic Scottish fare, you'd enjoy the food. The wine is flowing and the conversation at table is safely boring.

'My wife's an artist,' the gent opposite me says, having learned what business I'm in. It would appear that when you own a gallery, the only thing people want to talk to you about is painting or sculpting.

'Really. I'm so happy for you. Do you hang any at home?'

'She's not that good yet. You should see what she does. Would you like to sell her work?'

I smile and answer in the most polite way possible whilst avoiding the question and distracting him with 'I'm pretty distressed to find they want to cut back further on art and creativity programs in schools. How do you feel about that?'

No real answer. I feel I'm talking to a brick wall. 'No! Okay. Please pass the wine.'

Looking around the room, I can't help noticing that all eight women in the room are dressed in black and they're all looking like they'd prefer to be somewhere else. Err, me too.

The place goes quiet, the pipes are played and the ceremony starts. The whisky is served, and then more whisky and quite frankly, I'm thinking about bowing out and going home, when MPH saunters over to my table and asks, 'How's it going.' She sits down in a seat next to me and says, 'It's great fun; don't you think?'

I find it difficult to lie. 'It's the first Burns Night I've ever been to.'

'What do you think of men in kilts?' she asks, and then, pulling the chair closer, adds 'I love men in skirts. They're so sexy.'

'Really', I reply. 'I suppose it's good to let everything out in the open now and again.'

She squeezes my thigh and leans closer still.

'Bet you'd look great.' Then she stands up and leaves without saying where she's off to.

Am I the only man admiring this woman? She has a superb figure. Either it's God-gifted or crafted by hours in the gym. I don't believe she's wearing a bra either.

Oh well, attention back on the event, listening to speeches and in-house business jokes. The Managing Partner, sporting huge side-burns and red rosy cheeks, along with a cummerbund that's straining to let go, stands up, wavering slightly, to announce, 'We'll be continuing the evening at my favourite club.'

In for a penny, as the saying goes.

At least three quarters of the men stand to follow their host but only two of the women, Mary and her friend Tabitha. The pair of them are somewhat akin to a little and large show with Tabitha standing five feet in her kitten heels and Mary towering over her.

We head off down the street. It's like being back in school, one long queue of children all following the leader. Kilts, black dresses and few suits; it's quite a sight.

Three turnings later and we're standing outside the largest gay bar in town. I know of it but don't frequent it. The Managing Partner waves us all in past the bouncer who is suitably attired in an electric-blue sequined dress with matching eyelashes. He greets everyone in the lowest gravelly voice you can imagine, kissing the odd chap on both cheeks.

At this precise moment, MPH does a sort of pirouette and luckily, I'm near enough to catch her arm and stop her falling full length to the bottom of the stairs.

'Are you ok?'

'Nope!' she says emphatically. 'I have to go back to my hotel. It's not far.'

'Let me escort you?' I straighten her up and let go. On reflection this isn't a good idea as she begins to totter again. Without any fuss, I hold her arm and assist her back out into the fresh night air. Fatal. She starts laughing and utters something under her breath.

'Where to? '

'The Grand,' she hiccups.

She's staying in hotel no more than two streets away. A mere five-minute stroll. However, Mary decides her feet are killing her and flings her shoes into the road. 'Can't walk, won't walk and don't care anymore.' With that, she slowly crumples to the pavement.

Now hang on and stay with me. Options? I could try for a taxi; not sure any driver will let a very drunk woman, however tall and well-dressed, into his cab. Or I can be a gentleman and carry her back to her hotel. It wouldn't be a first for me but that's another story.

I decide to put her over my shoulder and nonchalantly stroll down to the Grand Hotel. She's singing blissfully out of tune and laughing all the way to the revolving doors and uniformed doorman.

'May I help you, sir?' he says, as if it's perfectly normal to see a man with an inebriated woman over his shoulder. What I don't like is the way he says *Sir*. It slips off his tongue like a crocodile entering the river. He's too smooth for my liking.

'This lady is staying here and I'm escorting her back.'

I get a look of total disbelief. You know the one, delivered with the most accurate guided missile technology.

'I need some help to get her to her room please.'

It really is becoming a farce, for now the night manager, and a barman taking a break are looking on with mock disbelief and MPH confuses matters further by opening her tiny handbag and offering twenty-pound notes to the men.

'Have you the key?' the manager asks like a mortician to a deceased corpse.

MPH is still on my shoulder and getting a little heavy now. 'I have a key' she pipes up and empties the contents of her bag on the floor. 'Oh dear. Silly me'

'Gentlemen, I really would like to get this woman to her room.'

At last the penny drops into acceptance and the manager presses the button to call the lift, collects all Mary's belongings off the deep-pile carpet, and leads the balancing act to the lift. So, there we are; the manager, the bell-hop and myself with MPH over my shoulder, happy as a drunken PA can be. The silence in the lift is explosive and even MPH goes quiet. I've never been in a more innocent situation whilst being hung, drawn and quartered at the same time.

We arrive at the fourth floor and duly march towards the room. The manager puts the credit card sized key into MPH's hand. Never mind that she's effectively upside down. She fiddles with it, trying to get into the slot. 'It's like posting a letter,' she giggles. But it clicks and the manager opens the door slowly and deliberately.

The room is unbelievably tidy, considering a woman has earlier prepared herself in it for the evening. On reflection, maybe MPH was planning a little something after the event.

'Well gents, what do you suggest we do?'

MPH isn't laughing anymore and I swing her down so she's the right way up, with her feet in contact with the floor. She looks a funny shade to me. 'I need to lie down.' With that decision made, she launches herself onto the large bed.

'I have to get back to my desk,' the manager says. 'At least she's safely back now, sir.' And he leaves the room followed by his bell hop, who I think just came along for the entertainment.

'I don't feel well!' she says.

In the bathroom, I soak a towel in cold water, ringing it out and returning to the bedroom. She's still lying on the bed but her dress has been entirely discarded and I see I was correct about the bra. There's no evidence of one anywhere.

'Don't you think you should cover yourself up', I suggest resting the towel on her forehead. She closes her eyes, lying quite still. I prop another pillow under her head and drape the blanket over her well-toned torso.

She opens her eyes, and her gaze is dazed. 'Don't you like what you see?'

'I think you have a magnificent figure and you're very drunk.'

Never ever attempt to sleep with drunken members of the opposite sex. It's just not a gentlemanly thing to do. Not to mention illegal. Informed consent and all that.

She sits up, grabs me by the shoulders and tries to kiss me; but instead manages to bite my lip hard. She looks pale and confused.

I say, 'I'll be going now,' and go back into the bathroom for the small waste bin to place it at her bedside. 'Just in case.' There's no response.

She's out cold.

I leave the side lights on, quietly closing the door behind me. Walking past reception, I hear the manager's voice. 'That was quick then.' I ignore the comment and head out through the revolving doors. *Well that's a hell of a first Burns Night* I think as I make my way to the taxi rank.

The next day is plainly hazy and foggy for some. At approximately quarter to one, with a lazy sun trying to peep through the city smog, a familiar woman gingerly walks into my gallery and makes for the nearest chair.

'Good afternoon,' I greet MPH. 'I daren't ask how you're feeling today.'

'I really shouldn't mix my drinks. I don't seem able to hold them like I used to.'

'May I ask what part of the evening you remember?'

A puzzled eyebrow accompanies her answer. 'I vaguely remember leaving the office. I've no idea how I ended up in my hotel room this morning.'

You know, sometimes, silence really is golden, as the song goes.

Julian brings us a black coffee and plain biscuits. Now that's what you call perfect timing. And a much better choice than the hair-of-the-dog, alcoholic, option.

SHAMROCK GREEN

The phone rings bright and early. Sometimes you can tell if it's a ring for something significant or a general enquiry, but today it seems to have a *we need you to do something for us* sort of tone

39

'Good Morning. Gallery here. How may I help?'

A rushed voice, Irish and out of breath, goes on and on about a high-ranking politician who's going to be talking at one of the largest breakfast meetings in the city and would I like the opportunity to be placed in front of the entire audience.

My mind begins to explore the thought but how much is this going to cost me? I ask the question. The answer is 'Nothing in real terms...all it'll cost you is a piece from the gallery to present to her on behalf of the organisation.'

It's a fair contra deal. It takes approximately five seconds to agree although I should first have asked the follow-up question. When?

Thursday! Three days from now. Oh, I love organisations that plan ahead.

What to do?

Actually, I do have the ideal piece of glass in stock. It's a sexy black charger with a shamrock-green base. In reality the shade of green is closer to lime but for the purposes of the Irish connection, shamrock green it will be. If you flick the edge of the glass, it reverberates with a beautiful bell tone, the sign of good quality lead crystal. It was made by a glassmaker I know. An amazing woman. I'll get round to her in due course.

Thursday morning, six am. I kid you not. Leap into my car, suited and booted, minus tie - after all one has to maintain some kind of bohemian look amongst the business community - and drive to the breakfast meeting.

There are twelve hundred invited businessmen and women in the hotel's banqueting room and the noise is alarmingly loud.

Each table takes its turn to walk up to the buffet and collect the usual, far too early, weird looking sausages, very pink bacon, scrambled eggs - far too yellow - and perfectly uniform shaped mushrooms, with one, just one per person, plum tomato.

Not one for this sort of delicacy, I decline and help myself to fruit.

Back at the table I get the obvious comments. 'Not eating then? Can't beat a good breakfast to start the day.'

Correct of course, but this is far too early and a massive fry-up certainly isn't my idea of a good breakfast.

'Not hungry,' seems a plausible response.

Curiosity satisfied, I'm introduced to all the others on the table. A tall bearded gent with an abominably loud tie shakes my hand. 'You're that new chap with the gallery, aren't you? Saw the article in the paper. My wife is a painter you know!' Deja-vu - it's a wondrous thing.

I smile, nod and say 'Yes.' It seems to get me off the hook.

'Would you pass me some toast?'

Someone bashes the microphone for silence and there are the usual greetings and messages before the guest speaker's announced and starts in on her address.

Before she's finished, I'm ushered to the side of the stage and asked to wait. Then I'm up and presenting the glass charger. I can't say I'm entirely clear about what I ought to be saying but it gets applause and a titter from the audience and a thank you from the politician. All done. I'm wrong. I'm pulled back on stage and thanked and plugged almost to the point of embarrassment. It's all been a worthwhile contra deal after all.

As with all reputable business breakfasts, it ends at nine am on the dot. I bid my farewells and dash out in the pouring rain to my car.

Sitting for a few minutes watching the steam build up on the inside of the windscreen, I enjoy the luxury of time to ponder on the last few hours. My phone, buzzing away in my jacket pocket, still on silent mode, breaks into my thoughts.

'Hello.' A woman's voice. 'Just a simple question if you don't mind. Is that glass thingy worth more than a hundred quid?'

'It most certainly is.'

Shit! I'll have to give it to the treasury. Rules are rules.'

'Not If I send you a receipt for ninety-five quid.'

'Oh. Thank you. By the way, my husband's a painter. Maybe you'd like to come to visit us and see what he does.'

She's right. For once I wouldn't mind a trip to see an amateur's work. Not if it means finding out how a national politician really lives in London. And perhaps I can sell her something else.

SULTRY RED

There are two things that go so well together; dance and painting. They equal Paintings of Dance, especially if it's the Tango. There's something so sensuous about this style of movement. As an artist friend of mine says, 'It's like making love on the dance floor without actually having sex.'

Flint is an artist who enjoys dance as inspiration. His bold, bright paintings are full of life and movement, loads of colour and flair. I'm pleased to sell his work and they're great value too.

I originally met Flint via a ceramic artist in the area and having seen two small pictures in a catalogue, contacted him to say I would love to sell his work. He's an outwardly shy chap, well dressed for an artist and has great deportment. You could say he almost glides into the gallery, even with his arms full of freshly painted canvases. He appears with six paintings at a time and usually within a week, they all sell. Easy work. Easy money.

He's a particularly good-looking chap, sharp chiseled features, broad shoulders, and an excellent mover on the dance floor, so I'm told. I'm sure most women find him attractive but I'm not sure he sees this himself as he's always quiet, polite and gracious. He has the loveliest of parents who occasionally call by to see how their son is doing. I find this endearing. Life in a gallery isn't always about the bottom line and seeing their smiles on seeing Flint's work hanging on the walls makes me feel good.

Funnily enough, Belinda never has a day off if Flint is coming in. Julian on the other hand, feigns indifference which I think most amusing. He actively arranges his days off to avoid Flint. I think he thinks *If you can't convert them then leave them well alone.*

With one such visit pending, I suggest to Flint some venues for sketching that might produce some dynamic canvases. We can start off in a Jazz bar, catching the atmosphere, possibly having a few beverages along the way, and then off to a live venue or nightclub.

Flint says this is a good idea and agrees with his partner that he can stay over at my place. His wife-to-be is a formidable woman. I'm not saying anything here.

Flint has a remarkable ability to capture atmosphere with just a few well-placed lines. At the club, sketchbook in hand, he takes up a position on the balcony, oblivious of everyone around him. Strangely, the area fills up with women in various lengths of skirts and styles of clothing, or lack of it. He has an immediate following, all female and all wanting to see what he's doing.

So here is some advice for young aspiring bucks. If you want to pull in a club, you have to look innocent and be able to draw. You'll have the pick of the entire place.

Flint doesn't speak to a soul. That's my role and my very real pleasure. We have several bottles of wine, as evidenced by the debris of empties and glasses around us, before a tall, long-legged blonde, in the tightest white dress, strolls in front of Flint. She just says, 'Paint me.'

He looks up, lowers his pencil and says in a quiet but positive manner, 'I never paint nudes in public.'

What a line! What a delivery! I'm not surprised his girlfriend is a little protective as to where her beau ends up. She shouldn't worry though. Flint is the epitome of the faithful man. Even if many of the women around him don't want him to be.

It turns out to be a successful night. We both achieve a satisfactory level of inebriation and Flint has a sketchbook full of ideas as well as a few telephone numbers written in lipstick on his pad. We take a taxi ride home and he can't stop discussing what we've seen during the night. It's a case of once he starts talking, he can't stop.

Several weeks later, Flint comes back with the night's work transposed into the obligatory six paintings but also a watercolour sketch. He's managed, without superfluous detail, to record the brass section of a funk band, glistening in the stage lights, and in another, a couple are embraced in conversation in the bar – you can almost hear what they're saying in the picture. The other images are dance floor pieces, vibrant in their use of colour. The last piece, the sketch, is a revealing study of the tall blonde, wearing very little against a blurred background. How did he do that? I swear to God that man has x-ray vision.

Flint is a success story in the making and I'm very happy to be part of it.

CLEAR GLASS

Is glass a liquid or a solid? Or both, at different stages of its creation? It has colour though, taken from the chemical content.

Imagine twelve hundred and fifty degrees of pure fire in a furnace. It's damned hot. We're talking burning gas and blinding white light accompanying the compelling smell of an industrial process.

Now add a tall, long dark-haired, incredibly good looking female glassmaker to the mix, and you get something even hotter and more dangerous. This particular glassmaker, Sarah, wears a dark blue boiler suit reminiscent of an Belinda's alternative apparel after getting soaked in the rain, and quite frankly it has a very similar effect. The expression is *horses sweat, men perspire and women glow*. This lady is glowing with a vengeance. How can someone be so sexy whilst beads, nay rivers, of perspiration pour down her face onto her boiler suit, vanishing down her cleavage to visit places only the mind can see.

She dips her metal blowpipe into the gather, collecting red, glowing, molten glass. Placing the end of the pipe to her lips, she gently blows into it. Slowly the glass expands, changing colour as it cools. Then, when she's measured the size of the glass, she begins to spin it, expertly turning the pipe, using old metal dividers to gently force the glass to open out, and blossom, morphing into a flat disk. It grows and grows and eventually when she's satisfied, she inverts the whole show and hits the base of the pipe, releasing the glass onto a metal tray full of paper and sand. As simple as that! Rest assured though, every moment has been honed and perfected. There's no room for error, lest the whole lot ends up shattered into a thousand pieces and she has to start again.

Sarah is a pleasure to watch and certainly makes glass buying even more attractive than one has any right to expect.

'Fancy a cuppa? I'm parched,' she says. Not surprising that!

'Tell me. Do you get many buyers watching you in action?'

'I try not to,' she says, flicking her hair back over her shoulder. She sees that I've noticed. 'It starts out all tied up and tied back, but somehow it never stays. Dangerous isn't the word at these high temperatures.

Anyway, I'm not too fond of letting people see me sweat buckets. It's embarrassing having my clothes end up soaking wet.'

I'd like to make a video of her working. I don't tell her that.

'Let's talk glass.'

'It's all about the relationship between the colours and the properties of the glass. Some glass melts at different temperatures and if you don't get it right...bang...it explodes. If it's cold and the wind blows through the factory, it can also ruin the finished pieces.' She sighs, collecting her thoughts. 'Sometimes I feel it's all too much and I should do something else. It's like a battle of heat and bloody mindedness to finish a piece. And it doesn't stop there. If as much as a little air bubble gets stuck inside, then as it cools down, that too can cause an explosion and that's another hour's worth of pain wasted. Nobody realises how much work and effort goes into making glass pieces.'

She walks over to her trusted friend, an old black metal kettle, and clicks the on-switch. Sitting down, her outfit parts, exposing her torso from neck to stomach. I'm not complaining.

'I've opened a new gallery now and I want to support local artists as much as possible,' I say, pulling up a crate to sit on.

'News travels fast you know? I'd already heard,' she says, and the conversation turns to partners and dogs. Hers not mine. 'It's too hot at home and I have to bring him to the studio. So, everyone in the industrial park takes turns to walk him and keep him happy. It's better than having him tied up.'

'We're talking the dog, not your boyfriend?' I ask tongue in cheek.

She ignores my stupidity. 'Let me show you something that I've never shown anyone till now. You could be the first to show it in your gallery.'

I always like a first but I'd thought today's adventure into the world of hot glass making by a hot glassmaker couldn't get any better. Then she leans down and reaches into a tall cardboard box, pulling out a wrapped object. It's long and black with a silver edge. It's a vase, matt black glass with a rolled silver leaf edge.

'Never seen anything like it,' I say. 'Anything else?'

'Yes,' and she pulls out a smaller piece, also masked in tissue paper. It looks very oriental and I know it'll work really well in the gallery. This time it's a small matt black bowl, again with silver dripping round the edge.

'These cost twice as much as the other pieces - it's so hard to make the silver stick to the glass.'

'I think they're superb. Different and very sensuous. And I want that piece you've just made too because I was here watching you when you do it.' I don't queer my pitch by telling her that looking at the pieces in the gallery will always remind me of the maker. And why not? There's so much ugliness in the world and a little beauty goes a long way towards happiness.

Sarah says she's had enough for the day, so I ask if she fancies a drink at the pub a few doors down. Smiling, she agrees.

'Back in a minute' she says and vanishes behind an old wooden door. Two minutes later, a totally changed person emerges. Her hair is loose, her sloppy sweatshirt just happens to fit in all the right places and it's accompanied by the tightest pair of jeans I've seen in ages.

'Let's go,' she says, turning off all the power and closing the battered old door. She slams the large bolt across and secures it with a rusty padlock.

'Beer o' clock.' She's smiling again.

'Did you enjoy watching today?'

'Honestly!' I raise my eyebrows. 'You are the hottest glassmaker I've ever seen.'

'That's easy,' she mocks. 'You've never seen a woman sweat before?'

'Not often in a factory and especially not in the middle of the day.' We wheel into the pub and straight to the bar. 'What can I get you then?'

'Pint of bitter, please'

The barman looks at me, then at Sarah, nodding his head in my direction. 'New one, is he?'

'Two pints of bitter, thanks.' I'm repeating myself.

Sarah laughs out loud. 'He always does that. Fancies the socks off me, doesn't stand a chance.'

'Do you always bring your conquests here to cool off?'

'It certainly looks that way.' Her eyes sparkle. Then she downs the entire pint in one go.

'Same again.' Then 'How old are you?'

'Why do you want to know?'

'I like to guess men's ages. Most of you are still boys and age is irrelevant. If you want a toy boy, you know what to expect. If you want a man with experience who knows how to treat a woman properly then you need to ask. The truth is I get so horny in my studio and Bob's on the way out. He's just not up to what I want or need right now.'

'I take it Bob's the boyfriend, not your dog?'

'Not for much longer. Don't think I should be telling you any of this. It's not very professional is it? But I have to tell someone.' She stops speaking and then looks directly into my eyes and asks, 'Do you mind if I have another beer?'

'Not at all'

She's consumed, nay guzzled, two pints on an empty stomach and wants a third while I'm still on my first.

'He doesn't want to sleep with me. Do you think I'm the sort of woman who doesn't want sex? Look at me!'

Well, I can only agree with her. 'You're a seriously sexy woman and after what you've told me, let alone watching you work, I'm sure you're fully justified.'

She leans in to me and whispers in my ear. 'So how old are you?'

'Nearly forty-eight,' I tell her, proudly.

She bites my ear. 'Not old enough. I don't sleep with anyone under fifty.'

'I can wait a bit.'

She laughs.

Funny thing is, I already know we're going to be good friends rather than end up in bed together, however much blowing and glowing she does for me.

PURPLE

There's something quite pleasant in only opening up at ten in the morning. You don't have to encounter the school run with its mad four-by-four drivers, oblivious to other rush hour traffic. It's one of my pet hates; such a waste of time. You end up sitting still in a queue of stationary cars billowing out their fumes. I smile at other drivers or nod or if I'm really into the radio, conduct along. It guarantees they stay away from you.

At 11.15 Julian sneaks in, horrendously and unusually late. He's wearing a full-length overcoat, a matching woolen scarf and dark glasses. It's not cold outside, it's not too sunny, and it's not raining. His garb is obviously hiding a story. Just a hunch.

He doesn't utter a word but sits down and lays his head on the desk, sighing. He remains in this position for five minutes, inviting curious attention and not moving an inch. It matters not to him that a lovely lady is buying a picture for her husband from me and is about to hand over her credit card. She looks over at him and asks, 'Are you alright young man?'

Julian raises his head. He turns it from side to side slowly as if to check it's still on his neck. 'This is not the day to ask me anything'. He speaks in a hushed, pained tone with strong overtones of *woe is me*. The scarf slips an inch revealing several empurpling bruises.

Not being a detective, I'd still hazard a guess that they're love bites. Well in true theatrical spirit, he has the entire floor, like a new sculpture displayed in the middle of the gallery.

'Do you realise what I've had to go through?' he yells out to no one in particular. We don't realise or want to. Furthermore, we aren't going to play ball, so I turn back to the Pattersons.

'Did you do anything special last night?' I ask.

Mrs. Patterson blushes and looks at her husband sheepishly.

Blimey. The wrong question to ask.

'Bloody cells. Bloody bins and bloody ripped Armani jeans. Brand new; ruined - totally bloody ruined.' Julian's working up into a cyclone. It would appear we've no choice but to take in the full performance. Curtains up, here we go.

'Okay, Julian. What happened to you?'

He shakes his head with a mock exhalation of air. 'I knew I shouldn't have gone to his house.'

'How about starting at the beginning?' I do try to be sympathetic to those embroiled in lovers' tiffs but Julian is too accustomed to finding the wrong sort of boyfriends, who apparently all treat him far too roughly, take his wages and abuse his friendship. His words, not mine.

Belinda slips away to the kitchen to prepare the drinks which will doubtless be needed. I detect a grin on her face.

Meanwhile, the Patterson's have decided, in addition to their picture, to purchase an exquisitely unique glass bowl. It's a radiant purple piece with swirls and cuts to let the light through. To the imaginative among us, it's a portal into the universe with hidden solar systems waiting to be discovered and reasonably priced at a whisker below two thousand quid.

Mrs. Patterson is caressing the bowl in a longing sort of way. 'It'll look beautiful in our lounge.' Mr. Patterson nods in agreement with his wife's decision, as if he has any real choice but to allow his credit card to take another bashing. And it's not even midday yet!

'Not at all' I say. 'Fancy a glass of wine to celebrate?'

'Most certainly,' says Mr. Patterson.

Belinda returns with fresh coffee and biscuits and I pull a good Rioja out from beneath the counter, with three glasses. Might as well join in the celebrations. It's a good way to cement a purchase and as far as I'm concerned, wine is an essential element to make the gallery run smoothly.

Without any apparent reason for the escalation of his temper, Julian suddenly sends his chair flying across the floor. He walks over to the newly sold glass bowl as if to take it off to be wrapped, raises it high above his head and turns it to catch the light. Then after a few seconds standing perfectly still, he lets it drop to the floor. For a moment the world goes into slow motion as the bowl aided by gravity falls straight down to its demise on the hard surface, and shatters into a thousand pieces. The noise is explosive and fragments launch off in all directions.

I look on in total disbelief and Mrs. Patterson freezes with her glass of wine an inch from her lips.

Julian steps carefully over the glass shards and heads for the front door. The last words that I can make out are that he can't stand it anymore. Then he's gone leaving me to face two incredibly upset and disappointed clients, a difficult clearing up job and what to do with the transaction.

No choice. I immediately offer to cancel the sale and ask for the card back. However, Mr. Patterson works for a bank and says that technically as he's already flexed his card and paid, he's now covered by the rules and can get a full refund. More wine needed I conclude.

It's strange to sit down with the Pattersons and act as if nothing has happened with all the mess around but one does what one has to do.

'Can you get another piece commissioned? asks Mrs. Patterson quietly.

'I'm sure after they hear the story of what's happened, they'll be delighted to make you a new unique piece.'

So, in a weird sort of way, we all end up in a winning situation; two bowls sold, two happy customers, plenty more wine consumed and Belinda secretly relieved to see the back of Julian.

For he's gone and never comes back.

RIOJA RED

There's a problem with alcohol. At what point do you refuse to offer a glass to a customer in the gallery? After all, it's not a licensed drinking establishment but we still need to recognise when enough is enough, especially when it isn't closing a deal.

It's a fine balancing act and may take years to perfect. My accountant keeps trying to say that wine isn't a justified expense on the annual balance sheet. I tell him it's a perfectly balanced way to run a gallery.

A foreign gentleman walks in one day and asks outright if I want to buy some organic Spanish wine. He says it's from his sister's vineyard. I'm sort of interested, especially after he tells me his life story. We're talking about diamonds and other precious gems, Africa, guns, converting to the Christian faith whilst living in the Middle East, and a desire to open a Sherry and Port bar in the city. It all sounds plausible if exotic, but I still want to try the wine before buying it. Sensible heh! He turns and walks out of the gallery door without a reply. So be it.

He's back in a bit carrying three bottles. He also has a glass decanter, corkscrew and very large wine glasses. 'So,' he says. 'Let us try the wine.'

The first bottle is a young vintage and personally, I don't like it at all. 'This is rough,' I tell him but he doesn't bat an eyelid.

He casually opens the next bottle. This is a six-year-old wine with a fuller body and superb cherry flavours. It's a deep, full-blown cracker of a bottle.

'Now this one I like', and he nods without commenting himself.

Then he opens the third bottle and tries it first himself. 'This is the wine for you.' He says at last.

I try the wine. It's magnificent. It has a bouquet that smacks of the expensive, a taste to match and a nice label.

'How many boxes would you like?'

There's only one simple, obvious question.

'How much are they?'

'I want twenty pounds a box but you must take several.'

This really is an incredible deal and for once I don't question either provenance or price, although at the back of my mind I do wonder if his sister actually exists. If there's a problem, we'll just drink the evidence.

'How many boxes of number three do you have? And they aren't stolen, are they?'

He looks marginally offended, 'My sister really owns the vineyard and I want to get rid of the lot and do something else with the money.'

A quick calculation is followed by the problem of where I'm going to store several hundred bottles of wine. A nice problem to have.

We decide on two shipments of fifty boxes each of number three and number two. A total of two hundred boxes of superb wine for cash on delivery. Sure enough he returns at four o'clock with the first shipment. Belinda announces that she can't be expected to carry boxes and duly installs herself behind the desk to make some phone calls. I love the selling incentive. Hump wine or sell art; after all, we're an art gallery. I take off my jacket, drape it over a chair and prepare for action.

The vintner wheels them in, six boxes at a time. As you can imagine, it takes some time to unload as the back of the gallery fills up and takes on the appearance of a warehouse.

I pay him cash, trusting the contents of each box and then make a few calls to friends to see if they'd like some wine. Actually, it turns out to be a fantastic deal - I make some money and keep enough back to last the year.

The trouble materialising is that we're all spoilt with the quality and several customers keep on coming in for the odd snifter. Far too often. Not sure how to discourage that.

Anyway, with the gallery well stocked with wine and some great new pieces of glass and art, it's a nice sunny afternoon, and a chap walks in wanting to buy some glass. It should be a simple case of sell, have a drink, wrap said goods, take the money and say goodbye. What could be easier? Alas this isn't going to happen.

He sits down to a taste of my newly acquired stock. So far so good. But then he begins to tell his life story. He's been abandoned by his wife for a younger man and although he's kept his glass collection, she's stripped him of his records, books and plants and he's devastated. The final straw is that she took the cat as well. You do have to listen to all this and be compassionate. Perhaps Wednesdays should become designated *sit on the couch and tell all* sessions.

Belinda's losing interest, bless her, and her advice is that he should get another cat. 'Back in a minute' she says. 'We need milk.'

I'm left having to listen to this chap pour out his heart. 'Have another glass of wine,' I suggest. He proceeds to go into detail about which records have been taken from him.

Then another customer comes in, puts down her shopping and sits in the second chair.

'My name's Jenny' she offers her hand whilst he's in full flow.

'Uh, Steve' he replies and shakes her hand quite hard.

This is going to be fun.

'How are you Jenny, Glass of wine?'

You know that moment when you feel like you don't exist in a room. Well these two are chatting away as if on a first date. They don't stop talking or for that matter drinking. Now you might think that I'm making up the next part, but I swear it's true.

After three glasses and forty minutes of non-stop chatter, Jenny leans over and snogs Steve's brains out. I mean there and then, in the gallery, and in front of me!

Well at least his record collection's now taking a back seat. They don't come up for air and continue to kiss and cuddle.

Belinda walks in. She's been gone ages. Where did she go for the milk? She looks at the couple, then looks at me, shrugs her shoulders and heads off to the kitchen.

'Pardon me for interrupting' I say slightly louder than normal. 'Don't you two lovers think you should book in across the road as I don't really think you can take this any further here?'

They stop and turn to look at me.

'What a great idea!' Jenny squeezes him tight, 'Shall we?'

'I'll collect my purchases later if that's ok?' Steve says looking somewhat disheveled.

'Fine, grab the moment.' I swear he's looking at me as if to ask permission. Then they both walk out, hand in hand; off to continue their tempestuous first date.

'Well,' I tell Belinda, 'at least he stopped talking about his records and that cat.'

'Yuck! That was so gross. How could she just do that? And they're so old!' she says.

I choose not to reply to her ageist attitude.

There but for the grace of God...

STICKY TREACLE BROWN

My opinion of installation art? Something that isn't for sale and usually bears no sense of commercial reality. It has its place in museums and art galleries, usually funded by our taxes, and provokes reactions and discussion within the art establishment. Or in simpler terms, it's a load of rubbish with hours spent producing something that, when finished, usually ends up wrapped and stored and never seen again till it's discarded on a tip.

I find myself invited to a degree show. In fact, I get invited to many degree shows at various universities around the country. And most of them I decline as basically too far away and too much effort to travel to at the end of a gallery day. However local shows are worth supporting and I suppose you have to look out for future talent lurking among the dross.

By dross I refer to the cards carrying hundreds of words explaining the artist's sentiment of a piece, trying to justify the bland workmanship hanging beside it. Or the usual reclaimed stuff littered around like decomposing dinosaurs wanting to be left alone, usually wrapped in resin or sheets or, in some cases, both.

At this particular degree show I end up not just close to the art but almost in it. Stumbling over an electric lead which has been inadequately gaffer taped down, I fall fully prostrate beside a tray of brown sticky stuff. I could have easily enhanced the installation by falling flat into the whole shebang but luckily not this time.

Rising from the middle of the treacle liquid pond are several metal spikes with flowers attached. They're a faded brown and very dejected or, simply, dead. They remind me of visiting the tar pits in California as a teenager but in truth this has far less going for it. I'm curious why anyone would produce such work after four years studying for a degree.

The Principal of the college strolls up to find out what I think of the show. I really want to say I'm totally underwhelmed but restrain myself and ask him what he thinks of the treacle bath.

'She's amazing, don't you agree?' He launches into a monologue about how society is glued together but spread thinly across a world in which only a few will escape and thrive. I try to look interested but my brain is saying one word. *Cobblers*.

'You must meet her. Natalya! Come over here.'

A tall, stunningly good-looking student saunters across with the air of a cheetah about to pounce. She has long blonde hair, a tight-fitting black jumper and a pair of sprayed-on, white jeans.

'How do you do?' she says in a deep voice, offering me her hand. She has piercing blue eyes. 'I'm Natalya. Who are you?' This is a girl on a mission.

'I own a gallery in the city.' I reply.

'Then I want to show my art in your gallery. I shall come and see what your place is like and decide what I need.'

It amazes me to hear her express such a complete and total expectation of being allowed to exhibit.

'I've never shown installation art but you're welcome to visit.'

'I'll come with my boyfriend in the morning.'

Just like that she walks off, dismissing me!

'Told you she was great.' The Principal smiles.

Do I detect a spring in his step? I begin to conjure up scenarios, none of them legal. Is he actually having a fling with this dangerously seductive student?

A few bottles of sponsored beer later, I decide my brain has been tortured enough and I aim for the exit. Standing outside with a cigarette perched on her bottom lip is Natalya.

'We could have some fun you know!' She exhales and blows smoke in my face.

'Really!' I can't help choking.

'My boyfriend loves to photograph me. He loves to watch.'

The intrigue grows by the minute.

'Okay, come by tomorrow, around eleven,' I say and get a taxi home.

Next day, precisely thirty minutes late, a small, timid, bearded chap, denim covered head to toe, including a peaked cap, edges into the gallery, holding a video camera.

'Please don't say anything till she speaks,' he says, quietly.

I look at him in disbelief and nod.

A couple of minutes later, in strides Natalya in a gold metallic nineteen-fifties style ball-gown, with a huge train. She walks past everything, stops, twirls around and stares at me. Then nothing. Absolutely nothing.

I can hear my brain whirring. *What's going on?*

'Action,' says denim boy and slowly but surely Natalya steps out of her gown in the middle of the gallery and stands there motionless in a black bodice with fish-net holdups.

'I really think you should come over here and dance me round the gallery!' she says.

'Um. Excuse me but this is an art gallery - open to the public and as amusing as it might seem, I don't think dancing round it with a semi-naked woman will do much for business.' In reality, I might be tempted but when all's said and done, we're a shop, not a cabaret venue and I'm a dreadful dancer.

'Grab him,' goes denim boy. Natalya steps in and jumps up, locking her legs around my torso and grabbing me tightly with her arms. By God, she's a strong lass.

'Now we shall do it, here and now. He loves to watch and I want to please him. Isn't he a munchkin?'

Is this *Candid Camera*? I've been set up. Where's the audience? Nobody comes to my rescue and Natalya keeps hanging on for some action.

'You're going to disappoint him and I'm getting very, very horny.'

'That's uhhh...wonderful, but this is neither the time nor place for the pair of you to perform.'

'He's not going to perform. We are!'

'One question then?'

'Hurry up' Natalya pants.

'What's the set up with you and the Principal?'

'Nothing! He hasn't got the stamina for anything adventurous. I'm sure gallery owners are far better, don't you agree?'

She has a point there but I'm afraid having denim boy filming everything isn't my idea of fun. Call me old fashioned if you will.

'Here's the deal. No camera, no open hours, no audience and you're welcome to find out what a gallery owner can do.'

'I can't do that. Milo would get jealous and he'd be so upset.'

'I live in a different world,' I conclude.

'No filming, no show.'

'In that case, it looks like you won't be exhibiting your installation here in my gallery. Sorry to disappoint you.'

Milo decides to speak. 'Got it all. Fantastic shoot. Thank you.'

'Are you for real or what?'

'I just love fantasy ideas and you were brilliant. Wait till you see the finished film. I assume you'll let me show this at college. We could even have a viewing here one evening if you like?' Natalya smiles and sheepishly adds, 'The Principal said you'd be perfect and would add realism to the part.'

'And what about the installation?'

'That rubbish! I hate pretentious art. I'm a drama student. It's so much more challenging!'

Game, set and match!

Before they leave, I ring the college.

'Peter, you're a bastard, but you know what, I'm up for it. After all, the only thing worse than being talked about is not being talked about. Thanks Mr. Wilde. Oh, and by the way, they can have their film show in the gallery too. Bye.'

'Okay you two, just for good measure let's have a glass of wine to celebrate.'

GREEN PATINA

I have an open-door policy. A person should be able to walk in and feel like they can look freely around and hopefully purchase or comment or leave without let or hindrance. I hate it when you have to press a bell and then someone stares at you and decides if they want to let you in.

Somehow it feels like you're guilty of something even if your halo's shining.

One late afternoon, I'm chatting to one of my artists - usual thing, a glass of wine and *how's life, oh no, he's left you again, you can't afford paints or canvas, don't know what to do*. Not a happy situation but blissfully improved when you offer an exchange of invoice for money for a sold painting. Then a drop more wine to celebrate. It's so important to keep both clients and creative persons happy.

A youngish looking bloke, wearing faded jeans and a white hooded top, walks straight in and marches over to a sculpture, at the back of the gallery on a tall plinth. It's a very heavy piece, made in bronze with a glorious green patina on a solid white marble base. He places both arms around the sculpture and lifts it up, turning to walk straight out the door.

I catch sight of his face and he has the look of a man stoned out of his brains on something.

I'm now between the chap and the door. Something's certainly wrong but part of me still thinks it's a joke, not a real theft in broad daylight. I go to stop him and he runs at me, pushing me aside. As I try to grab him, there are two more blokes, both wearing hoodies and one bastard waving a knife. He lunges straight at me, aiming for my sternum, but I've seized hold of the second man and shoved him against his mate. The knife falls to the floor and all three of them run out into the road where a battered looking blue car is waiting, its engine idling. They jump in and it speeds off, doors still swinging. In a moment of madness, I grab onto the back of the car and am dragged up the road, falling off and rolling on the tarmac. Not clever.

Actually, my whole reaction is a form of madness. I like and respect the sculptor who lent me the piece in the first place and it felt like I was duty-bound to protect it.

Now you're going to say, surely, you're insured and the answer is a resounding yes, but that isn't the point. Damned stupid heroics could have ending up being my demise, and as the mind has a habit of working overtime, it begins the mental torment of *what ifs*. I start to feel somewhat shaken. No other word for it.

I hobble back into the gallery and the arcade security team are there. 'We saw it all on camera and ran to you - not quickly enough to stop it though.'

Weird thing is, the whole scenario from the chap entering to the three of them getting away with the sculpture has taken just over a minute and a half. To me it feels like a whole era has gone by.

The artist comes back in, and she's visibly in much the same state as I am. 'I ran out the back. I'm so sorry. I didn't know what to do.'

'That's ok,' I say, trying to calm her down. 'Today we became a crime statistic.'

Then the police arrive. Well a detective and a quiet young officer who looks like he just left school. Must be a sign of my getting older.

'Right ho. What's happened here then?' Like a bad black and white television script.

My brain is galloping with what I should have done and what I might have done and what I didn't do. 'I've been attacked and nearly killed.' Slight exaggeration.

'Name?' The one in plain clothes puts pen to paper and begins what feels like an unwarranted interrogation. By the time he asks, 'Did you know the person,' my fuse is getting shorter by the millisecond.

'Do you have any surveillance system?'

'Yes. Do you want the footage?'

'I can't see any sign that says CCTV cameras are operating. That's a breach which might affect our ability to use the images in court. It's about protecting the privacy of the public.'

Good grief, sculpture stolen, man attacked, the criminal gets off and I'm in the wrong.

'We'll have to take the video as evidence and see if there's anything useable on it.'

'Do you have enhancing equipment?' I ask.

He stares at me; 'We send stuff away only on more serious cases. The expense, you know.'

I can't believe what I'm hearing. 'I'll copy the video for you,' I say, battening down my rising temper. 'I'll drop it off tomorrow'.

He's not happy. 'It's evidence,' he reiterates. I insist. He backs down.

We eventually return to description of stolen item, description of thief, and description of accomplices.

'We don't have to mention the knife; it's a pointless complication.' And a bad pun.'

'Why not?' I really am furious.

'It means more bloody paperwork.'

'It's aggravated assault' I say loudly. 'He could have killed me! Why come to my gallery with a knife if you don't intend to use it?'

The knife is still lying on the floor where it dropped. 'There,' I say, 'One bloody large killing tool, or is this something we don't need to record?' I, for one, want it recorded and sod the paperwork.'

The officers do agree to take it with them when they leave.

That evening, I'm supposed to be going to a charity ball. I feel I ought to go. You know...business as usual. Big smile, ha ha! I actually think I'm okay, but shock has definitely started to kick in. I walk into the hall to be greeted with a glass of champagne and find I'm shaking uncontrollably. Was I all right? A resounding *No*!

By sheer coincidence, the table I've been placed at doesn't have any artists, artists' mothers or wives of husbands who want to be artists. For once the Lord has looked down and intervened. I'm sitting by the Chief Constable and someone who turns out to be something senior for a TV news channel.

'Are you alright, son?' the chief asks, as though I'm a twelve-year old.

'NO!' I stutter. 'I most certainly am not.' Then I re-tell the events of my afternoon.

The guests sit in rapt silence. I have to say the chief cringed a little when he heard my description of his men's approach to questioning me as victim and vital witness but the head of news wants to know a lot more and a lot more he's going to get because he invites me into the studio tomorrow.

Anyway, tonight now requires quite a few glasses of fizz and wine to stabilise mind and body. I can't say I remember getting home that evening, but am a little concerned to wake up, still fully dressed, on the couch.

Yesterday seems like a bad dream but as it comes back to me, my hands are shaking and I reckon shakes don't normally continue after the unreality of a nightmare.

Back in the gallery, the papers have got hold of the story. The phone rings nonstop. It's sad to think it takes bad news to fill a gallery with nosey buggers or well-wishers but it doesn't lead to increased sales.

The worst moment is having to ring the sculptor and tell him. He doesn't seem unduly concerned as, whatever the outcome, he gets paid. A good philosophy I suppose but I prefer to know who's enjoying the works I choose to sell. It's a day to crack a bottle or two and Belinda is very caring, ensuring my glass is topped up regularly.

Alcohol doesn't usually make me mean but I can't help wishing that the little bastard gets nicked on another heist and shot at dawn.

The world works in strange ways. There's a similar grab and run attack in a designer shop a few days later. This time a member of the public is able to sketch the culprit on a tablecloth and the police have something concrete to work on in addition to my scratty video recording.

Business as usual means the gallery doors stay open despite the insurance company wanting them locked and actually we have a good few weeks, selling quite a lot of work. That can't be bad, but I'm feeling a little under the weather and my mind tends to drift into unhealthy thoughts. Even particularly well dressed, good looking ladies, don't merit my full attention. Something is definitely wrong with me. I really must do something about it.

A friend suggests hypnotherapy. I'm intrigued and pay a visit, but I don't think any of you reading this really want to hear what he pulled out of my head. It's not relevant anyway so I won't mention it. Okay?

Twenty-nine days after the horrible event, I receive a phone call from the police. 'Would you mind coming down to the station. We think we have something that needs identifying.'

No details. I agree and go straight over. I'm greeted by a pretty officer of the female variety, hair in a tight plait, well fitted uniform (not that I notice) and amazing eyes. I think I'm getting over my trauma.

It can't be proper to comment on her eyes, but I don't wish to stop myself. 'Excuse me for saying, as a would-be artist and gallery owner, I can't help noticing how blue your eyes are.'

'Sign here' is the reply. She indicates the open page of the visitor's book.

I wait a few minutes and then a tired-looking officer appears to escort me off to a dark green tired-looking room.

Strategically placed on the table, lying on its side, is my missing sculpture. Good grief!

'That's the piece,' I agree, checking the edition number, without touching the bronze. In case of fingerprints, you know. 'How come you recovered it?'

The abbreviated version is that a tip off lead to a raid on a house about ten miles away, and they found it behind a curtain, along with a load of other stolen artifacts and saleable goods.

'We need prints to see if yours are still on it.' Just as well I didn't touch the sculpture just now then. They should have warned me rather than relying on my obvious commonsense.

'What inks do you use?' I'm trying to take a professional interest.

'It's black.' End of interesting conversation.

The next day there's an identity parade. Back down to the station and I'm placed in a darkened room with one-way glass. It's an unnerving experience. They escort in ten men, all dressed in grey hoodies and all pretty much the same height. Considering how short a time I had to take in the thief's facial contours while grappling with him, I was never likely to pick him out of a crowd. I don't. Waste of time.

Fingerprints do the trick anyway and although he denies it, he's bang to rights. As they used to say on *The Sweeney*.

So now I'm a solved crime statistic with a reference number to match. Bully for me.

On a lighter note, I have to inform the insurance company the piece has been retrieved. They have actually requisitioned a cheque for the insured amount. Bugger! One more day and our financial position would have been much enhanced.

'Shit!' is the answer down the line when I tell the sculptor.

Mind you the episode makes the mainstream newspapers and a few weeks later I take a phone call from someone expressing an interest in buying the piece. So, armed with paper clippings and the newly restored sculpture, I drive for three hours to a hugely palatial house in the South of England.

A press of the doorbell summons a butler, of all things.

'I'm afraid the master has just popped out. He'll be back in an hour or two. He says to stay and have lunch and he'll see you later.'

He ushers me into a dining room with a table set for two dozen people. It's more like a film set than real life. I can hear a grandfather clock ticking away in the distance and a carriage clock on the mantelpiece competing with it. If it wasn't for the clocks the atmosphere would be hushed enough for me to hear my own heartbeat.

After a few minutes the butler returns with a steaming vegetable broth on a silver tray.

'Would sir like some bread?'

'That's okay, thanks,' I quip. 'Trying to look after my figure.'

He doesn't appear amused but on his next trip brings me a carafe of wine. He pours it into an exquisite cut-glass goblet large enough to hold half a bottle.

I rarely eat on my own and my mind works hard on imagining what normal company should be round the table with me. I conjure up a General or two, add Lady Whatchamacallit and her niece, a mad scientist and a director of some touring ballet company. That would make for a far more interesting lunch. Maybe throw in a philosopher or two - much better than eating on one's own. The conversation in my head goes exactly as I imagine it should.

The main course is served on a massive bone china plate with monogrammed initials in gold leaf on the outer rim. Roast beef, vegetables, roast potatoes and carrots. I hate carrots but am too polite to mention the fact.

Gravy is served in a silver jug, hallmarked *Birmingham 1840*. I have to lift up the jug for a peep underneath to get that information.

'Would sir like pudding or cheese?'

I'm stuffed and say so.

He shows signs of disappointment. 'The cheese is local and rather good, if you don't mind me saying so, sir.'

How can I refuse? Pleased, he skips out the room. Not really - he walks off in composed butler style.

Port flows with the cheese platter and by now I'm not only full but somewhat tipsy.

'Mr. Symes would like to show you the gardens, sir.'

That's my cue to stand and leave the table. Fresh air seems a good idea. You're laughing because you're ahead of me, I know.

We pass through the heavy oak door, along a corridor adorned with family portraits from the generations. It occurs to me that all the ancestors are staring at me like the house of horror in a Disneyland ride.

The sun through the stained-glass windows drapes the drably clad butler in a blaze of many colours. There's a motto for you: *always put colour in your life*.

'Please show our guest around, Mr. Symes.'

'It would be my pleasure.' Mr. Symes has no teeth yet beams from ear to ear. 'Follow me Sir'.

That's a bit of a problem. The wine and port have decided to kick in and launch a party in my head. I sort of side step along the old stone path and find I'm on a grass verge. There's a silence from Symes but he waits patiently for me to return to the straight and narrow.

'Excuse me,' I slur, struggling to maintain professionalism in the teeth of Latin names for every known shrub, tree and plant yet to be discovered in the Amazon. It keeps the brain active and engaged. 'Walk. Walk straight', I tell myself. 'What's that called?' I ask aloud trying to look interested and sober.

We arrive at length beside a large pond. I suppose you'd call it a lake really. It's surrounded by massive Hydrangea bushes, manicured topiary and a magnificent white marble sculpture positioned on a stone plinth in the middle of the water. It glistens in the bright light.

Mr. Symes says that it's placed there in memory of his first wife. Even in my pickled state I assume he's talking about his boss's wife not his own and I realise I've heard this story already. From the sculptor himself. The sculptor that is of the piece I'm delivering today. 'So, he'll have two...by the same man.' I can count.

'He loves his art, he does. Says it's his duty to collect and share in the beauty of creativity.'

Suddenly the earth moves, the horizon shifts and my vertical balance alters. Result; I fall head-long into the lake. I don't appear to be as sober as I'd like.

Bloody good port though.

I emerge coughing and laughing at one and the same time. All dignity has been abandoned and left at the bottom of the lake. Symes thrusts a wooden pole in my direction and waves it around for me to grab. Shortly thereafter a soaked gallery owner stands on the side of the lake, having learned the sobering effects of a cold dip. Another ruined suit.

The butler must have been watching us because he appears with a long, luxurious, white linen robe and a huge towel. Expressionlessly he offers me both. 'These might help sir.'

Butler, 1. Yours truly, nil.

Eventually we make our way back to the mansion. Squelching my way up the path, I feel like a stooge in an Ealing comedy.

'Would sir like a hot toddy?'

'Sir would not thank you. A strong black coffee will suffice.'

The telephone rings somewhere off in the distance, and a maid comes into the room to say that the master will be staying out for the evening. 'He says he hopes you've enjoyed his hospitality and apologises for not being around. He says the butler can handle the financial transaction on his behalf. And finally, he asks if you'd like to meet him in his club in London at a date and time convenient to yourself, sir.'

Her use of *Sir* is softer and much more attractive than the butler's but he's the one trusted with the cheque book. She curtseys and leaves the room. The writing of the cheque is an act of pure performance art. The butler sits down, takes out an exquisite gold pen from his inner pocket and fills in the details in beautiful copperplate handwriting. They must teach that in butlering school. He looks up and says, 'I believe that is correct,' tears it from the stub, and hands me the cheque.

I glance over it and smile. 'That's great. There's no charge for the after-lunch entertainment.'

I could swallow the silence.

'Please thank your boss for lunch and tell him his gardens are...truly memorable.

GREY

Grey is not a colour. It's a condition! How well do I remember this sentence? It's been with me all my painting life.

It's a Wednesday; a sunny morning, cold and crisp. You can see your breath vapourise into the sky.

The door is open and the heaters are blowing out an inviting warmth. In strolls a well-dressed gentleman, slightly long hair, trilby hat and an old-fashioned style of full-length, tweed coat with attached cape. He has a red kerchief tied round his neck. And his brogues, though well worn, are well-polished.

'Good morning. I'm looking for the proprietor.'

Now as you know, I don't allow random artists to turn up to see me without an appointment. Yet this man has a compelling aura about him and I'm intrigued by his take on contemporary dress codes.

'I'm he. May I help you?' I'm wearing a leather jacket, long hair and a loud designer shirt, without a tie. I'm examined in disbelief. 'I own this gallery,' I confirm.

'My friend has mentioned your establishment. You apparently have a good reputation.'

'That's a good start,' I say jovially.

'Do you actually sell this modern work? What sort of people purchase it? I must confess that I find it a tad difficult to understand the concept.'

This is a challenge to rise to. 'Not everyone wants cows and sheep, tits or tigers or cute gundogs on their wall.'

In an embarrassed fashion he nods. 'I'm a classical painter and yet I feel that this might be the right place to exhibit my work.'

'I'll have to be the judge of that. Would you like a drink?'

Belinda, taps my foot and mouths to me, 'You're mad.' I smile and watch her sashay out to put the kettle on.

The artist sits down to explain his compelling life. An hour goes by with hardly a word from me. It's now dangerously near wine o' clock and he suggests we should partake of some lunch.

I haven't partaken of lunch in ages. What a lovely expression. I like his approach to life, a man after my own heart. I tell him so.

'Belinda, you're in charge.' I have a feeling this is going to be a long lunch.

She tuts in disbelief. You'd have thought she would've been used to my bon viveur habits by now.

'There's a rather good restaurant round the corner,' he says. As if working here I wouldn't know that.

Like an ending to a vintage movie, we set off for the world of wine, food and good banter with a hint of gossip.

There's an amazing honesty to my new drinking buddy, and his knowledge of history and love of life helps the lunch along no end. As do two large gin and tonics before the three-course set menu, and the decision to wash it down with two superb French Red wines followed by two large vintage Ports. In fact, lunch flows seamlessly into afternoon tea without either the sandwiches or the tea.

I'm getting a premonition. You know the one; that feeling deep inside of a significant friendship in the making, despite the alcohol trying to cloud one's judgment. This is the start of something. I know it. This man just might be the catalyst to getting my own artistic career kick-started. Who knows?

In the end we shake hands and with a lilt in his step he leaves me to pick up the bill. I carefully reach the exit of the restaurant feeling like I've had a great time with a distant uncle who knows all the answers to everything important. Or it might be that I'm rather pissed.

I wander around the block to put my head back into a gear or two, and it's approximately quarter to six before I drift back into the gallery. A *Casablanca* quote comes to mind. It looks like it's the start of a perfect friendship. Please don't get me wrong. This isn't sexual. It's the coming together of two totally different people with a common liking or two; namely wine, women and passion - for art that is.

My thoughts are interrupted by a loud bang. Belinda has dropped the order book to the floor, deliberately. She regards me like a scolding teacher and spits out her grievance; 'We need another assistant. I don't like being on my own with all this expensive stuff.'

'It's not stuff.' My natural heartbeat reasserts itself.

'My Aunt...well I call her my Aunt...is looking for some part time work.'

My mind is elsewhere. I know it's dangerous but sometimes one is allowed to separate oneself from the reality of work, especially after a last glass of port.

'What? Oh, right. Fine. Ring her up and see if she'll come in.'

'She's in town tomorrow! I could get her to call by and say hello. I could take my lunch break with her.'

Bless women; they're always ahead of the game.

'Okay.' Giving in seems the easiest option.

Belinda is obviously excited. Don't know why. She always has an aura of nothing fazing her. Emotions don't usually register in her expression, let alone in her eyes. She even gains an unaccustomed spring in her step. It resembles happiness. Maybe I should be concerned.

The next day at precisely one o' clock she goes for lunch.

It's a quiet afternoon and I have space to reflect on the look of the gallery. I love the art; I love the artists I work with...and bless the customers - one has to like most of them. There are exceptions, but the truth is that gallery life is fascinating and varied – which would be no problem at all if I didn't constantly suffer the pangs of wanting to be an artist myself. I want to have my work in a gallery. I want someone else to buy my pictures. I want the time to paint. Ah yes, that magic concept, time. Suddenly an hour's gone. I've no idea where. I've been completely lost in a dream world.

A tall lady, long flowing red hair, wearing bright red fifties style lipstick and a smart, well-tailored, navy blue jacket is impinging on my space. Her heels are just about pornographic and her legs continue all the way past a tight-fitting, somewhat short skirt. Art has taken a giant step for mankind out the door. More primitive urges are kicking in.

'Hello. I'm Caroline...Belinda's aunt. My friends call me Charlie.' Her vocal chords are down in the female equivalent of the sub-basement. With that she lunges forward to take my hand and draw me devastatingly close to her.

'Belinda said you were in town.' I'm stammering a little over the words because my nose is being assailed by the classic aroma of Chanel no.5.

'Please take a seat' I offer her a chair and she sits, crossing her wondrous legs and smiles. 'I love art and all it represents.'

'That's a good place to start,' I say. 'Have you worked in retail before?'

'I had my own lingerie shop near Cheltenham. You'd be surprised what used to go on there; especially when the nags were running.'

I could imagine her as a very successful shop-keeper. I wager there were more male customers than female. However, was she the right sort of woman for my enterprise? She could melt glass with her overt sensuality. Ah well, in for a penny as they say.

'I'm great at weekends,' she smiles again for the returning Belinda's benefit.

'Thanks for lunch, Auntie'

Now I definitely don't know if I'm conducting an interview or a date match.

'Would you like to make your aunt a cup of tea or something?'

Belinda examines each of us in turn. 'Wine perchance?'

'This is a job interview!' That's me trying to scold her and failing dismally.

'And a celebration,' adds Charlie.

'Red or white?'

Belinda brings out a bottle of Sparkling Rose and three glasses. 'It's also Auntie's birthday.'

'Happy birthday. Welcome to the madhouse!'

There's no escaping it. Charlie is charming, bubbly and charismatic.

Belinda says she can't wait to have a weekend off. Conniving young woman! I'm going to be left with Aunt Charlie whether I like it or not.

The bottle is finished and Charlie leans over to kiss both my cheeks and says, 'Thank you.' Her departure is casual and I'm sure calculated to hold my attention. In my mind I can hear the rapturous applause of a non-existent audience.

GANJA GREEN

An Asian looking gentleman ambles in one day. He appears a little hung over and a strong coffee seems like a good idea.

'Hi. My name is Ang-Lo. We own the restaurant across the way I have a friend staying with me and he's an artist. A good one. I really think you will like his work. Come over for lunch and I'll introduce you.'

It's been a quiet morning so far and as I'm on my own, I put a sign on the door and close up. The sign reads *Gone fishing. Back later. Ring me if you need to buy something.* Hell, I own the place, and don't have to feel guilty. Not one little bit.

The restaurant is intriguing for someone like me who's never eaten Sushi or Sashimi before or any Asiatic cuisine, so it could be an interesting lunch.

'Greetings and welcome! Table for one sir?'

'Thanks; but I'm meeting Ang-Lo. Isn't he the boss?'

'He not boss. He party too much. Follow me'.

He walks us over a wooden bridge - large koi carp are swimming around in the pool underneath - into the main restaurant.

Chatting away with glasses of champagne are Ang-Lo, and the man I assume to be his friend, the artist.

'Welcome. This is Bruce. Have a drink.'

He pours me a glass of champagne.

'Cheers' he says finishing and re-filling his glass. 'Keep up.'

Bruce is in his mid-forties and in his smart designer jacket is nothing like you'd imagine an artist would dress.

'Where do you hail from?' I can't place his accent.

'Originally Australia, but that was a long time ago.'

Bruce from Australia, you're kidding. I don't say a word.

He hands over a printed catalogue of his work. The words are in German but who needs them when the images are so wonderfully dynamic. Much of his work features reflections of India's mighty river, the Ganges, or Ganga as he keeps referring to it. Then he's painted groups of Indian women and men in their colourful robes and saris. The pictures are certainly different. I like them. So why am I experiencing reservations in spite of finishing the second and third bottles of bubbles?

Lunch is served. It looks amazing; a work of art using raw fish served with sculptured carrots and cucumbers in the shapes of flowers and animals.

'Add some wasabi carefully' Ang-Lo grins, knowingly.

I'm a convert. This food is superb but then I dip some raw tuna into the wasabi and it blows my head off. Tears roll down my face as I try to regain my breath and the rest of my senses.

'That's hot, like Vesuvius.' It comes out as a squeak.

Bruce controls his laughter and continues talking about himself.

I'm already rather full and a touch tipsy, when the next course appears. It's an array of fillet steak, tiger prawns and fresh salmon with a bowl of rice and vegetables. There's enough food for a banquet.

Ang-Lo opens a bottle of Burgundian Red. Bruce knows the owner of the vineyard. Of course he does!

'You could visit my studio if you like. My work needs to be savoured at your leisure and there are several large canvases that don't translate in a photograph.'

'Where is it?' I ask.

'Not far from Baune. In Burgundy.'

'Why not.' A little trip to France. Just the ticket and tax deductible.

That really ought to be the end of the meeting apart from agreeing dates but we continue drinking into the evening. Finally, Ang-Lo says he'll come along for the ride. Well, why not?

I haven't driven long distances for many years. Not at all really since I left home at eighteen in a rather small car for a summer holiday, which lasted three years. When the time comes, I'm a touch reticent to go, if truth be told, given that I have a business to run. I just have to trust Belinda and Charlie not to wreck the joint while I'm away.

We set off at 4.30 am. to collect supplies from the wholesale market. Apparently, Ang-Lo is planning to cook when we arrive. Yes, we're to become the longest take away delivery service in Europe.

Less than four hours to reach my first encounter with Euro tunnel. My mother, bless her Irish heart, has told me to keep the windows closed, so we won't get wet. Before embarkation, it's coffees and croissants, obviously practicing for the French side, but the journey, once commenced, lands us on the continent in less than half an hour.

Ang-Lo has an insatiable appetite so it's an early lunch in a service station restaurant. This is nothing like our English motorway services - home cooked food and wine! I'm driving and do the decent thing, staying completely sober.

After several such refreshment breaks, we land in the best wine region in France. Trust me, the wines of Burgundy are superb.

Following specific instructions, we leave the AutoRoute to travel along country-lanes, with plenty of Charolaise herds littered everywhere. Over two more steep hills and lo and behold what appears in front of us is a monstrous, gothic chateau.

Bruce actually lives here.

In fact, he lives here on condition he restores the place and keeps it going. More or less all the money from sales of his work go into this twelfth century pile of stone.

We pull onto the cobbled drive and park by the ancient moat. The gatehouse is enormous. Our arrival sets the dogs off barking from the other side, ferociously. A lot of them. A small crack appears in a Judas gate. 'Come in slowly and you'll be okay. Their bark is far louder than their bite.'

We slide carefully through the wooden door and enter an inner courtyard like a Hollywood stage set. You might be forgiven for thinking that men in suits of armour are going to appear at any moment and blessed wenches to chase.

'We'll have a drink on the balcony,' says Bruce and leads the way into the dark interior of one of the buildings. The place has low ceilings, with huge wooden beams and a massive fire roars in a fireplace that's over six feet high. Bet that smoky smell permeates all his canvasses. A trademark of sorts.

The balcony overlooks the valley, the chateau being built on a high outcrop. Over in the distance there's a small church from which constantly emanates the peal of bells. It's a typical small French village on the other side of a river, with a population of not very many.

I'm taking in the breathtaking view, when a fighter jet flies low down the valley, thundering through and scaring every living thing. The noise reaches us in its wake. It's an odd sensation to be standing above a flight path.

'It doesn't happen too often,' says Bruce, pulling the cork and pouring the wine. He sips it after rolling it round the glass, inviting us to follow suit. Ang-Lo simply knocks his glass straight back.

'This is from a friend's vineyard not far from here. We'll visit him in the morning.'

Salut seems the appropriate toast

Ang-Lo takes his refilled glass and starts clattering around in the kitchen area.

Bruce examines me seriously, coughs and spits out a major concern. 'I've been badly treated in the past by dealers. I have real trust issues.'

Oh great. Eleven bloody hours driving on the wrong side of the road and a temperamental artist decides he doesn't want to work with me...GREAT!

'I can understand that.' I put on my most sympathetic tone even though on one level I want to kill him for wasting my time. 'But I have a belief in my gallery and so far, everybody I work with has trusted me. I've always paid my artists, some upfront on occasions, and as far as I know, I haven't disappointed any of them. So, if you feel it's not going to work, just tell me now. I mean I still want to see your paintings. After all that's the reason you asked me to come out here! N'est ce pas? Anyway, how many dealers have ever come out to see you in your studio?' I hope I already know the answer to that one.

'Nobody,' Bruce says softly, looking down at his canvas shoes.

'Exactly! If I like your work and I have a feeling I shall, then I need to understand you and what goes on behind the scenes so I can convey a part of you when I'm selling your paintings. To me it's a vital part of the relationship between clients and you and me. Don't you agree?'

'More wine?'

I don't speak. It's a closing technique. I'm good at this.

Bruce stands to pour the wine. Still no response.

He raises the glass to his lips.

'Cheers!' he says smiling. I think and hope he means *yes*.

'Salut,' I reply.

'Food's on the table' shouts out Ang-Lo from afar.

We pass through the courtyard and into what used to be the drawbridge tower. It's a magnificent room, lit only by candles and a large fire in an even larger fireplace. Gothic as a description comes close to under-statement. On an old table set for three is spread a banquet to suffice an army.

'I'm starving,' says Ang-Lo ripping apart the long French bread and sitting down.

We heave massive leather and wooden chairs into place and attend to our feast.

Throughout the meal, Bruce tells me a lot more about himself, his chateau and his art. In fact, he never stops talking, but he has the merit of sustaining the listener's interest. Any residual ice between us melts and I can see how much of an asset he could be, even if I have to accept some of his prima donna eccentricities.

We continue into the small hours and a bit like a summit between two countries, close the evening in a positive manner. That means see you at six am. We have to buy fresh bread and go wine tasting. Nothing like a three-hour sleep after a long days driving to set you up for a day out in the French countryside.

Three hours of sleep turns out to be a forlorn hope. The beds are as old as the chateau. I manage to lie in the middle of the ancient mattress without sinking so deeply that I'll risk being smothered. I think it should have been condemned in the middle ages. A dog starts barking way off in the valley and a few chickens cluck away in harmony, and it's already four in the morning. In two hours I'm going to be getting up. Might as well do it now. I venture downstairs and watch dawn rise over the valley from the balcony. It's breathtaking. I must have fallen asleep at some point and wake to feel a wet tongue licking my hand, which has developed pins and needles, draped over the back of the metal chair.

Two sets of eyes are staring at me in a hungry manner. Rolling, soft but menacing growls, emit from one dog and if the other is still, he seems no less potentially threatening. Twisting round in my seat I find a third hound now licking his lips rather than my fingers.

The odds are stacked against me. My communication skills in canine French are very limited. I point towards the kitchen and whisper 'Le biscuits'. Three pairs of ears prick up.

The church bells ring out.

It's five am. One hour to rescue.

Eventually Bruce appears and lights a wood-burning contraption. The dogs curl up around the old metal stove and relax. Funny; so do I. The relaxing not the curling.

'Did you have a restful night?' It isn't worth explaining so I confine myself to saying that I'm looking forward to breakfast. I'm vividly imagining freshly baked French bread.

'We have some time. Let me show you my studio.'

We head for the far tower. We duck through a low arch and start to climb a set of narrow, miniscule steps. They must have had very small feet in the fourteen-hundreds. Compared to my size twelves anyway.

Reaching the first floor, the sight is amazing; Bruce has painted the ceiling in cascading waterfalls. Cobwebs and old glass bottles fill the room, which contains only an old wooden table and a chair with no seat. A perfect setting for a *Carry-On* film. We don't stop. In the far corner is a steep set of wooden stairs, somewhat akin to a rickety ladder. An old frayed rope hangs down from the top, the only concession to safe climbing.

'Mind your head when you get to the top.'

Bruce makes the ascent look an easy jaunt. I grapple the rope and do as I'm told. I still hit my head on the stone beam.

Climbing through the hatch, I arrive in the turret. The studio has a wooden stove for heating, a wooden floor covered in paint and cushions, and a table under the window piled high with paper. There are a number of powerful paintings leaning against the walls, including a huge three-metre long canvas with a crowd of at least fifty people painted on it.

'How do you propose to get that out of here?' I ask. An obvious question.

'Voila'. He moves a stack of large canvases. Hidden behind them is an old wooden door. 'I swing them down with ropes, weather permitting.'

He wrestles the old door open and the view is stunning if you take your mind off the long drop to the courtyard below.

I'm impressed and say so, establishing a genuine connection with Bruce at last. We've broken through the barrier. Gallery owner and artist will henceforth get on.

'I'd love to sell your work.'

'I have others to show you in the library.'

I battle my way down the old stairs, this time to visit a safer outpost of Bruce's empire. The library, like the turret room, is full of paintings and several piles of newspaper.

'Ah. My boyfriend collects them. He never reads them and they drive me mad'

'Why don't you burn the lot down in the big fireplace? They must be a hazard in here.'

My suggestion is ignored. 'Take a look at these.' Bruce pulls a huge dustsheet off another stack of paintings.

I could easily spend an entire day going through his collection of stretched and rolled paintings but we don't have time. Not with bread and wine calling.

Bruce drives, leaving me free to envision the exhibition I can create. Selection from so many paintings should be an easy task. Then all we have to do is ship them back to Blighty and sell them.

Meanwhile, back in the car and hurtling down a little track with enough space for a goat or French sheep, Bruce pipes up. 'I have a great idea!'

Maybe he secretly wants to be a rally driver. Who knows I'm eating my seatbelt in fear? Ang-Lo looks equally terrified.

Luckily, we survive to reach the boulangerie. The place already has several people in it and conversation punctuated by shrugging shoulders and tutting is the order of the day. The place smells divine. I'm mad for the taste of fresh bread. Then I spot an egg tart beckoning for me to buy it. I can't ignore its call and eat it straight away in the car, the nutmeg flavour orgasmic on my tongue.

Armed with three huge French sticks and a bag of something or other, Bruce slams the boot shut and jumps back in, barely giving Ang-Lo time to take his seat before hitting the accelerator. We're going to achieve mac speed rather sooner than I'd like.

The area is known for its rolling hills and natural beauty but at eighty miles per hour everything is a blur, including the white cows which fly by quicker than storm clouds in a hurricane.

Hitting the brakes at long last, we slide to an abrupt stop. *Thanks be to the Lord*. We're in front of a lovely seventeenth century house with shutters on every window. A massive front door supports a huge brass knocker - a gargoyle with vine leaves sprouting from its mouth.

We don't even need to knock. The door opens and a well-dressed young chap, sporting a red cravat, red striped jacket and red corduroy trousers emerges. 'Have you remembered the buns?' he says.

'Antoine, this is my new dealer from England,' says Bruce. My new status confirmed. *Progress and promotion*.

'Good morning. Bonjour.' I offer my hand.

Antoine ignores me. 'I've had the most dreadful morning. Collette has walked out. She hates my cologne and the way I run the business. She has taken my dog. What am I to do?'

Bloody hell, it's a soap opera. Who's Collette?

Bruce put his arms around Antoine. 'It will all be alright,' he says in French. At least it sounds like French, albeit adulterated by some local dialect.

Then as if nothing has happened, Antoine shrugs him off and says, 'Let us try the new vintage.'

This is the bit where Ang-Lo wakes up properly, briskly setting off in Antoine's footsteps. We end up down in a cellar filled with a classic mushroomy smell and a host of barrels and bottles.

'Da cour! Right, today I am going to try my new mix for the first time.' He taps a barrel and pours three full glasses from a ladle.

Bruce does the vigorous twirling, sipping and slurping bit, pushing it between his teeth and sucking. Then he spits the whole lot out. Antoine does the same. I sip my glass and then sip some more. It tastes creamy and smooth. Ang-Lo already has an empty glass so I finish mine off.

Out of Bruce's bag come little baked round balls. They're light and have a cheesy aftertaste. We munch in silence. Then Antoine opens a bottle of white wine. Knife around the metal top, followed by an old corkscrew and pop, the wine is liberated for drinking.

Again, three glasses are poured and two men swirl and spit while two others knock it back with gusto. This is no cheap plonk but delightfully moreish, even at eight in the morning. Especially at eight in the morning.

'What do you think?' says Antoine at last.

'I'd like two cases please,' says Bruce.

'More wine!'

It's a warming but strange effect to be under the influence of alcohol so early in the day. However, as a suspicious sod, it occurs to me there might be a reason for all this softening up.

Bruce suggests sitting down. That's an easy task.

'I have an idea! I know you'll sell my work but I want to have an exhibition of something a little different'.

Antoine blushes and seems to shrink in stature, frozen in the act of refilling my glass.

'I've been using Antoine as a model for my project. The innocence of a wine maker relaxing.'

That might explain all the cushions back in the studio.

'He's naked.' Total silence falls. I try to catch Ang-Lo's reaction but he's studiously ignoring the rest of us.

'Are we talking meat and two veg?' I enquire.

'NO! It is quite tasteful.'

A challenging opportunity then.

Undeniably there haven't been too many naked male exhibitions in selling galleries and it could be an interesting marketing challenge. Not sure what Belinda will make of it.

'Here's the deal then.' Let's get opportunistic and strike while the iron's hot. 'First we have a show of your landscapes and river paintings. Then we follow it up a year later with your nude project. However, you'll need a sponsor.'

Bruce gives me a winning smile. 'Done. I've already got a wine merchant on side.'

'Well, that's just brilliant!' I say in total exasperation. Sorting the wine is going to be the least of our problems. What am I letting myself in for? It's either going to be a stress-fest or the social event of the decade. Got to do it though.

'Sold,' I say.

PART TWO

WHERE'S YOUR ART GALLERY NOW

THE CANVAS

Welcome back to the gallery. We've been trading for a few years in the art world now. The gallery has bedded in and the owner has embraced a lifestyle in which stress, fun, wine and women feature heavily.

If you've already read So You Want To Own An Art Gallery, you'll need no introduction to Belinda's Aunt Charlie, who has an agenda or to a business which swims in crateloads of good wine There are new customers to meet, as well as old friends and odd nutcases, and plenty of events, including Bruce's long-planned naked exhibition. Victor is mentoring the gallery owner, my good self, in the grammar of painting and in return everyone's liable to end up tipsy on seriously good cocktails.

Maybe the latest events will want to make you consider retiring early to take up painting or fishing or whatever else floats your boat.

I will apologise if you really thought I was giving you a manual on actually how to run an art gallery because I'm afraid you'll be disappointed. What I want you to do is to put your feet up and watch me trying to make a living out of selling art.

SWAMP GREEN

'Good morning Charlie' I say with a smile.

Charlie, my able assistant Belinda's long-legged aunt, is always a good start to any morning. She's going to be standing in for Belinda for the next two weeks. Belinda's decided to take herself off for a fortnight in Sharm-el-Sheik at short notice. 'It's a bargain and I need a break in the sun.'

Two weeks with Chanel Number 5 - this will be testing.

Charlie's skirt is usually a touch too short and revealing but she does have a great pair of legs, if it's acceptable to comment on them. She also has the ability to bend over like Betty Boop in those cartoons. Her back settles at ninety degrees to her legs, which remain perfectly straight, making her hemline even shorter. Now this isn't fair at only ten thirty in the morning.

The telephone rings. I answer it. That's the division of labour round here.

'Hello is Charlie there? I must speak to her!'

'One minute.' I hand the phone over to my new assistant.

'Hello gorgeous. How are you this morning?'

This is a selling technique new to me.

After several giggles and sweet nothings - I'm not earwigging but she does fill the gallery with her voice - she politely stretches over me to replace the phone in its cradle. She stares up at the ceiling and utters an explanation of sorts; 'A woman has needs you know.'

'I'm sure we all do, but we're open for business and I don't believe that was business. Please refrain from personal calls during opening hours. Thank you.'

'Shall I make you a coffee, sour puss?'

I'm not sure this is going to be a good idea after all.

A well-dressed couple with an unruly child hollering in the pram and trying to get out of its restraints, are the first customers of the morning.

'Quiet now, Teddy. Mommy and Daddy want to look at the nice paintings.'

The child wriggles and kicks and ensures everyone knows he objects to being where he doesn't want to be.

A few quiet words in his ear might help. I put down my cup of coffee and stroll over to introduce myself.

'May I have a little word with your son?'

Go ahead' says his father, looking exhausted already.

I bend down, enjoying the spectacle of little Harry Houdini failing to release his straps, his back arching as he grunts and kicks.

'Well now,' I say in a low whisper near his ear. 'I'm Shrek's older brother and I'll put you in the swamp right under the frogs and worms and eat you up later, when you're all soaked and mouldy, with my marmite soldiers for tea.'

He freezes and shuts right up.

I stand up, turn around and smile. Grown up, 1. Child, 0.

'That wasn't so difficult. May we offer you a tea or coffee. Something stronger perhaps and would your son like a biscuit. We've got some nice ones in the kitchen?'

'A large whisky wouldn't go amiss,' the father sighs.

'Sorry, no can do. The Sunday staff drank the lot. We've got a nice drop of Rioja. It's rather smooth and somewhere in the world it's past six o clock.'

'Perfect,' says the husband.

'We'd like something a little fresh for the bedroom,' says the wife. 'Don't we darling?'

The husband looks at me with helpless eyes, irresolute in what the future holds for him. Perhaps we could organise a kidnapping of his son for a bit of peace and quiet. 'How did you do that?' he begs, desperate for the answer.

'I've had to deal with many kids in the gallery. You just say something nice to them and they're fine. It never fails.'

Meanwhile Charlie is engaged in conversation with the wife. 'What do you want in your bedroom? Oops... I mean what effect would you like to achieve?'

Yes, we aim to please anything from bordello to nun's cell.

'Over the bed or over the dressing table?'

Charlie has a unique way with phrasing. I'm unprepared for what comes next.

'I love mirrors on the ceiling and long mirrors in my boudoir. Don't you?'

The husband stares at me in disbelief. I think he's lost in wishful thinking, until the wife takes the whole situation in hand. 'We want something a little more soft and cuddly. Have you any teddy bear paintings?'

'No. I'm afraid we don't have any wildlife paintings or teddy bear picnic scenes. Would you like to take a look in my stock-room? I can show you examples of what we do have. Let Charlie look after your husband and son for a bit.'

Revenge is sweet. A few moments with a nice sane woman sans child will sooth the nerves.

'Thank you,' she says. 'That's fine, isn't it dear?'

The husband says nothing, just stares at Charlie and nods.

We walked through the back door of the gallery into the stock room.

'Wow! Haven't you a got a lot of art?'

'We believe in having a good selection to tempt those who don't see what they like on the gallery walls. Take this painting for instance.' I pull out a pastel sunset over sea.

'That's beautiful' she says. 'How did you know I'd like this?'

'It's my inner teddy bear instincts,' I smile. 'Shall we show it to your husband?'

'Yes please. And I like the look of this painting.' She points out an abstract landscape in reds and blues with purple and orange highlights.

Nothing like a teddy bear picture whatsoever!

'Right. You hold onto this one and I'll fetch that one down. Follow me!'

We return to a gallery filled with rapturous laughter and a husband practically choking at the same time.

The child still isn't making a sound.

'Sorry to interrupt the entertainment,' says the wife.

Time for me to defuse an incipient atmosphere. 'By the way, what's your name?'

'Stella. My husband is George and this is little Teddy.'

Charlie relieves the wife of the picture she's carrying. 'Can I hang it over here?' she purrs. 'I think the light would complement it. Their bedroom has a large window with soft pink curtains. Hasn't it Stella?'

'Yes, it does.' Her disapproving tone is clear to all. She glowers at her husband as if Charlie has been discovered actually in her private sanctum.

Acting to calm the incipient storm, I try to explain a little about the painters and what they were striving to achieve.

The prickly static calms and Stella expresses partiality for the pastel. 'I like this one a lot.'

'Well, that's a good start,' I say.

'How much is it?' enquires George.

'Believe it or not, it's only £850 framed in the gold leaf moulding.'

'We'll take it', says Stella, not even consulting the husband. 'Do you deliver?'

'We do. With pleasure. Where do you live?'

'Not far from Evesham,' says George.

'I live near there,' pipes up Charlie. 'I could take it to you after work.'

I think not.

I ignore Charlie's offer. 'Would Wednesday morning suit you? I'll hang it for you. All part of the service.'

'That would be much appreciated,' says Stella. George looks a tad disappointed. I bet he is.

'Wednesday it is and thank you.'

As the three of them leave, Teddy starts firing up on all cylinders again.

'Charlie, if you ever flirt with married customers again in front of their spouses, I'll ask you to leave immediately.' That's not the threat I'd far rather carry out, involving the palm of my hand and her derriere.

Charlie saunters over to me. 'Who's a grumpy teddy bear then?'

This isn't going to be an easy fortnight.

She continues, 'Why don't we go for a drink after work? Just a bottle of pink bubbles; my round. After all, a woman has needs you know.'

BURNT UMBER

A eureka moment crosses my mind. It might be a good idea to spread out. I don't mean putting on weight, that's far too easy. All you have to do is keep on drinking and enjoying life in what little time's left in an eight-day week to while away in relaxation. Oh, hang on. You think a gallery life is just sauntering in at a sociable hour of the morning, having coffee followed by a two-hour lunch break, afternoon tea and a quick snifter before strolling home for a midnight snack. Really? Tut tut! How could you!

I've received an email. Yes, we're entering the modern world. It's an invite to exhibit at a new art fair over the border in Scotland. Now the very idea of exhibiting before had petrified me, I don't know why; couldn't really put my finger on it. I suppose I always thought there were enough potential buyers to sustain my humble establishment. Still there could always be more if I take my artists to a new country with new customers. How hard can it be? The gallery's been trading for over five years now and the time seems right.

Belinda won't like it; having to take over and play at being in charge. She prefers being a support or team player as she reminds me. Often! Charlie? Well the least said about her the better. She'll just be her usual loud self, always on the lookout for a victim. For victim read customer. Anyway, they'll have to sort out the gallery without me. I'm paying them and it's only for a mere six days. Make up my mind. It's time to call a staff meeting.

Belinda is looking tanned and refreshed after her glorious sunshine holiday in the home to a million flies whilst Charlie? She's is still looking desperate.

'Ladies. I have decided to try out an art exhibition in foreign climes. Scotland to be precise.'

There's no response. Nothing. Belinda stares at me with a *you really aren't being serious sort of way* eyebrow raised in disbelief.

'Oh, how wonderful. What shall I wear?' pipes up Charlie.

I ignore her. God help me! Can you imagine working away with this woman? 'We need to select six artists and two sculptors, a few not too delicate glass pieces and a good corkscrew.'

It's a guessing game, like going up the Amazon for the first time into unexplored territory and trying to barter with semi-clad natives whilst avoiding river fever. Ok, my imagination's running a bit over-board here; it is Edinburgh, so there might not be any mosquitos.

Bit of a happy coincidence occurs. I've been doing a bit of national newspaper advertising and a chap phones up wanting to buy the painting used in the ad. And where does he live? Edinburgh, no less. Fortuitous indeed. I offer to deliver it and hang it for him. It's a good sign methinks.

Back to the list. I need a van, plenty of wine, display stands, plinths, glasses to drink from, artwork, pens, visitor book, order book and, living hopefully, the famous red dots. Add a few smart clothes, hanging equipment, a cordless drill and yes, of course, the obligatory corkscrew.

Seems quite simple, you might think.

Actually, it's considerably more difficult and requires a lot of toing and froing combined with lots of list updating and crossing offs, calls, collecting art, reassuring artists, reassuring myself (not so easy) and, you guessed it, a shed load of money up front to pay for the stand. That's the gamble. Will it work? Will total strangers buy? Will anything sell? There's only one way to find out and that's without taking Charlie along, even though the fact is, I do need someone to help out. With an assistant, maybe I could even sneak out and sketch somewhere. I doubt it but you never know. I make a few calls to some potentials and luckily, a friend I haven't seen for a while happens to be free and decides to accompany me. Oh Good! I don't have to drive.

I won't bore you with all the details. Suffice to say that we wrap everything that's required, check and check again that everything needful is in the vehicular conveyance, including me, and off we go.

It's a long way in a van that doesn't have seats that slide back. At 60 mph max, the journey's a tad tedious and we stop off at several service stations for coffee breaks.

Eventually we arrive at a magnificent old hall with vans littered everywhere. We park and survey the set up. The first person we meet is an incredibly tall woman in a tight t-shirt with the slogan *So many men so little time* emblazoned across her cleavage. 'A good start' observes Harry with a smile.

She opens her mouth and a rash of expletives pour out. Basically, the stand company have screwed up and are running behind schedule by a full day This means nothing will be ready till tomorrow and seeing as the show was supposed to open at six, there is now plenty of time to panic.

In a moment of gentlemanly consideration, we offer to buy her a drink from the bar, the one thing luckily which is open. She agrees and consumes a pint of heavy in seconds followed by another, and all before we drink more than half of our own pints. Harry is intrigued with this display of Celtic wonder, or maybe he has a fixation on large-breasted, beer-drinking women.

Suddenly, he pipes up, which is most appropriate for Scotland. You see what I did there? 'Well, if all the gallery owners get together and help out, we'll have the place ready in time.'

You know what? That's exactly what we do. Nobody knows anyone to start with, but by the end of the evening and assisted by a plenitude (that means lots) of free drinks, we paint the stands and even help the one solitary electrician available to sort out where the lights are going to be located.

Alas no time left to get any pictures displayed and everyone has to leave their wrapped stuff by their stands for the morrow. There's only one thing left to do, find our accommodation and hit the town.

The place we're staying at is a typical Georgian building, massive front door and high ceilings. A young couple who'd been gainfully employed in the banking sector, and, judging by the toys everywhere, are now into child manufacture, own the place. There are three little ones crying at different decibel levels from all over the house. Memo to self, next time look for a child-free zone to stay in. Should there be a next time.

The nanny is French and looks helplessly incapable of looking after kids. The mother, a Londoner, Mrs. Okay-Yah is not faring much better although trying her best to be so *Okay, yah* in front of us.

'Hello. Welcome to the mad house. We have three gallery owners staying with us. You've got the third floor and the others are above you. Breakfast is at eight and my husband will cook his famous porridge.' I haven't heard of it and neither has Harry so it can't be that famous. We lug our cases up the stairs, dump everything and walk out in to the cold fresh air in search of food. And a drink.

We meander through a couple of streets and come across a tavern that looks inviting. There's live music and what's more, an available table. It's very sociable and almost completely full of young and not so young people, mingling and laughing their socks off.

A well-dressed, youngish and pretty staff person greets us. 'Very good evening gentlemen. You're not from round here I see. Welcome to Margaret's. Let's get you a table and something to eat. Follow me!' She turns, flicking her ponytail aside, and leads us to the one and only empty table which is near the stage.

Harry looks around. I swear he's drooling. 'All the women here are stunning. I reckon we're in for a great few days. How many tens do you think we'll see?'

'I'm sorry. Tens? What are tens?'

'You know. Perfect tens. Stunners, crackers; great legs and all.'

A guitarist wearing jeans and a black t-shirt walks on stage and introduces himself in fluent Glaswegian. In other words, we've no idea what he's saying. However, strumming his guitar and singing in a gravelly, bluesy voice, he's well and truly impressive.

'Steak for me' says Harry 'and how about a good red?'

We've started in style, so red it will be.

Two bottles later, and two men leave in a far more relaxed mood, heading back to the guesthouse to call it a night. I open the front door and enter the hallway; the place is now blissfully quiet even if there are still plenty of toys littering the floor.

'Tomorrow at eight. Cheers, Harry' I say, climbing the stairs to bed.

It doesn't take long to fall asleep in the head-to-toe burnt umber décor. Furniture, carpet, curtains and the bed sheets! Very imaginative, I think not. My mind cries out for colour. Good job I'm wearing red socks so I drop them on to the floor so they'll be directly in my eye-line when I wake up. That turns out to be rather sooner than anticipated. I stir to a gentle knock on the door and a slight creak as it opens.

To my surprise, the au pair's standing there, dressed in a Victorian-style, white cotton nightdress. Her hair is untied and cascades down her back. She creeps over to the bed. 'Monsieur, you must excuse me. I don't know how to say zis but I am missing my boyfriend. You remind me zo much of him. I ache for him here.' She grabs her breast, sighs and without so much as a by-your leave, climbs into my bed and snuggles up rather tightly to me.

I might be dreaming of course but as I put my arm around her shoulder and feel her warm body, I realise I'm not. Neither is she an optional extra off the tariff list, such as a guided tour of ghostly old Edinburgh town.

So, what is a man supposed to do?

Well I'll put you unashamedly straight on the matter. She falls fast asleep curled up in my bed. Absolutely out cold. I trust her boyfriend doesn't have the same effect on her.

At six o clock the light pours through a chink in the brown curtains. It wakes me up. I'm alone. There is no female in the bed. *Did that really happen*. But I can smell perfume on the pillow. *Oh well*. I get up, shower, dress and walk downstairs. A brisk walk round the block seems a good idea.

'Bonjour' the au pair waves, smiling. Someone's feeling happier this morning. I never realized it was that easy to please a woman.

The sun is bright for the time of day and the trees are rustling in the breeze. It's always good to collect one's thoughts whilst walking around a city, watching it wake up. Traffic is minimal and people by and large are relaxed. In a bit all there is to do is make my stand look great, hang and display everything and prepare for the unexpected. Famous porridge time beckons. I'm feeling refreshed, if a little concerned about the strange au pair but hey, who knows what today will bring.

Porridge is served. 'Would you like whisky on it?'

'Are you serious?'

'Oh yes. a wee dram with honey sets you up for the day, trust me'.

'Ok.' Here goes.'

'Morning, Harry' A tweeded, polka-dot cravatted, blue-shirted assistant enters the breakfast room in his best suede Hush Puppies. They would be blue suede, his shoes. naturally.

Harry chirps 'I had a great sleep. Lovely big bed. You could party in it.'

The au pair walks by smiling again. *Why is she smiling?*

Mrs Okay-Yah heaves in to view so she gets my sales pitch. 'Would anyone like complimentary tickets for tonight's private view, do you think?'

'We will certainly hand out a few for you' she says.

'Is it possible to have one? I do like zeeing art?' It's the au pair.' I am a free night tonight.'

'Settled then. Here you go. See you later.'

We head for the van. I decide not to say a word to Harry about you-know-what. Just in case. Next stop; deliver the painting to the Edinburgh client.

His home isn't difficult to find. He's on Gardner's Crescent. It's a beautiful, four-story, terraced property. You can see massive chandeliers as you peer through the tall windows.

The owner opens the door in his tracksuit.

'Good morning. Special delivery.'

I offer my hand but he ignores it. With good reason. 'Sorry, I'm all sweaty. Just back from a run. Ah, come in.'

Wow what a pad. The house is exquisitely designed. He's kept all the original style and features and filled it with expensive designer furniture and fittings plus some superb antiques and modern pieces.

'Where would you like this to hang?'

'Follow me' says Paul.

We walk upstairs, along a corridor and into an empty room, freshly painted and with nothing on the walls. It brings out my inner salesman. 'Fantastic place you have here. Would you like to come along to this evening's private view? You never know, we might have a thing or two to suit. There's one fantastic piece that would look great on this wall.'

'That depends on what my wife's doing this evening' Paul says. 'She runs the diary.'

After a quick coffee and a thank you for delivering the painting followed by a smart handshake this time, we're on our way again.

'Blimey O'Reilly, what a place' chirps Harry indicating to get us out into the traffic.

The exhibition venue awash with cars, predominantly Volvos and white vans. Everyone's running around carrying artwork in bags and bubble wrap. There is loads of it. How everyone will be ready for opening time will require a concerted miracle and superhuman effort.

Suffice it to say, we manage to set up our stand within two hours, which astounds and impresses me, particularly, as opposite us are two Scottish lasses in tight jeans and t-shirts. It's a pleasure to watch them work although all they've hung are three paintings and one isn't straight. What they are is a pleasant distraction. Harry says, 'To the rescue' and armed with his cordless drill, cocked and fully charged, arranges and hangs another eight paintings for them inside approximately fifteen minutes. They're delighted, as well as being a delight to look at. Harry's obviously pleased with himself too.

Time to prepare for the show; a quick change of outfit in the gents' loo and reappearing in a slightly unconventional jacket, a loud, colourful shirt, the obligatory cufflinks and a pair of dark, almost tartan trousers - blue with green and yellow fine lines. Actually, they're golfing trousers, but don't tell anyone.

Off to the bar, which seems like a good place to start.

It's shut. Oh well there will be enough wine afterwards.

The in-house speaker system springs to life. 'Ladies and Gentlemen, the show starts in ten minutes. The organisers would like to wish all exhibitors good luck and we hope you sell plenty.'

Me too. Am I nervous or what? It feels like my gallery opening night all over again minus Miss Top Hat and Tails. Looks like shades of tartan will have to do.

Harry is chatting to the taller of the two Scottish lasses, Shona. Her assistant is Iona and they are the luck of the Celts incarnate. I've never seen tartan waistcoats look so fetching. They fit just right matched with short pleated tartan skirts. All we need now are a few single malts and we'll be St. Andrew'd out.

The doors open and a stream of private viewers flow in a direct line to the free wine. Bless the human race. They're so predictable.

In no time at all the place is packed. There are well dressed folk in tweed, well-dressed folk not in tweed, art students in an array of clothes better thrown away and one old man, well into his nineties, looks like he's walked straight out of a Spike Milligan novel, complete with hairy knees, a long kilt and carrying the knobbliest walking stick ever. His hair is silver and worn tied back in a ponytail. He's wearing massive, aged-leather boots and off-cream woollen socks. A genuine highlander, I can't understand a word he says but by any other measure he seems a nice chap.

I'm freaking though; will anything acquire a red dot tonight?

'Excuse me?' I'm suddenly brought back down to earth by a middle-aged lady in a full-length cashmere coat tapping my arm "Would you mind selling me this lovely piece of glass?'

'Not at all madam.' I let Harry write up the details as I place the first red sticker on a price label. *One down. What a lovely lady*.

And it goes on with the art we've shipped north receiving positive responses.

'Not seen stuff like this.'

'You're different. Fancy a drink after the show.'

'What's your best price on this?'

It's music to my ears. Then I spy Paul talking to the gallery owner a couple of stands down from mine. He shakes hands and is walking towards us and thankfully his wife is with him. 'Good evening' she says in a glorious accent. 'We love the painting you brought up for us.'

'I'm delighted. And your home is exquisite' I offer them a glass of my own wine instead of the venue plonk.

'Darlink' she turns to Paul. 'I think we should have these two paintings for the hall and this table too. That big one will look good in the new snug and I'm sure we could find a place for this bronze.'

Am I really hearing this? I try to remain very calm on the outside, while my insides are going Vesuvian.

Paul says 'Well ole' chap, looks like your delivery service paid off. Sort me out the price for the lot and can you deliver them tomorrow morning?'

'With pleasure. We'll be with you for nine-thirty on the nose. Is that okay?'

'Perfect. We'll have the coffee on'. He shakes my hand again and she gives me brushing kisses on each cheek. Then they leave. For a moment I'm unable to breathe. They have just agreed to buy approximately goods to half the value of the entire stand.

Meanwhile Harry has just sold another piece of glass and is looking very pleased with himself. 'That's another grand in the pot. Yes!!'

'Well done, Harry. Great sale.'

'Are you okay? You look shocked.'

I say nothing and place red dots on the sold items.

'What are you doing? You don't need to pretend we're doing even better.'

'I've just sold this lot to Paul.'

'You've got to be bloody joking.'

'No, I'm bloody well not! I'm delighted. And the good news is we have to deliver it all in the morning.'

It doesn't take long for the news of our success to travel round the show. Gallery owners and onlookers are coming by the stand to congratulate us.

'Well done.'

'Bloody 'ell, fancy that.'

'Jammy bleeders! How much did you make?'

We don't have time to rest on our laurels. The opening night may already be a roaring success but it's not over yet and there are plenty of tens about too, so we're both pleased. Nay, ecstatic.

The au pair arrives in due course. 'Allo monsieur. It is a tres belle event. Some of ze art is, how you say, eclectic. I am sinking zat I might be missing my boyfriend a lot tonight'. She winks at me. I swear, she winks before wandering off in to the now thinning crowds. The wine's all been consumed and at last the evening's private view is nearly over.

'Ladies and gentlemen the show has now closed. We look forward to seeing you again tomorrow from eleven o'clock. Please make your way to the main exit, thank you'

I pour us out two very large glasses of red. 'Thank you, Harry. What an effin' amazing evening.'

'Cheers! Did you see that woman in the black leather trousers? She gets eleven out of ten,' says Harry.

We virtually dismantle the stand, wrapping the pieces we need to deliver in the morning and then load the van before joining the rest of the exhibitors for a get together over a wee snifter.

Harry makes a beeline for the tartan sisters and I thank the organisers for a great opening event. I mean we had a great opening even if others didn't fare so well. The luck of the draw.

Harry doesn't actually succeed in pulling either of the tartan clad lassies but he's not one to give in. We return to our accommodation, unload the art into the hallway for safety and retire for the evening. 'Let's see if we can beat the figures tomorrow.' says Harry, ever the optimist.

At about one in the morning, the door opens and the au pair slips under the sheets and to let you into a little secret, Jean Pierre wouldn't approve.

The rest of the show goes almost as well as the opening session. It seems to travel by in a blur of conversation and wine, with the occasional scrap of food thrown in for good measure to ensure my able assistant keeps his strength up for whichever of the tartan-clad girls he eventually pulls. I'm not at liberty to tell you which. A gentlemen's handshake on confidentiality is his bond and what happens in Edinburgh, stays in Edinburgh.

PURPLE

Purple is a great colour, made by blending blues with reds. Conveniently, it works superbly when it comes to highlighting dangly bits. Stick with me here.

Bruce's first show is a major success. We end up selling nearly three quarters of the exhibition and he's beside himself. A new audience buy into his art and lifestyle and enable him to pay off his debts...and buy more wine.

His devotees may come from all over the world, but the buyers were mainly from my mailing list. So why am I stressed? I'm mentally and physically exhausted. It's because it's akin to running a weeklong wedding albeit without a happy couple or any in-laws. That's an unfair comparison really but we're all happy after they've all gone. And none more than yours truly.

We went through more superb wine than the restaurant next door, the only discontent being expressed by a German lady with a distinct dislike of the French. 'Why haff you no Gutt German wines here in this establishment?'

'Madam, we're an art gallery not a wine bar.' You'd never know it from all the empties by the bins.

The woman's fingers are bedecked in rings with massive stones. She's wearing a full-length fur coat, horrendously strong perfume and an overly dyed, blonde hairdo. Only the bees in the countryside would ever be impressed by her hive. She was a rather well-built woman who preferred younger men. Need I say more? For some reason she spends too much time in my gallery.

Belinda finds her a hoot. Apparently, I'm not young enough for her. I've been saved at last.

Now I have to fulfil my promise to Bruce to host his more risqué exhibition.

Okay, let me explain. What Bruce has done is to take a male wine merchant of his close acquaintance, pose him on a collection of scatter cushions, throw the odd painting into the background and paint him over and over again. Fundamentally that's the show. Ah yes, not forgetting one little detail. Said male subject is naked. That should go down well.

Whilst I'm conjuring up a plan for making it happen, a couple of well-dressed gents walk in to the gallery. They apparently been advised to check me out. Let me state at this point, the t-shirt I'm wearing features a fairly blatantly heterosexual image and even though I've no problem at all with what anybody else chooses to do in their sex lives, I have no intention of batting for the other side. I'll leave that to some of my artists, clients, and friends.

One of the gentlemen looks uncannily like the late Freddie Mercury of Queen. The other, more seriously spoken asks to see the proprietor.

'Good afternoon. I'm the owner. How may I help you?'

'My name is Derek. We're looking for something a little different. Loud but not garish!' I smile.

'I want it big and colourful. You know modern like' says the other one. We'll call him Freddie Mark II. 'We've changed our whole house round to go contemporary. Out with his glitz and glitter and in with big and bold. '

I move out of sales mode. Well actually, I start the selling process. 'I think this calls for a glass of wine. Red or white?'

'Chablis darling?' says Freddie Mark II.

Belinda doesn't wait for any instruction from me. She beats a hasty retreat via the back door, returning a few minutes later with chilled Chablis. Bless that girl; I ought to give her a raise.

'So, what have you got that's big, umm?' says Derek. *Oh no, here we go! Its double entendre day.*

'Seriously, I say 'How big would you like it? '

The banter continues and the wine does flow. Eventually after twenty minutes I offer to bring out some pieces from the stockroom. I decide to show them work by three different artists, large, colourful canvases that don't require frames. One, by a female artist, is squiggles and blobs, very tasteful, a bit like the artist. The second is a dramatic piece by Bruce and the third a really red-styled sunset with showers of golden rain cascading down one side.

Neither customer likes the last one. 'It's too loud for my taste; looks like someone's peeing up the wall.' They do like the other two. 'How much?' asks Freddy Mark II.

Now here is where you have to be tactful in guessing what the budget will be. You could ask how much someone would like to spend but it's a blatantly crude approach and besides, nobody ever wants to say how much he or she is truly prepared to spend; it could be more than they say or considerably less if they're embarrassed or showing off. I decide my approach to price should be *reasonable*. Giving a little background about the artist whilst placing the painting on the wall for viewing from another angle always looks so much more professional than the hard sell anyway.

Just then two slightly drunk and obviously camp men mince into the gallery, walk straight up to the two chaps I'm working hard on selling to and exchange kisses. 'Hello luvs; we were wondering where you'd gone.' Oh my god! A committee of buyers is never a good idea, especially when one or more is already, to put it mildly, approaching paralytic.

Little drunk man pipes up. 'How much you spending now you tart?' He turns his attention to Belinda 'Where's my drink Girl? Get me a glass of wine.'

She glares at him with the eye of an eagle about to pounce on its prey and then chooses to ignore him, heading for the kitchen in a move straight out of a movie scene. *Drop dead pal.*

'Do excuse Brenda. He's such an alkie.'

'Well' says the man now identified as Brenda. 'No booze, no stay.' He exits stage right by the main doors.

'Just a normal day in a gallery,' I say with a smile, trying to lighten up the mood.

Luckily there's no need as Freddy Mark II comes to the rescue. 'Go and catch her up and make sure she doesn't fall in the street again. Go on. We'll see you later.' The silent one obediently does as he's told. 'Now, where are we? Oh, come on; let's have them both.'

'Invoice the club and we'll pay you tomorrow' says Derek.

'A club! What sort of club?' I ask.

'Well it's not exactly a gentleman's club. Is it luv? You could come down and join us later; we always have some entertainment on a Tuesday. Everyone dresses up and has a ball.'

'Well you never know' I say sheepishly, making a shrewd guess at what sort of club it might be. Then a brilliant idea flickers through my mind. 'You don't fancy sponsoring an art exhibition, do you?'

'We'll think about it darling. I'm sure I've just spent a fortune today. Give me a day to get my lips around the idea, I'll just finish another Chablis whilst I mull. Okay?'

With such perfect timing, Belinda arrives with more chilled wine. The hauteur mobilised for *the little shit* has vanished and we're all smiles again.

As they both leave slightly the merrier, Belinda pipes up, 'I heard what you said about the club. I'll come along tonight for a laugh as long as I can come in late tomorrow.'

'For a laugh at coming in late or what?' I smile.

She takes that to mean approval. 'Okay.'

The day is done and I take a corporate decision. 'Let's have a drink.' Somewhere in the world, the sun is over the yardarm.

'I think this show will be good fun after all' That's uncharacteristically positive for Belinda. I've got a good feeling all over.

'Red, white or bubbles?' I ask.

The next day from opening to around oneish is remarkably busy probably because I'm on my own. Customers, a delivery turning up unexpectedly and the phone keeps ringing. All good if you have a team working for you, but yours truly is trying to formulate the next exhibition and I keep coming to the same conclusion. Panic. *What am I letting myself in for?*

The phone rings again, seemingly louder than the earlier calls. I answer it in my usual calm, self-assured way. Should have been a bloody actor.

'Hello. Gallery here, how may I help you?'

'Hello darling!' It's Mr No name. Freddie Mark II. 'What a night we had. You should have been there. Your little assistant was a right diva, dancing and singing on the stage, flirting with anyone and everyone. She was more or less legless when we closed up. We put her in a taxi though.'

'Really!' is all I say.

'Anyway luvy, we've decided that a big gathering at yours and an after-show party at ours would the perfect notion. Little Belinda told us what's what. We'll cover the catalogue and fizz and you can do the rest. We'd like one of the pictures to go on the bottles of bubbly. Okay! Got to go, the cat's ripping the couch again. Nothing like a mad pussy is there?' Click.

Well what do you know? The show will go on cabaret style, no less. Time to ring Bruce. No answer. He's busy, so I leave a simple message leaving out the details. Sure he'll ring back sometime within the day. When he does, it takes a lot to explain what's occurred in the last twenty-four hours but I say nothing about Belinda who walks in rather the worse for wear. In sunglasses and a veil of silence, she heads straight for the kitchen.

Bruce suggests our new sponsors should come over to the chateau to discuss it and to show them the work. I say they've already agreed and maybe it would be nicer to offer that after the show. A safer bet in my opinion. The deal is struck; we'll wait till after the exhibition and parties!

Dear Lord, forgive me; I run a simple and humble art gallery that sells art, and the like.

Of course, everyday life has to go on as well and those boring things that makes businesses run, like bills, have to be handled. There's no such thing as being allowed a day off, you know. All hail the taxman and VAT and rent and stuff. My only rant...bloody paperwork. I hate it; every bloody sheet. It would be nicer using the time to draw or paint on sheets of paper, rather than covering them in numbers.

Sorry about that. Where was I? Ah yes, nudity; always a nice topic. Subtle covering up with a touch of risqué exposure isn't too bad either. I once happened to notice a rather elegant lady walking past in a long pleated, camel skirt and white blouse, her blonde hair blowing in the wind; and the same wind caught the split in her skirt, exposing just a hint of stocking top. I nearly knocked over a statue that somehow moved right into my path. That's both subtle and risqué.

Belinda speaks. Well not exactly true. She groans. 'Oh my God!'

'Care to improve on that?' I say.

'I didn't think I was going to make it.'

'Are you referring to last night or coming in today?' I raise an eyebrow, straight from the Roger Moore manual of emotional expressions.

'Someone spiked my drinks. I mean, phew, shit, I'm still ratted but I'm here. My head! You did say I could come in late!'

'Tell me later. Get some more water down you and go and sit out the back.'

'No, sfine,' she slurs, 'I'll be okay...honest.'

This, my friend is where you take control of your staff.

I ring the chemist across the road. 'Hi Jean. Would you do me a big favour and step over to take a look at my assistant. I think someone messed with her drinks last night. She's in a right state. Don't make it too obvious you're coming to examine her. You will? Thanks.'

She calmly walks in pretending to want a present for her friend or lover. Who knows? She's not wearing a wedding ring but she's a great chemist; great legs and, I believe, a great figure under her long white coat. 'Are you all right young lady?' That's not subtle at all.

Belinda looks vacant and unwell. She appears to be grey and purple all at once. Jean picks up the phone and dials 999. Within minutes, a paramedic arrives, takes out his kit and lays Belinda down at the back of the gallery.

He's working on her properly with machines that whir and print out something. 'I think she needs her stomach pumping.' he looks up at Jean who's holding Belinda's hand in support.

'Come on, you'll be okay. What did you drink last night?'

"Shloads of Vodka, and a couple or floor shocktails. I can handle my shrink...I'm fine.' Then she passes out.

I'm delighted to report that after a trip in an ambulance and the rest of the day off, granted by her generous employer, she's fine. So much for drinking on the job. Here's a lesson to you all, drink moderately and for God's sake don't turn up to work pissed, no matter what.

CERISE

I'm seriously hoping today will be quiet so I can sort out the dreaded paperwork. Or at least that's my plan. I make myself a fresh coffee, Java blue mountain, and sit down at my desk. Here goes; computer on, floods of emails and...a woman walks in.

'I have to show you my work...I absolutely insist. I've come all the way from Chelsea. Are you listening?'

Good grief. She hasn't even said *hello*.

I look up to be confronted by a tall, middle-aged woman dressed with attitude in thick woolly tights, pink Doc Martins, a very short woollen skirt, also pink, and a cerise scarf with her hair tied in a bun. You couldn't miss her in a crowd. Oh yes and a purple blouse with odd shaped and different coloured buttons.

That's the thing about art. It's all in the observation.

'Young man. I'm talking to you. Come here now.'

Oh no. My coffee will go cold. I was so looking forward to the caffeine rush I so desperately need.

I have to say it, just as I know what the answer will be. 'Good morning! Have you an appointment?'

'Don't be ridiculous? I want to see the art buyer or the owner, now!'

'He's not in today' I reply. She looks scary; her behaviour is scary and, I've a feeling, her art will be scary too.

'How old are you?' She eyes me up and down.

'I'm approaching a milestone birthday sometime in the next few years.' I attempt a smile but don't quite pull it off.

'Do you realise I have boys like you for breakfast?'

'That's nice. I prefer smoked salmon and scrambled eggs with a large orange juice.'

This is mad. Surely, she's not for real

'Do you have many girlfriends?'

'Do excuse me. I don't believe I can be of any assistance to you. If you'd like an appointment then I'll see when the owner is free.'

She ignores me and continues. 'What do you think of these then?' With that she undoes all the non-matching buttons of her blouse and exposes her breasts, right in front of my face.

Now I have to say they are mighty impressive and by any standard look real. Gravity isn't ruining her cleavage anyway.

'Don't you find art makes you horny...I do.' She undoes her bun, flings her head back and takes a deep breath. 'God it's good!'

I'm looking on in disbelief. *Someone help me please.* It's only Wednesday.

'You'll have to do' she sighs, unzipping the folder of the type we commonly refer to as a portfolio. 'Let me present my art.'

She's plainly not about to take no for an answer and strews sheet after sheet onto the floor. Each shows a naked torso.

'These look like they're of you,' I say.

'I love to see myself in the mirror. I have four in my studio. You should come and see me work sometime. Take a day off. I could paint you with me as well.'

Actually, despite the performance, her work isn't that bad. A bit raunchy obviously but much less dramatic than her entrance. In this context, that's a good thing.

'Madame' I say, rising from behind my desk. 'I shall tell the owner you'd like to see him and you may now put your work away, if you don't mind. Thanks.'

'I do mind.' She continues to produce more work from her bulging folder. There are couples in various coital positions and then she tops the lot with a drawing of herself naked on a horse.

No. I won't ask her if the horse was in the studio despite my inner devil cajoling me to do just that.

'Have you a CV?'

'No. But I do have a massive bed in Chelsea when you visit. Plenty of room.'

'I'll...uh...tell my boss that.' I thinking you'd need to get seriously fit to visit her studio. *Please go*, I'm screaming out in my head. On the outside I'm smiling and trying to look bored. I'm obviously failing.

'When will he be back? I can wait a while.' She really doesn't take no for an answer.

I feign a flick through the diary.' Says he'll be in on Saturday afternoon. You're welcome to wait but we tend to close up at night.'

At last she shows a sense of disappointment. I begin to think I can actually bring this episode to an end. She looks at me thoughtfully and says 'Well if you're staying, I'll stay.' *Oh, my giddy ruddy bloody aunt!!* She walks across and grabs my crotch. 'Don't play with my feelings. You know you want me. My trains at five forty-five. We have time.'

Luckily, and I mean extremely luckily, right then a rather petite lass walks in holding hands with her chap. 'Are we disturbing you?'

'Not at all please come in.' I bow. A warm sweeping welcome.

'Yes, you are!' Says the demonic life-drawer from hell.

Thankfully they're not easily deterred. 'We'll just have a look round.'

'Would you like a drink?' I offer. 'Wine or coffee?'

Before they can answer, Madame pipes up. 'You never offered me anything to drink. Or anything else for that matter.' She snorts loudly.

'Correct ...And I believe you're just leaving'

And this is what you call an ordinary day at the gallery? I pour the coffee down the sink, sod the paperwork and serve myself a large glass of wine.

BLONDE

Charlie looks like an eagle about to pounce. 'He's mine all mine.' She means the tall blonde young man who's just walked in. He's trendily dressed with a crisp white shirt and dark blue jeans that leave nothing to hide in the box department. Even the sun is shining on his immaculately quiffed hair-do

'Good morning,' she says with a tone of voice reserved in her sub-basement. 'May I help you.' He stops and eyes her up from head to tail and back again. We men are so obvious but then, as a friend of mine reminds me, Women are the way they are so men can look at them. *Comments on a postcard please!*

'I've just moved into the area and found you as I was walking around town.' Charlie's drooling. Poor chap stands not a hope in hell of escaping her clutches.

'Let me show you around the gallery and if you're at a loose end, I could show you round the area. I know all the right watering holes.'

'That would be great. We're filming for three weeks and it does get so boring afterwards.' Who's chatting up whom? He's a real smoothie. Charlie offers him a drink. On me! Naturally he accepts and they're chatting away. *Sell girl: sell!* She places her arm over his and walks him to the stock room 'I think we've the perfect thing for him' she says as she passes me, taking her victim to her lair.

Eight minutes pass and they return somewhat dishevelled with two pictures and an air of something having gone on. *Eight minutes?* Umm! I'm saying nothing.

Mike; his given name is Michael; sits down like a naughty school boy. Charlie is still fussing over him but to give her credit, she's hanging the two paintings on the wall as a potential sale. 'What do you think of these?' she preens.

He regains his composure enough to rise and walks over to view the pictures properly. 'I'm not so sure about that but I love this one.' He points as if performing on stage. 'May I collect it later?'

'Sure fire. We close at six tonight.'

'That's great. I'll buy you a drink later to celebrate.' He spins on his heels and exits central stage.

She looks at me with an air of satisfaction. 'That didn't take long did it?'

Now then. What was she talking about? Eight minutes! I shan't say a word. Honest.

Six o clock arrives and there's no sign of our actor. Charlie is looking dejected and rejected when suddenly blondie lands, a fashionable ten minutes late. 'I'm so sorry. You know how it is.'

A smile radiates all over Charlie's mush. *You know how it is. Tonight's going to be a good night.*

Time to leave her to it. 'I'm off me dears. Have fun'.

'Oh no. I insist you join us for a snifter!' says Mike.

Gallerists don't do chaperoning as a rule but why not. 'Just the one 'I reply.

We walk off to the nearest saloon. Set 'em up barman Cut.

ELECTRIC BLUE

I look up through the glass front door. It's a fairly ordinary sort of day; a bluish sky with a smattering of clouds against the background rumble of the city drifting by. And then to my surprise and pleasure, five girls walk into the gallery. Their names are Cindy, Sophie, Serena, Smiley and George. How do I know this? Well their names are emblazoned across their chests.

They speak and giggle in a sort of alternating unison. 'We're organising a charity run-walk-mash up, around the town and we want to use your gallery as a refreshment stop. All you have to do is sponsor a page and we'll include your logo on our t shirts and bring you in loads of people.'

Now there's a nice thought. Justified PR expense. Can't wait to tell the accountant the news.

'With pleasure ladies, in a good cause.'

The day arrives and two boxes of mixed cocktails in vials are delivered. They are horrendous shades; Glowing Green and Florescent Red with dashes of Electric Blue. God knows what's in them or what they'll do to you. But as the gallery motto states, put colour into your life.

We wait like a refuelling stop and wait and wait some more.

Suddenly a rosy-cheeked chap, sporting a long blonde wig, sweating profusely, in his pink leotard and black fish net stockings with the most incredibly high heels, staggers in through the doors.

'What an f-ing stupid bet eh? Drink now, please. These shoes are killing me!'

'The sight of you isn't exactly doing us any favours either,' I laugh, recognizing him as the MD of a local architects' practice. Think the last time I saw him was dressed in a kilt in a gay bar after a Burns night. Now he's at it again!

Within minutes the place is a heaving mass of fancy dress and outrageous costumes. It closely resembles a Rocky Horror reunion party. Stockings, heels tight bodices leather and satin, the lot. And that's just the chaps.

The women fare a little better. At least their legs are clean-shaven. Mind you, the odd lass has a bit of stubble but who's noticing? Or dares comment?

Smiley walks in, smiling divinely. She has a proper polished ring of white-toothed confidence. 'My logo looks great on you' I say admiring her electric blue T-shirt. Or the physique inside it.

'Do you mind if I hang around for a bit?'

'With pleasure' I say.

She looks into my eyes 'Come closer '

I'm already standing right in front of her. 'How much closer would you like?'

'Much nearer'

You couldn't put a ten-pound note between us. She pulls my head down to hers and plants a smacker of a kiss on my lips. She doesn't let go either but continues to kiss me and mess up my hair.

'Thank you. That's my challenge fulfilled. Fancy an encore?'

'I'm not complaining.' Smiley kisses me again.

'I've got to go and catch up with the gang. Bye'

Just like that. Gone

Belinda pokes me in the ribs. 'You've just passed the snog challenge,' she says.

'I'm not complaining,' I smile

COLOURS OF SUMMER (Part 1)

A letter arrives with a printed stamp from The Houses of Parliament. I'm invited to a party at the House of Commons. I love a good party. Been known to throw the occasional one myself, sorry private viewings I mean, not parties at all, as far as the taxman's concerned. This looks like it's going to be rather different.

There's a personal note attached to the invitation. *Do you mind being our guest list bouncer/ organizer?* Well I suppose it's a great way to get to meet everyone. I immediately ring to accept and say I'll be delighted to play the role of doorman!

Two minutes later the phone rings. 'Hello ol' boy. I've been thinking. You're a passionate salesman and you know your art but you don't understand the grammar of painting so I think you should come out to our next painting school to learn it. You can throw in the odd lecture as well. What do you say?'

Good grief I think. I get to paint abroad? How Wonderful! Sunshine, the odd glass of wine, painting and relaxing, my dream come true or what?

'When?'

'It's short notice but you won't regret it. Three weeks on Thursday' Regret it? In my mind I've already packed.

'Let me see if I can get a flight. And yes please.'

'Splendid.'

'Where is it?'

'Tuscany, dear chap, where else! Would you mind bringing out marmite and some rough-cut marmalade?'

'Consider it done.'

The line goes dead, there's no goodbye. Short and to the point. Check the dates. Typical! The party in London is on the Tuesday night so I'll have to dash back Wednesday and be at the airport for 6 am Thursday. Who says gallery life is boring?

Bruce rings again, 'I've booked a flight this Saturday. Shall I bring some cheese and mustard?' Life in the fast lane eh!

Sometimes I wish my pace of life would be a bit slower but who am I kidding? It's been like this ever since opening the doors of the gallery. I'm brought back into the moment as a couple of customers stroll in. 'Greetings my dears, wonderful day isn't it. You look like you have a gap on your wall to fill?' They don't. They're just mooching to kill time and are soon gone.

Belinda, in front of the computer, confirms a flight for me and queries my return date. 'How long this time?'

'It's only for ten days.' I try to sound casual. 'You can have this whole weekend off, if you like, with pay!'

'Sweet talking sod. Okay, you're booked. You fly into Pisa.' She presses the return key and signs out. I'm off to lunch.' My generous offer means another whole weekend with Charlie. Oh dear!

Bruce arrives at precisely wine o clock, towing a small luggage bag on wheels, and sits down at the desk. We'd be having a quiet day except that Charlie seems louder than usual, Effervescent she calls it. F'ing annoying I think.

'Oh, he's nice, just my type.'

'Charlie, I hate to disappoint you...' I stop, mid-sentence. Let the fun begin. She'll learn. 'Charlie this is Bruce. Bruce say hello to Charlie' I take a corporate decision to close for lunch. 'Come on, let's get a bite to eat. You too Charlie.'

'How fabulous.'

Bruce looks at me gone out, as they say in Sheffield. I put a sign on the door saying *Gone fishing. Back later.* Sometimes you have to seize the moment.

We stroll across to a little French restaurant and dig in for the afternoon. 'Fizz all round. Let's celebrate something.' Charlie's sitting near Bruce on the bench seats. Her skirt has risen and she makes no attempt to cover her thigh. You have to give her credit; she does possess a mighty fine pair of pins. Purely a natural observation! Bruce, however, is excited about what his show entails and ignores Charlie's exposed expanse of thigh. *Wine, women, men, whatever and song.* Although on a serious note, we'll be drinking some superb wines at the event again - always a plus. The show will be different but I'm now braced for this; I've started to line up all the gods of retail and more besides. *So, help, please let this be a success.*

Charlie's still unaware of the exhibition's content. 'It's predominantly the male nude,' I say in a low voice.

'Fanbloodytastic' she says. 'Let's celebrate dangly bits. My favourite pastime.' The champagne's already gone to her head.

Bruce is almost beside himself; not amused in the slightest. 'It's all about the trust and relationship within the art.' He takes a gulp of prosecco 'Who's she anyway?'

'Charlie's my part time assistant and can be very good in her own way.' I'm not going overboard in her defence.

'Mr. Bruce. This show is about sex and sex sells. Okay. However you want to wrap it up and explain it, is fine, but sex is my specialist topic and that's that'. She raises a glass.

He smiles at last, 'She's right. Charlie you're right. Cheers.'

I think it's time to change the subject. 'I'm going to paint in Tuscany for ten days. Rather excited to say the least.'

'I doubt you'll gain much insight in ten days and as for the wine...' He's such a wine snob. 'Although I've enjoyed many a good Italian red.' Bruce is obviously thinking of himself again but quickly brings the subject back to the exhibition once more. 'When will the catalogue be ready?' That's the thing with most artists; it's all about them. There's an inbuilt rivalry. I shan't call it jealousy for fear of being shot. After all, I'm only a gallery owner and apparently in their eyes, all I should do is sell art. Just you wait. One day it will be me and my art, not anyone else's. If I ever get the time that is to have a life outside the four walls of my retail establishment?

'Well Bruce ol' boy, you can judge what I do when I return. How's that? Touché!' The waiter arrives just at the right moment for refills all round.

'Let's have a bottle of French wine,' says Bruce, just one more hint of his distaste for most things Italian in his suggestion.

The rest of the lunch meanders by, aided by several glasses and Bruce is mellowing to the presence of both a dominant woman and a gallerist who wants to be an artist. We're about to leave when, by sheer chance, Freddy Mark II and partner stroll in, see us and come over. 'Darlings, how are you?'

'Well! What great timing. Let me introduce you to Bruce.'

Everyone kisses cheeks and another bottle of champagne is suggested, agreed to constitute a sound idea and called for. A magnum arrives and we chink away the afternoon. Bruce is back in his element; the men love him to bits as he revs up his performance levels and talks about his work, his home, his life his dogs, his wine...zzzzzzzz.

Still, it's all PR and they're paying for the sponsorship so perhaps we can dispute it being time wasted.

Charlie holds her booze far too well. That is until she decides to stand and duly falls backwards into Freddie Mark II's lap. 'Love the shoes babe,' says Derek as Charlie's legs fly high in the air. Everything else was on show too but no one said a word. It's good to know there's still chivalry towards the fairer sex.

'Oops! I think I'm a little tiddly. How's that happened?' She dusts herself down and realigns her skirt but remains none too steady on her heels as she carefully heads off to powder her nose.

'She's so camp' says Derek. 'Do let her work the exhibition as well.'

A second magnum later and we're all a tad merry. I decide to put Charlie in a cab and send her home.

'I say chaps, that's both my assistants you've rendered pissed.'

'Well, you only live once' says Freddy Mark II. 'I'm so looking forward to our show.'

We get up to leave for the second time, rather more intoxicated and considerably later than planned. Who cares? We stroll back to the gallery and there's a couple browsing through the window. 'Hope you've not been waiting too long?' I say unlocking the front door with a certain measure of difficulty, trying to present a moderately sober front.

'We've been admiring that bronze over there,' the woman says, pointing to a sculpture on a plinth in the middle of the gallery. 'How much is it?'

The alcohol is working too well. 'A mere twenty-four thousand pounds, madam. With a free bottle of wine.'

'Well darling, it's what you've always wanted.'

'I know,' she says looking lovingly into his eyes, but its ...'

'Shush.' He holds her hand tight and turns to me. 'We love it. If I pay now, would you mind delivering it tomorrow?'

Would I mind!!!!!!!!!! There's only one thing to say. 'It will be my absolute pleasure. What time would you like it?'

'Say tea time. We should be back by then'. He presents his credit card, which clears without question.

'I know I shouldn't but hey this calls for a celebratory drink. Champagne Okay?'

The woman glances at her chap and we all hear her quietly say 'I do love you.'

Cheers everyone. The sun is almost shining even if it hasn't reached the yard arm yet so I'm happy. Not such a bad day after all. 'Where shall we go for supper?' Bruce looks up from his book as if totally unimpressed with the latest sale.

'Jesus! Let's sober up first.'

Sunday arrives far too quickly for my liking. My brain feels a little cloudy, to say the least, but I am compos mentis to open the gallery. There's no sign of Charlie, and I vaguely remember telling Bruce not to come in before midday. At eleven-fifteen Charlie arrives in a white trouser suit wearing the obligatory dark glasses. For the first time in her life probably, she's reserved. By this I mean I get a simple quiet 'Good morning,' as she heads to the back of the gallery to make coffee. There are small mercies in certain staff being hungover. But hey, I'm not the sort of guy who'd take advantage of such an opportunity. Much. 'How's the head?' I call out. Loudly.

She comes back in and sits, all in slow motion but all she says is 'Why is he gay? What a waste of a male specimen. Oh, my head isn't talking to me! I don't seem to remember much of what happened yesterday?'

'Let's not debrief on that now. Please sort out this side of the gallery; it could do with a change around. You'll feel much better if you do something.'

'Thanks for lunch yesterday. What I remember of it.' Charlie stands and surveys the place. Well, I have to hand it to her, she's a true soldier and slowly comes back to life, regaining her ability to function, along with the gradual re-emergence of her natural loudness.

Bruce strolls in around one o'clock and stops Charlie working to show her some of the paintings. In the end I send him off to lunch on his own because we've work to do, and by a whisker at four o'clock the place looks superb.

One thing always works. As you move something around it takes on a fresh look and looks new. I don't understand galleries where the same paintings hang for months in the same place. And to prove it works a chap saunters in and stops by one of the freshly relocated paintings. 'This wasn't here last week, was it?'

'No sir. New in. What do you think?' Always engage with the customer.

'I've been looking for something like this for ages.'

Bless him. Wrap it up Charlie. Job done.

We close up and Charlie gives me a kiss on the cheek. 'Thanks again for yesterday; you're a sweetie'.

I escort Bruce to the station and head off to deliver the sculpture from yesterday's only sale. The one that made my day.

COLOURS OF SUMMER (Part 2)

Tuesday and I'm driving to London.

I hate driving but at least I can an exit the party when I like, a quick getaway so to speak. The city has a complete different set of road rules to the rest of the country I find. I'm not one for living in the fast lane and almost enjoy the sense of bumbling around like a country yokel. The result is that I'm undertaken, overtaken and sworn at in far too many languages Anyway I eventually arrive at my destination, a reserved parking space. How cool and I'm not even a member of parliament! I'm unable to share the exact location as it's a sworn secret and only the invitees know.

For the occasion I'm wearing my loudest shirt, bought for a bet with a friend who said nobody could get away with wearing it. Wrong! I win and I certainly stand out tonight.

I'm greeted with 'Fuckin hell! Who put you up to that?' I rest my case.

The guest list is three pages long. I don't personally know many of the names but I recognize at least 88% of the invited partygoers. I'm thinking this will be fun and as if by magic a large whiskey is placed in my hand. I know, I'm driving. But I need to look the part and I don't have to really drink it.

The order of play is as follows:

1. Let them in
2. Anything goes
3. Speeches
4. Food to order; no idea what that entails
5. Party hard
6. Leave discreetly

Within minutes, there are politicians, musicians, actors and every other manner of celebrity queuing up. I recognise a famous singer who's not on the list. He's clearly on his own and as I say, he's not on the list. This is cool. 'I'm sorry' I say. 'Invitees only.'

The response is the anticipated one. 'Do you know who I am?'

I do but I dislike his band and his music. Now I know how bouncers feel. Great. 'Hang on. I'll have to check.' Get on the handset.

'Is he on his own or has he got an entourage with him'

'Solo.'

'Fuck it. Okay.'

I tell him it's alright this time. He's not impressed in the slightest but *it's my job, mate.* Good grief. How many times do you hear that expression?

One stunning lady is already half cut, wearing a very short dress, ridiculously high heels and is bouncing off other guests. She lurches over to me. 'Where have we met?'

Well I'm sure I've never sold her anything. Nor have I ever appeared on her show.

'Remind me?' I try to steady her. She titters, leans over too far and falls into my arms.

'I'm sorry; I can't remember.'

She shoves me, harder than expected, back against the wall. 'You're not supposed to forget me, that really hurts.'

'I don't believe I've had the pleasure. Maybe you're mistaking me for someone else or someone else looks like me.'

'Shame.' She staggers off.

The temptation to drink that whiskey is getting stronger, but guests are still arriving. I feel like calling out 'Next!'

One old doddery chap looks like a politician and acts like one asking for a seat. I suspect his enormous bulk could shatter one of the old chairs littered around. However, I pull one over and he plonks himself down, beads of perspiration free-flowing from his brow as he pulls a red spotted handkerchief from his jacket pocket and absorbs his instant shower. Yuck.

Next up a group of luvvies all behaving in a frivolous manner and indulging in the worst dress code you can imagine. Do I need to amplify? No, I don't and actually, apart from the fact that they're obviously gay thespians, they turn out to be hilarious.

The place is filling rapidly, and only a few names remain which aren't crossed off. Virtually a full house. It's loud, boozy, smoky and blissfully entertaining. Most people don't know who I am and that makes it an even more amusing place to be.

Our host decides to hold court, shouting out, 'All right you lot. Quiet for a moment! As you know our time has come to move out of here. It's been fun with a few tough encounters you might say.' There's a massive cheer from everyone.

'I'm retiring from office and looking forward to relaxing full time.' Huge sighs and cries of *Shame. You'll never retire.*

'You'll all have to come and visit us up north. Right who wants food; hands up for burgers.'

There's a fast food takeaway a few doors away, and within minutes an array of chips, burgers, with cheese and without, fish and pies have been ordered and to get people started, a young lass brings around a tray of smoked salmon on very small brown bread pieces. A few minutes later and she returns sing the very glass charger I presented months ago to our host, as a tray. Well you might as well. 'Please don't drop it' I whisper to the lass,' It's valuable and I can't replace it anymore.'

The place ends up smelling just like a takeaway caff, the only difference being the alcohol and tobacco fumes.

I notice a couple embracing, and that's putting it mildly, on the stairway. She's not complaining as he practices his octopusical tendencies with limited success. That's show business.

I notice the party is beginning to quieten down and people are forming groups by profession. Isn't that weird how humans stick together. A gentleman in a yellow tweed suit and blue spotted bow tie, with a waxed handlebar moustache, approaches me with two drinks in his hands, 'I've noticed you're not drinking much. Here, I've brought you a rather nice red.'

'Most kind but I've got a long drive later.'

'Well, you could always come and stay at my pad. It's not far!'

Hells teeth, all these lovely female actresses and I get hit on by a colour-blind, badly dressed, old queen.

'Do I look gay to you?' I ask.

'Don't knock it till you try it love.'

'Sorry to disappoint you but I'm full time hetero in spite of my shirt.'

'It's so you though.'

'Thank you. I wore it for a bet.'

'Well, if you want to change your mind, here's my card.' He presents it with a flourish as though expecting a fanfare or drumroll.

'And if you ever want to purchase art, I've a gallery.'

Our host puts her hand under my arm, 'Come and meet a great friend of mine.' She pulls me into the front room and there, sitting on the floor, are two musicians I certainly recognise.

'He's a painter too and was scared to talk to you. Weren't you Thomas?'

'Love your music' I blurt out.

'Thanks. I've never shown anyone my art before. It's not like performing on stage or even being on TV, like. It's sort of more personal. Do you get my drift?'

'Totally' I agree. 'I dream about showing my own work, but I sell stuff far superior to mine. You're welcome to come up and show me your work or I can always come to see what you do wherever you are, assuming you're in the UK. Or if not, you could always pay my fare,' I laugh.

'Seriously. Hey that's a done deal, man.'

Work stops for no man, party or not. In fact, there are several musicians who have studied art and some are great. I wonder what his'll be like?

I would love to be the artist, I really would. I let the thought meander around my head. Maybe one day.

I'm so sorry.' Classic English shorthand for *I'm off, I really must be leaving you all*.

'You've been a hoot', or host says and she gives me a big hug.'

I slope off and head for my reserved parking space. There's a Policeman on duty standing by my car. 'This yours, sir?'

'Yes, officer.'

'Been partying, have we?'

'You could say that.'

'Drink much?'

'Not a drop.' The bloody truth. The large whiskey is untouched where I left it. I knew the gods were looking after me.

'Think I should breathalyse you, then.'

Oh, I've waited for this moment. 'With pleasure, officer. I've not had a drink since the weekend.'

'Go on then, bugger off. Don't park in this space again. They're reserved for special personnel.'

I think about putting him straight but say only 'Good night.' Open the door, sit down, belt up, smile and drive away.'

Say no more, apart from one thing, I'm bloody starving. Bloody burger takeaways, not bloody likely. Not like our receptions for sure. I put *The Who Live At Leeds* on loud and drive home, tummy rumbling in time to Keith's drumming.

COLOURS OF SUMMER (Part 3)

The next day I'm feeling somewhat shattered. It's all catching up with me.

'Morning boss,' Belinda hisses like I've done something wrong.

Do I detect irony or something? I wait and say nothing

"I hear I missed a fab weekend. Charlie rang and told me everything.

'I'm sure that's not entirely true. She didn't even remember getting back home. It was a little OTT.'

'A little!!!!'

I felt like saying that Charlie had drank enough for the England rugby squad, first and second teams but hold back. 'Your aunt was smashed in front of Derek and Freddy Mark 2. She thought she could add Bruce to her list of conquests and without trying, failed. Hey, but did she tell you, we sold the Roderham bronze.'

Belinda wants reassurance about my pending absence. You're in charge. Tell Charlie when she's to come in. There's some cash out back for whatever and we still have plenty of wine. I'm sure you'll be brilliant and sell lots. You've got all my details - where I'm staying and I believe there's internet access there. Am I missing anything?'

'It's not a good time to tell you this, but I think I want a change of direction '

Oh, bloody hell, that's the thing when you employ people, you're never really in charge and anything can and does happen. 'Listen, you're brilliant, and I for one would not stop anyone chasing whatever they want out of life. Just one question. Will you stay till after I get back please?'

'Of course, I wouldn't drop you in it. I have to apply for this course in October, so I can stay till then. Okay?'

Nothing but nothing is going to ruin this opportunity to paint; if necessary I'd have closed up for a week. But it's still a bombshell that's reverberating Well with this bombshell in my mind as I set off to pack and get ready for an adventure. Now where is Castiglione della Pescaia again? Tuscany's a big place after all.

I have to be at the airport ridiculously early, too early for a pint of Guinness at breakfast even. The plan is to meet up at Pisa airport and then the group will travel on by mini bus. The flight's on time and blissfully nothing untoward occurs on board apart from a chatty stewardess called Moira who lives in Swords, just outside Dublin. I know this as she says it all in one breath and, by the time the plane touches down, I've had a detailed breakdown of her entire life and family plus the three dogs and a horse. I only asked for a coffee with a Jameson's.

Pisa is a mad airport. You don't know who's leaving and who's landing, and everyone mingles irrespective of destination. I aim for the nearest bar, order a real espresso and read up about where we're going. There is nothing like being prepared and you're right to think it; I'm nothing like prepared. Think non-stop gallery life is easy? Why don't you try it sometime? Want to buy mine?

We're going to a fishing port. According to the newspaper it hasn't been discovered by the British yet. *Oh good, no English bars*. The thing about Tuscany is it's renowned for good wine and food - no egg and chips and pints of lager.

I'm people watching and lose track of time. I spy an elderly, very English looking couple standing in the middle of the walkway. He's sporting straw hat, cravat and yellow trousers with an old wrinkled linen jacket. Perfect old school, late sixties to mid-seventies and she's wearing a two-piece, floral pleated dress and matching jacket and she too sports a large-brimmed, straw hat. I walk over and ask if they're part of the painting group. Of course they are. Within minutes we're talking art. They have already been informed about me and my gallery. Or should that be forewarned?

A few moments later another couple of similar age in nearly identical attire appear followed by two lovely ladies straight out of some old Women's Institute poster. They're laughing and enjoying being alive it would appear. They make me feel rather young and gauche by comparison. Next to arrive is a teacher - well she looks like a teacher, maybe a head mistress, with her dark-dyed, chestnut hair pulled back into a tight bun. She's wearing an overly long skirt in drab green, a white cotton blouse, and a tweed jacket, with that velvet collar. She's straight out of St Tinian's.

Our host, Victor arrives in much the same garb as the other men except that his cravat is red and he's escorting a rather lovely looking middle-aged lady, he introduces as Penelope. She is very smartly dressed and certainly stands out. Methinks it's a classic Chanel number.

'Right, we're all here now. Follow me' says Victor and 'Good to see you ol' chap.'

'Likewise,' I say.' The marmite is in the case with the Oxford English marmalade in case you were worried.'

'Super.'

We head to the car park and a battered and beaten-up old Ford transit. The seats have seen better days and one rear door is held on with wire. 'Don't worry about her, she's fine, never let me down yet.'

'Are you going to drive,' I ask '...or have we got a driver?'

Victor looks at me sheepishly so I volunteer to drive. 'Just as long as you tell me which way to go.'

'With pleasure. Mind third gear it bounces out occasionally.'

It doesn't take too long to acclimatise to Italian style driving even with nine other GB passengers aboard. Use the horn and put your foot down. The journey takes approximately an hour and a half with the last bit all up-hill. The art wagon makes it, and we arrive at a large, typically Tuscan villa with shuttered windows and large doors. It's been recently repainted - say no more than two decades ago - but looks inviting in what you might call a shabby chic sort of way.

I look out over the bay, a stunning vista, and there's a large patio to sit out on whilst enjoying the scenery. There's a fountain, in working order and, hidden behind tall pines, a swimming pool. *Wow* is the word that comes to mind.

Plastic goblets filled with rose wine appear carried by a little bent lady called Liliana. She speaks no English and nods all the time. Victor coughs, taps a spoon and commands our attention. 'Welcome. Firstly, it should be a lot of fun. Secondly, I hope you manage to paint some future masterpieces and thirdly please drink as much wine as you like. Do help yourself. The fridge is always full. Supper will be at seven tonight. We have two more joining us later, as they're driving up from Rome.'

We're given our bedroom keys and then chill and mingle on the patio. Emily and Libby, the two giggling sisters, are still laughing out loud, 'We haven't been to Rome in years'. This makes them giggle even more.

I'm intrigued by the first couple who are rather quiet. We haven't been properly introduced yet. 'How was my driving then?' I try to start up a conversation.

'My wife isn't a good traveller. How do you do by the way? I'm Charles and my wife is Gladys.'

'It was a bit bouncy in the back' says Gladys.

We're so English, we never swap names at the beginning unlike the Americans, who ram their name down your throat as many times as they can in as little time as possible. I prefer our reserve.

'We own a little place in Portugal, still making port, but the children tend to run things now. She's the artist. I'm here for the sun.'

'I must confess to loving the odd bottle of port...once opened and all that.'

'This is my first painting holiday. I'm so nervous.'

I decide to venture up to my room. It's on the middle floor at the end of the landing. I open the door and the view that greets me is stunning. The windows face straight out to sea. I'm in heaven. The room is old and original. When I sit on the bed, the mattress too is old and original. I lie on it and crash out within seconds.

I sleep for two hours, waking up not knowing where I am. Ah yes, Tuscany by the sea. A quick change, freshen up and off downstairs. Everyone is dressed for dinner, except me. Oops! I'm on holiday for heaven's sake. We are all finally officially introduced to each other and move onto the patio

The table is set with tea-lights everywhere and the sun vanishes in minutes, the sky going a blue-black and the stars twinkling above. You can just hear the sea. It's truly magical. Supper is served at a leisurely pace, comprising endless glasses of wine, a Tuscan bean soup, veal and potatoes. To finish, we're offered Castagnaccio, served with a pudding wine, the classic Tuscan dessert.

Ten days of this and I shan't fit into any of my clothes.

Eventually Victor pushes his chair back, stands up from the table and says, 'Breakfast is at seven and the first talk will be at eight-fifteen on the patio. Remember to bring your notebooks. There's a night cap inside for anyone who wants one.'

We all move inside, the two giggling ladies bid good night and head for the stairs. The port couple, Charles and Gladys, follow suit and the rest of us sit around to partake in the green liquid Liliana pours from a tall shaped bottle into little glasses. She then utters something in Italian and leaves the room. Victor says she was wishing us a good time here in her home.

So, she actually owns this magnificent place and isn't the maid. I'm even more impressed.

The nightcap is rather moreish and we share a couple of top up rounds and suddenly it's one o'clock. Definitely time to retire.

Penelope is in the room next to mine. 'Isn't Victor sweet?' she says opening her door. 'Night sweetie.'

'Good night,' I reply.

Then it's six o'clock. My love of early mornings is zero and this is the second one in a row but the sun is already shining, driving shafts of light through the wooden shutters. At least I'm not the last one at the table for breakfast. If only just.

Victor's wearing red cords; check shirt and a bright orange cravat. Penelope looks stunning again, straight out of *Vogue*. I'm in T-shirt and shorts. The garb of the others falls in between our extremes.

When the classes begin, I'm seriously nervous. It's like being back in school, and I didn't enjoy school first time around. Some of the group are experienced painters; the rest of us are mere beginners but in minutes, Victor's entertaining anecdotal method of teaching relaxes us all. An hour flies by and we're told to find locations around the villa to paint whatever we like. That's it.

Where to start? The problem is that Penelope isn't far from me and provides a pleasant distraction. She's let her long hair down and is sitting cross-legged in a skimpy pair of shorts. Such a shame today is about landscape and isn't a life class.

Lunch, more talk, more wine, siesta, more painting. See my dears, it's not all work. I'm loving it.

Day three and another early start. We all head off in the van to Siena. We're going to the central piazza known as Il Campo, for lunch. It's about an hour and a half normally by car but Victor drives considerably slower than nearly every other vehicle on the planet and talks all the way about the history of the place. He does however claim to know the best restaurant to eat in and the best views to paint. We eventually arrive in Siena after Victor breaks his personal best record of two hours and disperse each to do our own artistic thing.

Whilst minding my own business, sitting on a little fold up seat and trying to look like I know what I'm doing, an old man in dungarees and an even older oil-skin jacket places himself behind me. He starts to talk in Italian tutting and commenting on every brush stroke I'm making. It's totally distracting.

'Anglesi?'

'Yes.'

'You are not so bad. Why you paint in acquerelli? My daughter is artista. She is molto bene.'

I'm trying to keep painting when a woman with legs up to her neck, in the tightest fitting jeans, and with the silkiest, darkest long hair turns up to greet the old man, hugging him and kissing him on both cheeks amid a flood of voluble Italian. The only word I recognise is 'Papa.' She peers at my painting and laughs. Well at least I'm evoking a reaction.

'You should go to the Florence art academy. It is where I am studying'. Her English is impeccable.

'Where did you learn to speak such good English?'

'I went to Cheltenham Ladies' College. I wanted to come home to study my art here. The food is so much better than in England.'

You could have fooled me. She looks like she's never eaten so much as a single sweet or fattening morsel. Whereas me? If I even think of a Guinness, I put on weight. She must be a mind-reader because the next thing she says is 'Come, join us for coffee and a cake. One won't hurt you.'

'Don't mind if I do.'

We stroll over to a table in the shade and her papa orders three coffees three cakes and three amaretto. What a perfectly civilized way to spend my time in Siena.

The old man it transpires isn't so old at all; he has five daughters, which probably explains a lot. From the group photo he produces out of his battered leather wallet, they're all stunningly good looking. Sophia is the middle daughter. She shows me images on her phone of her work, and they're superb; classic to a fault, almost from a different era. I tell her that I sell contemporary art and she says she'll visit next time she's in England. We part on excellent terms and I venture to find another location to paint in. The amaretto's warming effect ought to inspire a masterpiece. Half an hour to lunch though. A sketch will have to do.

I'm really enjoying the routine of this trip; the early starts, lectures, painting, lunching, drinking, dozing, more painting, more drinking, eating and sleeping. Add in learning loads, laughter and lovely locations. What's not to love?

I earn my keep on the eighth day. It's my turn to give a talk on presentation, a simple chat about how to make your art stand out when selling or simply displaying it on one's wall at home. Many artists fail to see beyond the painting. They're too close to the subject and end up using anything handy to frame their hard-worked masterpiece. For that an outside pair of eyes helps; just as even the writer of a masterpiece on gallery management can benefit from a good editor. Luckily no one falls asleep. The sisters titter, and one stands up, 'Excuse me. Would you like to come to our home and sort out all our paintings for us when we get back? We'd make you a rather nice lunch?'

What a nice request. I can do no other than agree.

The afternoon meanders as we head off to the port to paint again. It's such hard work...in a quaintly timeless area where the clock stopped sometime in the 1950's. I pull up my little seat and stare out, taking in the odd chugging fishing boat and the disgruntled gulls demanding their fair share of the catch.

It really is the first time in ages that I've not thought about the gallery for more than five minutes. Shame on me, but I'm so absorbed in painting and the brushes seem to flow on their own, leaving me merely the conductor, watching the image transform on the paper. Victor saunters over, says nothing, and moves away again. Is it rubbish? Who knows? It's the first time he hasn't said anything, constructive or otherwise, about my work.

A long pair of legs emerging from a multi-coloured sarong, slowly and seductively moving towards me, are a definite distraction. The legs speak. 'You are with Victor?'

I find I'm looking up at a six-foot; blue-eyed, dark-haired and stunningly good-looking woman.

'I'm part of his art group. Can I help you?'

'He is ignoring me and I am missing him. Tell him I must see him.' That's disappointing but lucky old Victor!

'And who shall I say is asking?'

'I am Veronica,' and she turns and walks off as coolly as she arrived.

I pack everything away and meet up with the rest of the crew in a little bar on the quayside. We have a quick snifter and a chat, comparing notes as all budding artists do. No. Actually it's more like, *My round, what are you drinking?*

Victor looks lost in thought, making notes in his little battered leather book, when I pull him aside. 'I have regards for you from a lady I met on the front. She said her name's Veronica and she wants to see you…'

I haven't finished talking when a blushing Victor interrupts. 'How do you know Veronica?'

'I don't know her at all. She walked up to me while I was painting and…'

'Right. You've not seen her. Okay? And don't mention her name in front of the group.'

'Mums the word ol' boy. Let's do lunch when we're back in England. You've got to tell me'

'Some things are best kept secret.'

'Really?' I'm smiling now. You see, art, paintings, selling, privacy and juicy bits, all part and parcel of the everyday life of a gallery owner. 'Maybe I should write a book one day, Victor, what do you think?'

I think Victor is not amused. He calls out 'Time to go' and we head off to the jalopy for more food and wine, which you know could become habit forming.

As it's the last evening, we show our achievements and sketches, displaying them propped up on chairs and tables on the patio. It's a great mix of styles and colours. Some are really good. I cannot comment on mine. Liliana serves up drinks and I find myself impelled to make a little speech.

'Ladies and Gents'. Maybe I should say my lords, ladies and other dignitaries, however I digress. 'I'd like on everyone's behalf to thank

Victor and all of you for making this a fantastic time. I've enjoyed every second. It's such a change from being in my gallery and so I've decided to make you all one of my special cocktails to celebrate I shall call it a *Tuscan Sunset.'*

I produce, from the carrier bag at my feet, a bottle of gin, a bottle of vodka, a bottle of vermouth a bottle of Drambuie, some pink grapefruit juice and a bottle of grenadine, all secretly purchased earlier in the day. *Tuscan Sunsets* turn out to be smooth and don't taste that strong but don't be fooled my friends; the second one affects the knees and the third illuminates the night sky. Funny really, as nearly everyone in the party manages to drink three of them.

'Good grief ol' boy! You've managed to inebriate the whole group.'

'Well, it should loosen up everyone and after all it's a colourful bit of Tuscan fun.'

Penelope saunters over and sits herself down right beside me. 'This is our last night. Don't you think we should do something frivolous?'

'Any suggestions?'

'Indeed, but not here.'

Victor is holding court and retelling something historical about the area to gales of alcohol-induced laughter.

Penelope whispers in my ear. Is she kidding? I think not.

I excuse myself to step outside for fresh air and to take in the beautiful view. Everything appears to twinkle on the horizon. Must be the fishing boats. I feel an arm around mine.

'I've wanted you since we met at the airport.' It's not Penelope but the headmistress to my shocked surprise. 'You men are all the same. You play it cool knowing deep down what's going on.'

'Honest, we don't.'

'Well it looks like I shall have to show you.' Without hesitation she grabs my hair and pulls me into a kiss full on the lips. I try hard not to respond and she breaks away at last. 'Oh, I'm so sorry. I seem to have allowed myself to be carried away.'

'That's okay. My cocktails have been known to have special after effects.'

'I don't usually kiss strange men.'

'I'm not that strange but I promise not to say a word if you don't.'

She does it again, goes right ahead and plants a smacker on my mouth, then turns around and states 'I'm off to bed.' She brushes past Penelope on the way into the villa.

'Am I missing something?'

'No, I don't think so!'

'Were you snogging that woman? I'm sure I saw you in a rather awkward looking embrace. Really! How common!'

'Penelope, I'm merely a humble gallery owner.'

'Well humble your derriere up to my room right now. That's an order, not a request.' She too turns and leaves.

Well, there go. Two women having beaten their retreat; what else follows? Maybe I should be a gentleman and retire to my own bed? On the other hand, maybe not. Good night.

Breakfast is later than usual and quiet. Everyone is quiet, and Penelope is exceptionally quiet.

'Morning everyone' I try for a lilt of verbal sunshine.

Eventually the day slowly matures and heads reassemble themselves.

Charles taps me on the arm 'What was in those cocktails old boy? You must give me your recipe! Gladys was beside herself.' Charles winks appreciatively.'

'I'm afraid that's a trade secret...but for you I'll write it down. Do be careful though. It has a habit of making people do things they sometimes can't remember.'

'Spot on dear chap. Spot on 'Charles is a reborn Tuscan sun-setter.

Penelope is looking different today. It's not her very chic white, two-piece, linen outfit. It's that she's wearing a wedding ring. She's almost apologetic as she asks, 'May I buy one of your paintings? I love the one of the port you worked on yesterday.'

'It would be my pleasure but please accept it as a gift.' Either Penelope has no taste or I'm not as bad as I think I am. At painting that is.

She notices I've noticed her wedding ring. 'He's an old sod who doesn't care what I do or say. You ought to come and visit us sometime if you're ever in Suffolk.'

'Thanks. I might just surprise you one day.'

Victor pulls me to one side and offers me the opportunity to host an exhibition based on several trips he's made to Venice. I agree, knowing his entourage will follow devoutly and maybe, just maybe, Penelope will come along, minus husband.

We bid our goodbyes back at the dreaded Pisa airport. What a great time I've had. My passion for selling is now reinforced by a greater knowledge of how to paint myself. Life will never be the same again. I wonder when, or indeed if, I'll ever get the chance to paint again.

ULTRAMARINE BLUE

It's half past four and neither wine nor tea, not a drop, has passed my lips all day. Parched is the word that springs to mind.

'Hello may I come in.'

'Certainly, please do.'

She's wearing a plunging V-neck dress, which just shows a hint of leopard-patterned, or it may be cheetah, bra.

'I'm just about to crack a bottle. Fancy a glass?'

'That's very nice. Yes please.'

I produce two Swedish designer glasses and bottle of Rioja from my stock room in which boxes of wine no longer outnumber paintings but be reassured, there's still plenty left. It's just that they now all fit, nicely stacked in the corner.

'Mm this is good,' she says. 'Now, my name's Margo.' She places her expensive looking pink patent handbag on the desk and looks me straight in the eye. 'I'll come right to the point. I can help you and your gallery can help me.'

'Well, that's a good opener. Pray continue.' I pour more wine into our glasses.

'I have a client who wants to launch an unusual website.'

'How unusual?'

'We'd need to black out the windows.'

'And?'

'We'd use a few scantily clad models and for a backdrop we'd love you to put up any art with a nude theme!'

'That's kind of you but what's the benefit to the gallery?'

'There's lots of wealthy clients and you never know.'

I sip my wine, pondering what sort of website she means.

Margo smiles for me. That's fatal 'Can we put a speedboat outside the entrance?'

'Anything else?'

'I can get a Ferrari and an Aston Martin or two to park on the street!'

'Hang on. I'm a gallery not a footballer's playground. How much will your client pay for the evening?'

'Nothing in cash. But we'll provide everything; champagne, girls, a magician, DJ, the lot and you get to go on the website.'

I must be mad! But then as I've found out on more than one occasion, you have to be mad to own an art gallery.

I find myself saying 'Why not?' I still don't know what sort of website she's promoting.

'Fab. Are you free for an early breakfast tomorrow? At seven? It's one of these business breakfast clubs they have there.'

I hate early starts. 'I suppose so.'

'Right. See you at the Grand Hotel tomorrow.' With that she smiles, picks up her bag, turns on her smart designer heels and leaves. Nice pins methinks.

Belinda expresses caution. 'What's that all about? She's after you. You can tell. Did you see the way she flicked her hair? I'd be careful if I was you.'

Thankfully Belinda isn't me and I'm not Belinda. 'Well, there's nothing like a good reception to grab some media interest for the gallery. And no harm having a bit of fun eh! They only want to hire the place for a night.'

'Yes, Boss'. Belinda smiles knowingly, like all true intuitively women learn to do from birth. All I do is own the place. How silly of me to believe I know what's going on in it!

In the hotel lobby I get a professional kiss on both cheeks from Margo who places her arm on mine and steers me over to her client. 'George Lambert, how do you do!'

'I do well above middling thanks.' His hand isn't as large as mine but he's strong and uses the pretext of a handshake to try to crush my knuckles. It's all about animal dominance. Luckily, I know how to lock my upper arm and grip just as hard. My mind is already having second thoughts about him as a client and all the hairs are up on my forearm.

'Come meet Cynthia, my partner in crime,' says George.

Standing by one of the tables is another dangerous-looking individual. A blonde woman. Correction. A peroxide blonde with fake boobs and a facelift that must have cost a fortune. How red are her lips? Dangerously red. She eyes me up and down. 'Margo says you're wonderful!'

'What can I say?' I reply.

'You must come back to ours after breakfast. This is an ungodly hour to gather. I never drink champagne before nine.'

I can't see a wedding ring, but she is flashing enough diamond rings to blind you on a sunny day. I deduce that she's not Mrs. Lambert.

'Sit by me and tell me all about yourself. I'm sure you're not boring.'

'Where would you like me to begin?'

'Are you married?'

'Not that I know of.'

'That's a good start.'

'I own a gallery and...'

She interrupts. 'I know and what else?'

'You're going to hire my gallery for an evening.'

'Are you for hire'

'I'm sorry. Am I for hire? Are you kidding?'

'Not at all. I have friends who'd adore hiring you for an evening.'

It is only twenty past seven. A stupidly early hour to be propositioned. This is without doubt the strangest of breakfast meetings. *She means I could be an escort*. There's a thought. I park it and pour a large coffee. Let's change tactics.

'So, what do you do'?

'I just love to have fun and work as little as possible. I'm a catalyst you could say.'

Umm. All right. Change subjects again. 'How many bods at this reception?'

'Maybe sixty. Give or take a few.'

'We can accommodate that.' I'm trying to sound less apprehensive than I'm now feeling. *Why did I say yes?*

Some bigwig from the Chamber of Commerce calls us to order then and we have to endure a boring talk from a boring man who owns a naval chandlery.

Cynthia smiles. Her botoxed brow doesn't move. 'Some chains are fun but his are way too big. Even I can't imagine things to do with an anchor chain except hang an anchor on it.' A hand squeezes my thigh and Cynthia smiles again. all mock innocence. 'Let's go. The chauffeur's outside and my watch says it's almost time for bubbles.'

Margo, Cynthia, George and yours truly make a quick exit. No time for after chats or business card exchanges. Outside a black stretch Chevrolet with tinted windows is waiting, beside it a chauffeur wearing a smart grey suit and a peaked hat, is holding the rear door open. It's like a scene in a crass, B rated American movie.

Good grief, it gets worse. The interior is furnished in red leather seats with a wood veneer surround. Margo opens a small hatch, extracts a bottle and pours out four glasses of *Veuve Cliquot*.

'Well it is after nine, now. Cheers darlings'

We arrive at what can only be described as a mansion where the gates open automatically and you hear the scrunch of white pebbles under rubber as we slowly drive up to the front door. The place itself is massive and accessed through a pair of *Hammer Horror* doors with highly polished brass knockers which are flung open for us by a maid in full uniform.

'Drinks in the lounge Madame?'

'By the pool. It's more relaxing'.

We follow Cynthia over the marble floor to the swimming pool It's like no other place I've ever seen. There are luxurious couches covered in soft satin and two massive chandeliers hanging over the water. The pool has that expensive ultramarine look to it. A wonderful colour.

'They must be Murano. The tiles.'

'Correct. I had them commissioned a year ago.'

We sit at the far end looking out over a magnificent garden. Crass has morphed into class. 'Wow, it's beautiful. Do you have many sculptures dotted around out there?'

She doesn't answer because the maid appears with a silver tray of smoked salmon blinis and, you guessed it, more champagne.

Margo is sitting chatting to George and Cynthia says exactly what I'm thinking; 'Nobody should do seven am! I'm exhausted' Then she downs her entire glass in one. 'Can you swim?' she holds her arm out for the glass to be refilled.

'Not often enough.'

'Why don't you have a go? I'll join you.'

I protest 'I didn't come prepared. No shorts.'

'No need, house rules. Nobody swims in anything but what nature provides.' She stands up. Strips off and dives in. Artificial or not, she has an excellent physique.

Margo follows suit but George walks off talking into his mobile phone. 'Come on grumpy drawers. Get in!' shouts Margo.

When in Rome as the saying goes. Clothes off and splash. At least my suit's not getting ruined this time. I'm in an indoor pool with not one but two naked ladies. What can I say?

'What's the website all about then?' That's aimed generally at either or both women. Distraction technique.

'Shhhh! This isn't work time. Bubbles required!'

The maid appears with another bottle to top up the glasses. George is nowhere to be seen. Margo swims right up to me brushing her body against mine. 'Said we'd be good for each other, didn't I?'

Cynthia is sipping her champagne by the edge of the pool. 'What would you like to do next?'

'Well in truth I really should be going. You know gallery to run and all that.'

'Why don't you stay for lunch?'

'I really should go. Ladies it's been a delight but art calls.'

Cynthia just says, 'Don't be so prissy. Lunch is going to be served at twelve-thirty Then you can go if you must.'

It's a tough call. What should I do? Looks like I'm going to be late for work.

CHARTREUSE

A young lady pops her head around the door. 'Excuse me. Please will you have a look at my dad's work. He doesn't live too far from here? It wouldn't take long. You see, he never leaves the house and the place is stuffed to the gills. It's good stuff, I think. Please would you?'

An unusual approach for sure and intriguing. 'I will. With pleasure.' Sounds like something I shouldn't miss. 'I'll pop over later this afternoon. How's that?'

'Smashing. I'll tell him'

I love impromptu occasionally and today is an impromptu sort of day especially as Belinda's in a tidying and rearranging mood.

'I'm off to see a reclusive artist.'

'That makes a change. What is it about artists? Why aren't any of them normal?'

'And your point is?'

'The gallery is a magnet for odd bods, you know. It's a bit like a selection of my ex boyfriends. Just saying.'

'Young lady! It's what makes the art world rotate and besides I know you still love it. You could always be a stock broker.'

'Not bloody likely!'

Time to leave. Belinda is unimpressed and likely to stay that way.

The address I've been given isn't exactly just round the corner. It's a few miles away to be precise and getting there takes longer than it should because I'm held up en-route by not one but two separate funeral cortèges. The countryside is obviously bad for health and longevity these days. To cap it off I end up behind a refuse wagon and nothing and nobody is more important to our bin men than slinging green and brown plastic wheelie bins around to cause as much havoc as possible.

The bell doesn't work.

I knock hard on the old, blue-painted, wooden door. After a while the door opens and a head appears. A pair of beady eyes looks me up and down. 'I'm not sure I want to let you in.'

I could just turn around and leave to satisfy his insecurity but instead I tell him I'm here because his daughter pleaded with me to come. 'She said your paintings are worth the journey. So, can I see them, if only to satisfy her.' That does the trick. Graham opens the door fully and backs away. Entering the hallway, I'm confronted with loads of stacked canvases. There's a narrow path to the kitchen and an old kettle with the red whistling top is merrily boiling away.

'Cuppa?'

Progress in the trust stakes. 'I'll have a glass of water if you don't mind. How long have you been painting?

'About twenty years, give or take.'

'Let's have a look then. Where shall we start?'

'Upstairs?' We climb to the landing to be confronted with hundreds more canvases, all stacked on top of each other.

'How many have you painted?'

'Quite a few, I guess.'

It's obvious he's been constrained only by a total lack of space. The two bedrooms are full to the ceilings and the bathroom has a stack in it too.

It seems the landing will have to serve as a viewing area. Graham sort of sidles into the first bedroom and then suddenly there's a crash followed by a certain expletive and a white Persian cat races through my legs and shoots down the stairs looking positively guilty. Well that would explain the cat hairs sticking on more than a few on the paintings.

'It's so fine and it sticks to the varnish all the time,' explains Graham.

Distracted I'm peering out of the window. There's a shed out there, sadly looking like it's seen better days. 'Is that your studio?'

'It was, but it's pretty rotten so I don't use it now…and all my trains are out there in boxes.'

I decide not to pursue the benefits of having a Tri-ang train set tootling round the studio whilst blissfully painting away.

Graham excavates six canvases, holding them precariously balanced on the banister rail. 'This is one of my least favourite pieces.'

Why show it to me then? I don't say that aloud because it's brilliantly wacky, a naïve, colourful, figurative picture on a garish, chartreuse background. Two glaring eyes haunt the middle ground, in the face of a David Bowie lookalike – apart from being bald.

'Not exactly a user-friendly colour, is it?'

'I got it cheap in a church bazaar a while back.'

His strange, humorous, almost alien, figures emerge as the theme of most of the paintings. His colours are bold and certainly different. 'I think you'll scare the public. I love them, but you need to clean them up and defuzz them.'

Three hours have passed, and we're still working our way through the upstairs paintings. I can't see any more; my head is clogged full of new images. The best thing to do is arrange to call again to view the contents of the downstairs collection another day.

'Well, I would like to show your work in my gallery.'

'If you say so.' Graham isn't showing signs of positivity or great joy. Sometimes I feel I shouldn't bother. All in a day's work, though, dealing with negativity and cynicism.

The following week I plough through another two hundred or so canvases and eventually select a grand total of thirty-six.

'Who on earth do you think will buy my work?'

'That is my gamble and my department. I really believe they will sell.' As I'm loading the car though I'm wondering if this might be a challenge too far.

I pull up outside the gallery and Belinda and Charlie assist with the unloading.

'He's weird' says Belinda

'Has he got a woman?' asks Charlie 'I bet he's a bit, you know...kinky.'

'To be honest, we never discussed his sex life. Why don't you ring him up and ask him, eh?'

'Ooh! Who got out of bed the wrong side then?' Those ten days in Tuscany already seem a light year away.

'Sorry, ladies. Drinks on me when we close up.'

'Agreed,' they reply in unison.

A woman's' perspective is very important in art and on reflection their first opinion of Graham's work rings alarm bells. Good grief, I'm beginning to listen to others. How refreshing. My dream team decides they like two thirds of the work and their suggestions for what to do with the rest contain several repeated expletives. I listen and agree with their selection and reasoning.

With the day's done, we lock up and head to the wine bar. My girls - correction, the staff - never forget a promise. The wine is poured and the day slows into chill mode.

'Well, did anyone miss me while I was out?'

'Didn't notice you'd gone' laughed Charlie

'Who are you anyway?' Belinda clinks my glass with hers.

'Cheers.'

For once I realise I'm seriously tired, physically and mentally, and we've several large shows ahead plus Victor's Venetian show we've now added to the calendar. The waiter arrives at our table and asks if we'd like anything else. There's only one answer in the circumstances. 'Another bottle of the same please, and a jug of water.' At least water is good for you.

PAYNE'S GREY

Payne's Grey is a very useful and a very dangerous colour. Just the smallest amount does wonders but use it to excess and the blackness in it is damning and ruins everything.

Mrs. Topping is on the phone. She's wailing and shouting out nearly simultaneously. We're a gallery, not a domestic abuse help-line. From what I gather between the sobs and tirades, Mr. Topping has been a naughty boy. How naughty it's not for me to say, but apparently the nude painting over the bed is causing a lot of stress in Mrs. Toppings life.

'He's always staring at her. I originally bought it from you thinking he'd love it but that bitch has taken over our lives. He's obsessed with her.'

I try to calm her down, saying it's only a painting. Apparently, that's entirely the wrong thing to say.

'No, it's not,' she wails. 'I've met her. He's bloody well having an affair with her.'

How can anyone have an affair with a painting? I manage not to say that to her.

'He decided to take up life drawing. There she was in his class. That bitch is over our head in our bedroom and he's shagging her senseless.' There's a momentary silence and then an enormous crash of glass followed by further wailing.

'Hello! Hello! Mrs. Topping, are you alright?'

The phone is picked again and she says, 'I've done it. Smashed the little whore to pieces. I'm so sorry for the trouble. I just had to speak to someone.'

'Are you okay?' I hope I sound as concerned as I feel I should.

'I've broken the painting...hic. Do you think it could be repaired?'

Apparently, the truth is she's as drunk as a skunk and jealous as hell of a mere painting. As I say, it's not my role to judge anyone and I like to think that I show genuine concern for the people I meet in my business capacity. Mrs. Topping is crying down the phone and no man likes to hear a woman cry. It upsets us beyond belief.

'Why don't you come in and have a nice glass of something special next time you're in town.'

'Oh yes. Thank you. Good idea. We'll come in later.'

I didn't mean today. Oh God! 'Do you mean with Mr. Topping?'

'Me and Mr. Topping's credit card and my bestie, Lucy.' Her mood has changed completely. Methinks it's time to batten down the hatches and prepare for war. I mean I'm an old-fashioned romantic at heart. I like the world to be nice and peaceful. I'm not into violence and disharmony, and the Topping conversation has genuinely upset my psyche.

'Are you alright Boss?' Belinda enquires.

'I'm a bit shook up with Mrs. Topping's drunken battle cries and woes down the phone. She's bloody jealous of a painting.'

Belinda heads off to the kitchen, returning with the glass of red wine she knows I desperately need. Bright girl, our Belinda. I drink it down in one.

'I'll never figure out the female race.'

'You're not supposed to,' Belinda chuckles. 'Let me handle her when she arrives'

'With pleasure.'

We spend the next hour sorting the catalogue for Bruce's show. 'What do you think we should call it?' I ask.

'Willies on parade.' We both break into peals of laughter.

'No, seriously.'

We eventually settle on a title, after half-heartedly exploring *Hard and Soft*, *It's all in the dangle*, and best of all, *Let me paint your...*

The title of the show is to be *Trust*.

Belinda assembles the images; she's good on the computer, unlike myself, who hasn't the foggiest idea which buttons to press.

Time flies and Mrs. Topping and Lucy walk in. dressed to kill. Literally.

'Good afternoon, ladies. You look like you're on a mission.'

Mrs. Topping is dressed in a smart dark grey suit with the tightest three-quarter length trousers and high heels. Payne's Grey at its best.

Lucy is in rather too tight a blouse and blue flared culottes. She's teetering on a pair of severely dangerous high heels.

'I'm so sorry about before, it was most unprofessional of me.'

'As long as you're alright, Mrs. Topping.'

'Call me Tina. I've told you before,' There's a smile cracking her well made up face. Belinda takes control, producing a bottle of fizz.

'Thank you my dear. I want something different above my bed. There's room for something special there now.'

Belinda offers Tina a chair beside the computer screen and shows her some of Bruce's paintings. The girl has a wicked sense of humour and before long Tina Topping finds one she loves. 'That will show him. Just look at those thighs. Makes me want him right now,' she says, in an undertone.

I suppose if Mr. T. turns out to be bisexual, he might like it too. Keep schtum on that thought.

'I want it. When can I have it?'

'The work arrives next Tuesday for the exhibition opening on Thursday.'

'Well its mine. Can I have it delivered on Friday?'

Belinda writes the order and, bless her, asks for a credit card.

'How much shall I put through?'

'All of it,' says Mrs Topping. 'How much is it?'

Belinda looks at me helplessly.

'It will be up at ten and a half but for you Tina, we'll say nine thousand.'

'That's perfect, and I want that beautiful glass piece on the table too. It's a rainbow and I feel like I've found the crock of gold. My grandfather was Irish you know. Drank himself to death on Poteen.'

'The Irish have a lot to answer for then. Distilled potatoes is only good for arthritis, one of my uncles used to say.'

'How about another glass of bubbly?'

I'm happy to play barman this time.

Lucy picks up a glass bowl and holds it up to the light. 'You don't mind if I touch it?'

'Not at all.'

'I love the way the light bursts through and the cuts are superb. This would look so good on my dining room table.'

Before I can say anything, Tina says, 'Add it to my bill.'

'Don't be silly, Tina, 'I couldn't possibly.'

Oh yes, she can. Neither Belinda nor I say a word. We let the two ladies fight it out. Luckily for us it takes mere seconds to reach a blissful conclusion and the piece is added to the bill.

Tina places her hand on my shoulder and gives it a squeeze. 'Will you come and deliver my painting for me?'

'It will be my pleasure,' I assure her

The two ladies leave in a far more jovial mood than they arrived in. *What's that expression? Retail therapy.*

'Well that's one willy down. Nineteen more to go,' says Belinda in a jubilant mood.

'Well done that girl' I say.

This really is a great way to start a show and the work hasn't even arrived yet. It does next day in two huge crates deposited outside the front door just as I arrive to open up. The crates contain enough wooden boards to make a garden shed, I reckon. Armed with my trusty electric screwdriver, I unscrew at least two hundred brass screws. Slowly but surely the containers release their goodies. Bruce has packed the paintings magnificently with each canvas wrapped first in shrink-wrap film and then in bubble-wrap. They take forever to unwrap but eventually the contents lay spread out around the gallery leaning against my skirting boards.

Without a shadow of a doubt, this is going to be a very different exhibition to anything else I've ever shown. And *showing* is definitely the word for a room with twenty naked men, even if, in fact, each picture is of the same man.

By the time Charlie and Belinda arrive for work, I've managed to hang half the show. 'No comments please, it's too early.' Charlie seems genuinely fascinated while Belinda looks somewhat ambivalent.

The whole show is hung within an hour of opening up, apart from a spot of tidying up here and there. A few sculptures to dot around and the gallery will be ready. All we need now is a lot of luck, a lot of red dots placed on paintings and a damn good opening night. I've been very selective with my invitations this time, as our sponsors have already asked quite a few of their clients and acquaintances.

Thursday. Bruce walks in at midday.

I wait for his comments on my hanging.

'I think they read well,' he nods in approval. First hurdle over. Now we wait for the opening bash.

There is always a sense of panic to any show we put on. I mean you just never know who'll come, in spite of the RSVPs so catering and liquid refreshments are a guessing game. At least this time the champagne is arriving by the box load, and Bruce's wine merchant and part-time model has donated forty bottles of Alicote from his own vineyard.

Freddy Mark II arrives in a fluster. 'I have the stickers for the bubbly; we need to stick them over the labels as the wine merchants have slipped up. You don't mind doing it, do you? I'm so busy! See you later.' He spins and dashes out the door. That's all we need, fifty bottles to be relabelled, Rock n roll.

The wheels begin to turn. The caterers arrive and set up, and I have to ask them to move as they're taking up too much space on the floor.

The caterer argues 'We need four trestles.'

The owner of the gallery is adamant. 'You can't have them. Two's the max. This isn't a bloody garden fete!' I'm feeling the pressure obviously.

Belinda and Charlie disappear to get ready, leaving Bruce and I, to cope, before any further storm hits.

'Good luck with my show, I wouldn't trust anyone else to put this on.'

'Thanks for the vote of confidence' I reply, sitting down for the first time all day.

There's a knock on the front door and I look up to see a tall, bearded chap wearing a red-sequined ball gown, blocking the entrance. 'What time is kick off, sweetie?'

'It's seven,' I say, unfazed.

'Oh bugger. We're early.'

I think he's expecting me to let him stay, but my tradition is to allow no one in till just before an event starts. 'I'm very sorry. We have to close up for a while to finalise everything, but we look forward to seeing you again soon.' I lock the door and switch off half the lighting. Big beard doesn't object, luckily, and strolls off with his little friend, who's in a shocking purple suit, arm in arm.

Bruce changes his attire in the kitchen. He re-enters wearing a golden-silk, Indian style jacket with black satin trousers. I think we need Oscar Wilde to complete this scene. Freddy Mark II and his partner, Derek, arrive in matching, pale-blue suits, brightly coloured shirts and cravats. I'm keeping it simple, like Johnny Cash, sporting a black suit, black shirt and black dress shoes.

Belinda walks in wearing a full-length dress with just a hint of cleavage showing and a red scarf that matches her lipstick. Charlie is in loud mode, but something inside me says she won't be as loud as some of the guests. She has on a bright yellow jacket, white blouse and matching yellow skirt, longer than normal but still above her knees, finished off with very high, golden heels.

Bring it on; the gallery team are dressed to impress!

The guests start to arrive and it's more akin to a Hollywood red-carpet event. I've never seen so much sparkle, especially on the men. Suffice it to say the artwork is competing with the guests for attention. For once I don't know most of the guests so it's a bit like being at a distant friend's wedding However, there is one fundamental difference because this wedding is all about selling Bruce's male nudes to over-dressed men in OTT makeup and, in several cases, ball gowns.

There are some women too, mostly with the obligatory short spiky hair. The photographer is beside himself, trying not to focus on anything too risqué as his newspaper is read by *everyday folk*. Where's the Sun or Mirror when you want them?

Champagne flows and the noise levels rise with laughter, coarse and hilarious. Nobody seems to recognise Antoine, then subject of Bruce's paintings, when he arrives in a very smart woollen jacket, pink striped shirt and black slacks with loafers, looking dead normal. It's because he's dressed. I think that's for the best in this crowd.

Within minutes the place is packed, the canapés are consumed and the bottles are emptying at a record rate.

Belinda bumps into me, 'It's madness, total chaos. How am I supposed to sell anything?'

'Stay calm. Just wait till Bruce says a few words.' I try to sound convincing.

Freddy Mark II takes the microphone. 'Shut up you lot I can't hear myself think.'

The place goes silent. Let me hand you over to my partner, Derek Audrey.'

So that's his surname. Audrey. I didn't know it till this moment.

Derek now takes centre stage to deliver a short but blue comedy routine, to rapturous applause, before declaring the show open and introducing Bruce as the star of the show. More cheers and then Bruce is standing there in total silence in front of everyone.

He takes a gentle cough. 'Trust is something we all need in our lives. I paint to survive and survive by painting. My relationship with wine I trust to my dear friend and my own taste buds. My trust in art is with this gallery and I trust you enjoy what is displayed and acquire some. Right now. I trust it's to your taste and I humbly thank you all for coming here tonight.'

There's a huge cheer and rapturous applause.

A man in with a fairly reserved dress code taps my arm. 'I want this one. It so reminds me of you, love'. He means the chap beside him in a blue dress with long satin gloves, not me. Red dot number two. To my considerable pleasure several more paintings are snapped up in a flurry of red dots.

The champagne is certainly flowing. Charlie looks frustrated at being unable to find a man to pounce on and Belinda is chatting to two women who look like they're both hitting on her. She still manages to place a red dot on one of the smaller paintings for them. Good girl.

Eleven-fifteen and all the champagne is gone. Mr. Audrey strolls over. 'What a lovely evening, darling. We've so enjoyed our little soiree. We're going to move down to the club for the after party. You simply must come. Bruce and Antoine are coming. Bring the girls too.'

What can I say? *What a great idea*. Not! 'We'd love to. I'll just check if Belinda and Charlie can make it.'

No points for guessing their answer.

'Yay,' says Charlie. 'Party time.'

'Count me in,' says Belinda.

The crowd disperses rather quickly, allured by the pull of more booze down the road. Bruce is sitting sipping a large glass of wine and looking a touch perplexed.

'What's up, matey?'

'I was thinking maybe I shouldn't have sold these so quickly. I'm never going to revisit this series again.'

There's no pleasing some folk; I want to throttle him. It's been the most delicate and difficult exhibition to mount, which, in case he hasn't noticed, has been a magnificent success. There are only four paintings left unsold and it's not even day one proper yet.

'Let's go join the party. I'm sure you'll feel better soon.'

'I suppose so. Antoine enjoyed the evening.'

We lock up, leaving the battle ground mess behind and hail a taxi. I have to admit to bailing out of the ensuing party at about two in the morning, leaving them all to it. Bruce is dancing away, Charlie has a crowd around her and Belinda is still being chatted up by the same two women. Only Antoine is nowhere to be seen.

As I'm leaving, a silver haired gent eyes me up 'Are you with your wife?'

'I'm not married.'

'Who's that then?'

He's the artist. We've just had an opening at my gallery.

'You're not a couple then?'

'No. I could say I'm his dealer, but I don't like that terminology.'

'Fancy lunch sometime this week?'

Heavens above, I'm being chatted up. 'Sorry, I hate to disappoint you, I bat for the other side.'

'Don't knock it till you try it dearie!' Deja-vu. This is like the man at the party in London. *What vibe am I putting out?*

'Here's my card if you ever fancy...'

'And here's mine if you ever fancy some art for your home.'

I walk out into the early hours of the morning and hail a cab'

'Taxi!!' I'm going home alone. Thank God.

COOL WHITE

Graham's work is selling rather better than I anticipated. So much so that it doesn't seem out of the ordinary when a chap walks in showing great interest in one of the pieces, although he talks just a bit too fast and his eyes are dancing round his head. I'm no expert on drugs, but I'd be inclined to suspect cocaine's involved.

In short after forcing me to listen to a shed load of musical management bullshit at double speed, he says he wants to use Graham's work for his all new female rock band. There's one painting in particular in which fingers are entering the eye sockets in the skull.

'This will make a fantastic cover for the new single. It's called *Not My Eyes*. Man, you should hear them. Fuckin' awesome.'

'Okay. How much would you like to pay for the right to use the image'

'It'll be great PR for you and the gallery and I'm sure the dude would love to see his name on a disc.'

'Don't think so. You can buy the painting and a licensing fee for commercial use of the image.'

'I can use another painting from another gallery.'

'But you like this artist.'

'Alright. Fuck it. How much?'

We don't haggle long and he hands me an Amex card.

'Fancy a drink? Seal the deal.'

'Do you have Jack Daniels?

'Wine or coffee?'

'I'm not much of a drinker. Okay. Glass of red.'

'With pleasure'. Hope he calms down. I'm feeling the stress of his treble speed conversation and wired thought processes.

He sits down to quaff the wine, head slowly turning left and right, looking around the room, humming.

'We could do a photo shoot in here; it's got a nicely faded feel

'I beg your pardon?'

'Yeah man. I mean a coat of paint and a few mirrors and - voila, show time!'

'Nice thought but I'm not really looking to change things. I like my gallery the way it looks.'

He downs the wine in one. 'Ten grand man; think about it.' He stands and walks out the door. He's back five minutes later. 'Forgot the painting, man.'

Belinda's stayed out the way the whole time and reappears only when the coast is clear.

'What was that all about?'

'Some bloke just bought a painting and told me to repaint the gallery.'

'Well it is looking a bit shabby.'

This isn't what I want to hear. Is no one on my side? Although, looking around, I have to admit a lick of paint wouldn't go amiss. You get used to your surroundings and if it takes a coked-up customer to point it out...Bugger!

The next day the cokehead's on the phone. 'Dude, I've been thinking!'

'Hey, that's great. So have I.'

'The record company will pay 15k if you let them use your gaff. They only need it for a couple of days. What do you say?'

'What colour would you like the walls painted?'

'Deep red and black.' He waits a micro-second for my gasp. 'Nah, kidding. A cool white will do.'

I takes me two milli-seconds to decide. 'Done. When?'

'Monday.'

Square it with Belinda and Charlie. 'Ladies, we need to clear the gallery for a few days.'

'Why?' asks Charlie?

'When?' asks Belinda.

'Saturday. It won't take long.'

Why am I doing this? Ah yes, fifteen grand. That's why. Lick of paint time and a film crew coming in on Monday There's a degree of mental resistance but I even know a client who can paint the place on Sunday. So why make excuses to avoid the achievable?

The weekend traverses without any glitches despite Belinda announcing she has to finish at six-thirty 'Coz I've got a date and need to get ready.'

'Fine' I smile 'We'll finish before then, wont we?' And we do, just.

With true Rock 'n' roll timing, nobody from the band or label arrive on the Monday till eleven and even then, it takes six large coffees from some unmentionable coffee chain to get things underway.

Did I forget to say I'm a coffee snob?

The band arrives looking like they've just been let out of school for the day but, after a mere twenty minutes of makeup, lights, action, reappear in slashed leather and black lace demonic outfits, ready and able to attack a host of zombies, and to save a poor, lost, virgin soldier who, according to the shooting script, needs a good sorting out.

In actuality, the girls are all really sweet and polite. Unlike the camera crew, who couldn't give a toss about my gallery or the subject matter of the film so long as they get paid. Just an observation.

To my considerable surprise the reclusive Graham breaks his habitual shyness to come into town today of all days. He walks in to find one of his paintings blown up and replicated six times around the room and filming in full swing.

'I wanted a word with you.'

'Sure thing. Let's go round the back.'

'I don't think I can cope with all this.

'My dear chap, it's all good exposure. What would you rather do, leave them all in your house piled up for ever more?'

'I hate them all. I want to destroy them now.'

Great. If that's how you feel, let me get you a knife and you can shred away. See if I care. But do let them finish filming first. The band sound really good.'

By the look on his face, I know he's deadly serious, so I take him through to the stock room and get him a Stanley knife. Guess what? He slashes each of the paintings leaning against the wall. He's actually enjoying himself and getting in the mood I suggest he puts his head through like an old Edwardian pier mock-up and take a photo, for posterity. Although a bloody gun might have been more useful than a camera. There we are surrounded by ripped up canvases and broken wooden stretchers. 'I trust you're going to tidy up and throw this bloody mess out?'

'I feel much better, honestly. It's been bugging me since you came to my house'. The sweat is pouring down his face.

Why do I bother? Graham, you're a total fruitcake.'

'I promise I'll paint you more - far better than this lot of rubbish'

'I wait with baited breath.'

Out in the gallery, the girls are still miming to their forthcoming new release and life goes on as per any normal Monday on planet Earth.

'Mate!' The director looks in my direction.

I hate being called that. 'Do you mean me by any chance?'

'Yeah, whatever your name is. I want another stiff and you'll do seeing as you're doing nothing. Make up! Tart him up!'

I can see the tabloid-heading now; *Gallery owner prematurely deceased in own shop.*

But why not? Graham's destroyed his work and I'm seething inside. Within minutes, I'm a dead carcass.

'Lie there now and don't move till I tell you. Got it?'

Think of the money.

The gallery looks very different lying on the floor. The girls look rather taller from down here too. Then they strut over and each of them positions a foot on my torso. Okay, so now I'm a stiff with eyes glazed over, enjoying the view.

'Cut. Perfect. That's a wrap.' The director looks pleased with himself. There you go, I'm immortalised and all in one take. I doubt anyone would believe what's happened today.

When they've all cleared out and gone, the place is quiet again and Graham returns to talk to me. 'I'm sorry about what happened before.'

'You know what Graham, I've risen from the dead and guess what? I just don't care.'

INDIGO

Indigo and its depth works a treat for night paintings. It's dark and occasionally sultry, like the woman who paints mysterious nocturnal abstracts with bright yellow city lights.

There's a definite relationship between the work of the female artists I meet and their height. The shorter they are, the larger the paintings. This is certainly true for Samantha. Her voice is gravel, pure sex down the phone, and she stands a good four foot three inches depending on which way the wind blows.

She lives with her chap who is jealous of anyone, particularly male, who talks to her, so you'll understand what it's like when I want to visit her studio.

I originally espied her work hanging in a little framer's shop. He has a cupboard – sorry, a bijou studio he uses to show paintings by local artists. There was something intriguing about her work that I liked. So, I ring her up, and arrange to see her.

At a front door, which has seen better days, I'm met by a bloke who's roughly shaved - hardly designer stubble, more unkempt, greasy hair stuck to his scalp like an old mop. His image is reinforced by tatty, worn-out jeans. I take an instant dislike to him and he looks at me like I'm his life-long enemy.

'Is Samantha in?'

'Why?'

'I have an appointment to see her work.'

'I'll check she wants to see you.'

I sense a huge problem. I'm not wrong. 'You have ten minutes. She's over in that room.' He points along the ripped wallpaper of the corridor. I slide past him, stepping over quantities of non-matching shoes and wellies and a sleeping dog and land outside a brown-stained wooden door. I Knock quite hard and turn the sticky Bakelite handle.

Samantha's kneeling on all fours on the floor, her derriere in a very tight pair of jeans facing me as I walk in. What a pleasant greeting. She's painting on a square canvas and her hands are covered in indigo paint.

'Hello Samantha. Who's the bodyguard?'

'You've met Robin then. Don't mind him'. What a voice. She stops and rises up to her full diminutive height.

'Do you smoke?' That would explain things.

'No,' she says. 'I gave up cigarettes years ago. Just little spliffs now and then'. Her voice is down in the dungeon. It's almost a growl with a purring undertone thrown in for good measure.

Hanging off nails are a number of unfinished paintings, with as much paint on the wall as on the canvases. Little sketches on lined notepaper are stuck with drawing pins onto the plaster and an old Dansette record player is spinning *Wild Things Run Fast*. I know it well. I own a copy of the album too. 'Love Joni Mitchell.'

'Me too.' She changes gear and subject. 'How does your gallery work?'

'Rather well apparently!'

'I've been stung before; down in London'

'I don't believe any of my artists have ever had a reason to complain. I pay everyone.'

'That's comforting.' She gets back down on the floor and continues to paint. Watching her in action is almost hypnotic.

I sit myself down on the floor cross-legged. There are no chairs in the room. We just chat away and she continues to paint. Suddenly there's the door loudly bangs open and Robin storms in. 'What the hell do you think you're doing?' His anger is clearly directed at me.

'Conversing. Why?'

Without warning he stomps over and kicks the record player. The stylus makes a loud screech as it skids off the disc and crashes with the player to the floor.

'That's my favourite record, you bastard!'

'Screw you, bitch!' He grabs a jar of murky blue paint-clogged water and hurls it at the wall. Jackson Pollack, eat your heart out! It splashes everywhere, missing me by a few millimetres.

I refuse to engage and fight, which clearly is what he wants. 'I like Joni Mitchell. That's a great album you've ruined.'

Samantha is sobbing curled up in a foetal position and my calm further fans the flames. 'I don't want you in this fucking house! You can't have her!'

Before I can think of a suitable reply, Samantha leaps off the floor and jumps on him, screaming and pulling at his hair.

'I love you when you're angry, you bitch' Astonishingly that's from Robin, laughing hysterically whilst spinning and banging into the wall. Samantha doesn't let go. She continues hitting him, screaming as she does so.

Breaking free, he runs out, down the corridor, kicking the sleeping dog and slamming the front door on his way out.

'I'm so sorry.' She flicks her hair back and wipes her eyes, smearing indigo over her cheeks. 'We divorced years ago and he won't let go.'

'Are you sure you're okay?'

You see you never know what's been going on behind the surface of a painting. Some people just look and say, *That's nice. That'll suit our lounge*. Do they think about the life of the artist? I doubt it. Not unless the artist is about to die and escalate the value of his or her work. Buyers are mercenary bastards. Well here's a case of beautiful paintings, deep, sultry and powerful, the camouflage for a woman being mentally and physically abused by her ex-husband.

Samantha looks up at me and her eyes are full of sorrow. At the same time, they're very beautiful. 'What am I supposed to do?' she asks. Then she kisses me...on the nose.

'Let's have some fun. I know, let's go for a walk. The park's just across the way.' She wipes her hands on a multi-coloured, terry towel, and throws it down on the floor. 'Come on slowcoach!'

We stroll across the road and turn left into one of the last of this country's proper Edwardian style parks with its tidy flowerbeds, exploding in a colourful array of carefully matched flowers. Over in the distance is a bowling green actually in use by a gaggle of elderly ladies and gents. *Hurrah for England*.

Samantha runs off like a mental afghan hound unleashed, hair flying everywhere as she leaps and skips laughing out loud. I sort of meander in the general direction of her wake and stop to watch the octogenarian bowls tournament.

Samantha arrives back at my side. 'When was the last time you made love outside?'

'Not for a long while and just for the record, I've never played bowls either.' It seems the disarmingly right thing to say.

She has rosy cheeks and a beaming smile of happiness, 'I feel like I've been set free, thank you.'

'I don't believe I've done anything untoward apart from viewing your work.'

'Silly boy. You're exactly what I need, right now.'

Technically speaking, Samantha isn't one of my artists. Not yet. Neither is she staff, so normal rules don't apply. There's just one simple set of questions to be addressed. Would she like me to sell her art or not?

Would I like to sell her work or not? Would I want to miss an opportunity for some fun? Ah that solitary word, fun. *Would it be fun?*

YELLOW OCHRE

There's a debate that contrasts yellow ochre with raw sienna. Actually, it's more or less the same colour in oils but one is opaquer in watercolours, assuming you care to know that? Anyway Venice, as an artist's playground, has a lot of washed out colours and yellow ochre figures to a great extent.

Or should that be raw sienna?

Victor wants his Venetian show in October and of course October is when Belinda's planning on leaving the gallery. Time to look for a new member of staff. It dawns on me that I have no more than six weeks to find someone new.

'Belinda! Pardon me for asking, but when exactly in October are you going?'

Belinda bursts into tears. 'I don't want to talk about it now.'

'That's all well and good but I really need to know. We've got Victors exhibition coming up and you've been brilliant and I'm beside myself and I really need to know if it's the beginning or end.'

'It's neither. I changed my mind. They cancelled the course. I don't want to go and I thought you meant you were pleased you were getting rid of me.'

'Are you kidding.' *Women!* 'That's great news; I mean, I'm really sorry it hasn't worked out for you. I want you to stay. Would a pay rise cheer you up?'

I can't begin to tell her how relieved I am. Joyous in fact.

Even if none of us is actually indispensable, great members of staff do make your life so much easier. I'm deeply relieved by Belinda's news.

'Well then, I'm putting you in charge of the show. The whole shebang. So that's it, start now. Catalogue by the weekend please and you choose which image we use for the theme.'

The subject is closed. Belinda appears as relieved as I am. That's retail my dears. It's just like relationships; it's all about communication.

The phone rings. It's Victor. 'My dear chap. Do you need an extra member of staff? My niece, Abigail, needs a month's work placement as part of her university degree. Wouldn't it be fun, if she could help at my show?' He's either weirdly tuning in to my operating frequency or it's the most useful of coincidences.

'Victor ol' boy, tell her to ring me. Belinda is going to look after all the exhibition details and I dare say she'd enjoy having a personal assistant.'

I put the phone down as two elderly ladies, very smartly dressed and what you might call proper, stroll into the gallery. 'Good morning ladies; may we offer you tea or coffee?'

'Are you the young man that owns this establishment?'

'I believe that I do.'

'Good. My name is Woodridge. This is Emily, she is my sister and a wonderful artist and I believe you should inspect her work.'

'How do you do, Emily.' Emily quietly shakes my hand. There's an air of mischief in her deep blue eyes.

'I have some photographs here in my handbag if you would like to see some?'

'With pleasure.'

What I see is unexpected. The photos depict bold landscapes, quite naïve but full of energy. They're simply divine. I fall in love with the quality of the colours. 'If you don't mind me saying, these are brilliant. I love them.'

Emily blushes. 'You won't mess me around, will you? My last boyfriend was an incorrigible flirt and it upset me so.'

'Emily, I don't mix pleasure with business unless it involves a glass of wine or two. May I offer you both a drink?'

'Do you have Cinzano?' The older Miss Woodridge pipes up.

'We might indeed. At the back of the fridge.'

Charlie picks up on the hint straight away and nips out to buy a bottle. She returns quickly and steps out from the kitchen with two iced drinks of the requested tipple. Always ready to please. Not difficult to achieve, given a local wine shop, three doors from the gallery. A Godsend.

We all clink glasses and formality merrily melts way.

We sort out a date for me to visit Emily's studio and as they stand to leave, Emily's sister leans in to me and says, 'Young man. Do you think you might manage to play something a little more classical in your gallery next time we visit?'

'Grateful Dead or Glenn Miller? I quietly respond.'

'Schubert would do nicely.' With that they leave without another word, Emily towed by her Sergeant-Major of a sister.

'How about that then?'

'Aren't they sweet. I'd kill for that art deco brooch Emily was wearing.'

I love being surprised, in a nice way and more times than most it's the older artists that are full of them. However, there's one drawback. Although young at heart, they're an aging collection of wonderful characters and the inevitable is bound to happen sooner or later. We can't play God though and serious art buyers are only too aware of the fact and always seems to want to know how old an artist is. Maybe I should put born and expected to die dates on the labels. Greed you see, I don't like it. I remember lending a painting to a couple who were umming and ahhing about a particular piece. I said to hang it on their walls over the weekend and see if it suited. No obligation. Unfortunately, on the Sunday afternoon I had a phone call from the artist's wife to say he'd died and she wanted all the available work back, obviously expecting an explosion in his market value. I seemed debateable whether the piece I'd lent was available or not. I suppose it was but on the Monday morning I rang the couple to see if they had decided to keep or return the painting. Luckily for them they did want it and agreed to pay for it by credit card there and then. Only then because they loved the picture not the prospect of monetary gain did I reveal that the artist had died the day before.

Back in presentsville, Charlie sits down beside me at the desk. 'I've been thinking! You were so nice to those ladies. In fact, you're really such a sweetie, I think we'd make a great pair. You're kind and gentle and I've had enough of liaisons, I want to settle down and be naughty with one person for a long time. What do you say?'

My jaw drops. 'Charlie, are you serious? You must want something. What do you want?'

'No really, you're just my type and...'

I cut her off, 'No. Your type are males, tall, short, not so short not so tall. You crack me up.'

'I'm chatting you up here and you don't believe me.'

'I'm flattered, but I shall have to let you down.'

'You're so good with older woman, I thought maybe we ...?'

'Heavens love, you're only a month or two older than me and I feel like I'm entering my prime. Sorry to disappoint you.'

'Well it was worth. You should at least let me show you what you're missing.' A more determined salesperson I have never met. 'Well, what are you going to do when you're older eh?'

She always has a way of making me think.

'I want to be an outrageous bohemian artist.'

'Well boyo, a little practice wouldn't go amiss then. Would it?'

Belinda is oblivious to what's going on. Her head is stuck in the Venetian show. Bless her. But thankfully she's physically present in the gallery. I'm saved.

'How's it going, Belinda?' I call out to her.

She doesn't answer, and then I notice she's got small headphones in her ears. I walk over and, removing the headphones, ask again.

'Pink Floyd. It helps me think. *Wish You Were Here*. It's my favourite.' Well at least she has taste.

'Charlie's up to something. I can feel it in my bones.'

'Don't tell me she's after you again. She always says she'll get you one day.'

I don't know what to say. Apparently, there is one rule for the boss and a hundred that can be broken by the staff. Sometimes I think I'm the outsider here in this retail world. Maybe being an artist would be an easier life. Not so much guess work!

Charlie is full of smiles as she slinks up to me. 'Cup of tea?'

'What's the time?'

'Three o clock'

Wine o clock methinks. 'Glass of red then, please.' Memo to self, maybe I should drink a little less. 'A small one, not a flagon'

In truth I now know I have a problem with the permanently frisky member of my staff. I'm out of my depth. Best is to ignore it.

'I love Venice. It's such a romantic city. Isn't it?' Charlie's trying a different tactic.

'Well you can dream about it when the show's on and work your magic helping Belinda sell them to customers."

'That's the easy bit. Is Victor available?'

I smile thinking of Victor being attacked by Charlie. *Phew, I'm reprieved; it's over to you Victor. She's all yours dear friend.* Now there's a thought.

'What's so funny?'

Nothing at all.' I feel much better.

'I think the paintings are too cheap. They're magnificent and should be loads more expensive,' suggests Belinda.

'Well put that to Victor and let's see what he says. I must say I agree with you.' She is completely right and rising to the challenge.

'Really, that's so cool, thank you.'.

She rings Victor, who agrees without hesitation and we more or less double the prices. Here's hoping they sell anyway.

Another phone call, this time from the framer. All the works are ready to collect but for one slight problem; the framer himself has broken his ankle, slipping on his stairs at home and can't drive. *Can we collect them?*

A tall slender, well-groomed girl walks up to the desk as I'm hanging up. 'Hello, I'm Abi, Victor's niece.'

'Ah yes, we've been expecting a call from you. Your uncle said you might like to some work experience in a gallery.'

'I forgot to ring but I did have a look at your website and I can start as soon whenever you want. It's okay isn't it?'

'How can one refuse? Right, first things first. Come with me. We're off to collect your uncle's work'. We hail a taxi and Abigail's work experience formally begins.

Twenty minutes later at the workshop, I ask the driver to wait as outside his cab and we pass through the battered red door. We don't need to ring the old brass bell on the counter. Bill, the framer, is sitting there in a wheel chair looking stressed. 'Bloody stupid cat; went between my legs. Six weeks I've got to be in this ruddy cast.'

'Shall I sign it for you?' I won't repeat his expletives.

I introduce Abigail. 'This is Victors niece. You've just framed his show.' He sheepishly apologies for his outburst

Abigail nods 'I've heard worse. Mater dropped a vase on her foot once. It was rather expensive and it rolled onto the tiled floor and shattered. Her language was far worse; trust me.'

I like this girl. Her initial air of innocence, camouflages the woman in waiting.

All the paintings are bubble wrapped and thankfully numbered, making it easier to identify when hanging and labelling, but then dear reader, you know this already, don't you? It's a tight squeeze getting them all and the two of us into the taxi, but we manage it. Abigail's a natural packer. Experience Lesson One completed. Score 10 /10.

Lesson two is about unpacking, unwrapping and arranging paintings in an orderly fashion, without losing sight of the allocated numbering.

The static from the bubble wrap plays havoc with Abigail's long hair, which is flying away and standing on end. Belinda comes to the rescue with a can of something or other. I think it's called bonding. The display of friendship not the hairspray.

Belinda asks to be allowed to hang the show and I let her do it with Abigail's help. I find it amusing and rewarding to see how well I've developed her hanging skills and her managerial talents. It's not all plain sailing though. Belinda is on the fourth rung of the ladder when she utters a cry. 'Help, my finger's trapped in the cord!' Somehow the picture cord and the hook have attached themselves to her middle finger.

'Permission to touch? Do excuse me.' I lift her by her waist off the ladder, still connected to the painting. I return her to the floor; aware now that she's somewhat heavier than I realised or that I'm older than I like to remember and don't want to damage my back. 'How on earth did you manage to tie yourself up?'

'How on earth did you manage to lift me down?'

'I surprise myself sometimes.' I untangle her slightly blue looking middle finger from the painting. Thankfully the painting's undamaged.

The show's hung by teatime. I angle the lights for maximum effect. Lighting is so important to bring out the best in a painting. Please remember this little tip as so many electricians put stupid picture lights at the wrong height and the light doesn't even reach the painting. Just a little moan and dig.

'Voila! I think we should all have a celebratory drink. How about a nice bottle of Italian Red?'

The paintings have an exquisite glow to them and you can almost hear the colours rustling with atmosphere trying to escape from behind the glass. I have a good feeling about this show. I feel it in my stomach. Normally before an opening I experience a tension and nervousness, like a growing knot deep down. This time a serenity is developing. I'm sure it won't last but for now its drink o clock time. 'Cheers ladies. The gallery looks great. Here's to all of us.'

With two days to go, we're ready ahead of schedule, and everything's running smoothly. Now all we will need is a happy, buying audience.

I'm sure I mentioned two of my artists in my last book; Peter and Patricia, a husband and wife team. Today they drop in for unexpected visit. They tend not to leave their respective studios much so it's a pleasant surprise to see them.

Patricia says, 'I thought you might like a pot of my gooseberry jam.' She delves into her enormous black leather bag and follows the package with some helpful advice. 'Be careful. It tastes as sharp as a kitchen knife.'

'How lovely to see you both and how did you know Gooseberry's my all-time favourite jam?'

'I didn't, ducky. Pot luck one could say.'

Peter walks among the paintings 'I really like these. Very different from what you normally show. A touch of real class with a hint of innocence.' Peter's examination is slow and meticulous. 'Ah! He has a great palate too.' In the trade we call this intense scrutiny by the term *scanning*, and it's often conducted by rival artists before ever introducing themselves to mere mortal gallery owners.

'Drinks my dears?'

'Cup of tea would be lovely,' answers Patricia.

Belinda slips away to put the kettle on.

Charlie introduces Abigail. 'This is the artist's niece and she's been a great help the last couple of days. And these...,' she turns to Abigail, '...are my favourite artists!'

I cringe inside but Abigail's too smart for Charlie's mischief. She's already done her homework in my stockroom. 'What a pleasure to meet you, Peter. Variety is such an asset and I have to agree with Charlie. I'm struck by the boldness in your oils and the unusual use of greens and Patricia – your hand sewn pieces, - I'll own one, one day. I'm too used to Uncle Victor's paintings. We grew up with his work everywhere round the house.'

Peter smiles, clearly enjoying the banter but Charlie's nose is, for some reason is put out of joint. *Game set and match to Abi.*

Patricia says, 'I think we should have one of these, sweetie. I love the light bouncing off the water.' Now this is a real compliment. An artist buying another artist's work in the same gallery they themselves show in. Very reassuring indeed. The magical red dot is placed on the said painting. Sold.

'Assume you want it left for the show. We can't make tomorrow evening.'

'Thanks, I'll drop it out to you afterwards and let you know how I get on with the jam.'

'How's your own painting coming on? Bet you never get any time mind you. I always say that a few minutes a day sketching is the best way forward.'

'I'll bear that in mind when I get a moment.'

Charlie says, under her breath 'Yes a moments fun would be a great idea. As for sketching, that's something else!'

Finally, it's Thursday and Victor plans to arrive early so we can chat about things What we certainly can't afford is to have a liquid lunch today. He's already late when the phone rings ominously. 'Hello ol' boy, spot of bother I'm afraid. The cars a bit broken. I'll leave it and taxi up to you.'

I knew it was going too smoothly. 'Are you okay?'

'I'm alright. Car isn't.' The phone goes dead. *Well at least he is still alive, so I can't put prices up just yet!*

'You look like you've seen a ghost,' says Belinda.

'Just a hiccup, I hope. Artists car demise, artist still alive.' *Can anything else happen, a world war or an earthquake or something less trivial perhaps?*

Abigail is less calm when she learns of Victor's delay. 'What's happened? Is he alright?' I'm sure he shouldn't drive. He's positively the worst person to sit behind a steering wheel.'

Having driven with him myself, I agree with her but it won't help to say so. 'He assures me he's fine and will be here soon. We have a couple of hours to go so let's all chill and break all the rules and have a drink. Any one for a nice cup of tea?'

That inspires general laughter and Belinda emerges with a cold bottle of fizz *and why not?* Victor arrives to find all of us clutching half-empty, fluted glasses, and Charlie immediately places a drink in his hand. 'You just might need this.'

'Oh, thank you. Hello Abi dear. How's Mama?' It's to be business as usual; the car incident forgotten and on with the show.

Victor seems delighted with his exhibition and even more so once he spots that there's already a sprinkling of little red dots to be seen. 'It's rather splendid don't you think. I took the liberty of asking a few more friends to pop along who already have some of my work. Ah! Here they are now.'

He means the vintage couple straight out of a 1950s movie. She; magnificent fur coat. He; double breasted, pin-striped suit. Vintage; in their seventies but well preserved. They start to chatter with Victor as soon as they're in the door. Let the show begin.

Within minutes the place is a hive of loud conversation with Victor greeting everyone and introducing guests to each other. Wine is flowing, fizz is bubbling and even a peppermint tea is produced on demand.

Soon to my satisfaction red dots are flying. Belinda grabs me by the arm. 'They're all gone, every painting's gone. It's sold-out.'. At that precise moment a voice I know only too well says, 'Hello darling, who is that young thing on your arm?' It's Penelope and she's not wearing her wedding ring.

'Welcome to my gallery. How lovely to see you. This is my senior sales executive, Belinda.'

Belinda says hello and vanishes into the crowd. What is it with female ESP? I'll never know.

Victor's in his element and taps a spoon against his glass. 'I'm delighted you could all make it today. Venice is such a magical place and there's so much going on throughout the day.'

'And night' someone calls out from the crowd. There's a titter of approval and Victor actually blushes.

'Well now, I've just been told that my show is a sell-out Thank you to the gallery for doing such a splendid job of hosting and hanging the show. I believe my niece has been involved in the process too. Well done Abigail dear, I won't embarrass you any further Thank you dear friends for all your support, wine and port over the years and for coming from far and near. There's only one more thing to say and that's cheers.' He gets the explosion of applause he thoroughly deserves.

'We shall have to celebrate afterwards,' Penelope says. 'I'm going to mingle, darling.'

It's hard to say how I feel at this moment, a mixture of happiness, delight, confusion, and relief. All accompanied by a touch of mischievous anticipation for what may happen later on.

I reckon this sums up being a gallery owner. You just never know what's going to happen next.

OLD RED LEATHER

Imagine a junkyard filled with enough *stuff* to fill three stage sets for *Steptoe and Son*. Add a few dogs, sheep and hunks of stone and you more or less have the place I'm visiting. However, there's one small difference. This place precariously overhangs a canal and looks like it's going to fall in at any moment. I proceed carefully. Very carefully.

The old green door with massive rusty hinges carries a sign. *Knock very hard*. I do exactly as requested and wait.

The more I look around, the more I spy. It's a very interesting zone; a throwaway museum of artefacts, strewn about randomly in a totally non-artistic way, waiting nervously to be adapted or utilised to make something. What that could be, I've no idea.

The door opens to reveal a completely dust covered chap in overalls and old hobnail boots. 'Greetings. Mind the flooring; it's a bit dodgy in places.'

Standing amongst breezeblocks, lathes and a colourful abstract in process mounted on an easel is an old-fashioned, chrome and red leather barber's chair. In addition, there are mirrors leaning up against wooden poles and crates. In all my years of visiting studios, I've never seen this sort of set up before. I have to ask. 'Work in progress. Installation perhaps?'

'No mate.' He laughs. 'I cut people's hair occasionally. Some of the women love it. Me names Rudolf but everyone calls me Randy'. A white dust covered hand is projected in my direction. I shake it carefully, trying to avoid a Saharan-scale sandstorm. Luckily, I'm not wearing any black clothing. Eureka, I've learnt from past experience!

The dust still flies everywhere, including up my nostrils and inevitably clogs the back of my throat. Trying to cough and still sound like a professional gallery owner, I attempt to strike up a relevant, fact-finding conversation. 'So what *cough* do you *cough*, *splutter* like to *cough*, *cough*, *gasp*, like the most in your art.' I stagger and reel into the barber chair.

'Well,' Randy says. 'All of it. Do you fancy a haircut?'

'No thanks. I like my hair as it is'

'Well, there's something about stone that really gets me going. Mind you I love to paint. But I get bored. Sculpting is what I really like...and the female form.'

His eyes are deep blue in his powdered face. You can see that there's a rough edge, an uncut diamond feel, about him.

'Don't you think you should wear a mask?'

'I should, but it stops me thinking!'

He roots around for a couple of mugs and pours nearly boiling water from a battered and dust covered kettle. 'Tea or coffee?'

'Weak tea please, no milk. No sugar.'

'Blimey. That's gnats piss. That ain't tea!'

We chat and I find him hugely likeable. He's refreshing and most certainly different. Mind you, I have to add that my gut instinct is saying *Lock up your daughters*, especially after he begins telling me some of the tricks he's got up to on his chair. All in the good name of art - I don't think!

Everything, the banter, the probing questions and answers, is all a means to an end though. It's a game or warfare; getting to know your opponents' cards even if you're not in a smoked filled room full of poker players. Money is the crux of it all. Will this sell? Will that work? Will you try to sell it for me? How much do you make? How much can I make? Will you try some back at your gaff? It's all the same, no matter who you're dealing with; a guessing game to get it right. Right for the customers and right for the artists and of course right for me who has to make a few bob if only to cover my time and all the overheads.

He feigns disinterest in money and he's not alone coz nobody wants to under-sell himself or herself and I've got to guess it just right. It's a highflying, juggling act, aided and abetted by careful assistants back my gaff. I like that word. *Gaff*. All my attempts to create a great successful art gallery, admired by many, reduced to a simple word. *Gaff*. Love it. It takes all the seriousness and all the goings on behind the scenes and throws them up in the air. I own a gaff. Isn't that just bloody perfect?

'Yes,' I say. 'I will take some pieces back to my gaff...if you clean them and remove all the dust.'

Randy looks at the stonework on the floor. 'A quick polish'll do the trick and I'll wrap them in blankets so you dain't ruin yer motor.'

His accent is pure Black Country, in case you haven't guessed. It's a refreshingly rare, old delight. I can't wait to invite him in to meet some of his future clients and collectors.

'Can I take a photo of you in your studio? It's for my new website so people can see what you're like and get a sense of the atmosphere surrounding your art'.

'Yeah. Why not?' He poses as only a natural could do.

My mind's racing ahead. I wonder if Charlie will try her luck with this one? Methinks there won't be any resistance from him. We shall have to wait and see. After a while, my car is laden with more than I care to think about. I'm sure the shock absorbers are none too delighted with half a quarry in the boot. However, the journey back's uneventful as the weight irons out any bumps and potholes in the road. Bless our country. The roads are crumbling. Long live the British Empire. Time for a radio four play for today!

Driving's the only head space I get. I enjoy listening to the airwaves. It's where I get to use my imagination whilst calming down and relaxing. Shame it's so rare that I get to hear the whole play and I never ever get to enjoy the whole of a five-part drama. Got no time. One day I suppose might. Something to dream about.

I arrive back at the gaff and enlist the help of my trusted team. 'Ladies, we have a new bod joining the stable. Help me bring these in please. Wait till you see the photos!'

After the pieces are strewn round the gallery, we play the *how much do you think we can sell them for* game.

Surprisingly it's Belinda who comments on the photo. 'Cor. He's a bit of alright then.' Think she approves. Charlie just seems bemused and if I could mind-read, I wonder if I'd find her thinking about a potential threesome.

Saturday morning arrives and in he walks, a stickily-built chap sporting a denim jacket, turned up jeans, heavy polished boots and a bobble hat. He has noticeably large bushy sideburns. Engelbert Humperdinck would be proud of those. He resembles nothing so much as a Liverpool docker.

He slowly turns 360 degrees with his hands on his hips before giving his opinion. 'Nice gaff, chief.'

'Fancy a cuppa. No gnats piss, honest!'

'Smashing.'

'Ladies, let me introduce Randolph.'

'Everyone calls me Randy.'

Charlie's ears pick up and I swear I hear her mutter, 'I bet he is.' She turns to me and delivers that knowing smile of hers.

Belinda looks equally smitten - like she's about to donate her knickers and throw them at him. For a moment the gallery seems to have become a stud farm where willing cows wait in turn to be mounted by the bull. Everyone knows this, and my role is only to play at farm hand. What joy.

'You can play games after work, thank you. Belinda, show Randolph his inventory. I said *inventory*! And get him to sign the paperwork.'

'With pleasure,' she drools. They sit down in the far corner emitting chuckles and giggles at regular intervals. I've never seen Belinda acting so girly and coy. It's hilarious.

I stroll over with his cuppa. 'Here you are then; one cup of builder's brew.'

'Maybe Randy would like something stronger,' Belinda says, lovingly lost in our sculptor's eyes.

'I don't drink luv. Ta anyway. Tea's me favourite tipple. I used to drink like a horse and get into way too much trouble. I just about manage now with tea. Lots o' cups mind.' You would swear Adonis was talking with bells and angels flying around.

Belinda is seriously mesmerised and loses his attention only because a couple walk in to browse and the woman starts admiring one of Randy's pieces. In a jiffy he ups and introduces himself as the artist. Within five minutes she asks to buy the piece. Now that's amazing. It's a sort of sexual magnetism that does it, I think.

Belinda glides over to escort them to the desk to do the paperwork. That's an expression in the trade meaning *to pay*.

'It's alright this place. And your brew's good too.'

'Well, thank you. Hopefully we should continue to thrive a few more years now we have your seal of approval.'

Randy winks. 'Let me know if I can help out at any time. I forgot how much I enjoy selling. Easy innit when you know how.'

'Alright. I'll take a flyer. Let's do a meet the artist day with you. Turn up in your work clobber, but not as dusty please. Let's say two weeks Sunday. That's the 17th.'

'All right chief. Done. Ta very much.'

WISHY WASHY BLUE

Have you ever looked at a woman's hand and found it difficult to count the number of diamonds on her fingers? No? Well let me tell you!

This is a woman in her fifties in a full-length fur coat. 'Good morning. Are you the owner of this establishment?'

'I am indeed. A very good morning to you.' It seems like the right way to respond to her formality.

She glides over to the desk and sits down. Her seamed stockings flirt as her coat and dress fall away and she crosses and uncrosses her legs. A mighty fine pair of pins they are too. Very distracting.

'I have a problem and need some advice.'

'May I offer you a drink, fresh coffee or a fruit tea perhaps?' Why am I talking in this manner? Because she started it.

'My uncle has left me a folder of paintings and I have no idea what to do with them.'

'May I take a look?'

 She opens her large leather bag; I can see the Mulberry emblem by the handle. From it she produces a red-ribboned folder and places it on the desktop. 'Here you are. Tell me what you think?'

I open the folder carefully exposing several tissue-covered watercolours. To my surprise they're all by a well-known deceased artist. 'Do you know who these are by?' I ask.

'No idea. I collect jewellery.' As if I hadn't noticed. *How does she keep her wrist so straight?* 'I simply have no inclination to put artwork on the walls. They ruin the wall paper.'

Good grief. I've heard many reasons for not hanging a painting before but this gets first prize.

'Well Miss... I'm afraid I don't recall your name...'

'I haven't told you yet. It's Maeve Denninger and it's Mrs.'

I do love being put in my place especially in my own gallery. Smile and start again. Opening the tissue carefully I expose a painting worth in excess of twenty-five thousand pounds. Well, the last one fetched that much at auction and here there are twelve of them, all at least as good. Not my style though and certainly not what I'd sell in the gallery. 'This artist has been well published over the last sixty years and it looks like some of these are originals and they've never seen daylight.' I'm intrigued

'My uncle told me he purchased them direct from the artist and then forgot all about them. They sat collecting dust on the top of his wardrobe. He offered them to me as a present two weeks ago and sadly he dropped down dead last week of a massive heart attack.'

'Do you actually own these then?' My eyebrows are raised, waiting for the answer.

'Technically yes, but the funeral is next week and then the will has to be read.'

It's beginning to sound a bit too good to be true. My radar's spinning and lights are flashing in my head. Gut feeling, natural instincts, call it what you will. It's pushing me to believe these are stolen. Fortunately, there's an amazing website that one can use to check if works of art have been nicked.

'Let's check some prices for you.' I walk over the computer and type in the code to bring up the private site. Yes, the first is certainly stolen. There's an image of the print with the word *stolen* emblazoned in red across it and the rest of the paintings in the folder are mentioned too. Taken from the publishers no less.

I look up facing a pointed gun levelled at my nose. Take a deep breath. 'I don't believe you need to shoot me today...or any day.'

'You will do as you're told.'

'You have my undivided attention.' *Where are my staff when I need them?* I'm alone with a well-dressed, gun-wielding female thief. And a maniac to boot. I think this is where a TV commercial break would be most welcome.

I repeat 'Why would you want to shoot me?'

'Coz you're a man in a man's world and you bastards treat us female artists as secondary citizens and inferior to you bastard men."

'Okay I get it but you do hold a gun to my heard giving a distinct advantage to this situation.'

I try to smile and diffuse this dangerous situation. My insides reverberate, screaming with the thought that I'm going to die.

'Question. Do you think I should represent your art in this gallery?'

She stands up, walking around with the gun aimlessly pointed at the ceiling. She turns and spits out "How the fuck should I know? You know everything and you've refused to answer my requests.'

'Listen, I'm really sorry you feel this way but my approach is simple. Make an appointment and I see you at a mutually convenient time.'

'Fuck that! Now's the time and I want to be here in your gallery I am the best artist you will ever know.'

Seriously she's the most deranged artist that ever walked through my door. And I mean ever.

'I think we're getting off on the wrong foot here,' she says, tossing back hair.' I really am an amazing artist and I can be ever so nice and obliging.'

'Well I'd be most obliged if you stopped wielding and pointing that gun of yours.'

'Ha! Fooled you. It has the safety catch on. Watch.' She squeezes the trigger. There's an enormous bang and part of the ceiling comes down with dust everywhere. My ears are ringing and my heart is actually beating outside my body.

'What the FUCK. Isn't life fun? It's the same with sex don't you think. Fast loud and dangerous.'

'No, I don't.'

To my considerable relief the sound of the shot attracts the attentions of a passing police patrol. Two officers no less, pushing open the door. 'Is everything all right, Sir?'

'Oh, we're just having some fun, aren't we darling?'

Can't they see from my pleading expression that I'm at the mercy of a madwoman here?

'We heard a noise that sounded like gunfire coming from in here.'

'Not at all, officers. Darling, put the kettle on for these fine gentlemen, won't you?'

I'm totally not in control of my own life. *Help!!* One officer appears to have an *I don't believe you look* on his face so I mouth a warning at him. 'She has gun. Help. She's mad!'

'I didn't quite catch that, Sir.'

'Would you like tea or coffee?' I speak deliberately slowly and nod in a negating way.

'Are you all right, Sir? Something wrong with your neck?'

Maeve is holding the gun out again 'He's fine you bastard.' She aims it at the second police officer.

He says calmly to his colleague 'It was gunfire we heard. See, I told you so.' He slowly crosses to Mrs Denninger and in an act of casual bravery, pushes her with his flattened hand hard enough to knock her over. She falls against a glass bowl, sending it flying across the room. It shatters into far too many pieces to count and she drops the pistol as she goes down.

He picks up the gun with a handkerchief and sniffs the barrel. 'Freshly smoking I'd say.'

'Is it yours, Sir? A lovers' tiff. Are we being a naughty boy? Are you okay, Miss?'

'I'm fine,' she says. 'But he won't let me exhibit here and he's vile and vicious and I want him arrested officer.'

I can't believe this is happening at all.

'No' I shout back. 'She walked into my gallery and all hell's broken loose. She's mad. She has just tried to shoot me.'

Belinda appears from nowhere. About bloody time! 'I heard a noise, boss. Is everything all right?'

'Who's she? says Maeve 'I've not met her before. Is she your little bit on the side then, you bastard? How could you do this to me?' She spins round and sets off for the entrance.

'Not so fast, Miss' First officer is beginning to put his cogs into gear. I think we hear some whirling going on. 'Do you work here sir?'

'Yes, I do.'

'Do you work here ma'am?' The officer means Belinda.

'Yes!'

'Do you work here madam? He points at Maeve.'

She shouts back. 'I just want to exhibit my paintings. I'm an amazing artist and they won't show my work. Arrest them officers. NOW!'

The penny drops. Second officer grabs her arm. Fairly gently. 'Would you like to come with us my dear and we can file a complaint. Let's go together.' He walks Maeve Denninger out of the gallery and miraculously into a waiting police car, parked outside.

'It looks like she's on the loose again. Such a shame. Some people should be locked up, not medicated in my opinion.

Did I hear correctly? My ears were still ringing from the gunshot. I think I've just been presumed innocent till proven guilty.

The officer continues unfazed. 'May I take a few details? Is this your gun?'

'No officer. It's her's. I only met it for the first time today whilst it was attached to that woman. Which hospital has she escaped from?'

'They don't escape you know. It's care in the community. After all, they do have rights you know!' He turns, flips his small black notebook closed and walks out the gallery without a by your leave or even handing over the usual business card in case I remember anything else. There's only one word that springs to mind and I'm too polite to use it.

Belinda collects up a bundle of papers from the floor and presents them to me. 'What shall we do with these wishy-washy watercolours?'

'I'm not doing anything. They're in your hand and I say *well volunteered*. They're all yours! Every fucking last piece of wishy-washy paper! I need a bloody large drink! Or a holiday! You deal with them! Bloody hell! Nearly shot dead in my own gallery!'

'Oh dear! Are we having a bad day then?' says Charlie bringing forth a large rioja.' Her entry is perfectly timed, unlike being shot in the ceiling. Which isn't a tax-deductible expense.

Today is not a perfect day, whatever Mr. Lou Reed might have to sing on the subject.

STRONG GREEN

In all the years I've worked my gallery, I've only occasionally been asked to give a talk but today's one of the days. A group of business people called the CRBL gather quarterly as an excuse for a glorious piss up, consuming vast quantities of beer and wine, usually both and claim It all back on expenses. How nice! After all this time, my accountant still doesn't accept that wine is an integral tool for selling in art galleries. And it has to be good wine too - none of your three for a tenner stuff!

Anyway, I have to be booted and suited like a sheep to fit in. Well sod that! I'm sporting tweed trousers with a shocking purple stripe, a bright orange spotted shirt and no tie, and a vintage leather jacket with two badges on it, one saying *What's the use of getting sober* and the other *When you gonna get drunk again?* The latter refers to a brilliant Louis Jordan song covered by Joe Jackson on his *Jumpin' Jive* album – see I'm a mine of useless information!

Herein lies the lesson; orange and purple are complementary colours, so they harmonise. How I wear them possibly might not but who cares? Not I. I hover around the gallery somewhat nervously. For what reason I cannot fathom, Belinda pays me a compliment. 'You look really cool for a change.'

'For a change?'

My head is whirling even though I do have a good idea what to say. I've even made a few notes but you have to be careful and read the audience properly. Anyway, enough of pacing the gallery floor. Here I go.

'Have fun' Belinda waves with a mock smile, as if sending me off to the slaughter house.

My taxi arrives and we drive across town to the Cornwall Hotel. It has a smart Georgian facade with two huge columns and vast oak doors. A large doorman, dressed in morning suit and top hat, opens the taxi door and the look on his face is a priceless. He obviously recognises a well-dressed gent when he sees one.

It's showtime. I proffer no tip and walk deliberately through into the heady atmosphere of a mausoleum. The place is exceptionally quiet. It has that padded cell quality. Not that I've ever been in a padded cell. The carpet is a rich green wool, several inches deep and carries a monogram in the form of a letter C in a shield, emblazoned at ten intervals. Not that I notice petty details like that you understand!

Following a CRBL sign and an arrow takes me to the Admiral Suite, along a corridor with a collection of old nautical paintings and prints hanging on both sides. The suite is the furthest room from the reception and the door is closed. Such a friendly warm place. Reminds me of a graveyard I visited in Rome back in the eighties. I open the door to be greeted by roomful of women in business suits. Some wear smart pencil skirts but most seem to be in trouser suits. There are two butlers with mortician's faces pouring teas and coffees from silver polished pots into delicate bone china tea-cups. There's not a wine glass in sight. To be daring, they're offering a selection of apple, cranberry and orange juices as an alternative. What a refreshing change! In fact, quite novel. I think this is going to be quite interesting. Possibly.

A well-set blonde hairdo casually strolls up to me. 'You must be the gallery chap. We are looking forward to your talk. Which museum are you from again?'

'Actually, I'm not from any museum, I have my own gallery which promotes living artists.'

She looks stunned. 'Shula said you were a curator in her notes. She sends her apologies for not being here this afternoon. Are you sure you're not from a museum?'

'Quite. I left my establishment an hour ago and as far as I remember, it was still selling contemporary art.'

'Stay here a moment. I'll get Sharon. She'll know what's what.'

You know that feeling when you've entered the room for a function and after shaking a few hands the penny drops and you realize you're in the wrong place, with the wrong wedding party or even at the wrong funeral.

Sharon hastily appears, 'There seems to be a misunderstanding. We were expecting a talk on how to curate an exhibition.'

'Ah well that's more or less what I do.' I mentally rip up my notes on how to run an art gallery. 'I curate exhibitions with the aim of selling all the works. It saves storing them afterwards.'

'Really!' Sharon sounds more interested now.

'Really!' I nod. I'm not sure I'm out of the shit yet but it sounds good. 'I've curated exhibitions as far away as Edinburgh you know.'

'Follow me.'

I do as I'm told. We walk to the head table and take our seats. I'm sitting with Sharon on my left, a lady called Phyllis to my right and along from her a woman who looks just like Margaret Rutherford in a black business suit. I know that's not an easy image to conjure up but give it a go.

Lunch is served. Cauliflower soup followed by quiche and salad. I hate quiche; it's a pointless scrambled egg mush in a pastry.

Margaret Rutherford stands to go through the formalities and then hands the room over to me. Well there's only one thing for it. Sink or swim and believe me, I've learnt to swim.

'Ladies, what a privilege it is to stand here in front of the best-dressed lunch group I've ever attended in all my years in the art world.' There's a silence in the room so I continue 'Far too often one has to do breakfast meetings at some ridiculous o'clock, lunch-time previews and openings and all too often these are noisy, badly dressed events. I know I shouldn't say this, but in the art world you tend to notice these things. They're attended by people, mostly men, who bore the pants off me. I make no apology for not wearing a tie, I couldn't find one to complement this shirt.' Suddenly there's applause followed by a ripple of laughter. Bloody hell, I've nailed it!

The rest becomes easier with the talk changing direction. I throw in a few anecdotes on how to hang paintings in the right way, a few anecdotal tales of art, artists and clients; it's apparent that a little gossip goes a long way, no matter how well one is dressed.

Question time, and a very smartly fitted suit stands up to ask about my policy on female artists. I say, 'Madame, I would never take on a female artist. They're far too dangerous for the likes of mere mortal men.'

She smiles and you guessed it; 'My mother is an artist. How can I get her into your gallery?'

'Through the front door, and a drink will be on hand if she likes. We offer a fine selection of teas, coffees and wines. It's my humble opinion that wine oils the wheels of the art world.'

Then it's done. 'Would you like a drink young man? We have a policy to refrain till after the speaker has finished. Sometimes you need one then you know?'

'That's a lovely idea. Thank you.' Need one? Try three!

I'm presented with a bottle of port and thanked by Phyllis. Everyone stands to give a round of applause and a bar miraculously opens up at the rear of the room. I swear it wasn't there before. I'm saved. I've lived to tell the tale.

I walk into the gallery and Charlie is busying herself with a young chap. She turns and sniffs at me. 'You smell of perfume!'

'Good afternoon to you too. I've been in a hotel suite with a whole lot of well-dressed ladies of business.'

'I bet you have,' and she continues to woo her unsuspecting client into something rather special for his bedroom wall.

CRIMSON RED – THE FINAL CURTAIN

A letter arrives in a brown envelope with an unusual postage stamp. It's splattered in some foreign language I don't recognise. Belinda opens it in her usual debonair manner and stares at the contents awhile. 'I don't think you're going to like this one bit.' She hands the letter to me and heads for the kitchen. 'I'll get you a drink.'

> Dear Sirs.
> We act on behalf of clients who have purchased the building you occupy who intend to redevelop the block. Accordingly, we are serving notice under BLAH BLAH BLAH to vacate the premises by the 3rd November this year.
> If any problems arise from compliance with this correspondence please put them in writing to our office for due consideration.
> Yours sincerely
> Mr. Nonentity

Shit shit shit! They can't do this surely? I've been here twenty years, give or take. I don't know how I feel. Numb? Frozen maybe. Surely, they cannot do this without more notice? Surely not? Or can they? A thought crosses my knitted brow. It's a sign. I could move...I could cry...I could....I should, I would. There is only one thing to do.

I will party. The gallery will show its appreciation to all its artists and customers over the years. After all, if in doubt, there is only one thing to do and that's to party hard.

'Belinda. You can come out now'.

The door opens sheepishly to admit a red eyed assistant. Belinda's bottom lip quivers. 'Is this for real?' she mutters.

'Bloody well looks like it. I'll ring my solicitor and find out. This will cost. I can feel it in my bones and my bones' bank account won't like it one bit.'

A thought. The wine shop is going to have to close as well. So, we'll have to make this an even larger do than when we opened up. I must be mad. Although...here's an opportunity to do what I've always wanted. To paint.

Charlie arrives late in her usual, effervescent *I met a man last night self-persona*. 'I love a party. Who's the artist this time?'

Belinda begins to cry again. 'It's not an artist. It's the end. It's the death toll party. The gallery is being knocked down.'

'We can open another somewhere surely?' Charlie's voice rises a decibel or two 'No! They can't do this. I love working here. You must find somewhere else to open. Surely?' She looks me hard in the eye. 'Does this mean we can at least...'

'Don't even go there.'

'You're such a spoilsport sometimes.'

'Shall we advertise we're closing. A pre-obituary statement.' Belinda drops back into work mode.

'I don't think so. Let's Just invite some friends.' I too begin to well up inside. 'One last time eh!'

'Everyone knows you. Invite everyone.'

'Listen up my dear trusty team. Sometimes in life shit happens for a reason. You have to look at the positive and today's is in the fridge. Bring forth that large bottle of champagne. It's under the Chablis. Let's start the wake now.'

The pop of the cork may not change the atmosphere but the second glass of fizz starts to thaw the women.

'To my great team.'

Charlie gives me a large hug, squeezing too tight. She whispers in my ear. 'You really don't know what you're missing. Thank you for the fun. I'll let my little dream win.'

'Maybe in another life! Shall I come back as your gardener or your butler?'

The invite we decide to issue does not say we're closing down. We pick something more dramatic. *Le finale.*

However, today still has to be business as usual. One has to keep paying the bills.

The first old customer of the day through the doors is Mrs. Topping, with a young chap on her arm. She's wearing a long pleated, cream skirt with a matching, almost see-through, blouse. The smile on her face lights up like a heading on a Sunday paper. 'Ah champagne. What's the occasion?'

We all look at each other. Nobody's sure what to say.

'Love,' says Belinda. 'All you need is love!'

'Well, we'll drink to that, won't we Brad?'

The three of us smile knowingly at each other. *We know what you've been doing!*

'I'm looking for a little something as a thank you,' says Mrs. Topping.

'Let's see what we've got hidden in our stockroom Mrs.T. Follow me.'

She lightly trips along in my wake and whispers in my ear. 'Isn't he a dish? I feel like I've come back to life. Mind you I'm still disappointed you haven't phoned me. You should have.'

I'm almost speechless. 'My loss.' I nod. Then to business. 'May I ask how much you'd like to spend on this thank you?'

'Just a couple of grand,' she says. 'He's better value than joining the gym.' She pokes me in the ribs with her elbow.

I show her a few things, unwrapping boxes and pulling out etchings. I don't believe she really cares what she buys. She's come in to display her new workout. How sweet. Memo time; never underestimate the power of a woman on a mission. Actually, change that. Never ever underestimate the power of a woman full stop.

This should put the bloody feminists to rights.

My accountant rings telling me to put all the paperwork in order and remind me that I have to keep every bit of it for six years for tax purposes. Oh, such joy.

It doesn't take long for the news to spread. Well there's no news like bad news and it does bring people in. The masses gather for the cull. Everyone wants a bargain. I suppose it's human nature to grab what you can. I decide to abstain from drinking till closing night. Don't ask me why. It's a protest of sorts or a self-depriving punishment for all the good times. To the outside world it's business as usual but inside I feel like this is the precursor to doing what I want to do. What have I got to lose? My sanity went out the window years ago. I must stop talking to myself.

The sad thing is there are still good artists wanting appointments to see me and I hate saying no. Some don't believe I'm refusing them and are quite rude. One chap actually wrote to say spent five years building up the confidence to ask. Maybe I should reply *Come back five years ago*. No that's not fair. Time travel doesn't exist. Apart from rushing forward towards foreclosure.

It all hits home when the landlords enter with two suited gents. Their trousers are too short so they must be officials. One has a clipboard and the other a memo tape recorder. He flicks the mike on and off annoyingly.

'How long has that pipework been on show?' says official number one. Is he talking to me?

I say nothing. The landlord repeats the same question.

'Before you gave me the lease, I believe. You should know!'

Official number two clicks his mike and mutters something.

'Is there any reason for you to just walk into my shop unannounced while my business is open. This is an invasion of my rights as a tenant and I request you leave now. Make an appointment, preferably after the end of November '

Over at my desk I pick up the phone and dial the local paper. 'Hello, is that the press office?'

The landlord says, 'Can I have a word?'

'Any particular reason?'

'There might be a problem with that pipe.'

'Well now you tell me! That's your problem matey, not mine. When you've ripped the whole building down I'm sure you'll resolve it.'

'We'll have to renegotiate your exit terms based on the pipework. It's not legal.'

'I give you ten seconds to remove yourself from these premises or that pipe of yours will be shoved right up your...' I stop myself from saying the word. I'm physically shaking. 'OUT!' I shout. 'NOW!' Even louder.

The three men leave. It feels like war's been declared.

'Blimey, I wouldn't want to get on the wrong side of you' says Charlie flicking her hair back. 'At least, not in the daytime.'

'Right, that's it. The biggest damned party ever. Bring it on. Ladies to war!'

It's impossible to guess how many will attend, which means it's impossible to cater correctly, so we decide not to have food, just massive bowls of sweets, biscuits, wine gums; all things stupidly silly and childish. There'll be live music too. Where the hell will they go? Who cares? Let's stuff the place to the ceiling and go out in style.

As the day draws nearer a knot grows in my stomach. Am I doing the right thing? Why not open somewhere else? Except that I've been there, I own the t shirt - printed and designed it myself. But what will Belinda and Charlie do when we close? Memo; give them glowing references and a farewell bonus.

And on the other hand; no more paperwork, no more VAT or insurance and all the myriads of stress just to function No more 24/7 active alarm systems. Peace, yes peace. No more customers, artists pain in the derrieres, and no more breakfast meetings. I'm going to be an artist, broke or not.

It's a sunny day, and I sit with Belinda and Charlie having a coffee before the expected mayhem breaks forth. Usually a pre-brief has involved a quick snifter across the road in the wine bar, but today we're espresso fuelled. 'There's only one thing I want to say to you two; sell everything, anything that moves, you name it; deal and deal again; take no prisoners. Let's go team.' We stand up to leave.

'Paying for the coffees, sir?' The waiter hands me the bill.

'Sorry, I'm a bit preoccupied 'I put a tenner in his hand. 'Keep the change.'

There's a massive bouquet of flowers leaning outside the door. The unsigned card says *Goodbye and good luck*. I haven't the foggiest idea who it's from. Belinda scoops them up, finds a vase and displays them right in the middle of the gallery.

People start to trickle in from about midday. It's a help yourself bar, coz for once we're going to all be hands on deck selling off everything. Slowly the gallery fills and the noise levels increase. You can't hear the music now for the noise of conversations getting louder and louder. There's a violin player trying to move around serenading anyone who wants to listen. Whose stupid idea is this? I take no responsibility this time. In passing he says to me in a lilting Irish brogue. 'I can't hear a feckin' thing. I'm not sure if me fiddle's even in tune.'

'I'm not sure I know why you're even here, if that helps!' He appears a tad upset and fiddles his way into a corner.

Artists mingling with customers isn't usually a recommended combination but it's the dying moments of my gallery and I don't care. You can all do whatever you like. And that's exactly what everybody's doing. Even I get the odd pinch on the bum. Really, you just can't trust the public these days.

Belinda grabs my arm and shouts in my ear, 'How much do you want for the desk?'

'What do you reckon? A ton!'

She laughs out loud 'That's exactly what I'm thinking.'

Lots of everything is selling. 'Will you throw in that vase if I buy these paintings'. *With pleasure madam, please pay over there*.

The music is blaring; people are actually dancing. If it stands still long enough it will sell. Charlie's on top form, Belinda's the cavalry and all the sweets are being devoured. Strangely we haven't run out of booze yet.

My trusty chair is sold. The countless decisions made in it, good riddance. *Yes, I'm sure it will look lovely in your office, thank you.*

You'd like a piece of the gallery as a memento? 'Do you like pipework? I have a rather unusual bit for sale if you like. Oh, never mind. How about a glass cabinet with some superb glass to display?'

Belinda pulls my arm. 'Someone wants to buy the plan chest. Come into the stock room now.' I follow her, marching quickly. She slams the door, throws her arms around me and kisses me on the lips. 'You're wonderful. It's been the best job ever.'

I hold her close. 'Thank you. Do you want the plan chest? If so it's yours.'

'No, I've already sold it. I just had this urge to kiss you.' And she returns to the fray.

I'm humbled, with a genuine feeling of having achieved something. Before I owned my own gallery I'd never had a business of my own before and my assistant chief tells me it's been the best job ever. The kiss is the best bonus I could ever deserve.

Back in the main room, the world is going into fast forward and everything and everyone is a bit of a blur. My mind goes back to the opening, my naivety in opening the gallery *How the hell did I get myself into this*? I suddenly feel very sad. I should feel proud. I hear the *Harry Lime* theme playing in the back of my mind; the zither striking my heartstrings. I shout out for everyone to be quiet and wait a few seconds. 'Friends, clients and artists, lend me your ears.'

I feel a tear rolling down my cheek. Not now! Don't cry. Come on, hold it together. 'This gallery wouldn't have been anything without you all. The symbiotic relationship between artists, customers and staff has, I always like to say, put colour into all our lives and I want to thank you all, especially my dream team who've put up with my little idiosyncrasies over the years. Looks like everything is selling and remember, everything has to go. Except me.'

'How much' shouts somebody in the crowd. There are massive cheers and the room is full of laughter. My back is being slapped as if I've just won a heavy-weight-boxing match. We party into the evening and beyond. The last guest, who I'm sure wasn't invited, leaves at three minutes to two in the morning. The gallery is no more.

'Well ladies, that's how you throw a closing down party.'

'Where shall we go now? 'Charlie asks

'Is she serious? says Belinda. 'I'm cream crackered'

'Home I believe is a good idea,' I say

'Can we come with? How about one last glass of something. Just the three of us?'

'Come on Belinda, the night is young and you're supposed to be young too. Trust your aunt!'

'Can't think of a reason why not.'

'Taxi!'

Next morning I'm standing outside the shop looking through the plate glass window, staring at my past. It's all gone Everything's been collected and the place is empty. As vacant as the week before we opened, all those years ago. What will never go are the memories and friends and all the mayhem stored in my head. Still, I've given the keys back to the landlord without wishing him well. How remiss of me. And that's that.

The twenty years seem to have flown by in a moment. I feel emotional again before the sense of freedom reasserts itself, a release you could say despite my brain screaming out in total panic, *What the hell am I going to do now?*

The answer's on the road in front of me. A woman walks right up to me. She's wearing a sloppy, cream-coloured jumper, along with a great pair of legs, revealed by sprayed on drainpipe jeans capped off by a pair of very expensive, crimson patent-leather, stiletto, ankle boots. Not that I notice such details.

'Hello, stranger' she says in a familiar gravelly voice, I recognise immediately. It's Miss Top Hat and Tails.

How odd. The last time we met was when I'd hired her for the opening night of the gallery

'Hello. How are you? Where have you been? I've not seen you in years? What are you doing in this neck of the woods?'

'Hang on Whoa! So many questions. Not a lot. Been working away, you know the sort of thing. I've been thinking of looking in to see you for ages so I thought I'd see what you're up to. Have a spot of lunch or maybe something else. What's happened here? What you done with the gallery?'

'The gallery's closed forever. Had to get out. The landlord's redeveloping the block and I'm about to embark on the next phase of my life.'

'Oh yeah. What's that going to be then; a teacher, or let me guess, an art consultant. You know, something boring?'

'Not in the slightest. I'm going to do what I've always wanted to do since I was a teenager.' I take a gulp as if was about to confess that I've lost my virginity. 'I'm going to be an artist myself.'

'No kidding! Really. You! That's so funny. Fancy a muse?'

'I've never been more serious. I'm going to look after one artist, me, from now on. So, what are you doing the rest of your life?' My heart stops for a moment, thinking what I've just said.

'I fancy an adventure. Life should never be normal' she says.

'You might have to stick around forever though. That's the deal'

'Don't you mean committed?'

'I rest my case,' and offer her my arm. She puts hers through mine and we walk along the pavement to nowhere in particular. *Lunch with a muse. Now there's a start.*

She squeezes and looks up at me. 'Nice biceps. I like a man with good muscles. Oh yes, and a cute bum.'

Life is good.

PART THREE

NOW YOU'RE THE ARTIST...DEAL WITH IT

PROLOGUE

Do you know me? I'm an artist. I've kept this notion hidden deep inside me for decades. I owned a gallery once upon a time, which at least meant I was right beside the art for many years.

I still have a good eye and the opinion that I might be right.

I've been tested and tried through life's little journey and have come to the conclusion that the answer's not as simple as pouring a large drink. The very existence of life is sex and sex is a powerful motivator. If something is sexy, curvy and colourful then I'm likely to be attracted to it.

If a torso has a beautifully smooth back...surely then life is smooth and beautiful. I'm somewhat naive but hopefully that's a redeeming quality. I am possibly available to the opposite sex but you know what. That's none of your business

Now you're the artist. Deal with it

I've closed my existence as a gallery owner and opened my life as an artist. A painter. No, I don't mean a decorator, using large brushes with few colours.

Now, I need to find a place to hold an exhibition, somewhere where I'm not known. I mean will people accept me as the artist, or will the past catch up on me and no one ends up buying my work; *he's that gallery chap, shouldn't he be selling the work and not pretending to be the artist.*

Why not! Why not me? All of my life I've been selling things; I've sold everybody else's work. So, how difficult is it to sell yourself? Let me tell you; it's almost impossible. Almost, but not quite. So, come join me on my next outing. I need you to as it's a lot less busy now. Or is it?

ACT 1 SCENE 1

Do you like happy ever after stories? Me too. However, this is not one of them. Well at least, not the first part.

It all started when Miss Top-Hat-and-Tails turned up at the gallery doors literarily just as I'd been forced to close up. There was a connection one might say...after not seeing her for many years. We went off for a drink and as in all good films, it just happened rather quickly.

She landed at my place and dug in for a while.

Why did I let her into my life? I mean surely after a twenty-year gap, I should have realized that something was not right; might never be right.

But my head was closed to reason.

It didn't take me long too find out that she was a touch mad. Actually, she was barking. Apparently, she left her husband and a shed-load of bills, and she keeps on reminding me that her dog is being held captive, a prisoner against its will and somehow, now, it's all my fault.

Are all women like this? I know I worked with some pretty unusual members of the species but I have to say Miss Top-Hat-and-Tails takes first prize. She's the messiest woman on the planet. She's a walking hurricane, twister and tropical storm rolled into one. In fact, she's bloody mad Her idea of life is sex and sleeping. That's it. It's nowhere near how I imagined it would be. Happy ending time. Not so sure. Think it's time for an attitudinal shift. Fancy waiting all that time! Don't get me wrong; she was fun for a while - well maybe a week or two - but now it's like having a demented pack hound around. Today I'll take the initiative and do something about it. I feel a real sense of relief with my decision when suddenly the door slams open, hitting the wall with such force it carves a hole in the wall.

'I've had enough of you and your *want to be the artist* bullshit. All you do is go off and paint. Haven't you anything better to do. My friends think you're a lazy bastard.'

'Hello to you too.' I keep my distance. 'Had a bad day at the office?'

'Why can't you be normal?'

Despite wanting to say something, to respond with wit and intelligence, I stand and bow. 'Define normal'

'How do I know where you are or who you're with. For all I know you might be out shagging every day!'

'I should be so lucky'

She picks up an aspidistra plant and hurls it, pot and all, at me, luckily missing but it explodes all over the carpet. Plant and pot are no more.

'Ikea pots - not that durable then. Never liked it anyway '

'Screw you!'

With that, she turns and frog -marches up the stairs slamming the bedroom door. I hear a herd of disco-dancing elephants resonating through the ceiling. Doors are slammed, and then something else is smashed. I wonder what that could have been? Finally, after ten minutes the tornado emerges with two cases stuffed to the gills.

'I'm out of here forever. FOREVER!'

The doorbell rings, perfect timing coincidently. I open up and there, standing head and shoulders shorter than me, is a chap in his mid-fifties, sporting a tweed jacket, yellow-spotted cravat and pink cords His shoes are scuffed.

'She's all yours matey. I assume that's who you've come for.' I hold the door open, trying to refrain from looking relieved and look remorseful.

Alas it doesn't work. I'm unable to stop my face smiling in anticipation.

'Have you forgotten anything?'

She ignores me and then she's gone.

Peace. What a wonderful word. Oh yes and calm. Yes calm

The house is calm.

I close the door and walk into the lounge to pour myself a relaxing Irish whiskey into my favourite cut-glass tumbler. I sit in awe of what's just happened. How the hell did I put up with her this long? There certainly was something about her, but from now on, Miss Top-Hat-and-Tails will be identified as Miss Mad Hatter - with horns. How come she never turned up in all my years of having the gallery? If she had I'd never have ended up with her as a house-guest. Madness lurks everywhere. What an eye opener.

ACT 1 SCENE 2

I walk into the only shop in town selling stationery and art products.

'Can I help you?'

'I think I'm beyond help,' I reply looking at a rather pretty young assistant

'Oh, I know you. My mom came into you your gallery once and you got her drunk

'Really. What's her name'?

'Isabelle, she was a sculptor but you didn't like her work enough.'

'Was I that blunt; surely not?'

'To be honest she fancied you then, but you showed no interest in her.' Her look is one of distain.

'Well, I'm very sorry to have disappointed her. Please tell her I'm sorry and add that she has a very pretty daughter '

'You old men are so schmoozey. She died a couple of years ago. She stopped for a few seconds 'Are you buying supplies for one of your artists then?'

'Actually, it's for me. The gallery has closed. I'm the artist. I'm now on the other side of the counter.'

'Really! You takin' the piss or something? What do you know about painting? Suppose this is all about a discount eh. I'm not authorised to give you any and the manager's away.'

I smile politely and glance down at her chest. That's where her name badge is pinned. 'I'm truly sorry for your loss, Lucy. You're welcome to take it out on me. I've broad shoulders but I really would like to buy some watercolours, brushes and paper today, if you don't mind.'

'I'm sorry, it just sometimes all gets too much and I want to explode. It's not fair; she was only fifty-one.'

'Tell me more about your mom, then.'

This seems to have a cathartic effect and slowly she calms down, the angst leaving her knitted brows.

'Shall we drink something? I always had a well-stocked wine supply and good fresh coffee and tea in the gallery. It was amazing how many people needed to sit and unburden themselves after a drink or two.'

'Would you like a coffee. It's a bit sludgy' Lucy asks.

'Looks like you could do with a G&T more like. Nothing untoward mind. Perhaps after work; a quick snifter.'

'I don't mind at all. Come back at five fifteen.'

'Alright. I will.'

I leave the shop without purchasing a thing, surely that's not right and walk aimlessly through milling shoppers and beggars. Why are they always wearing new trainers?

Several hours later, a quick pit stop and shopping for a folding seat, I wander back to the art shop.

Lucy has done her hair and put lipstick on.

'Hi' she says as I walk up to the counter.

'Drink o' clock I believe.'

I've put a small selection of tubes of paint and three good brushes aside for you. It's only £48 with discount. Oh yes, and a watercolour paper block. It's got a lovely texture.'

She smiles as I hand her my debit card.

'Where shall we go then?'

'The Whistle,' she suggests. 'It's not far. Bet you've never been in it before?'

'Haven't even heard of it.'

We walk out the shop and turn down the road. She walks at a hell of a lick.

'What's the rush?' I up my pace and we reach the Whistle in record time. We arrive before a badly painted, matt-black door, which is chipped and scratched all over. It miraculously opens without being touched.

A chap with the largest of holes in his ear – it's akin to that of an Andean tribesman from somewhere up the Limpopo - and with a major tattoo overdose, greets us. 'Oh gawd! What have you brought in this time? He's ancient!'

'I've framed better artwork,' I throw back.

'Oh, hark at him. It talks as well.'

'Leave it out, Mary,' Lucy snipes and leads the way through the almost pitch-black corridor. We walk into a blue-lit lounge with lots of mirrors and stands with quite erotic sculptures. Jazzy, bluesy music plays in the background.

'What a cool place, I love the sculptures.'

'They're my mom's.'

'Really. She never showed me anything like these.'

'She was too scared. Thought you'd be able to move her other stuff.'

'What a shame. These are really powerful.'

A woman, all dressed in black and with matching piercings everywhere on show, slinks up to Lucy and plants a smacker on her lips.

'This is Beth. She's my partner,' she says, squeezing her hand.

'Hi Beth. Care to join us for a drink?'

'I'll have a pint later. Got to keep an eye on the staff.'

'She's the manager here,' Lucy announces proudly.

'Do you think I could come again with my notepad and do some sketching in here. The reflections are great. It's still life and life drawing rolled into one.'

'As long as you promise to behave,' Lucy smiles and nudges me in the ribs.

'This place has been right under my eyes all this time and you're right; I never knew it was here.'

ACT 1 SCENE 3

Lucy clears it for me to revisit the Whistle and sketch anytime I like so long as I try to do it inconspicuously.

This time the bouncer lets me in with a wink.

Within a few minutes of setting up, a wiry, overly-dyed, blonde-haired chap sits down right beside me. 'Watcha doing sweetie?'

'Sketching.'

'Really! Don't you ever need real models?'

'These don't argue back and can sit for longer. Plus, they never need feeding or paying.'

'I'll pose for you. I love stripping off. Where do you live?'

'I'm not local. It's okay. I prefer these stiff ones.'

'Well, we all do that love!'

I start drawing again, trying to ignore the chat up. The mirrors add an extra ambiance and dimension to the figures. I get lost in the moment, which, as it so happens, lasts over two hours.

'God you're so boring!' peroxide-blonde boy states. 'All you've done is sit there all day, scribbling away,'

I grin at him. *Funny little shit.* I think not.

My freethinking mind is crying out to tell him to piss off but my conscience says *don't think that's a good idea.* I smile without saying a word, lay down the sketchbook and put everything else in my bag of tricks.

'Finished. Time for a drink.'

'Yes please. Large vodka, no ice.'

He doesn't give in, does he?

'I don't do men. Ever! Get it?'

'Lucy said you were available. How disappointing.' He walks off like a cat having been offered a bowl of the cheapest cat food.

'Cider, please.'

The barman nods. 'Wouldn't worry about Troy. He tries it on with everyone and anything. Shall I add a vodka to your tab to keep him happy?'

'Only if it has something in it to silence him with. A small one. then.' Reluctantly giving in.

The place is filling up and it's only three fifteen in the afternoon. *Don't these folk work?*

'You staying for the afternoon, tea-dance disco. All drinks half price,' the barman asks.

'Thanks, but no. Hopefully the sun is still out.' I down my cider and turn to leave only to have Beth tap me on the shoulder.

'Keep your eyes off, Lucy. Know what I mean!'

'Seeing as she tried to pimp me off to one of your regulars, I think you'll find you're quite safe.'

'He'd shag a dog if it was tied to a lamppost.'

'Seriously, you've nothing to fear. Would you like to see what I've been doing?'

'If you insist.' Beth doesn't look interested in the slightest.

I pull out the sketchbook and open it to show her the day's drawings.

'Holy shit. They're awesome! I thought you were after a bit of skirt. You really can draw.'

'Thank you.'

'You're forgiven. Drink?'

'I was leaving, but go on then. Cider, please'

'Two ciders, Chas.'

She turns to me and you can see the cogs whirring in her mind.

'We could do an arty class here. Fancy giving it a go? I'll pay you?'

'Music to my ears. Anytime to suit. I do have quite a free diary these days.'

'Towards the end of next month, then. I'll come back to you.'

'Let's drink to that.'

I clink glasses with her.

ACT 1 SCENE 4

A couple of weeks pass by. My mobile rings, I let it ring out. It rings again

'Hello! It's me Lucy. I need your help.'

'You setting me up for another blind date?'

'Beth's dumped me for another woman.

Please I really must see you? Not The Whistle though. Please come to the shop tomorrow at closing time. Don't say no. '

'Ok I'll see you tomorrow.'

'Unless you're not doing anything later. I'm not trying to sound pushy. Am I?'

'Are you ok?'

'Not really.' Her voice is wavering.

'I'll meet you in an hour outside the shop then. '

'Thank you. Thank you!'

My house is still calm but it would appear that on the other side of the door, the world for some, is in *a state of chassis* as Sean O'Casey wrote I believe in *Juno and the Paycock*.

I stroll up the stairs and view my bedroom. It is still in carnage with the wardrobe door hanging on one hinge. The bed linen is still strewn over the floor and my clothes are flung all over the place.

I ought to tidy it up. But you know what, I don't care. It will wait till I return. I pick a jacket off the floor and put the hanger back in the wardrobe.

I decide to walk into town. It's not too far and I try to make sense of something or other. Needless to say, I arrive outside the shop early and Lucy runs out and hugs me very hard. Then she starts to sob into my chest uncontrollably.

'Thank you. Thank you Thank you. I knew I could trust you.'

'You don't. Joke. But you can. Come on. Tell me everything. I've a great pair of ears and very broad shoulders.'

She starts by explaining it's her first girlfriend and she was never really sure if it wasn't just a dangerous lesson or love for another woman. She'd had boyfriends but they were so immature by comparison.

Beth had treated her like a princess but it very quickly turned to domination in everything. What she wore, what she ate? Who she should see? She was feeling imprisoned she thought she needed a mother figure to replace her mom Now she was scared. 'A mad blonde woman approached me wanting to know what was going on between you and me. She said I must be sleeping with you and told me she would have spells put on me that would kill me. Then Beth saw me talking to her and things got messy. They were shoving each other round and pulling hair n stuff it was a catfight. It was awful. I've done nothing. Who was she? Why me? Now I've nowhere to live and I'm scared.'

She goes on to describing the mad hatter to a T.

'I'm afraid I do know who you are talking about That's my very recent ex as from not so long ago. The very one. And yes. She is bloody mad. F'ing crazy.'

Having worked with woman for nearly twenty years I have learnt never to offer a male thinking constructive answer. 'What would you like to do?'

'I dunno! What do you think?'

I am very nearly cornered. 'What are your options?'

'My dad's in Spain, haven't spoken to him in years and my sister's in New Zealand.'

'Maybe consider smaller steps. Have you no friends around that you can bunk up with for a short while?'

'Beth took care of all of them.'

Well without wishing to sound like a dirty old man, I could offer my guest room for a week to get yourself sorted.'

'I don't want to put you out but that would be fantastic. Thank you. I'm always thanking you.'

'Yeh yeh. Can you cook and are you tidy? Coz if you're not tidy, I reduce your stay to 48 hours. Got it.'

We laugh and a very relieved young lass is saved for another day.

'Were you married ever?'

Why? Does it matter?'

'You're sort of kind and nice.'

'I've had my fair share of loonies.' I grimace with the thoughts. 'I like calm. It's the new me and I'm trying to keep it that way.'

'I'll find someone to suit you.'

'That will also reduce your stay to 48 hours. You've been warned.'

Her boss steps out the shop and lets Lucy leave early.

'See you tomorrow on the ball!' Then she turns to me 'look after her, she's had a very traumatic day.'

'Right ho boss. Come on Lucy, me thinks you need a drink.'

We walk down the road aiming for nowhere in particular and finding it after ten minutes 'Here's perfect. I like the music, the beer and it's never loud or outrageous.'

We walk in to one of my gallery days watering holes.

'Where you been hiding?' The barman pours me a beer without asking follows with 'and you miss?'

'Vodka, Red Bull, thanks.'

'Gallery had to close; didn't you hear?'

'Oh yes, sort of, I tend to remember the important bits like how's the beer?'

'I take a large gulp 'Perfect.'

He leans over to me 'Ain't she a bit young for you?'

'I'm not with him you creep,' Lucy pipes up. She attempts to throw the contents of her drink over the barman but I catch her arm in time.

'Whoah! Calm down lass. That's a large vodka.'

'He's an insulting prick.'.

'Indeed he is. Big feet big mouth and no manners. Right George?'

'Fuckin A!' Sorry little un, was only teasing. If I don't pick on you then I don't like you right. It's me trademark. Tetchy bint. Next drink's on me; alright?'

'Another large Vodka Red Bull then, prat.' Lucy glugs and finishes her drink in one go slamming the glass down hard on the bar.

194

Far too many rounds later we take a taxi back to mine. 'Beware the remains of an earthquake.' I open the door and to my surprise find the TV missing and my favourite chair gone as well. The kitchen cupboards are open and empty. There are broken glasses strewn over the floor. My crystal glass has been shattered into a thousand tiny bits, abandoned in the sink. How kind.

'Ouch'.

'Are you sure it's safe here?'

'Safe as any war zone!

Your room is upstairs to the left of the bannisters. Shall I mount an armed guard for you?'

'I thought you said you want a calm life?'

'Trust me. I do, it's a mere hiccup in the journey of life.'

'Maybe they are in cahoots. God poor you fancy having a deranged lesbian and a mad psycho coming for you.'

'Are there any differences?'

I am certain this has been the work of the mad hatter wreaking havoc. I bolt the front door and bid Lucy good night.

The mess and the missing will have to wait.

Next morning, I walk down to find a very tidy kitchen and a note on table.

Thanks for sanctuary. Gone to work See you later if you don't mind letting me in. No key. L x

ACT 2 SCENE 1

The sun is shining. The bedroom will wait. I excavate some clothes, grab my bag and head out, hopefully trying to avoid the human race for a change. First things first; get a key cut for my visitor and then off to paint.

There is a lovely spot on the canal, which is slightly sheltered. You might think you were in the country. It's blissfully quiet. No urban noise. There's a heron standing, most statuesque, by the bank. Perfectly still, he stands observing his surroundings. He's an amazing creature, a throw-back from a past age.

I follow his example, watching the gentle ripples and shadows in search of the best idea to blossom.

The bird will find its fish and I shall find my place. Sorry!

Three hours later we're both successful; well, the bird caught a perch after five minutes and I happened to take a while longer but I'm satisfied and haven't spoken to a soul.

I arrive home around five fifteen relaxed, physically and artistically. At precisely 5.30 pm the doorbell rings and I open the front door to find Lucy beaming on the doorstep.

'Someone's looking happy. Welcome to chilled mansions!'

'I've not looked forward to leaving work in ages. And it's thanks to you. Are you going to show me what you've done today then?'

I pull out my pad and open it to the current watercolour.

'Voila.'

'Good grief. You can actually paint. I love your style.' There's a note of near disbelief in Lucy's voice.

'Thanks. I'll keep on going then. Shall I?'

'No, no; I mean I didn't expect you to be any good. I thought you just sold the art!'

'Well you're not the first to say that.'

'Changing topics quickly; would you like a hand to clear up your mess upstairs?'

'I think I'll manage. Tomorrow's another day.'

'Ah, come on. Two pairs of hands and all that. It'll take minutes then and save you more time. Besides I'm sure you don't really want to sleep in that mess. I couldn't.'

'Yes, miss. Um, by the way, who owns this establishment?'

And forty minutes later my room is like a freshly-made hotel suite.

'Blimey. Never looked so tidy since I moved in.'

'My pleasure, it's the least I can do. If you don't mind me saying though I couldn't help notice that there's some clothes you should get rid of or at least take to a charity shop.'

'Ouch. Arrow in my heart. I didn't add dress guru to lodger status.'

Lucy smiles and raises an eyebrow. 'Well you got to look the part too you know. If the old you has had its day, then the clothes go too. We could go shopping next week.'

Suddenly I feel my generosity is being challenged and a young, wee snapper is digging in.

'No. We will not go shopping next week.'

Lucy falters and freezes.

Until I add, 'We can go tomorrow. Thursday late-night opening.'

She walks over and throws her arms tightly around me 'You're brilliant.'

ACT 2 SCENE 2

I look out of my bedroom window. The sun is low in the sky with the light casting super long shadows.

She has put the kettle on because I hear the whistle screaming out, breaking into my more creative thoughts.

'Tea or coffee? Where's the cups?' She shouts up the stairs.

'Middle cupboard,' I reply. 'Strong, black.'

She clinks and rattles the entire house, and then presents herself in my best white shirt with the cuffs rolled up half-way to her elbows. The shirt has one button done up across her stomach, leaving her breasts exposed magnificently to the shaft of sunlight glaring through the window.

'Don't move,' I command grabbing my pad and conte crayon from the floor. Always be prepared. Always sketch every day and always have something or someone to draw. Unfortunately, a someone is not always an option.

She doesn't listen to me and places the cups down on the bedside table by shifting the contents off with a swift flick of her foot. She's rather supple and bounces onto the bed; 'Draw me or have me now. Your choice?'

Well when faced with such a demand, I believe it's always safer to follow instructions and do whatever the woman wants. It's twenty minutes before I can pick up my pad and sketch her lying prostrate on the bed, her long hair lying pleasantly bedraggled over the pillow.

She is fast asleep.

My place has a sense of quiet again.

ACT 2 SCENE 3

I'm attending an art class around the corner from where I live, so it'll be a gentle walk and if there's wine on offer then a gentle swagger back.

It's being organised by Beryl. She is using her classes to supplement the upkeep of her massive four-storey house. Her husband, a judge, walked out on her about six months ago, leaving a rather fit-looking woman to replace her with his twenty-three years younger, even fitter new model, previously his personal assistant. An apt title that, I'm sure.

Beryl is a woman who oozes sensuality without trying. Her clothes are always immaculate and I've never seen her without smart high heels to complement her long legs.

'Darling!' Worry not. She calls everybody this. Men, women, even the milkman. 'So good of you to come along,' and without taking a breath, '...that will be eight pounds please.'

The room being used as the studio is freezing. There's no heating on and goose bumps are gathering everywhere; not just on me. The room has seven ladies standing around a large table chatting away, sipping elderflower presse. It's like a Chanel verses Jaeger competition. Every one of them more suitably dressed for a lunch date than for an art class. I feel I should have worn a cravat but I don't possess one, so jeans and a tee-shirt have to do.

Beryl introduces me to each of the woman in turn; 'He used to run a gallery in town and now he's come out as an artist.'

I certainly don't like that expression. The connotations could be readily misconstrued. Maybe I should have worn a more blatantly heterosexual tee-shirt.

'One always feels safe with your type,' Sybil says, reassuring me with a pat on the arm. See, told you so.'

Seeing as I'm the only man in the room and my arty hen party now assume I'm gay, it's apparently safe to proceed with the class. What did they all think I would do?

Beryl puts on an old cassette player and Ravel's Bolero starts to play. 'We shall paint to music. Feel free to express whatever comes to mind.'

Really. Whatever comes to mind! Surely not!

I mean this is the music for Torvill And Dean's stunning climactic ice dance routine. And the climax is exactly that. An orgasm to music.

Let's go for it. Lots of paint splashing everywhere with bold bright colours swirling off the paper. None of your thirty second quickie, I'll have you know.

One of the other artist's blushes, looking at my new musical masterpiece. 'It's very expressive. I painted an orange.'

'Nice,' I reply.

'Thank you.'

An orange! Poor husband!

I'm quite enjoying this sense of freedom although I prefer to be outdoors in good weather, taking in the elements along with the atmosphere *en plein air* as the saying goes, akin to eating al fresco.

Everything is good outside!

Shirley decides to sit beside me. 'I've a great idea. Why can't we do a life drawing exercise as part two of this class? You'd make a great model.'

Her voice is just loud enough for everyone to hear.

Beryl claps her hands. 'We shall refund your class fee. You don't mind surely.'

Seeing as the place is freezing, I don't believe anything might appear. I mean I'm going to be naked with eight well-dressed women. Dream on. Make that seven. The one who painted an orange might take all night!

Beryl hands me an old-fashioned maroon smokers' jacket. 'You're such a sport. Won't this be fun? You can change through that door. We won't look.' She giggles like a school girl.

I walk through the door. It's even colder in this cupboard-sized locker room. I can hear all the ladies laughing now. Surely, they've seen a naked man before. Maybe they can't remember when it was.

Anyway...

Here goes.

I stroll into their lair...sorry, studio. And sit in the middle of the group on a cold metal stool. Well that should completely stop anything untoward happening.

'Here goes,' I say again to myself. I must be bonkers.

Although I'm not in bad shape to be frank. A bit of toning up here and there and maybe a full wax. Ouch not for me. That's going too far.

I drop the jacket to the floor and pose.

Mabel nods her head whilst sharpening a crayon and lets the bits fall to the floor. 'I hope you'll stand for us later?'

'I sincerely hope not,' I smile.

A titter reverberates around the room.

I remain perfectly still and my body is stiff from the cold. Never mind blue in the face, I'm blue from head to toe and everywhere in between.

Furthermore, I've never heard a room full of women so quiet before.

Hypothermia, an interesting topic, but not something I was considering studying in depth. Now I feel I'm gaining a masters in the subject. Suddenly and without warning my teeth chatter and an involuntary shake envelops me.

'Oh, hang on love; I've nearly finished,' says one of the women.

'I'm totally finished,' I chatter. 'I'm frozen.'

'Oh dear,' says Beryl. I'll put the heater on.'

She could have done that in the first place! She leaves to return with a vintage two-bar, electric fire circa vintage. You can see the red and black wires hanging loose from the plug!

'Is that thing safe?' I enquire.

'Don't worry. It's never let us down since we moved here in 1964. It cost a small fortune, this heater. Top of the range as well.'

She plugs it in and it splutters to life, humming as the two electric coiled elements are called into action.

It does have the desired effect. Heat. Dry, electric, dusty smelling, singe-tasting heat. But she is right. It works.

So, I do as I'm told and this time, in glorious vintage heat surround, stand with my right hand on the stool and my left leg crossed over my right. A relaxed violin stance without the fiddle. Watch it now!

Surprise, surprise. I'm invited back to the class another time. I get dressed and check what the budding artists have painted! Well, one thing is for sure, I've never seen myself look like this collection on paper before. Even my mirror is more complimentary. And that's saying something.

'I've tried to capture your inner strength.'

I nod and move on.

'You're very good you know. Lovely arms.'

'Thank you. I've heard that before.' I smile. What did happen to Miss Top-Hat-'n'-Tails? Oh yes? She left me.

'Let's all have a drink to celebrate.'

Beryl is beside herself and beaming; 'You must let us sketch you again. I won't charge you!'

I don't think I'll make a living being a life model; at least not as Beryl's rates. 'Thank you. Maybe when summer arrives.'

'Will you open the bottle please. It's a Chardonnay, Australian.'

I give her my loveliest smile. I break the seal and unscrew the lid. Aldi, four pound ninety-nine. You've got to be joking!

I pour the harsh yellow liquid into plastic cups.

Some habits I just cannot give up. Drinking cheap wine is a no go. Ever!

'You're not joining us for one?' Beryl takes the bottle and fills her beaker to the top.

'I don't drink white wine.'

'Would you like a drop of whiskey? I think there's some in the lounge downstairs on the right of the hallway. Pop down and have a rummage.'

'Maybe next time,' I reply.

So, it won't be a stagger home.

'Ladies, there's only one slight disadvantage to this life class. I was unable to draw. Who's volunteering next time?'

There is total silence in the room.

'Young man, I would never show myself undressed. I don't believe my husband's seen me unclothed since our wedding night.'

Shirley moves in right beside me. 'I'll undress for you if you fancy coming around to mine sometime. Not here though.'

Art can be a very precarious pastime and it's all in the name of research. Sometimes you have to make sacrifices.

ACT 2 SCENE 4

Lucy is looking a little subdued.

'Can I get you a drink; a whiskey?'

'What's up, me dear. You sound like you have the problems of the world on your shoulders, spill 'em.'

'Well...'

She is picking her words deliberately and slowly.

'I've been having some serious thinking...'

'Yes. And?'

'It's just that I've really enjoyed your company and all, and I don't know how to put this kindly.'

'Spill it; I'm not in the mood to play guessing games.'

'I'm trying to. Wait a tick.'

'I'm waiting!'

'I think it's time to move out.'

'Oh, is that it. Phew, I thought it was something serious.'

'It is; to me. I don't want to fall for you. I mean you'll be a hundred when I won't even be seventy. I don't fancy pushing you around then in your wheelchair, or worse.'

'Well, that settles it then. I'm not into seventy-year olds either. When you leaving?'

'I'm going to stay with my Dad in Spain. I decided to get in touch with him and he asked me to visit. So, I've bought a plane ticket. I've not flown before in me life.'

'Would you like a lift to the airport, to make sure you get on it. When are you going?'

'Next Tuesday. I handed my notice in at work today.'

'I'm sure they'll miss you Lucy. As long as you're doing what's good for you then I'm delighted. Although I dare say I might miss you a bit.'

She throws a cushion at me. 'It's from East Midlands Airport. Is that okay?'

'Sure thing, as long as it's not some horrendous early start.'

There's a silence and a little girl looks at me with mock innocence. She tilts her head ever so slightly and shrugs her shoulders. 'Six in the morning. Okay?'

'Glorious. Best time to catch the light. Are you sure you want to go?'

'I've nothing to lose and besides I think I need an adventure. I want to find out more about me.'

'Good for you.'

Lucy potters around the lounge, pours two whiskeys and hands me one. 'Thank you for everything; for being there and saving me. I've something special for you for later on.'

'I love surprises.'

'I'm certain you'll like this one.'

She clinks glasses, then humming something or other, I've no idea what, and leaves the room.

ACT 3 SCENE 1

I decide to take a long break in the south west of England.

Whilst sitting in a pub, I spot an advert in the local paper about an art group that loves adventures outdoors and painting en plein air. Obviously, it is totally dependent on the weather but I ring them up and arrange to join them.

Luckily, it's a sunny day. And I mean a glorious blue sky with a few wisps of cloud floating by. We are to meet in a car park at Ivybridge, off the main road, the A38.

The trip is to take in the moors and some of the tors. Haytor is the first port of call. These craggy, split rocks are from a long-ago deceased volcano. They are the remnants of the lava plugs.

The views overlooking the moors and the surrounding landscapes are spectacular by any standard. We arrive at the location and disperse around the locale. After a few minutes of walking and spying, I find a spot I like, unravel my chequered picnic blanket and squeeze different tubes of paint onto my travelling palate. I need only a few moments of observation before I apply the wash and nestle in to paint my new masterpiece.

One of the women in the group is sitting on a fold up chair about a hundred yards from me sketching away. I can't help noticing she's wearing a long skirt with ankle boots and a green crocheted top.

Meanwhile I'm really trying to focus and am getting into this particular painting. It's all flowing nicely. The rocks have a sparkle and sheen to them and the atmosphere is intoxicating. Off in the distance I can hear sheep bleating and crows squawking. I find myself humming and whistling, quietly lost in the moment.

The woman, the one I couldn't help but notice, stands, slowly, dusts her skirt down and leaves her sketchbook on the grass. She walks carefully and elegantly over to me and, without saying a word, lies down on my blanket. Then she pulls back her split skirt, exposing her black stockings.

I don't know who she is apart from the fact that she was on the coach and therefore must be one of the group.

'What do you think of these?' she asks.

'Not bad,' I reply, callously returning to my subject. You do have to concentrate when working in watercolours. Make every stroke count.

She hoists her skirt higher and arches one leg. 'This is one of my favourite poses in my life drawing classes. It makes a good subject to paint,' she says.

That's all very well but I haven't finished my landscape and that takes precedence.

She looks up at me in an appealing manner. 'I'm horny.'

'I'm not,' I reply, continuing to paint. For heaven's sake, I don't even know your name.

She removes her minuscule thong and lies in full glory in public on the top of the hill.

'I really need sex now! Surely, you're not going to refuse me. Look!' She parts her legs and arches her back.

Now when you're offered something on a plate, let's be honest and say it might sound a good idea, but the idea of having a bit of rumpy-pumpy in public with someone I don't know, does not. Call me old fashioned; I do have boundaries.

She starts rubbing herself and moaning louder by the second.

'Anyone would think you're having a good time,' I say trying to lighten up the situation and still continue painting.

Suddenly she screams out, 'I want to do it now!'

Around us I can see lots of people including the group, looking in our direction. You'd have to be stone deaf not to hear her demands reverberating around the hillside.

'Okay, joke's over. Who's putting you up to this? It's not funny anymore.'

I said it in a quiet manner but she shouts back; 'You're such a self-important prick. Who do you think you are?'

Her demeanor has changed completely and alarm bells are ringing. I think she's a bit off the wall.

'Why can't a woman demand sex when she wants to have it? I suppose it's fine when a man does. You're all shits, every single one of you.'

I'm feeling more than a little nervous now and she's shaking in rage. She stands up, rips her skirt off and pulls the blanket off the ground scattering everything off down the hill.

'Fuck you and your painting. I hate your whistling too.'

She picks up one of the sable brushes and makes a lunge at me. Holy Mother of God, as a good Catholic would say and I'm not even catholic. She just misses my face as I sidestep.

I try to diffuse her with reason. 'What's the matter with you? You don't know me. You have no idea who I am. Calm down for heaven's sake.'

This apparently does not diffuse anything about the situation.

Several members of the group are walking over towards us. This has the same effect as a red rag to a bull and she makes another stab at my face and just catches my cheek.

'You stole from my lover. You sold his work and made a fortune from his art. You're all leeches in the art world. I should fuck you till you die.'

Then she lets out another almighty scream and collapses on the grass in a semi-naked heap. She's sobbing hysterically and rolling around on the ground.

One of the other chaps in the group asks me if I'm okay.

'Why?' I reply. 'Is this her normal behavior. I've never met her before in my life. She's completely mad.' My hands are shaking as I try to retrieve my scattered equipment.

Meanwhile, the madwoman has stopped sobbing and is now lying in a foetal position mumbling to herself.

Another man, wearing a pair of velvet loons some forty years after they were last in vogue, pipes up 'She's one of those strange model types; a bit temperamental; you know what I mean.'

'I bloody well do now. Why didn't one of you say something?'

'Well you know how it is. She's been okay for a while now. Something must have set her off. She's from Totnes. They're all a bit soft in the head down there.'

I didn't realise how dangerous it is to be an en plein air painter. It would appear that fresh air and good light are not enough to complete a masterpiece. One needs an adrenaline rush to add drama to your subject.

I know what I need and that's a stiff drink.

A few of us walk down the path to the parked coach and within a few minutes everyone including the mad woman are back on board. She says nothing as she walks past to a seat behind me but seated, she mutters one word. 'Bastard,' she whispers.

I stand and walk up to the front.

'Driver. Please let me off at the nearest pub. It's an emergency.'

'Right ho, then my handsome. It's about mile and bit.'

It's the longest mile I've ever ridden on a bus and when it stops, I jump straight off. I watch the coach pull away and see a hand in the back widow gesticulating a none-too happy salute in my direction.

Then I remember what I was whistling that she took exception to; 'Hi ho, hi ho. It's off to paint I go.'

Several months later I exhibit the painting in a mixed show and I'm delighted when a lady approaches me and asks about the subject. She feels she knows the area.

'Madam, I say politely. There is so much more to this painting that I'm sure you won't believe me if I tell you.'

Anyway, I'm delighted because she purchases it.

All in a day's work methinks. I had titled the picture *A Lucky Escape*.

ACT 3 SCENE 2

Today's trek along the coastal path is accompanied by hundreds of gulls and a squall that keeps knocking me in the back. The waves are behaving like horses running wild and the crashing of water on the shale applauds as the tide ebbs away.

Perfect conditions, albeit a tad windy.

The view is sublime. A headland with trees. A few scattered boats, bobbing on their moorings. A pathway meanders off round the remains of a Second World War gun emplacement. It's quiet and there is even a bench with a little plaque in memory of Uncle Bob who loved looking out to sea.

I sit and open my flask of coffee. Yes coffee; it's far too early for a snifter. Even for a practicing artist.

I love the sea. I connect and lose myself thinking. Whatever needs to leave my mind does and travels far away to leave more room to ponder and fill with anything new that comes along.

I have peace for a full fifteen minutes when an elderly chap walks by, stopping in front of me and blocking my view.

'Great view from here,' he says.

I smile and reply, 'Yes, it was.'

'What are you doing then; painting or something?'

'You could say that. Would you mind moving either to the left or to the right.'

'I'll sit beside you if you move your mess.'

Trying to discourage him I say, 'I never speak to anyone when I'm lost in my art.' I try to sound pretentious; it fails.

'I love art. My wife used to paint. She loved Elvis Presley and Tom Jones. He's still alive mind.'

I make no effort to respond.

'She passed on a few years ago. She'd have loved watching you paint.'

I hold my brush poised in anticipation of whatever else he will say. I can't concentrate.

'Are you anyone I should know?'

'You never know. Maybe in a hundred years,' I say with controlled frustration.

He nods for a few seconds and continues 'I knew Bob. Great mates we were. We played darts at the pub up the road every Tuesday.'

I give in. 'Do you still play then?'

'My arthritis keeps playing up now. It's so painful in my throwing arm; just about lift a pint these days.'

'You should try a half pint. Less weight.'

He goes quiet. I dip my brush in the water and nearly get to apply it on the paper...

'Fancy a beer then?'

'Thanks, but no. It's not ten thirty yet. I'm going nowhere till this watercolour's finished.'

'I didn't mean now exactly. In a couple of hours. It only opens at midday.'

'We'll see,' I reply trying to placate him. I'm smiling externally while inside my body is shouting out *Please go away far away. As far away as possible. Now.*

He is quiet at last. I cautiously begin painting again. He nods occasionally, giving the odd cough to remind me he is still here. The gulls continue soaring against the wind above and the crashing waves nearly make everything seem alright.

Strolling from around the gun emplacement is a tall man. He's wearing a smart black overcoat and a multi-striped Paul Smith scarf. He is walking rather slowly and deliberately towards us. *Keep going* I want to shout out.

Alas he walks straight up to the bench and greets us. 'Lovely view innit?'

Londoner. Why make a statement then add the question. It is either a lovely view or not. Look!

'What you doing?'

'Painting.'

'He's painting the headland,' the old man pipes up.

'That's nice. Let me see.'

So, another spectator has joined me. They both get acquainted and talk louder.

'Gents please, a little softer if you don't mind.'

'Mate!'

I hate being called mate.

'It's not like you're having to fink or summit.'

I don't reply. Mantra time. Make every brush stroke count. Does that include poking his eyes out with my sable brush?

I apply a calming blue wash to the paper

'She only bleedin' ups and leaves me. Left the dog mind.'

'Why don't the two of you sort the world out in the pub up the road.'

'Temperamental bloody artists, they're all the same.'

The old man tuts, 'I was only telling him how much my wife loved Elvis and Tom Jones.' Finally, they do both walk off to the pub.

A dog bounces over and cocks his leg on the bench. 'Piss off' and he does smarmy little sod. Ah yes en plein air. Nothing to beat it.

An hour later and I'm pleased with my efforts; thirsty too. So, I head off for a well-deserved pint.

'Where you been? You been ages.'

'Painting.'

'Fort you dropped off the cliff. How can you do all that wishy-washy stuff for so long?'

'What do you do?' Do I care?

'I.T. mate.'

'Ah yes. Push little knobs in front of a screen all day. How fascinating.'

The barman pulls a pint.

'Your round, mate. I'm Kelvin by the way; we're on the Doombar.'

'Two Doombars and a cider ta.'

It's costly business, minding one's own business.

'Go on then; let's have a butchers.'

I reluctantly pull the pad out from my bag.

'It's alright that innit!'

'I concur.'

'You what?'

'I agree.'

'He agrees. My wife would have liked that.'

'Here you are. Have it. It's a present.'

'I'll buy you another cider then.'

It's a deal. I turn around to Kelvin 'Some of us are generous arty types you know.'

Venture costs, time, paint, paper, and two more rounds. Ah well I'll put it down to setting up expenses.

Here's to another attempt tomorrow.

ACT 4 SCENE 1

Sitting on a bench by the River Tamar.

Watching the sun go down.

Slow boats and sails.

Union Jack flag gently blowing in the breeze and the sound of kids running down the hill.

The occasional laughter and an odd dog bark

The sea sparkles and a haze forms on the distant land; it's idyllic.

I venture over the border into Cornwall. Apparently to Cornish folk, this is a separate country while to Devonians it's a place over the bridge where no one goes or should ever go.

Well, not being either, I venture across one of Brunel's masterpieces, completed in his life time, and turn down the small road onto the

Cornish side of the Tamar. This happens be amazingly located right by a pub with a bronze, life-size figure of Brunel, complete with his tall chimney hat standing proudly in front.

I stroll up and down the river and find a great view of the bridges plus all the old boats bobbing around. After a few moments, I realise it's a bit chilly and the wind is ripping through my jacket. Brisk fresh air. It's bloody freezing but I'm determined to paint outside although the wind is reminding me of the temperature. My brushes are rolling freely on the bench but luckily my paper is attached in book form so at present won't fly off down the river.

The real problems are my fingers. They're turning blue but at least the sun's out and it's not raining. I'm sticking it out.

After ten minutes I notice several large muddy, grey-brown swans paddling downstream in formation. Another moment cruises by and they all turn towards the bank and waddle out. I do believe they're eyeballing me. They continue their journey in my direction, akin as much as anything to a gang of bikers, well pissed-off for some inexplicable reason, hissing and looking menacing.

Valiantly, I continue sketching, keeping an eye on the gaggle as they continue their approach.

The lead bird has attitude, I swear. He walks up to the bench and pecks at the brush Next, another picks up a tube of paint and suddenly six large, feathered gangsters are going for me. A polite *Shoo* has no effect. 'Scram sod off.' I stand and flail my arms about to defy my assailants. No joy. One goes for my knee, which I must add, hurts and makes me jolt. This is not funny I am being attacked by these creatures. So much for sharing Mother Nature.

I move quicker than normal further down the jetty only to find they're following me. Suddenly there's a loud bang and the birds stop and turn their necks towards the pub. A rather portly chap with massive sideburns hurls a pail of something or other in their direction and all except one waddle over to sample the contents. The last bird hisses one more time making a lunge for my shoe and only then does it turn and follow the gang.

I go to repossess my paints which have been scattered everywhere. Little bastards. Correction; large, ugly bastards.

The safest place appears to be the pub. I walk in and stand by the fire.

The staff are laughing. Is that at me? 'Hells teeth, my handsome. That were right amusing. We were going to place a bet to see who'd win.'

'It was bloody close,' I say. 'Whisky please. Large one, no ice thanks.'

'You're not from round here then,' says Mr. Sideburns.

Another chap leaning on the bar says, 'Them birds hate everyone. You were sat at their landing spot. Tut tut. Shouldn't do that again if I were you.'

Seems like I'm the entertainment for the day.

'Them birds rule the jetty. You should see how they be when they don't like the colour of a launch or a jacket. I saw a woman throw her vest at one bird. Boobs popped out an all. She was in a right tizzy. Nice pair mind.'

'Enough of this bird talk, feathered or not; are you still serving lunch?'

'Only got a couple of pasties left.'

'But you have a sign saying home cooked food served all day?'

'Ah that was up till yesterday. Chef left in a huff. There's a chip shop back up the hill. You can bring it back here if you want to sup a decent pint with it.'

I smile, nay grimace, at the barman. How jovial and helpful. The thought of lashings of gravy on a hot roast lunch evaporates from my mind. 'Doombar please. Back in a tick.'

It's no warmer as I pace up the steep street to the steamed-up window of the chip shop.

'You from the pub then?'

'How can you tell?'

'Never seen you before and you're the eighth stranger today. Chef must've left again.'

'You're right on all counts. Haddock and chips, mushy peas, no salt and vinegar, ta.'

'Here you go,' as he shovels the fresh hot chips onto the paper and extracts a long juicy piece of fish from under the glass of the counter. 'Better take some extra chips for them lot down there.'

I pay and stroll back down to my freshly poured pint.

'Chippy says to give you all some chips.' I place the wrapped bundle on the bar.

Two plates arrive with ketchup. Voila.

'No charge,' says the barman.

The birds are a distant memory as I tuck in. Three pints later and I feel warmer, fuller and a little drunk. Only a little mind you.

'Anywhere cheap to stay round here?'

The barman, now known to me as *Tim the Keg* tells me his sister has a B&B not far and rings her to confirm a booking.

Great service. More beer. The place has filled up, the company's good and the sun is setting. It's tough being an artist.

ACT 4 SCENE 2

The B&B is clean and simple in taste; white Ikea furniture and everywhere painted white to match. I wake to find the sunlight already peeking through the curtains.

I'm not wasting any time indoors. I skip breakfast and polite conversation with people I don't want to talk to and venture to my next location, the Jenny Cliff Café, situated on a headland not far from Plymouth. The views are dramatic, and yet it has an air of time standing still, with the breakwater and Drake's Island enhancing the panorama.

There are yachts and large boats moving in slow motion and a big Union Jack flag gently curling around the flag-pole beside the café. It seems the whole of Plymouth has woken early and the air is full of the sound of kids running down the hill with peals of laughter, as well as the odd dog barking away at anything that moves.

The sea sparkles and a haze forms on the distant land.

It's idyllic. Again.

I set out my equipment on a bench and lo and behold a seagull decides to drop his morning's breakfast on me. Now some folk say that's a sign bringing good luck. I say something entirely different but the wind kindly carries my harsh words out to sea.

There is one slight problem I find out to my detriment. The bench I choose is placed precariously close to a large drop behind. Wait for it. A sharp breeze starts by clutching the paper and redistributing the sheets all over the grassy slope. Then the wind very carefully pushes one of my brushes through a gap on the seat and sends it rolling down the verge. Okay, I'm being challenged. I get it; firstly knighted by bird shit, followed closely by the hazard of a windy gust and now, as I try to retrieve a brush too far, I slip and fall backward down the slope; a triple reverse roll and thud. I look up at the sky and then nothing. I don't know how long nothing lasts but I open my eyes and it feels a lot later than when I inadvertently closed them.

There are three youngish lads maybe aged nine or ten staring at me.

'You alright mister?' says the first lad.

'We've been watching you for ages seeing if you're dead like,' says the second lad with a look of disappointment on his face.

'I said you were,' says the third lad.

'Hah! See, I win. He's not dead. Look he's moved.' The first lad punches the air with his fist. 'Yes!'

I suddenly realise my head is hurting; nay thumping, and my ribs aren't talking to me. I try to sit up and fail miserably. Diagnostic time. Ouch! Maybe a broken rib or two, large bump on head. Nothing too serious is the general consensus; fell over a ridge and hurt myself.

'Are them your paints 'n' stuff up there?' The second lad points upwards.

'Yes,' I reply.

'Shit,' says the third lad.

'Don't swear, tosser,' says the first lad to the second lad, shoving him hard.

'We only played a bit with them,' says the third lad sheepishly.

Then they run off rather quickly.

215

I slowly manage to stand up and, even more slowly, climb back up the slope to see what's happened to my equipment. My rather expensive pad is full of drawings of battleships, racing cars and planes, all emblazoned in the green colour of a certain football team identified by the statement *Plimuth Argle rools*.

One tube of zinc white has been emptied of its contents in a long line along the grass. There goes twenty quid.

I'm too sore to be bothered and open my hip flask, which by an excellent coincidence holds just the right amount of Irish whiskey to ensure I remain in a state not to care.

Eventually the pain recedes and I produce quite a nice sketch, even if I say so myself. I drain the whisky and walk over to the café.

The place is packed with well-tempered parents and their noisy kids. Or is it well-tempered kids and noisy parents? Six dogs, which are all sitting quietly, tied to a rail by the front door, eagerly espy me as a potential dog lover.

I walk up to the counter. The assistant, looking like an art student greets me. 'That was a stupid thing to do. You looked so funny. Are you okay?' She has a strong Geordie accent.

'You're a long way from home. Thanks for noticing the entertainment; no charge. I could murder a strong black coffee and some toast please.'

'Do you want clotted cream with that?'

'Err, no thanks.'

'Everyone has clotted cream with everything down here.'

'Well not me.'

'I'm doing my own art down here. Can I look at what you've been painting?'

'With pleasure; when you bring my order over.'

I find the only available table - with a rickety chair - it must be my chairful destiny to seek out and locate all potential seating dangers. I take out my sketchbook and pencil and try to catch the buzz of this obviously popular café.

'Here's your toast and coffee. Have you got a tab?'

'I won't do a runner, I'll pay you.'

'Naw man; a tab, a fag, a ciggie!'

'Sorry, don't smoke.'

'Nither mind like. Let's see then.'

I open the pad to show her my latest watercolour.

'It's canny like.' I think she means it's good.

'I'm sure it is, but what do you think as a student of the arts.'

'It's alright, that.'

'Thanks.'

'Do you sell them or just paint like?'

'I'm collecting for an exhibition and I have sold a few along the way.'

'You should do big oils, man. No one treats watercolours with respect. I mean they're all nice like but you don't get dirty and covered in paint.'

I smile,' I can do dirty but not while I paint.'

She ignores my attempt at repartee, turns and ventures back to the bustle indoors.

I just love taking the time to watch the world go by. It's something I really never had the time for as a gallery owner. After fifteen minutes of doing absolutely nothing, a rather large bloke, tattooed from head to toe, walks across my line of sight.

'What you looking at mate?'

'The world going by.'

I still hate being called mate.

'Well stop looking at me, right.'

'I wasn't aware I was exclusively looking at you - or your collection of tattoos come to think of it.'

'You think you're so bloody clever, your sort; bleedin' arty-farty types. You queer or something?'

The mood is not quite what you'd expect from a quiet Devon café.

'Bill, piss off. Leave him alone. He's a nice quiet artist.' The Geordie assistant, turned savior, is back.

'He's staring at me all funny and I don't like the way he's looking around.'

'Why don't you let me do a sketch of you?' I chip in trying to diffuse the situation.

'You're weird, pervert. How'd you like I rearrange your head all over that table.'

This is going in the wrong direction. 'Not too hot on that idea I'm afraid.'

Next second a large volume of water splatters over Bill launched with precision by Miss Geordie. He's standing there soaking wet and open mouthed with nothing coming out.

'Wet on wet; great technique; looks like you've applied just the right amount of water.'

'He always causes a fuss here, big wuss. A coffee on the house for the aggro?'

'Thanks, that's nice' Meanwhile Bill retreats to his Ford Ka. Which to a car snob like me says a lot about him.

She returns with a coffee. 'Okay watercolours can be fun too.'

We both chuckle. 'Would you have really drawn him?'

'We'll never know. Will we?'

ACT 4 SCENE 3

I blame my Irish descendants and Guinness for the next episode. I'm walking around Plymouth as it's wet and not at all like a summer's day. The wind is blowing too hard to paint outside so I merrily find a watering-hole up some side street. It's an Irish bar; a bit like walking into a real Dublin pub with a wooden floor and dark interior. There are Celtic signs and just about every Irish flag imaginable hanging from the ceiling.

There's a rather petite lass with hair tied back tight, propping her elbows on the bar, waiting for something to happen. The place is quiet apart from a couple hunched together, an old chap reading a paper and an even older, yellow Labrador chasing a slightly mangled rubber ball across the floor. The dog stops when someone's foot or a barstool leg blocks the ball, it barks, the ball is kicked and the dog chases off, skidding across the floor to catch it again.

Riveting you might say – or not - but something told me the old black 'n' white stuff ought to be worth sampling.

I go up to the bar. 'A bit wet out.'

'Yeh, always is down 'ere,' says the barmaid.

'Pint of Guinness, ta'

'Where you from then? You're not from down here.'

'For sure, I'm visiting and taking in the scenery.'

'Don't sound like you come from London. Weird lot them are.'

'I'm not; try further up the M5.'

'Oh, I dunno, as long as you're not from Stoke-on-bloody-Trent.'

'Any reason you don't like Stoke?'

'Tosser of an ex. Up his own, he was. Stick to the Navy, my dad used to say.'

'Was your dad right then?'

'Not bloody likely. He buggered off with my mom's best friend and my ex-husband was an officer down here. He's pissed off and all.'

By the time I've heard her life story without letting her have the least idea where I'm from, the Guinness is poured to perfection.

'Here you go.' The barmaid looks pleased with her skills, and rightly so.

'Thanks.' I take a sip. It's smooth, creamy, not too cold and slightly addictive. This is a bad sign; I'm sure another might beckon shortly.

There's a knock against my foot. I look down to see the dog staring up at me. Must be my turn. I gently kick the ball, but the dog just looks and plonks his full weight on my feet.

The man reading the paper looks up at me. 'It's all right; he's getting on a bit. Give him a moment.'

I can't easily negotiate the extrication of my foot as I'm right up against the bar. Oh well, it's still raining so there's nowhere else to go.

A few minutes later and with a large yawn, the dog shuffles to his feet and slowly strides over to the ball, which is in the middle of the empty floor.

I find a table in the shaded window and take my sketchbook out. How do you capture this place? It's great. I start by supping some more to help me absorb the atmosphere. To my surprise, the Guinness has gone and I have to persuade myself to have another.

'Same again please.'

The barmaid is looking a bit inquisitive. 'What you doing then?'

'Trying to capture the ambiance of this place.'

'The what?'

'Ambiance, atmosphere, the mood; it's great.'

'You not spying or nothing?'

'No, an artist.'

'I ain't done nothing wrong, honest.'

'I said I'm an artist. I'm trying to sketch the inside of this pub. Capture its character '

'You better stick around for later then if you want character. Mick's band will be playing. They're well good, proper foot tapping stuff, right characters, the lot of them.'

'Well, there's no law against staying indoors to paint en plein inside, lesson three.'

I think it's funny, the barmaid doesn't. She curls her upper lip and walks off. Obviously you need to be on the Guinness to appreciate my sense of humour.

I resume my non-spying, trying to catch the atmosphere on my note pad. Within the hour the place has filled up and the dog is having a tough time of playing ball, but still continues to bark only now at many more feet.

The noise level has risen considerably; it's more like grand central station and two more staff have miraculously appeared to start serving the ever-growing masses.

Another few minutes and it's impossible to concentrate on my sketching.

A mightily tall chap with long, flaming-red hair strolls in carrying a violin case. 'Look after this, will yaz?' and he places it on the table over my pad. He returns with four pints of Guinness, deposits them on the table and goes back to the bar returning with another two pints. 'Have one on me, the lads will be here in a bit.'

'That's most kind.'

'Not all; we're going to be sharing your table. Sláinte.'

'Sláinte. Are you in the band?'

'Ah sure I might do a turn if asked; you never know yer luck.'

'I used to be in a band you know.'

'Bet you didn't play the penny whistle.'

'Nor rattle the spoons; guitar actually, long time ago, when I had hair. We used to do a mean version of *Whiskey In The Jar*.'

'Ah Jazus, you don't need hair to play a musical instrument. Were you any good?'

'I suppose so.'

'I'll ask Mick for youz and you can do a turn twanging your strings. I'm sure one of the lads will lend you a guitar.'

Meanwhile the Guinness is flowing too freely.

'My shout, same again.'

'The lads aren't here yet, have another one of these.'

We clink glasses again and make a toast to *once a muso, always a muso*.

I am now feeling very relaxed. I've not eaten lunch although they say that Guinness is as good as a meal in which case I must have drunk four courses, but who's counting?

Mick and his cronies walk in. They all seem to have long flaming-red hair, and all are sporting beards as impressive as *the gold diggers of '49*.

'How ya doing little Billy?' Mick slaps my Guinness-sharing pal on the back.

'Ne'er better, ya big bollox.' And turning to me, 'Micks me little brother.'

Little is not the operative word here; the pair of them would make great prop forwards for any Rugby team. I'm tall but they both tower over me.

"I was told your band is full of character and worth waiting for. My round I believe. Guinness all round I assume.'

'Right ho so. Wait and find out.'

Swaying ever so slightly, I make my way to the bar. On returning I find the brothers are looking through my note pad.

'Was just havin' a peek. Did you draw all this lot? They're fecking great.'

'Guilty as charged.'

'Sure, why don't you do a painting of us playing and we could use it, like for our next CD.'

Billy pipes up, 'Live in the pub.'

Half way through my fifth pint I agree. Then nature calls.

How the hell am I going to capture this band live? The floor is full and there's no sight line to speak of at all. A drunken idea emerges; I'll stand on the table. I actually manage to get to the bar and ask someone if it's okay, as Mick wants me to sketch the band here and now.

The someone happens to be the manager. 'So long as you don't fall off and break your neck, I don't give a flying...'

So here I am, armed with charcoal, pencil and pad, standing on an old table in an Irish bar in Plymouth, sketching a mad Cèilidh band, whilst under the influence of far too may pints of Guinness.

Now that's what you call artistry.

Mick's band is really good and the place is going for it. I nearly get knocked off the table by overzealous dancers and more or less finish the task when Mick looks out at me.

'Hey fella, come and join us. Sean, give me artist friend a guitar there.'

Oh well, there's only one thing to do; I clamber down and join the band to play - you guessed right - *Whiskey In The Jar*. My fingers are a bit rusty but they seem to work, and what's more, we get a loud cheer.'

'Thanks a lot Mick.'

I stay with the band for a jam before taking my leave by jumping off the raised stage; well, more like a palate really but *once a muso, always a muso*. I smile with contentment. That was fun.

'I didn't quite catch your name fella,' says Mick.

'I didn't give it.' I reply, being patted and thumped on the back as I try to meander back to the safety of the table to collect my gear.

Three girls - well I say girls but they're more like Amazonian tribal bouncers - are leaning on the bar. There have more tattoos on them than a tattoo parlour advert. Scary.

'Were you that bloke on the table before?' says the largest of the three. She sports an amazing, blonde, dried-out peroxide hair-do and purple lipstick matched with her leopard skin-patterned short skirt and unbelievably high-heeled, purple shoes. She and her friends look as if they have walked straight out of a Beryl Cook painting. Cook is, as you know, a famous artist from Plymouth.

'I am that man.' I take a bow.

'Aren't you a bit old to be standing on tables lover boy?' says Amazonia Number Two.

I wonder whether I should explain my actions; oh heck, why not? 'I'm an artist and I was catching the band for their forthcoming CD.' Well it sounds good, though why I'm trying to impress these ladies I'll never know. Well I do but I won't admit to the Guinness effect.

'Oh, an artist. Well, we are models, aren't we girls?'

'Yeh! How about drawing us?'

'Unfortunately, I'm leaving here tomorrow; otherwise it would have been a pleasure'

'You don't know what you'll be missing,' giggled Number Three. 'You'll have to come down again; we're always in here on a Friday night.'

I give another bow and hastily leave the pub. It seemed wise.

ACT 5 SCENE 1

Time is so different to when I was running the gallery. It does seem like years ago, when life was permanently on fast forward and going all the time, compared to now, sitting on a park bench with my sketch book and paints out, watching the world go by.

I still feel like I might be missing out on something. I don't exactly know what but it lingers in the back of my mind, unless I'm lost in the mood whilst painting.

Today is slightly overcast, with plenty of moody light and long shadows. Overlooking my bench is a lake with geese and ducks gently cruising along.

I watch two figures come into view. I assume it's a father and son. The father is slightly dragging his son along the path but they stop by the edge of the water. The father messes around with a hold-all and removes a remote-control speedboat.

'Come on stop messing around. Hold this now.'

The son doesn't look impressed. 'I don't want to play. I want an ice cream; I want to go on the swings; I hate your stupid boat; I don't want to be here; aaaaah!'

Yes, it's a father and son bonding time.

'You'll bloody well stay exactly where you are and watch. This is great fun. Wait and see.' The father is looking somewhat stressed and you can see he's physically turning a sort of heated red in the face; a heart attack in the making.

The ducks, thinking there's food on offer, swim faster to the two figures only to find to their disappointment there is no bread. Instead the father places the boat in the murky water and fires up the engine from the control unit. A whirring bubbly noise scares the ducks which scatter and fly off in all directions. The geese hiss as the boat tears across the water scaring all in its path. It swerves and speeds along with no regard for the wildlife. The man is a bully to animals and based on what I witnessed, a bully to his own offspring.

'Boring, boring, boring,' the lad shouts at his dad.

Suddenly the father lifts his arm and hits the lad, knocking him to the ground. He gets up and charges his father trying to grab the remote control. The father lets out a mighty sweep of his arm knocking the lad off his feet and straight into the water. It is at this point I feel an obligation to butt in and stop minding my own business.

I rush to the edge hollering, 'Oy! What do you think you're doing?'

'Mind you own f'ing business,' comes the reply.

The lad is spluttering and making a fuss even though the water is only a few inches deep.

'Now you're in for it you little urchin. Come here.' He grabs the boy by the scruff of his neck and yanks him in the air and more or less throws him onto dry land.

'There's no need to be so damned violent to this boy; you're hurting him.'

'I'll bloody well hurt you in a minute if you don't piss off!'

Weighing up the situation, in a moment of stupidity, I lunge at the man and shove him hard into the water. He falls, waving his arms and throwing the remote-control unit into the air. It lands on the grass and the batteries fly out.

The father steps out the water and strides towards me. 'I'm going to kill you with my bare fists,' and he aims a punch at my head. I sidestep and shout out for help. Luckily some people have seen the incident and are running over - either to help or to enjoy the spectacle. Meanwhile the boat is merrily spinning along on the water without the aid of any control. It sort of gently loops the lake and is heading for land exactly where we're standing.

The father takes another step to bring me within range of his fist, only this time I bend down, charge and force him back into the water where back-peddling in the mud, he slips completely and goes down with a huge splash. You can almost hear the ducks laughing. The boat continues its journey and collides with its owner, who picks it up and hurls it at me. It misses and explodes onto the grass bank nearby, making a last mosquito whirr and then silence.

'Look what you made me do,' he bellows. I'm going to sue you, you piece of shit.'

The boy is smiling and jumping up and down, 'Yay dad, you're great; this is the best fun ever.' A fatal mistake as the father stops, takes a look at his son and then begins to chase him. The son takes off as fast as he can, easily out-running his father and legs it up the path, up the hill and out of sight. The father, out of breath, slows but still follows doggedly after him.

'Are you alright, sir?' A policeman taps me on the shoulder.

'I'm fine. It's just I saw this bloke hit his child and felt I had to do something.'

'Do you mind if I ask you a few questions?'

We cross over to the bench and sit. 'Are these your bits sir?'

'Yes officer, my painting bits, for painting.'

'I see, then. So, I take it you're a painter?'

'Yes officer. I specialise in watercolours.'

'That's most interesting indeed. Can't say I know much about painting but my ex-wife enjoyed doing it. She's taken up with her tutor. I prefer writing myself. Poetry and the like. I find I'm able to escape from this humdrum life, which frankly ain't what it used to be when I joined the force.'

'That so? Is there anything you want to ask me regarding the incident?'

'Ah yes, nearly forgot where I was. Who started the fight?'

'Actually, I would say the father was bullying his son, and after I saw him hit the poor lad, I upped and pushed him to stop him hurting the boy.'

'I see.' He paused for a while, nodding 'And then what?'

'He fell in to the water and the lad ran off up the hill over there.'

'Did the man hit you by any chance, in response to your attack?'

'I wouldn't say it was an attack; I wanted to stop him from hitting the lad. After all he's a minor, and his father was taller than me.'

'So, he didn't hit you back?'

'He did threaten to kill me, if that's any help.'

'I'll make a note of that, thank you.'

This is sounding more like a *Carry-On* film by the minute.

'Can you describe your attacker?'

'Taller than me, middle age, maybe forty plus, greying hair, eyes a bit close together and a thin long nose.'

'Quite observant, aren't we?'

'It's all about observing; that's what painting is about you see. Look, look and look some more.'

'Even while being threatened?'

'Even while being threatened.'

'You do realise that you've just described Dr. Whittingham. He's one of the science teachers at the school over the road. I happen to know he is rather strict, and quite a few of the parents have filed complaints regarding his behavior. Do you wish to make a complaint sir? I'll need to fill in another form if you do.'

Ah paperwork, I'm glad it isn't just me that hates it. 'No, let's leave it alone. You do what you have to do. I'm going back to my painting if you don't mind'

'Right. Well in that case the matter is closed.' The officer shuts his notebook. 'But if you want some advice, leave him alone in future; he's not a nice man. Although apart from that, it's nice to see members of the public looking after the little nippers.'

'Thank you, officer.'

I feel like I've been told off in a strangely polite manner.

He walks off and I look out at the lake. The ducks and geese are gliding about again as if nothing has happened. Perhaps nothing really has apart from a broken controller lying abandoned on the grass.

The shadows have lengthened and I return to thinking how nice and quiet my life is these days.

ACT 5 SCENE 2

There are some fundamental similarities between painting and running an art gallery, namely women wine and art; now isn't that a pleasant coincidence.

I mean, how can you really get into the mood without a nice smooth Rioja or a Montepulciano? However, something too robust is not good for thinking and believe it or not, I do have to concentrate. In fact, looking at something is an exhausting process and requires several glasses of wine to aid that concentration. Well, that's what I believe, except that now I'm sure it's not a justified expense to set against tax. My accountant will have a word or two about that, no doubt. The obvious answer is to add on the cost of a bottle of wine to the painting. After all the paints cost enough to buy and handmade paper is a fortune.

Am I boring you? Well at least some wines on offer at three for a tenner are drinkable.

Hey ho; after a brisk walk to the local wine shop, aka the supermarket, I stroll down the road to the reservoir and find a nice spot with a bit of shade and a bench. I do like benches. I spread everything out on them; a mobile studio, so to speak.

Today I have my face to the sun and the shadows are doing exactly what I want them to do - that is until two rather good-looking blonde women, immaculately made-up, stroll up rather than jogging by in ill-fitting lycra. They look like they've stepped straight out of Vogue magazine.

'I used to study art years ago.'

'Really, you never mentioned that before.'

'He reminds me a bit of my old teacher,' the first blonde nods in my direction.

'Excuse me,' I pitch in. 'Less of the old; oh and good afternoon ladies, it's a lovely day for painting.'

'I'm sure it is. Actually, do you give lessons. I'd love to have a bash again.'

'Actually, I do.' Well why not; after all she started it.

'Tina, why don't you join us, it will be such fun.'

I'm not making this up, honest.

'I haven't the foggiest idea what to do.'

'Oh, come on. I insist.'

Tina allows herself to be persuaded and two blondes take up the offer of a lesson in watercolours.

'Where would you like your first session?' I ask. a bit reserved. Me reserved, that's a first.

'Come to our home. How's next Tuesday at three o'clock?' She presents a card and grabs Tina's arm in excitement.

The name on the card is Caroline Kendall DBE.

'You're going to love it, trust me,' I say and as they start walking away; 'That will be fine.'

ACT 5 SCENE 3

Tuesday arrives and I head out to give my first lesson. This involves driving up a pebbled drive to a large Elizabethan pile. I knock and a butler opens the door.

'Ma'am is waiting on the patio, sir. Follow me.'

The interior is exquisite, befitting a stately home with antiques everywhere and classic paintings, mainly Victorian, on every available wall. Passing through a large lounge on the way to the patio, I can't help but notice a large Turner landscape. Yes, a real JMW Turner hanging innocently amongst the other paintings.

We continue out to the patio to find Caroline and Tina drinking champagne whilst sitting on wicker recliners. They are both dressed as stunningly as at our last encounter.

'We were wondering if you'd turn up,' Caroline coyly smiled. 'Do have a drink before we start.'

'Thank you. It's my motto.'

She's wearing a casually fitted white blouse and matching Palazzo trousers. Her hair is loosely tied up and, I have to say, she looks drop dead stunning.

Tina is wearing tight jeans, and a bright red t-shirt – it bears a depiction of Snoopy and Charlie Brown cuddling. She too has her hair tied back and is almost equally gorgeous.

We move to a large table and the butler refills the glasses.

'Well now, to begin...' I produce two pads, several paints and palates and little receptacles for water. The butler returns presciently bearing a jug of water.

The view is magnificent, dotted with sculptures, water features and an arboretum of trees.

'You have a glorious garden. Where shall we start?'

Tina does in fact know something about how to paint. She was hiding her light under a bushel that day at the reservoir and Caroline, I would say is, a good amateur and some guided practice and tips will help her improve significantly.

An hour goes by before Tina stands abruptly; 'Sweetie, this has been wonderful but I've just remembered; I have to collect Sasha.'

Far be it for me to enquire just who she has to collect and why so I say 'Glad you've enjoyed your time; here's to another session.'

'Ring you tomorrow.' Caroline stops painting and blows her a kiss which I wouldn't have minded intercepting. 'Now then Mr. Art-Teacher, what else can you show me?'

'I haven't brought anything else today; maybe pastels next time if you like.'

'I'm not talking painting. Do you like Degas, Chagall, Dali?'

'Indeed. I went to Fugeras once; what a great museum.'

'Follow me.' She stands and walks back into the mansion. 'Come on, we haven't got all day.'

As the saying goes, in for a penny...

We climb the dark wooden stairs and on the next level there is a wall that has painting after painting of some of the truly great twentieth century artists. There is even a Picasso. Worse still, they're all real. Wow!

Caroline beckons as she continues along the corridor. She opens a set of double doors and my gaze meets a massive bed, covered in a soft, green embroidered satin quilt with hundreds of scatter cushions.

'This is what I want to show you.'

She doesn't mean the bed. As we turn the corner, hanging on the wall is a Monet. Jesus H! Whoa. It's bold and as fresh as the day it was painted.

'What do you think of my little collection?'

'It's wonderful. You only expect to see them in galleries.'

She gently settles her immaculately toned body down on the bed. 'They are my darlings. Come here now.'

'Now?'

'Now!'

Far be it from me to argue with a lady. I do as I'm told.

The Monet looks great from a reclining position...when given the chance. It still looks superb an hour later as well.

'I think that was a good lesson today. How about a week next Thursday for lesson number two?'

'Why not.'

'By the way,' Caroline winks. 'I think you're much better than my last art teacher.'

ACT 6 SCENE 1

An old raffia hat!

One of life's challenges when you sit outside is the sun. Have you noticed that your head gets hot? Mine too; what a coincidence.

With the onset of globalization, it's difficult to find a suitable hat that I don't look a twit in. Okay? Most hats make me look silly but I need one that actually suits me and does the job.

Hence, a raffia hat with a brim and touch of class. Walking into a charity shop, there it is, in front of my very eyes, lying quietly on the shelf behind the assistant. Bless; she looks about ninety-five give or take a week.

'May I try that hat behind you?'

'That was Alfie's favourite, you know.'

'Can't say I do.'

She passes me the hat and I notice her hands are well manicured and look in great condition. She catches the line of my gaze and says, 'I used to be a hand and forearm model in my youth.' She stops and sighs still holding on to the hat. I take it from her and place the hat, slightly angled, on my head.

'What do you think?'

'It really suits you. Alfie would be proud. Mind you, he was far more dashing than you.'

Well, if ever there was a better selling line to date, I've never heard it.

'Perfect. I'll take it.'

'You don't see men wearing hats these days. Such a shame. I don't mean those stupid peaked caps that they put on backwards. What do they look like?'

'I totally agree. I want this for protection from the elements whilst I'm painting outside.'

'Well don't let the wind blow it away. It's an original. Alfie always bought the best. Can't say I remember where or when he bought it. Might have been Italy or maybe Antibes. We loved traveling away together.'

'Oh. So, Alfie was your husband then?'

'Good grief, no. He was married to a right old battle-axe. She never went anywhere. Lovers, dear. We were passionate lovers.'

'In that case I shall take extra care. You never know; maybe it will become my good luck and schmooze hat.'

'Wear it in good health, my dear and enjoy every day of your life.'

I thank her and leave the shop. I think it's a good omen

Finished with the top hat and on with a raffia one. Bring it on.

ACT 6 SCENE 2

Every artist should have a studio.

It's more professional they say.

Well, I don't have one. I paint outside and this suits me. My front room is sort of a studio, reserved for wet days.

My telephone rings and one of the artists I used to represent in my gallery days asks if I know of anyone who wants to share his space as he's finding it difficult to make ends meet. Suddenly I find myself saying 'I'll take it.' I must be mad, I decide.

The studio is in an old factory in need of serious restoration, or to put it more bluntly, being knocked down. The old wooden reception area is tired and falling apart, the sign to the toilets has a sort of *don't bother using them but this way if you must* feel to it. By the way, they're conveniently situated on the ground floor, at the end of a long corridor with walls spray-painted to give a mottled green effect akin to a mould outbreak. Most inviting, I don't think. And the rickety stairs should be condemned. There is a lift but I think it's probably safer to use a parachute.

I climb the oily smelling stairs to find the smell not only continues but gets stronger on each landing until I reach the fourth floor. At least it's good exercise. There is a sign on the lift door *Not in use.* Someone has a sense of humour.

I walk past three chipped old grey-painted doors and I come across one which has a sign - *Artist at work: Enter at own risk* - painted in red, with matching drips.

I knock loudly and wait. I knock again and eventually a bolt is flung and the door opens revealing a splattered artist.

'Hello, mate.'

I hate being called *mate.* I may have mentioned this before.

'Hi, Sid. Long time no see. How's tricks?'

'Don't ask; been trying to do up the house. The missus is havin' another one and I'm supposed to be showing in Bristol in under a couple of months an' I'm nowhere near ready.'

'Glad I asked.'

I look around. There are pianos all over the place and canvasses leaning everywhere. If I'm being slightly critical there's not a lot of space for anyone or thing to add to the general melee.

"Where would you like me to work from? On top of that old baby grand perhaps?'

'Yeah, well, it's a bit tight at the moment but if you help me shift some stuff around, I'm sure it'll work out.'

'I think there might be enough space if I worked on miniatures.'

'I just need a few shekels in to help me stress levels.'

'Sid, let's be honest, there's no room in here for you, let alone anyone else.'

'I suppose not. Don't suppose you could lend me a few bob; five hundred quid would do it.'

'Tell you what I will do; I'll buy that one over there.' I point to a large piece hanging off a nail slightly skewwhiff. 'Then you sell it at your show and pay me back. How's that?'

'Mate, that's just amazing. Thank you, honest.' There's a pause. He looks at me. 'What if it doesn't sell?'

'When have I ever picked one that won't sell?'

So, now I'm five hundred quid down with no studio. See; told you I was mad.

'There's another room going up for rent soon. It's on the top floor.'

'Oh joy; does it leak, is the floor safe?' I try to sound interested.

'It's got great views.'

'Call me old fashioned but I'm not really feeling this place. Pardon me for asking, but how are you going to get those pianos out of your place with no functioning lift? Hire a crane perhaps?'

'Funny you should say that. Next Thursday...doing exactly that. Fancy helping?'

'This I shall have to see.'

I do trundle further up the stairs and peer into the void. It's dark, web-covered and like the rest of the building, it smells of old oil and engineering. It's dark because the windows are filthy. On the plus side, it's not going to cost much, so I venture into my new studio. I'll take it.

'Great,' says Sid 'and that means you'll still help me next week shift those pianos.'

'How can I refuse. Sounds like it's a good time for a beer, eh?'

Sid agrees instantly and we stroll down the stairs.

'By the way, you're lucky too coz there's toilets on your floor.'

'Aren't I the fortunate one then. Come on, let's go and celebrate.'

ACT 6 SCENE 3

I am kneeling and trying to sort out one of my plan chests, for artworks and the like, generally trying unsuccessfully to organize my stuff. There's a knock. I hoist myself up, dust down my trousers and open the door to find a very serious looking, youngish lady staring quite blankly at me. She's wearing a smart overcoat, unbuttoned to reveal a well-fitted red dress.

'How do you do?'

'Sometimes better than other days.'

'What's your name?'

'Prudence; my friends call me Pru.' She walks in and peers around.

'Thanks for responding to my advert.'

Without turning around, she says, 'Do you want me to take my clothes off?'

'Not at all. You look fab in what you're wearing.'

'I need the ladies!'

I point the way. 'Down the corridor to the left.'

She drapes her coat over my chair and saunters off. What a great pair of legs she has. I can't help but notice.

Next minute there's an almighty scream followed by several expletives and finally a loud plea for help. Is someone being assaulted? I swiftly traverse the corridor to the loo and knock. 'Are you ok?'

'No. I'm friggin' well not. 'There's a rat staring at me with a giant tail. It will bite me. Help, help, help! Kill it now!'

'May I step in?'

'Bloody well hurry up,' she screams.

I push the door. Fortunately, it's not locked. Pru is standing on the toilet seat holding her skirt.

'There,' she points and screams again.

I have to smile. 'That's Hubert. He's a gerbil and believe me, he's totally harmless. He prefers lettuce to females.'

Pru isn't impressed. 'It's a rat. They're filthy bastards.'

Poor Hubert is frozen with shock and hopefully unaware of being misdiagnosed as a rat. I bend down and pick him up, putting him in my pocket.

I offer a hand to assist with Pru's descent off the loo. She really isn't impressed in the slightest.

'Maybe a drink might help.' I suggest.

Pru does not want a drink; Pru does not want to stay; Pru is a stuck-up pain in the arse - or so Hubert would say if he could talk.

'What sort of filthy studio is this anyway?'

Pru is shaking I believe more in anger now more than from being petrified by poor Hubert.

'Well actually I was just sorting out my artworks, sketches, the like before you came in. It's a rather tidy studio thank you. You should see some of the places I've seen in my life.'

"Do I care?'

Blimey. I reckon she has got up the wrong side of the street let alone her bed...and dragged her negativity with her.

I try to get back on track. 'So, would you like to model for me or not?'

'No more f'ing animals lurking around?'

'No. Hubert has had enough for one day. He'll put the kettle on later, if you ask him nicely.'

Pru stares, cracks her face and walks over to the chair where she simply sheds her dress in one move and sits down. 'Come on, I've not got all day.'

I pull up a stool and grab a pad, a Conte crayon and some charcoal.

Her face is as motionless as her body. She has, however, a wonderful torso and she's in great shape. At least as long as I don't have to draw her mind.

The time flies and after five sketches, I'm done.

'I suppose you want me to come again?' Pru steps into her dress and flicks her hair back. She glances at my work. 'S'alright. You should see some of the crap I've had to sit through.'

'Alright then, same time next week. Would you mind wearing that dress for me as well.'

Pru looks at me, or more likely through me. 'Whatever.' She grabs her coat and turns to the door. 'Pay me next week. I'll only spend it.' And with that she's gone.

I walk over and close the door. Takes all sorts, and she is certainly all sorts.

ACT 6 SCENE 4

It's a harvest moon and the light is illuminating the entire outside with an eerie glow; except for a solitary moonbeam shining through the window, kissing her derrière, making for a very pretty sight. Her blond hair is strewn over the pillow like a preened mermaid, that is apart from the lack of a tail. Memo to self, I must remember to sketch this image.

My eyes close again and suddenly I see a man sitting on a bench by a lake. He is engrossed in painting and does not notice two youths in hoodies approaching him.

'What you doing old man,' says the first, grabbing the pad and flicking through the pages.

'Fuckin waste of time; twat!' says the second, pushing the man off the bench.

He falls to the floor and tries to stand up but is kicked hard in the chest. 'Didn't you do art in school when you were younger?' he manages to exclaim.

'School,' shouts the first. 'You havin a laugh?'

Suddenly I am feeling the pain in my ribs and the image is swirling. I see my watercolours being thrown into the water, ripped out one by one from the pad, crumpled into a ball and flung out. I watch paper balls transform into blackbirds flying upwards and away, laughing, mocking me. 'Crap. Crap. Crap,' they keep repeating.

'No. Not my pictures. Please stop!' I'm shouting out as I see a foot about to kick my head in.

'Jesus Bloody Mary. Are you alright?'

She's holding and shaking me and I'm back in the bedroom. 'Whoah. What a nightmare I was about to die!'

'Come on old man. I'll prove you're not going to die. Well at least not yet,' as she gently places her body on top of mine.

'If you insist.' Thankfully I live to see another sunrise.

ACT 7 SCENE 1

Majorca is a lovely island in the Balearics. I have been invited out on a ten-day course to give a few lectures about art and presentation and due to careful planning, have arrived early and having sorted somewhere to stay in Palma. Strangely enough on getting there I can't help noticing that my hearing is detecting a lot of Teutonic accents.

Not being too savvy on info web surfing, searching as I call it, I've booked a reasonably priced hotel just outside the capital. At the hotel on checking in, a very pretty receptionist looks at my passport and then straight at me and states 'This is a German hotel! You are English!"

'I only want to stay one night; is that okay?'

'But this is a German hotel and everyone in the hotel is German.'

'Great. I don't have to speak to anyone then. What time is breakfast served?'

'It's at eight a.m.'

'Until?'

'Breakfast is served at eight a.m.'

She stamps the paperwork, hands me the key and turns to her assistant, addressing her in German and that's it. I'm checked in.

I dump my bag and stroll outside to find a quiet bar. It's still strange being on a Spanish island and all you can hear are German-speaking people.

I stroll past three very loud and full bars and enter the fourth. The music is a bit oompah-oompah but bearable so I order a large beer and find an empty table. I quickly take out my small sketchbook and try to capture the atmosphere.

Ten minutes go by and a large gent of huge girth strolls up to my table. 'Herr Englander?'

'The very one.'

'Ja! I hear you are staying in my hotel.'

'Do I really stand out that much?'

'It's a very rare occurrence, in fact a first.'

I didn't ask him how he knew who I was. Am I being followed?

'Your hotel looks very nice and clean and the room is fine, thanks.'

'Vy aff you chosen my hotel?'

'I guess it was a lucky dip that did it. Fancy a beer?'

I don't drink vis my clients or guests and don't let my staff do ever.'

'Okay.'

'Permit me for asking once again why my hotel?'

'Is there any reason as to why I shouldn't stay?'

'Zere is a very important conference on at this moment with a lot of important persons and you don't exactly look like you fit in. Zat is all. Vot exactly do you do?'

'I'm an artist. I'm here on a two-week art course stroke holiday and I arrived here a day early.'

'Zat is so. Anything else. You're not a journalist by chance. Zos dreaded Zeitung; I hate zem.'

'No, I assure you, I am an artist. I paint in watercolours and love watching the world go by.'

'All right. We shall say goodbye to you tomorrow morning, Herr Englander. Till then. Auf wiedersehen.' He spins round and walks out of the bar.

Another chap promptly taps me on the shoulder. 'Excuse me. How do you know Herr von Rotenberg?'

'I don't. However, I am staying at his hotel up the road.'

'Good. Very good. We shall look forward to seeing you at the conference. What's your specialty?'

'En plein air,' I reply.

He looks puzzled.

I avoid everybody till the next day and check out quickly. After all it's a German hotel and I'm a Brit in Spain. Makes sense; no?

The journey by train to my next port of call is without incident. That is until I get out of the station and can't find a taxi. There is a small cafe bar with three old men sipping beer. 'Anyone know where I can get a taxi?'

They continue drinking and talking to each other. When I repeat my question, I get a blunt, 'Espanyol signor.'

'A taxi?'

'Non taxi.'

A thin, wiry chap comes from out behind the bar. 'There is no taxi here.'

'Where can I get one? Or a bus maybe.' I show him the location on my map.

'Si. Si.' He nods and then shouts out, 'Pedro!'

An even thinner, wirier lad emerges He says something that sounds suitably Spanish and taps me on shoulder. 'Come'

I follow him as he mounts a vintage rusty Vespa. He has no helmets and it splutters to life as if suffering from an attack of asthma, as I climb on. Luckily, I have a small bag, which I clutch with one hand, grabbing the tail rail with the other.

Even luckier is the fact that it doesn't go very fast.

He also seems to know where he's going and fifteen minutes later, we drive up a dirt track to my destination. I give him some notes and he tootles off beeping his rusty horn whilst the sheep and goats stop chewing the dried grass to watch him vanish down the track.

'Hola, you look mucho dust.' A nice greeting from someone I assume to be the house keeper. 'They are by pool - I show.'

I follow her around the courtyard through an arch to a large pool with a group sitting around it fully dressed. Must be English.

'Hello ole chap what have you been up to?' Vince is cravatted and corduroyed and it's only about twenty-seven degrees! 'Unusual method of transport. The local Pedro, no doubt.'

'Correct in one.'

'Maria will show you to your room. Go freshen up and I'll introduce you to everyone.'

The housemaid takes me back to the house. It's the Spanish equivalent of an old Manor House with three floors and I'm on the top floor. It's all olde-worlde with an eclectic range of objects and paintings littered everywhere.

My room has a faded quality about it but it's clean and smells fresh. The view overlooks the fields with the sea far off on the horizon and the crickets are chirping away. I like it. There's even a shower concealed behind a curtain and soon I'm clean, not so faded, and fresh for action.

'Good afternoon everyone. I'm here to offer a few lectures over your painting holiday and with a bit of luck do some painting as well if you let me.'

Vince does the introductions but I don't remember most names apart from a Harriet, and a Michael although I think there are two of them. I used to have great staff in my gallery days that would prompt me.

Rose wine is served and Vince runs through the itinerary for the next ten days. Oh dear. Breakfast at seven again with lectures starting promptly at eight I've never been my best at this hour of the day.

You might ask how come I can talk about painting so authoritatively only having been a practicing artist myself for a couple of years. Well twenty years plus spent right beside the artists whose work I was selling and time spent in their studios have helped me immensely. So, it's natural to pass on ideas and observations. Strangely I never see my own work as great art but then it's not up to me. Others like and buy it, so who am I to complain? The one common thing with painters is that sense of never being satisfied which I suppose helps drive us on.

The first lesson is a gentle warm up. Mixing colours and vanishing points. Men get perspective and women get colour. For us men, it's the hunter instinct in us. Maybe I'll find a cave when I return and leave supermarkets alone in future.

The lesson concludes and we head for the trusty old transit still held together by string as well as something unknown to most garages - sheer luck.

First port of call is Alcudia, an ancient, walled town with a bull ring just outside. Remind me to avoid that. The Square is buzzing with cafes and bars spilling out and a world chattering away with itself.

We order drinks and disperse to sketch. Across the table from where I'm sitting is a young dad with his daughter attempting to spoon feed her a rather large ice cream. There is more on her face and dress than appears to be going in. For some reason she must be the only child ever born who doesn't like ice cream.

'May I take a photo? I'll send you a copy.' She looks gorgeous, a perfect picture.

'Hurry. Before my wife returns. She won't be impressed!' The little girl stops her battle and beams looking at my camera.

'Takes after her mom. A proper model.'

Image taken, I help him both clean up the mess. Just in time as said wife returns with two shopping bags.

'Mama! 'The daughter raises her arms as if having missed her mother for decades.

'Thanks,' dad says with a thumbs up.

'My pleasure.'

'Who's that?' says the wife.

'He's just an artist out here. Nice chap.'

'Fine. Let's go.'

'Bye.' I wave and the little girls sticks her tongue out. That's gratitude for you. I return to enjoying the solitude in a crowd of an uninterrupted couple of hours.

Vince strolls by. 'I say ole boy you've come on a bit.'

'It's called practice, just as you told me to do.'

'I miss your gallery.'

'Well I'm not going to stop you looking me up for lunches anytime you like. Besides I'll always help you hang shows if you like.'

'That's exactly what I wanted to ask you. I've been asked to show at my club in London.'

'I'm your man.'

'I knew I could rely on you.'

Vince, happy, walks away to visit the other group members, and cast his beady and hopefully encouraging eye over their works.

For a moment I lose myself in the thoughts of a former gallery owner who's exchanged a vibrant, constantly on-the-go lifestyle to one spent sitting, watching the world go by, and channeling all his energy down the barrel of a brush, trying to make a piece of paper into a reflection of what my eyes can see. Some of the artists I used to represent have gone now but I can still hear them giving me hints. *Paint what you see not what you know.* Or *look, look and look some more*...but none of the friends from my past ever explained how you feel inside. It's an unusual solitude; plenty of time spent alone but not lonely; the polar opposite of running the gallery.

Do I miss my old life? Well, in truth, after applying a cool-blue wash on the wall I'm painting, the answer is a resounding...No! However, late lunches, wine and the occasional chat up still goes on. So, ah yes, being the artist is fun – in a different way.

I've fed my mind so it's back to painting a beautiful, old, wooden door surrounded by a huge, many-layered, stone arch. There are a couple sitting on a bench to the left of the door. They kiss; that's the title of my painting - better than *The Scream*.

Time flies until I hear Vince rounding up the gang. 'Lunch will be served back at the house.' *And not forgetting copious glasses of rose* I titter to myself.

Sunshine, painting, food and wine leads to only one thing; a nap till three. Refreshed and ready to give my first talk, constrained by Vince's instruction to keep it clean. Moi! There's that little knot in the stomach and off I go. Ask me to remember exactly what I talk about and in hindsight I've no idea but I'm bombarded by questions, including the most important one, 'Will you make a cocktail like the last time in Tuscany?' My infamy follows me.

Beatrice is a lovely petite, perfect size six Jaeger. An octogenarian with sparkly green eyes, she glides up to me, and puts her arm through mine 'Young man, I really enjoyed your talk. You have a naive approach to life I believe.'

'Madame, I don't believe I ever want to grow up.'

'Me neither. Call me Bea.' She whispers it, confidingly.

I blush and have to compose myself 'You'll have to give me some of your secrets.'

'Younger men, my dear. Can't be bothered with old fogeys. Life's too short you know.'

I'm being chatted up. What's not to love?

ACT 7 SCENE 2

Is it selfish, being an artist?

I used to ask that of my artists in my gallery days Most replied with some variant of a reciprocal question; 'What do you mean by selfish?'

I walk down into a field I've been given permission to enter by the owner and continue along the dusty track, surrounded by clucking hens and cockerels. I spy an old prewar car, a Citroen, exposed to the elements as the covering tarpaulin has multiple holes and weeds growing through, which makes it an interesting object to paint.

I set up my stool and begin.

It's rather warm and dry and I'm delighted to say my trusty second-hand hat is working a treat.

A cock emerges through the tall grass and takes a peck at my paints. Followed by another and suddenly the place is awash with feathered folk attacking everything. No amount of shushing and flapping my arms works. These birds mean serious business and seem to have a taste for watercolour blocks.

As I try to gather up my equipment, an elderly chap who looks as dusty as the path, accompanied by a scrawny mutt, slowly strolls up to me.

He starts talking in some dialect that I don't know. The dog just growls and wheezes.

'I'm afraid I've no idea what you're saying. I'm a painter under attack.'

He starts gesticulating at the car and then at the birds and then more vigorously at me. The penny drops. I realise I'm invading the nesting ground of the shagadelic palace for the cockerels.

The old man is still pointing at me.

'I have permission to be here.'

'Mad Englander' comes a reply I can understand while the dog's growling grows louder and now it's clearly snarling.

See painting outdoors is not as carefree as one would like. I gather up my stuff and begin to walk back to the gate. The old man spits at the ground and there's an ominous metallic click behind me. I turn around to find him pointing a gun at me. It looks like a semi-automatic pistol. I'm a little more than concerned. What's that expression? *Smell it? I'm sitting in it.*

He indicates with the gun to move. I follow orders.

We walk away from the gate and down the hill to the other side of the field. The dog keeps growling. Eventually we come across a rundown stone hut with an old brown wooden door hanging off its hinges. There are old tools, broken farm machinery and scrap metal everywhere with an abundance of chickens all over the place. A couple of rusty buckets hang from the guttering, which would make an interesting rustic exhibit in a garden centre.

We walk into the dark interior and he points to a stool, which I duly sit down on. The dog places itself beside me and collapses to the floor.

He starts shouting at me and I've no idea what he's ranting on about.

An elderly woman shuffles into the room. She is quite stooped and her hands are gnarled. 'Hola signor. You like something to drink?'

'Why has he got a gun trained on me?'

'He no trust anyone especially men.'

'All I was doing was painting that old wreck, I wasn't going to pinch it.'

'He the old guard. Franco his hero.'

With that the man straightens up, beats his chest and then spits on the floor.

'Please tell him to put the gun away.'

She utters something to him and he turns and walks out in disgust. The dog follows, still growling.

She pours a milky liquid out of a pot and offers me a stone beaker.

'Here Horchata. Drink.'

I don't drink milk but feel like I shouldn't mention it.

'Is good,' she nods at me.

I try it. It's sweet and refreshing.

'Show me signor artista sus pintura.'

I get the gist of what she's asking and reach down for my pad. Somehow, I still feel I'm under house arrest.

'Here you go.' I pass it to her

She studies each page nodding. 'Bueno.' She looks up and asks me to paint her home. At least I think that's what she says.

'Okay. Pronto or mañana.'

'Is ahora. Non pronto.'

'Okay.'

I stand, picking up my bag and walk to the entrance.

'Momento'. She finds a huge parasol and cushion and follows. I have a guard with me which is worrying. Strolling around outside looking for the perfect viewpoint of the wrecked cottage, I spy the old chap not that far away.

'Um. This is a good spot.'

I stop and set up. The woman throws the cushion down behind me and puts the parasol up. She sits to observe me in action.

Slowly the painting comes to life. It's a hive of red beaks, rust and a ramshackle building in a scorched field landscape. Actually, I'm quite pleased with it. The woman has not uttered one word so far. A couple of hours pass and then with one more dash of red beak, I'm satisfied.

'Finished. Finito.'

The woman slowly gets up and scans her home and then the painting, then her home again. 'Is good no?'

'Is good yes!' I reply.

It's the first time she smiles since our initial encounter. I know what's coming next.

'I have?' It's more a statement than a question.

'Only if I can finish painting the old car, automobile, yes?'

'Coche,' she replies. 'Si car.'

'No man or gun?'

'Si, is okay.'

I'm still not convinced.

I hand her the painting and she walks off home with an air of accomplishment. Meanwhile I eyeball the chap as I trudge back up the hill to my original destination.

As I find the place and set up again, I feel like everything is watching me. Birds, man, dog; even the field has eyes. It's uncomfortable. Slowly a cock struts up and pecks at the watercolour box.

This time I ignore him and his companions who follow. I'll just accept being surrounded by inquisitive future coq u vin. However, I do manage to complete the picture without strangling one bird in the process.

The sun is beginning to cast long shadows. Mosquito time. They love me. I hate them. I pack up and beat a hasty retreat to my lodgings.

Some day!

I don't believe anyone would believe it - forced at gunpoint to paint a commission without pay!

The rest of the break surprisingly passes without any drama at all, much to my delight. It is replete with plenty of wine, painting and even relaxing. Dare I describe it as idyllic. Sadly, it's soon time to return to England. Victor drives me to the airport and after parking up, pulls at my arm. 'I say ole chap. I must admit to missing you and your gallery.'

'Like I said before I'll do lunch anytime. Come and visit; come and stay even. Besides I'm going to be helping you with your next exhibition, so what are you worrying about?'

Victor considers for a moment.

When he speaks again, it's in a serious tone of voice. 'That's just it. Actually, I have something to tell you. As a matter of fact, I'm not in the best of health. I'm sure it will all be okay, but I thought I'd let you know.'

'Care to amplify that statement Victor?' I know him too well to push.

'I'll let you know when I've seen the specialist. Not a word to anyone!'

He shakes my hand and saunters off, leaving me deeply concerned.

ACT 8 SCENE 1

'Hello, boss.'

'Charlie, how the devil are you?'

'I'm great sort of...' There's a pregnant pause 'Well I'm getting married and I've a great idea for a present.'

'You're getting married. Wow! Who's the lucky chap?'

'Do you remember that blonde actor?'

'You're kidding me.'

'No. Not him. One of his friends.'

'You must tell me all over a glass or wine or two.'

'Are you free tomorrow?'

'I'll clear the decks. This I gotta hear. Wine o'clock. Where do you fancy?'

'Can we meet at yours first?'

'Okay. Till tomorrow then.'

I pour a glass of wine, pick up my brush and continue painting. Good grief. I've not seen Charlie in three years. Mind you, I've not seen Belinda, my former faithful gallery assistant either. I wonder what she's up to.

You know, it's so different now to gallery life. All I do now is try and look after me and that's not always straightforward.

The bell rings. Charlie is standing on the doorstep, looking stunning, still sporting a very short skirt and tight blouse and her obligatory high heels but she's shed a bit of weight.

'Well, fancy seeing you. You're looking very, how shall we say, fit!'

'Gym and less booze. So, can I come in?'

'Seeing as you're not a vampire please do.'

She plants a smacker on my cheek and walks in. 'Am I pleased to see you.'

'Tea, coffee, wine, tomato juice?'

'This will do nicely. And it's chilled.' She produces a bottle of champagne from behind her back.

'Okay. I'll get the glasses then. You must spill the beans.'

When I return, Charlie is lying seductively on the couch.

'That would make a good pose for a sketch.' I'm smiling. My thoughts regretfully are not entirely innocently disinterested.

'I want you to paint me for my fiancé. I want to surprise him.'

'Haven't you already?'

She throws a cushion at me. 'you don't mind if I go topless, do you?'

'Let's have a drink first.'

'I thought it would be a great idea. He can ogle me all the time in the bedroom - in case I'm not there.'

'Maybe you'll want a series dotted around the house,' I quip.

'There's a thought.'

We clink glasses.

'So, tell me. Who, how, why, when; in any order?'

Charlie takes a gulp. 'We met at a party and in a mad moment - most unlike me - I gave him my number and he kept on ringing. I gave in and he's really cute so we're getting hitched three weeks next Thursday. But I'm still not sure! Maybe it's nerves. I've not been married in years, decades. What do you reckon? Am I in good shape?'

She removes her blouse and bra.

The simplest answer is affirmative. 'I have to say, Charlie, you are in great shape.'

'And they're all mine too.'

'When are you free for a sitting?'

'How's about now? I'm undressed. Shall I remove my skirt?'

'No! No, that's fine, honest. Let's do a head and shoulders.'

'I've been working so hard on my glutes. Look.'

She pulls her unbuttoned skirt down at the back to reveal a tight derrière in equally great shape.

'Perfect. So, shall we do subtle or raunchy?'

'I'm easy' she laughs.

'Wrong answer.' Although I fear, the truth.

She rolls on to her front and rests her head on her elbows. 'How about a Marilyn Monroe pose?'

I pull out a pad and some charcoals and do a quick sketch.

'Move that arm a bit to the left and raise your chin up.'

After only a few minutes I'm happy with it. 'Well done. Here take a look.'

Charlie raises an eyebrow 'It's not half bad, that. I'm most impressed. I heard you were doing okay with your art. Rumours seem to run true. Now then. How about convincing me I'm doing the right thing with this marriage dilemma?'

'Charlie. You never cease to amaze me.'

'Well you're not breaking any rules. It's not like I work for you anymore and besides...'

I must be mad. 'No. Tell me about your fiancé. What's he like?'

'Oh, you know. Tall, fit, young, blue eyes; a real munchkin and all the girls in the gym certainly would.'

'So, he's a trophy then. What about nice romance, togetherness?'

'Who has time for bloody romance these days?'

'Doesn't the sanctity of marriage mean anything to you?'

'Thereby lies the problem. Eternity seems quite a long time. And there are so many men out there. Well, I have to say you're not helping in the way I want. Maybe you should become a priest. I thought artists are supposed to have fun?'

'We do. But that doesn't mean I have to sleep with everyone.'

'I'm not everyone! I worked for you.'

'Exactly!'

She gets dressed and pouts her lips. 'You're a meany. I really thought you'd succumb to my...advances.'

'I think you should save it for your hubby to be and exhaust him more often. Now about your sittings...'

'I don't want a painting. I want you.'

Quickly changing topics, I refill her glass 'Well in that case, please accept this sketch as a wedding present. We might as well finish our drinks.'

'Tell me something?'

'Yes.'

Charlie asks in a sheepish manner 'What about Belinda. Would you sleep with her if she came round?'

I look Charlie right between the eyes, saying nothing. Then I wink and raise my glass. 'Cheers, Charlie. I'm saying no more.' I clink her glass and drain mine quickly.

ACT 8 SCENE 2

The only problem with painting outside in this blessed country of ours is the weather, from which we can deduce the real reason why the paints are called, watercolours. The English do have a particular attraction to them.

So, when it rains, as of now, I'm stuck indoors. The view from the hills. I'm reliably informed, is breathtaking but not today.

I decide to don my waterproof jacket and stroll through the village. There's a lovely cafe displaying wickedly fattening cakes in the window and if I'm not mistaken some sensuous croissants. My nose detects they're freshly made - with butter.

One fresh ground coffee and two croissants later, smothered with blackcurrant jam, I'm looking at the rivulets making patterns down the curved glass front. Some are larger and racing whilst others meander, in no hurry to dive onto the pavement. Can you easily tell I'm bored rigid?

A woman dashes in, long hair soaking and curling round her shoulders with one strand clinging to her nose.

'Usual dearie' says the assistant.

'Yes, please Mary, and one of those croissants too.'

'They are rather moreish,' I pipe up. 'I've had two.'

'Lucky you. I bet you're going to tell me next the weather is perfect for rambling.'

'Afraid not. Useless for painting as well.'

'Are you an artist?'

'You could say that but today I'm a croissant connoisseur.'

'Hi I'm Sara without an *H*. I own the Bartlett gallery just up there. If your artistic temperament can drag you further up the road, call by. I don't think I shall be too busy today.'

She turns and exits, leaving a spreading puddle on the floor.

Funny really. I think I would have said the same sort of thing when I was a gallery owner. I ponder a while longer and venture outside to capture the essence of soaking wet high street. An antiquarian bookshop is open and I dip inside.

'Dry your hands before touching any books, if you don't mind.'

'Good morning to you too,' I respond. 'Art section please.'

The miserable owner stares at me, looking down at my shoes then at my jacket, and gives a tut. 'Right at the back. Shelves eight and nine marked *Art*!'

I could set up a service industry academy here. I love it when people make you feel important and want you to spend money with them. Well not today, *you grumpy sod*. I give a smile as I walk back through the myriad unsold books. Outside it may be wet but inside smells dank. The further back into the shop the muskier and danker it becomes. I fiddle with a few titles but it's off-putting and I reckon I'll develop mould myself if I stay any longer.

I don't pull any punches on my way out. 'The place smells as mouldy as your temperament. Good day.'

I'm ignored.

After walking by a few so-called antique shops - more like bric-a-brac tat - I find the Bartlett gallery.

On display are selections of Victorian paintings as well as more modern works. Suddenly I feel awkward. I'm the artist not the owner, the roles have changed, reversed. Well I was asked to call by. Here goes.

'Greetings again Sara-without-an-H.'

'Make yourself comfy, I'll be with you in a moment.'

I do what every artist does in galleries. Study the artworks. Scan them. Artists never just look and admire. They scan the image from the top corner to the bottom and back. Scanning.

I wasn't too hot on the Victorian landscapes. A bit too pot-boiler for my liking but then I come across a Turner original. It's stunning as is the matching price tag.

'What do think of this little beauty?'

'If I could paint half as well, I'd be a happy man.'

We're always on the lookout for good work. It's not easy you know. There's so much tosh.'

'I agree, actually. I used to say exactly the same thing. I had a gallery once. You have to keep on searching for that something extra that jumps out.'

'Tell me more.' She bends down to pull a bottle of champagne from an under-the-counter fridge.

'Well; well; what a great idea. I used to keep my fridge in the kitchen at the back of the gallery.'

'Sometimes you need it to hand.' She laughs, pulling the cork at the same time.

'Cheers you!'

'Cheers to you too!'

'What do you paint?'

'Contemporary, naïve; quite colourful, really.'

'You'll have to show me some.'

'I can show you what's in my sketch book later if you like?'

'I think I'll like. You can tell, you know from the way the person is, what their work going to be like.'

Good grief. She does sound like me. And there was I thinking I used to be unique. How positively refreshing.

We finish the second glass after talking about all things related and unrelated to gallery life. Next minute it's 1.25. No one has walked in. The phone hasn't rung. Rain stopped play.

'There's a great pub a bit up the road. Fancy a bite?'

'What about your gallery?'

'I'll put *gone fishing* on the door.'

'Sounds a great idea.' Sounds like something I'd say as well.

We head off full tilt to The Kings Head. It's not a cheese and raw onion cob place. Silver service and a cracking menu. It's still raining. Sara is attractive in a challenging way. She's full of beans and full of life. I'm feeling quite rejuvenated in her company and I love her I don't care approach. Who does she remind me of? Lunch comprises lots of good wine and food and like all good lunches ends late.

'I suppose I better do some work.'

'I'll walk you to your establishment then.'

We settle the bill. I offer to pay, and she refuses. I leave the tip. We laugh. She puts her arm through mine as we amble back. The rain has finally ceased and I bid her farewell.

'Bring your art back later; say half six?'

'If you say so. Bye for now.'

Well I'm not painting but it's certainly a colourful day.

I dash upstairs and sort out three of my pads, have a quick shower and spruce up with a splash of aftershave. Go with the flow ticker-tapes through my mind. Does she want to see my art or am I being naive and childish. Do I care? This is fun and I've no one to answer to except myself.

I buy a large box of chocolate Maltesers and at six twenty I stroll back to the gallery.

Sara-without-an-H is on the phone. She's twiddling her hair and appears quite agitated. 'Bloody artists!' she explodes, slamming down the phone.

'Hello. Bloody artist here, as requested.'

She looks up 'Grrrrrr; sometimes I wonder why I'm doing this. There's got to be an easier way to make a living.'

'Ah but is it as much fun?'

She stops and nods. 'You do know how it feels don't you?'

'Been there, done that, and printed the t shirt. Here you go. I got you a little thank you for lunch.'

'How did you know I love Maltesers?'

'Who doesn't. They stress bust just at the right moment of crunching. Especially when you pop in more than one at the same time.'

'You're really funny.'

'Been in the art world for ages; that does it.'

She is calm again. 'Come on. Show me your art.'

I produce my books and lay them on the desk. 'Over to you my trusty gallery owner.' I'm now feeling naked. How ridiculous.

She says nothing, just turns each page over, studying my watercolours. When she finishes the second book, she looks at me and blows a slight whistle. 'Well!'

'Well?'

'They're nothing like I imagined they would be. That's the first time I've got it so wrong. Well, I never.'

I'm a little concerned as to what she means. 'What do you really think then?'

'Love em. All of them; love your style, the freshness, the honesty, they're great. You're not how I imagined your work to be.'

'Wow. Thank you.'

I'm nervous asking the next question but don't need to as Sara gets in first; 'I'd like to try a dozen of these if you don't mind. I really love this piece. She holds up the book and places it on the shelf before stepping back. 'Just a simple wooden frame and a large mount. Bliss.'

'How do you operate with your commission structure?'

'Fairly' she winks and smiles.

'I'm happy with that. Let me buy you a drink to celebrate?'

'Good idea. I better sort George out first.'

'George?'

'My cat. He needs feeding.'

'Do you live far from here?'

'Ever-so close. It's the annexe behind the gallery. Through the courtyard.'

We lock up and go through the back door into a cobbled courtyard. George is sitting bolt upright against a stone carving by the door. I'm not a lover of cats but this one looks majestic. He's also looking at me with an inquisitive air of disdain. He's naturally first in queue and that's all there is to it.

We walk in to a long lounge full of art and antiques and with a huge, gold-leafed mirror on the far wall.

'French, I believe.'

'Correct. Louis XVI.'

She feeds George who in turn, totally ignores me.

'Lovely place you have.'

'Oh, it will do for now. I converted it to live in when I got divorced.' She looks reflective all of a sudden.

I change the mood. 'Come on. Let's go. It must be well past wine-o' clock. Bye George.'

George continues to ignore me.

We return to the same watering hole. I order a bottle of Malbec and a jug of water.

Sara is bemused with the water. 'Why?'

'Coz it's good for you. Two litres a day and all that.'

'Tosh.'

The wine goes down rather too quickly and is followed by several more bottles.

Sara leans over and whispers in my ear 'I don't think I'm going to regret this.' She kisses me full on the lips. 'My place?'

'If you insist.'

She pokes me in the chest. 'Move it mister!'

It's raining again. Ah yes, the bliss of living in England.

So, I'm lying in bed pondering on what to do now.

She's still asleep beside me as the church bells ring out to say it's eight in the morning. Where am I? I'm in a rather nice bedroom somewhere in the country, but not in my hotel. My head begins to spin a little, reminding me of a tad too much alcoholic consumption from last night. Well to be fair, it was only five hours ago. What's her name? Ah yes Sara-without-the-H. She owns a gallery. The thought hits home. I've just slept with a gallery owner. Fancy! All the years of protecting my staff and artists as an owner and never actually sleeping with one. They were my rules. Well now the brush is in the other hand so to speak. Enough. I'm starving, so I slowly get up.

'Not so fast lover boy,' says Sara lifting her head and turning over to grab me around my waist.

By nine o clock my body is demanding breakfast with menaces. I run down the road to get fresh croissants. When I return Sara is in the galley with a fresh pot of coffee brewing.

'I didn't think you'd do a runner on me.'

'What with fresh croissants as good as these down the road. You're joking.'

'I don't normally pounce on men you know…'

'I'm honoured; but does that mean you won't take my art?'

'Perish the thought. Of course, I will. When they've sold, I might even have some more. Paintings that is.'

'Naturally' I reply.

I leave the paintings with her and amble back to my hotel. Who says art has no fringe benefits?

ACT 9 SCENE 1

I have now collated forty watercolours and framed them with the help of the framer that I've used for years. I am driving to my first solo show. It's petrifying; I can't believe how terrified I'm feeling. All those years selling other artists - easy - but now it's me. Just me and my art in the hands of another gallery owner. What if nobody likes them, or nothing sells? I take a gulp and tell myself to shut the f*** up. How many times did I have to reassure my artists before a show?

Forty miles to go. I pull in to a petrol forecourt. Coffee that should help. 'Black Americano please, easy on the water.'

The assistant looks at me and shrugs her shoulders. 'It's busted, can't make one. We've got soft drinks or there's a *Costa* in *Smiths*.'

It's a sign, I don't need the coffee.

'Thanks, but no thanks.'

'Whatever,' and she turns to talk to her mate.

I get back in my car, switch *The Who* on full blast and it's *I get on my knees and pray.* Then *We won't get fooled again'* Maybe I'm fooling myself being an artist; maybe it's all a dream; maybe I'm chickening out; maybe I'm becoming an arse! Hold on, even my framer likes the work; and his assistant wants one of the Venetian paintings, she told me - that is if it doesn't sell in the show.

People try to put us down...talking bout my generation. Why am I putting myself down? This is my generation, my time to be what I've always wanted to be. The speedometer is registering 85 mph. Slow down idiot; it's the music and my whirring brain. Luckily there are no cars in front. I ease off, open the window and let the wind buffet my face.

Arriving, I'm lucky to find a place to park nearby. Something's going right. I walk down the hill to the gallery. It's a steep hill; the pavement is cobbled; I miss my footing and fall headlong into the entrance.

An elderly gent peers over me. 'Good afternoon. Are you alright? Let me help you up.'

The man offers his arm and I pull myself off the floor. 'Thanks, I'm okay, I think. Dramatic entrance eh? Luckily, I've left all the paintings in the car.'

'Most fortunate then. Mind you, you're not the first to fall into this place. I'll get on to the council and let them know it's happened again.'

'And there I was thinking I was unique. It sort of reminds me of a time many moons ago where I was walking the streets, canvassing for business and I walked into a shop, slipped on the wet floor and knocked a card display and loads of crisps all over the place. I left my card and as I walked out the awning gave way and I was drenched. I had the nerve to go back in dripping and say *I'll be back.*'

The chap laughed. 'I'm George, Sybil's father. She'll be back in a jiffy. Fancy a tea or a coffee; maybe a wee dram of something stronger. His soft Scottish accent rolling over the words *wee dram* has the desired effect.

'A wee dram will do just fine if you don't mind.'

I sit down and look around the place. It's a nice, compact gallery with a mixture of loud paintings and pretty touristy clutter. I make no comment apart from '*Cheers,*' and down the whisky in one.

Sybil walks in with her arms full of bags and a massive bunch of flowers. 'Och, hello. See you met my Dad.'

'I did at that.' The accent's catching.

'Where's your work then?'

'It's just in the car. I'll go fetch it all in now.'

With that, I carefully step outside and proceed slowly back up the hill. Even more slowly and carefully, I return and stack the watercolours on the side wall.

Sybil raises an eyebrow; 'Och, laddie. They're far better framed than I thought they'd be.'

'Years of being in the trade, I suppose. Glad you approve.'

She rummages through them, and sort of mumbles or hums; I can't make out which.

'Would you like me to help you hang them?'

'No thanks, I'll sort it. Why don't you take Dad across the road and buy him a beer? I'll join you soon.'

'I'll nay object,' says George.

So far so good.

We walk in and head for the bar only to find it inhabited by a loutish yob, somewhat out of place in this quaint local watering hole. He is being lewd; crude and abusive to the young female bar staff.

George taps him on the shoulder. 'If you don't stop, I'll take your lights out pal!'

The yob spins round and throws a punch, but George simply grabs his arm, spins him round, arm-locks him, and marches him outside. All in the space of a blink. I can just about hear a stream of non-Shakespearian dialogue, followed by a thwack, and then George walks back in, dusting his sleeve.

'Are you alright lassie?'

The timid assistant is visibly shaken but appears in one piece. 'I'm okay really, George. Thank you.'

'Aye it's nothing.' George turns to me; 'What you having?

'I'm speechless. How did you do that?'

'Military my son. Army training, you ne'er forget it.'

You know the saying, never judge a book by its cover. Well, here lies a classic case. What else will Madame fate have in store?

'My shout. You helped me up before.'

'Alright laddie; it's an IPA in my tankard, and a wee Glenlivet. Thank you kindly.'

The manager walks over to George. 'Don't you think you're maybe too old to be bouncing and defending Sally's honour?'

'I'll not drink in here with the likes of scum like him, so if you don't mind, either you sort it or I'll change pubs.'

'Okay. Okay but don't do it again.'

'I reckon he won't be in here for quite a while, shall we say I have my persuasive techniques...Now then, tell me about yourself.' He turns to me reverting to gentle old man and pulls up a stool.

A few beers later and Sybil lands alongside us. The barman puts a gin and tonic in front of her. She hasn't uttered a word.

'Don't you love the local establishment, the service, friendliness of most of the clients and staff, I repeat...most.'

'I'm thinking of putting your prices up a tad. They're much better than the photos you sent. Och, that's not fair really, having met you as a gallery owner, I didn't think you'd be this good. Do you get my drift?'

'Oh, fine by me. I can handle subtle insults. How much more?'

'I reckon we should get an average of seven hundred and fifty for the medium, and say twelve fifty for the larger pieces, give or take.'

'I'm in your hands; I've priced that many works before but damned if I get mine right. Same deal, plus framing?'

We shake hands. Love it; a pub is the proper place to conduct business.

Sybil finishes her drink 'Where are you staying, or are you travelling back. Same again please.'

'No, I'm stopping in a little place, I've booked up the road.'

'Well next time you must come and stay with us at the Vicarage. It's massive. Come and stay after the opening next week; stay for a few days if you like; the views are stunning.'

'That's very kind and generous of you. I think that'll depend on whether my art sells or not.'

'Nonsense. Trust me, I don't pick losers.'

We all raise a glass. I try to act totally calm.

We shall see.

ACT 9 SCENE 2

One week later

The whole week I've faffed around unable to paint or do anything useful. I go to the pictures but can't concentrate. I've not slept properly and I've avoided the world.

So, I arrive at the gallery looking a touch exhausted.

I walk in and get confronted with a gallery full of my work. *Whoah, it's really happening.*

'What do you think?'

'The gallery looks great, thank you. I'm truly humbled.'

Sybil walks over and gives me a kiss on the cheek.' Guess what. We have already sold six to one of my collectors; and she's dying to meet you this evening.

'Six!'

There in front of my eyes are red dots by the titles. *Wow, someone really likes my art.* I'm amazed.

'That's fantastic.' I compose myself and add 'Thirty-two to go then.'

'I told you I pick winners, wait till later. Come on, let me show you the Vicarage; it's only up the road. She puts her arm in mine and sort of marches me out of the gallery.

It all comes back to me, the anxiety of a private view, the catering, the drink, the artist, the staff, the costs, the time, will they or won't they sell? Here a gallery owner is reassuring me with a few sales under her belt that it will be okay. Very strange indeed.

The Vicarage is mid Victorian, large and beautifully adorned with paintings of all genres and furnished in an eclectic mix of antique and modern furniture

'What a great place you have. Love it.'

'Thanks; I've collected since I was young. And I'd like to have one of yours here.'

'Really!'

'Seriously. They've grown on me. You have a distinct style that reaches out. It's sort of naïve but with a hidden message.'

'I just try to capture what I see, but I suppose what I see has to reflect how I am at the time.'

'Don't change. It's funny but I'd never put you as the person who paints like you do.'

'Well, maybe part of me has never grown up; maybe never wants to.'

'Follow me.' Sybil leads the way up the large staircase.

There's a superb Grandfather clock at the top of the stairs, the face exquisitely decorated and the casing glowing after years of polish and TLC. The tick is almost hypnotic.

We walk along the corridor and Sybil opens a large door. 'Here you go, make yourself at home.'

My room looks out over a well-kept garden. Further on there are rolling hills. She's right; the view is stunning through the four large leaded windows. I'm sure she didn't make this sort of wealth from the gallery.

That remains a matter for a later conversation. I won't dwell on their home; suffice to say it's all beautifully set out with superb taste. I could easily stay for a few days or so. In fact, that is exactly what I shall do.

I shower and change, freshen up and stroll back down to the gallery which has filled up with a cacophony of friends, clients and freebie hanger-on-ers. I walk in and seeing as most people have no idea who I am, stroll right up to the young lass with a tray and relieve her of a freshly poured prosecco.

'You're only allowed one, my lover, that is, unless you want to buy a painting.'

'Thank you, I'll consider that. Cheers.' I carve a path into the crowd, heading for the counter.

'Are there you are' says Sybil. 'Come and meet one of my best clients.' She winks and I follow in her footsteps.

'This is Barbara and Gerald. They simply adore your paintings.'

I shake hands noticing Barbara's huge diamond ring, glowing like *the Edison Lighthouse* on a clear black night.

'Why don't you tell us what inspires you to paint?'

Now really, how am I supposed to answer this? *Hello, coz I want to* or *Don't you just love the view*, or *Are you so stupid asking such a mad question*. I take a breath and concoct an utterly mindless answer.

Barbara prods Gerald. 'See I told you I knew what he would be like. Isn't he adorable? You're just like your paintings, full of empathy and naïve at the same time. Bliss, sheer bliss.'

'What can I say?' I take a small bow. Gerald looks at me and I raise an eyebrow.

'What do you do? I can see he's bored rigid.

'I play golf these days; retired you know. Stockbroker. Got out at the right time, you know what I mean?'

I feign total understanding. 'How interesting' I remark 'Do you like art?'

'Seems like I've no choice, if Barbara wants them, then we get them. Do you like wine? I've just bought a vineyard.'

'Nectar from the gods.'

'Good, good. You can come out and paint the chateau in the summer,' and with that remark walks off leaving his wife and me out there on the dance floor, so to speak.

'He likes you. I'm so pleased. Darling Sibyl, put us down for those three extra ones; he won't know.'

And that is how the evening continues. *Hello - how are you - who are you - thank you - another red dot - another happy customer.* So, result, a delighted gallery owner and a bloody ecstatic artist.

I walk over to the bearer of the drinks tray. 'I've considered the art and need another glass to help me decide.'

She considers me carefully. "You know I shouldn't let you, but don't say anything to anyone, go on. Be discreet, okay?'

'I promise. Cheers' and walk off in to the crowd.

The memories of my own gallery's private-view receptions flood back. The noise, the total knot in my stomach, the fear of failure, the last man standing, the after party, the mess, the next day and cut...

This is my private view, my art, me!

I'm truly stunned; every painting sold, every single one. The show has sold out. I don't know how I feel. Like a rabbit glued to the headlights of an oncoming speeding vehicle. How did this happen?

Sybil cracks open a bottle of champagne. 'See, I told you I know what I'm doing.'

I have to agree; she knows what she's doing.

But do I?

FINALE

I'm staring at a blank piece of paper, thinking about what to paint, and nothing is coming to mind when the phone rings.

'Hello this is Abi.'

Ah, that feisty nephew of Victor who hasn't spoken to me since working in the gallery. My something is wrong radar is on full alert. I don't even say *hello* but go straight into 'What's up?'

'It's Victor, he's...' There's a very long pause. 'He's dead. I had to tell you. I'm so sorry.'

'Oh no...my dear, I am so, so sorry. He told me he was sort of not well, but never said too much.'

'He wouldn't...fuss. I'll let you know the details when they're finalised.'

The phone went dead.

My dear friend and mentor, gone. That is so not fair.

I open a bottle of Rioja and pour a massive glass, staring at the walls, losing myself in the tragic news.

Paint, sell, paint, sell, paint, paint, paint. Live, die.

Enough, it is affecting my life. I'm supposed to be enjoying myself, life is fun, I mean I paint, I eat, I have fun, I sleep occasionally but the frustration is growing deep inside of me. Something is missing, something is not in my control, something is *aaaah*.

I've had enough, don't ask me why? It just is enough; plain and simple, I've had enough.

Oh no, not Victor. I walk out of my studio, leaving the door ajar, run down the stairs and march, not stroll, to the edge of somewhere steep; where I am...don't know. I just keep walking muttering to myself. 'What's it all for, I mean what's the bloody point. I feel like my head is bursting and I'm shouting but there is total silence, only the heavy sound of my large feet striding to somewhere but I've no idea where I'm heading. I keep walking, ignoring traffic signs, puddles, litter - bloody litter everywhere; why can't people pick it up; is it that difficult? Everything I see is annoying me.

I want to paint so that people will like my art. Is this really what I want? I want to be relaxed and satisfied with what I do but it's not happening; it's all about bloody other people and what they want, what they think. I'm just fed up to the gills. I'm not a puppet, I'm sick of being nice to everyone. It's not in my nature to be cruel, yet I'm hurting one person – me.

What's that song, *I can't get no satisfaction*? Well fuck you Jagger and the bloody Rolling Stones, you're right I've tried I've tried I can't get no...no, no, no!

I stop at the top of the hill and look out over the panorama. All the lights are starting to twinkle. The sun has had enough and is pissing off to warmer climes. Nobody gives one iota about me. What's that famous saying? You're only worth something when you're dead. I used to say that to customers in the gallery; 'Would you like born and expected to die dates on the artist!'

That's it; I'll end it all now. Simple.

There is a loud horn parping, laughing at me, it continues getting louder as a blue mini skids to a stop.

The door opens and a woman is shouting at me. 'What do you think you're bloody well doing out here?'

'I'm thinking about trying to kill myself. Why?'

'That's the most fucking stupid idea I've heard all day'

She walks over to me. She's wearing a full-length navy coat with a maybe-real maybe-fake fur wrap. 'Got a light?'

'I don't smoke, I just seethe these days.'

'I've been following you since you stormed out of the building, I've seen that look before.'

'Oh, don't tell me you're a bleedin' do-good Samaritan. That's all I need.'

'Perish the thought!' She unzips her bag and hands me a card.

I can just make out the writing;

Lizzie Collington
Art director, publisher, and agent.

'So?'

'I've been monitoring you for quite a while now and was hoping we would meet under more social conditions. However, this might be just the right time. Would you like to hear more?'

'My art will only be worth something when I'm dead and then only after many years of decomposing.'

'Oh diddums; are we feeling sorry for oneself?'

'Are you taking the piss?'

'Of course. If you're so determined to end it all then I've a much better idea. Why don't you fake it? Voila. Fake your own death. Then you can read your obituary in some local paper and attend your own wake if you must. Then vanish for a while. Take a holiday, somewhere warm by the sea. Whatever floats your boat.'

I say nothing; just stare out looking for an answer. I'm gazing onto a world that doesn't give a damn.

Then I start to nod and smile.

"That's just bloody hilarious. The whole thing is a bloody joke, life's a joke, art is a joke, and death is a joke, well sometimes. It's all a bloody show, every bloody second on the planet. It's a bleedin' performance. Lizzie you're a genius. You know what. I like it. It's a much better than ending than I was coming up with.'

'See, I'm full of great ideas. I've got another one that you really might love.'

'Really, there's more?'

She walks up closer to me putting her arm through mine and subtly steering me away from the edge. 'Step away from that ledge and climb into my car. I'll show you what's fake or not.'

'Anything you say Lizzie, anything you say.'

'Where would you like to go?'

'Give me somewhere warm with lots of sunshine, empty beaches and no bloody people!'

'How about the Caribbean – pink beaches and palm trees kissing the sea?'

'Now you're talking, my dear.'

'I can easily arrange that. What's more, a good friend has a little mansion hideaway I think you would adore.'

'I'm all yours,' I say fastening the seat belt.

Shew turns the key and the engine roars into life. She slams the car into first gear as the wheels screech burning rubber in objection.

'We'll talk contracts later; much later,' she says as we vanish over the horizon.

THE END

ACKNOWLEDGMENTS

There are numerous people I'd like to thank and I reckon you all know who you are. There are also some people walking around totally oblivious to my observations and sadly there are some who are no longer with us. They live on in spirit and great memories.

Printed in Poland
by Amazon Fulfillment
Poland Sp. z o.o., Wrocław